HANDLING LOVE

WELCOME TO HARDY FALLS

BETSY HORVATH

VARIOUS MINDED BOOKS

Various Minded Books
PO Box 792
Quakertown, PA 18951
Email: admin@variousmindedbooks.com
www.variousmindedbooks.com

Publisher's Note: This is a work of fiction. Names, characters, places, and incidents are a product of the author's imagination. Locales and public names are sometimes used for atmospheric purposes. Any resemblance to actual people, living or dead, or to businesses, companies, events, institutions, or locales is entirely coincidental.

Edited by: Kendra L. Clayton

Handling Love / Betsy Horvath. -- 1st ed.
ISBN 978-1-943725-05-2

ACKNOWLEDGMENTS

I'd like to send out HUGE thank yous to my beta readers – Monica, Ann, and Chris. I appreciate it more than I can say. You guys rock!

Many thanks to Dina for her awesome insider information about restaurants. The dishwashing scene's for you, babe. Thanks also to Ann for having entrepreneurial experience hard-won in the battlefield of business, and not being afraid to share it.

Last, but not least, massive thanks to my wonderful editor, Kendra, who tried to keep me on the straight and narrow. Any commas used inappropriately in this book are my fault, not hers. I take full responsibility for all splices.

1

____

"Go talk to my aunt," Hannah Frederickson said as she strode into the taproom of the Country Time Bar and Grill.

Her bartender, Deacon Black, looked up with a puzzled expression on his pleasantly rough face. He was standing behind the bar cleaning shot glasses in anticipation of the regular Wednesday night crowd. Well, maybe "crowd" was too optimistic, but they usually had a pretty good turnout when the bowling leagues were playing next door at Murphy Lanes.

"Huh?" he said.

"Go talk to my aunt," Hannah repeated. She walked behind the bar, slid past Deacon, and headed for the bottle of whiskey sitting on a nearby shelf.

"Now?" he asked, turning to watch her, obviously still confused. "We're going to open soon, and she lives across town."

"No." Struggling to hold onto her patience, Hannah grabbed one of the clean shot glasses he had stacked neatly on the back counter and poured a generous amount of the whiskey into it. "I want you to go to my office, pick up the phone, and talk to my aunt. She's on hold."

Deacon narrowed his bright blue eyes and tossed the rag he'd been using on the bar.

"Why?"

Hannah knocked back the shot, sputtered a little, and poured another.

"Because," she said, "I cannot possibly have heard her correctly. I need you to talk to her, and then tell me I'm having either a nightmare or a hallucination."

"What's going on?" he demanded.

"Just go talk to her!" Hannah shouted.

"All right, all right. Jeez." Deacon turned and stalked down the short hallway to Hannah's tiny office.

Hannah chugged the second shot, then picked up his discarded rag and began to polish the top of the old wooden bar. She heard Deacon talking, his voice growing louder, and she polished faster. By the time he slammed back into the taproom, the oak bar gleamed as never before. Hell, she'd practically set the thing on fire.

He walked up to stand beside her, and Hannah stopped her manic polishing to look at him. The expression on his face made her heart fall through the soles of her feet, down into the basement.

Oh, God.

She cleared her throat.

"Aunt Hildy didn't really say that Uncle George emptied my business bank account, took all of my money, and left town with his assistant, did she?"

"Bastard." Deacon said.

Oh, God. It was real.

Hannah's knees gave out, and she sank to the floor behind the bar. It was clean, but she wouldn't have noticed if she'd stuck to the vinyl.

"Is Aunt Hildy okay?" she asked.

"She actually sounded kind of relieved. Except for the whole money thing. She's sorry about that."

Hannah nodded. That was nice.

Deacon got another glass and poured himself some whiskey from the bottle she'd left on the bar. "She said when she got home from work—"

"She's a cashier at the Wal-Mart."

"—there was a note on the kitchen table telling her George and Crystal—"

"The assistant bimbo."

"—were heading somewhere warm."

"Bastard."

Deacon downed his whiskey. He did not sputter.

"The note said he wanted her to tell you he'd taken your money. He didn't want you to find out when the creditors started calling."

"Decent of him." Hannah dropped her face into her hands.

"Did you check your bank account balance?" Deacon asked. "Maybe George is just playing a practical joke or something."

Yeah. Because George was such a light-hearted trickster.

"I got online while I was on the phone with Hildy. It looks like he left me fifty dollars," she said into her hands.

"If you knew that, why the hell did you bother having me talk to her?"

"I didn't believe it." But it was true. It was all true. "Why did I let him talk me into being my accountant?" she moaned. "Why? I know what he's like. It was only a matter of time before he snapped."

"The bigger question," Deacon said, "is how he got access to your business bank account."

"Oh, that's easy," she said, still not looking up. "I gave him signing authority."

"Uh huh." He paused. "Why?" His voice sounded strained.

"After my father died, before you came back to town, I was really busy, and it was hard to keep ahead of the bookkeeping stuff. Uncle George said he did that kind of thing for other clients." She sighed. "And yes, I know I should have started paying the bills again, once you were working here, and I had more time. But I let him keep doing it. It was nice not to have to worry about everything."

Of course, now she had a bigger issue to worry about than finding the time to write out a couple of checks.

Oddly, when she finally looked at Deacon, he seemed relieved.

"Okay," he said. "So he paid bills for other clients. That means he must be bonded."

She hadn't thought there was anything below the basement, but she could feel her heart bouncing into a dark pit much further down.

She swallowed.

"Um, bonded?"

"A surety bond," Deacon said. "If he was handling your cash, you made sure that he...was..." His voice trailed off when he saw her expression. They stared at each other in silence for a moment.

Deacon squatted beside her, the material of his jeans stretching across his thighs. "Uncle George wasn't bonded?" he asked carefully.

She shook her head.

"I thought you said he handled money for other clients?"

"Well," she shifted on her butt. "Not exactly their money. For the other clients he handled the books, and they wrote the checks. But he said he would handle the money for me. Because I was family. He gave me a good rate."

"Why didn't you make him get bonded?" Deacon shouted.

"He was my uncle!" Hannah shouted back. "I trusted him!"

Then, to her horror, she started to cry. Deep, gulping sobs.

Before she could turn away or try to hide, Deacon heaved a sigh, sat on the floor next to her, and pulled her up against his chest.

"Come on, now," he said, stroking his hand down her back.

"I can't believe Uncle George did this to me! The b... b...bastard."

"It'll be okay," Deacon said, as he held her tighter. His arms were strong and they felt good wrapped around her. Without quite realizing what she was doing, Hannah found herself clinging to him, her fingers knotting in the soft fabric of his dark blue Country Time polo shirt. She hoped she wasn't getting snot all over him.

"All of my money is gone," she sobbed.

"I know, Hannah."

She couldn't seem to stop crying. His chest was warm and broad, and he smelled good, and he was holding her, and he'd never done that before, not even when they'd known each other in high school.

Of course, he was her employee now, so it wasn't surprising he never held her. Employees didn't usually go around holding their employers. It was probably weirding him out that she was crying all over him. She tried to get herself back under control.

Sniffling, she pulled away. He let her go, and they looked at each other. Then he shoved to his feet, reached down, and helped her up. She stood, feeling suddenly awkward, and grabbed a tissue from the box behind the bar, blowing her nose as discreetly as possible.

"Sorry," she muttered.

"Better?" Deacon had backed up a little, but he was still watching her with concern.

He wasn't exactly a handsome man, Hannah thought, considering him. He certainly wasn't pretty like his brother, Sam. Yet somehow his face managed to be both hard and sympathetic, framed by receding brown hair kept so brutally short it was little more than stubble. His profile easily could have been stamped on an ancient Roman coin.

"I guess," she said, suddenly aware of the heat and hardness of his body in the confined space.

When she'd known him in high school, before he'd left home at eighteen to join the army, he'd been young and…soft. The years between then and now, the traveling he'd done, the work on oil rigs and in construction, had added layers of solid muscle to his tall frame and some intriguing lines to his face. She'd heard him say he lifted weights regularly because he didn't want to get a gut.

Whatever he was doing, it really worked for him. They'd had a sharp increase in female customers since he'd started working at the Country Time.

He was a drifter who wouldn't stay in town forever, but while he was here he was a definite asset.

Maybe she could get him to go shirtless while he was tending bar to try and attract more women.

A vision of Deacon, shirtless, and maybe dancing and spinning bottles while he made drinks, flitted through her mind.

Yeah. A *definite* asset.

"You have to revoke George's signing authority," he said, pulling her from her admittedly inappropriate thoughts. "You'd better call the bank and do it right away."

"Sure. Because there's so much money left to worry about."

"You want to get him off the account."

"I know that, Deacon." Just because she'd cried all over the man didn't mean he had the right to treat her like she was a complete idiot.

"And you'll have to report this to the police. You have to tell Chief Kline what happened and swear out an arrest warrant, so George can be found and picked up."

"I know that, too," she muttered, wadding up the tissue and throwing it away. "I'm not completely stupid. I know I have to do that." Her stomach jumped. George might be a thief, but he was still her uncle. It made her a little queasy to think about having her uncle arrested.

Deacon could apparently read her mind. "You have to do this, Hannah," he said.

"I know." Then she turned and left him before she broke down and cried all over him again.

Back in her office, Hannah dropped into her chair and logged onto her online banking site to check her balance one more time. What if she'd made a mistake? What if she'd somehow opened the wrong account, and she still had all of her money, and Deacon was right, and that note from George was some kind of sick practical joke? It could happen.

Nope, she thought, looking at the numbers. No joke.

If only she'd made George get bonded. Then she'd have insurance.

Insurance.

She sat up straighter, hope suddenly zinging through her.

The Country Time carried liability insurance, right? Wasn't there a clause in there somewhere about employees stealing? Wasn't George basically an employee? Maybe she would be covered...?

Fingers scrabbling across the desk, she grabbed the phone and called Chet Hinkle, the local insurance agent who'd been handling their policies forever.

"Hey Chet," she greeted him when he answered, trying to sound casual instead of desperate. "I need to ask you about the Country Time's insurance policies."

"You do?" Chet's voice brightened. "Want to schedule a review?"

"No!" She realized she'd snapped the word and took a deep breath before continuing. "No. I, um, was wondering if I was covered for, uh, employee theft."

"Employee theft?" Now Chet sounded confused. "Are you having a problem?"

"Of course not. I'm just interested." She gripped the phone receiver tighter. "Can you look at my policy?"

"Sure. Now?"

"Yes." Hannah tried not to grind her teeth. "Now."

"Sure, okay. Hold on and let me get your file."

After what seemed to be an interminable length of time he was back, huffing slightly, as if moving from his chair had taken an effort.

"Okay," he said and she heard papers flipping in the background. "Let's see what we've...huh."

Hannah's blood chilled.

"What?" she demanded.

"Huh," Chet repeated. "Hmmm...uh huh. Oh."

"For God's sake, what?" He was killing her.

"I remember this now," Chet sounded cheery again, happy things were falling into place. "Before your father died, I met with him, and he cut back on the Country Time's insurance coverage. My note says he wanted to reduce premiums."

"Okay," Hannah said slowly. "And what does that mean for employee theft coverage?"

"Well..." More rustling. "According to the file, he reduced employee theft coverage to a thousand dollars. With the deductible, that's basically nothing." He laughed. "Guess he trusted his employees more than you do, Hannah."

Hope no longer zinged. "I guess," she croaked.

"Hey, it's all there in the addendum," Chet told her. "Didn't you read your insurance policies when you took over the business?"

She hadn't. She'd been too busy coping with her father's death and trying to run the Country Time without quite enough staff. Maybe George would have mentioned it to her if

George had been a better adviser. But it was pretty obvious now that he'd been following his own agenda.

Chet must have shifted to the computer while she'd been absorbing the new blow he'd just delivered, because the sound of tapping keys had replaced the shuffling of paper in the background.

"Looks like you still haven't paid your premiums for the quarter," he said, sounding genuinely concerned for the first time in their conversation. "Better tell George to get that check out. You don't want them to lapse."

Right.

"Sure you don't want to review your policies?" Chet sounded hopeful. "I could come over and—"

She hung up on him.

Running her hands through her hair, she tried to think. Apparently insurance would not be riding to her rescue.

Thanks, Dad.

Of course, maybe she should have actually looked at the insurance policies before now.

Her next step was to call the bank to cut off Uncle George's access to the Country Time's checking account. On a whim, she asked the woman who'd answered the phone if they would replace her funds.

Once the woman had stopped laughing, Hannah made an appointment to see a lending officer about reactivating a line of credit her father had taken out a few years ago. She hadn't needed to use it since his death, but she was going to need it now. Big time.

After the bank, she called Police Chief Jacqueline Kline to see what she had to do to have her late mother's older brother arrested. Josie Kline, Chief Kline's daughter and one of Hannah's best friends since sixth grade, had always said her mother was scary protective when it came to people she cared about. So, Hannah wasn't entirely surprised when the other woman said she'd be over in a few minutes to personally take her statement.

Because the Country Time had just opened, Hannah asked the chief to come to the back door in the hopes of avoiding stirring up the customers. As promised, the other woman arrived fifteen minutes later, a young patrolman in tow. As soon as she stepped into the kitchen, she wrapped Hannah in a tight, motherly embrace before letting her go to study her face, her brown eyes serious.

"What the hell happened?"

Hannah shrugged. "I told you on the phone. George ran off with all of the money."

Chief Kline nodded, took off her uniform hat and ran a hand through her cap of dark hair. "I need the details. Tell me everything."

"Okay," Hannah sighed. "We'd better go to the office."

She led them to the office through a side door so they wouldn't have to go into the taproom. But she knew her attempts at discretion had probably been a complete waste of time. Sure enough, when she relieved Deacon at the bar so he could go talk to the chief, she got enough speculative glances to assure her everyone knew something was up.

At least June and Mary Alice, the two servers scheduled for the evening, weren't there yet. Hannah did not look forward to telling June what had happened. The woman wouldn't hesitate to let her know she'd been a complete dumbass.

Then there was Grace, the other server. Kevin, her part-time cook. Jason, the second bartender. Billy, the dishwasher. God, what was she going to tell them? What *could* she tell them?

Maybe she just wouldn't tell them anything.

Hannah considered that option while she drew a beer from one of the taps for a bowling league guy who'd come in early for a pre-game brew. She frowned into the mug as she filled it, ignoring the way the man watched her with ill-disguised curiosity.

No. She had to tell the staff. Hell, at the rate things were going, they'd hear the gossip before they got to work.

Deacon came back behind the bar and touched her shoulder without speaking. Hannah nodded in acknowledgment, gave the bowling league guy his beer, and went back to her office.

Once Chief Kline and her officer were satisfied they'd gotten all of the information they needed for now, Hannah ushered them out through the kitchen. Thank God Kevin hadn't been scheduled to work; it was still deserted.

"We'll do all we can, Hannah," the chief said, after she'd sent her officer out to the car. "I'll put out a warrant on George, so if anyone checks they'll know he's wanted. We'll freeze his accounts, flag his credit cards, and that sort of thing."

"What about Aunt Hildy?" Hannah asked, alarmed.

"I'm going to go talk to her now. We'll see what we can do."

"Thanks." Hannah shook her head. "I just don't understand why the bank didn't call me when the account was emptied."

Chief Kline shrugged. "Why would they? George had signing authority, so he could basically do whatever he wanted. The online records you showed me indicate he transferred the money to a variety of accounts. Your bank probably hasn't even noticed."

"Wonderful." Why the hell was she paying those monthly account fees if the bank wasn't even looking at her account?

Chief Kline cleared her throat. "The problem is, if he closed the other accounts and pulled out the cash, or if he transferred the money from them to other identities, we're going to have a hard time finding him."

"Yeah," Hannah sighed. For all she knew, Uncle George had set up twenty false identities.

"I have a small department," Chief Kline said. "I barely have enough people to handle traffic accidents and the occasional drunk and disorderly. I'll bump this up to the staties, but you're going to need a lawyer, Hannah. And if you want to find George before he spends all of your money, I think you should consider hiring a private investigator."

Hannah stared at the other woman. "And pay him with what? My charm?"

Chief Kline nodded. "Good point." She settled her hat more firmly on her head and patted Hannah's cheek. "I'll be in touch."

"Thank you," Hannah said, meaning it.

"Just doing my job." The chief grinned at her, then tapped her on the nose. "Call Josie. If my girl hears about this from someone else, she's going to be pissed, and I don't want her bitching at me."

Hannah's stomach clutched. "Yes, ma'am."

Chief Kline chuckled and left.

Hannah went back to her office, closed the door, and sat behind her desk, rubbing at the wicked throbbing in her temples. She considered calling Josie and getting it over with, but she just couldn't face her friend.

She checked her bank balance again, instead.

Still fifty dollars.

And she was still screwed.

2

Hannah had dug out some ibuprofen and was drinking water after swallowing three tablets when there was a brief knock on the door. It opened, and Deacon stepped into the office.

"Who's tending the bar?" she asked automatically.

"June's here," he said, closing the door and walking over to drop into the visitor's chair. "What did Chief Kline say?"

"She's putting out a warrant for George's arrest and talking to people," Hannah told him. "She's also going to send the information on to the state police so they can spread the word —or whatever it is they do. But to find my money, they have to find George. She wasn't encouraging."

"I was wondering if your insurance would cover—"

"I already called Chet," she interrupted him. "My father dicked around with the policies a couple of years ago. They won't cover squat."

"Too bad." He frowned. "Are you going to declare bankruptcy?"

She ran a hand through her hair. "Jesus, Deacon. I just found out about George a couple of hours ago. I think I can take a minute to think before I decide what I'm going to do about it."

But she already knew there was no way she'd declare bankruptcy. If she did, she might as well close; it was extremely unlikely any of the vendors would agree to keep working with her afterward.

Hannah refused to close the Country Time Bar and Grill.

This bar, this place, had been in her family for four generations. Her father had counted on her to keep it going. He'd trusted her. Her employees depended on her. She'd been training to run it since before she could legally drink in it. In a lot of ways, it was home. She would be *damned* if it was going to fail on her watch just because some old asshole couldn't keep his hands off her accounts.

Deacon tapped his fingers on his knee. "Well, whatever you do, I guess you're going to need some legal help."

"Yeah." Hannah had been thinking about Chief Kline's advice and come to a rather distasteful conclusion.

"Did you call your attorney?" Deacon asked.

"No," she answered absently. "Bob retired and went to Indonesia as a missionary, remember? We had his farewell party here a couple of months ago."

He rolled his eyes. "Of course I remember. Are you telling me you don't have another attorney?"

"No. He gave me some names, but I haven't called anyone yet." Because she'd been too busy. But in hindsight, she should have made the time.

"So call Bob. There are phones in Indonesia."

"Not where he is. Besides, what's he going to do? Fly in to the rescue?" She snorted, picturing the big, silver-haired lawyer. "Right. He probably has malaria or something by now. Bob never did have much common sense."

He also hadn't been especially spiritual, as far as she could tell. Which was why she'd always wondered if he'd really become a missionary, or if he'd had another reason for disappearing so completely. Like, oh, jail.

"Then call one of the attorneys he recommended."

"Deacon." Hannah folded her hands on her desk and leaned towards him. "I hate to mention this, but at the moment I don't have enough money to hire a flea. Bob would have done me a favor because he'd been friends with my father. I guarantee you none of the people he recommended will work without a retainer."

"Good point." Deacon crossed an ankle over the opposite knee.

Hannah shifted back in her chair again, watching him warily. She wasn't exactly sure how he'd react to the decision she'd made.

"I do, um, have another option. For legal advice, I mean," she said.

Deacon studied her expression for a moment, then dropped his foot to the floor.

"No," he said.

She drew in a deep breath.

"I think—"

"Hannah—"

"—I'm going to call Sam."

"Sam, my brother."

"Your brother Sam, the attorney."

"Your ex-boyfriend. The same guy who slept with one of your waitresses," he said, as if seeking clarification.

"And who is an attorney, yes."

"In the backseat of her car."

"While he was an attorney."

"In your own damn parking lot."

Unable to remain seated, Hannah lunged to her feet. She paced the few steps it took to get to the wall, then back again.

"Look, I don't like this any more than you do. But Sam is an attorney. A good attorney. I think."

"I wouldn't know. We haven't exactly been on speaking terms since I punched him in the face."

Well, she still felt a little guilty about that. After the police had caught Sam and Louise in the parking lot and charged them with public indecency, Sam had come back into the Country Time, apparently to try and talk to Hannah. She'd never found out what he would have said because Deacon, only back in town for a month or so, had jumped over the bar and punched his brother in the face. She hadn't been able to stop him.

Admittedly, she hadn't tried very hard.

"Sam," she pushed on, "is an attorney who will not charge me anything."

Deacon blinked. "Huh?"

"I said, he won't charge me anything." If she worked it right.

"How do you know?" he demanded.

Good question.

"Because he dumped me when we dated in high school, and after I gave him a second chance, he screwed one of my waitresses in my parking lot. I'm going to play the guilt card."

"That's a hell of a lot of guilt."

"He's sure got it."

"I don't trust him, the self-centered prick."

"Look, I know you two have issues—"

"Issues?" Deacon sounded highly offended.

"But he works for a big firm in the Lehigh Valley, and he must know some private detectives. He can help."

"Maybe he can, but will he?"

Another damn good question. Hannah paced over to the room's tiny window and stared out, arms crossed over her chest. Honestly, she didn't have a clue whether or not Sam would cooperate. After all, she'd made sure he'd known he was *persona non grata* at the Country Time. They hadn't even spoken for two years. But she had to believe he'd help her, if for no other reason than to rub her face in the fact that she needed him.

"I don't have a choice," she said.

"There have to be other options for legal counsel."

"Free legal counsel," she reminded him, turning to face him again. "Preferably pretty good free legal counsel. Someone I can find quickly who might have a lead on a private detective."

"There's got to be another way," he argued.

"Well, I don't know, Deacon." She threw up her hands in frustration. "This is my first embezzlement, okay? I'm doing the best I can. There might be other options. Maybe a lot of other options. Maybe better options. But Sam's the only option I know about, so I'm going to start with him and take it from there."

Deacon huffed out a breath. Belatedly she realized seeing his older brother again might be difficult for him.

"You don't have to be around when I talk to him," she offered. "I'm going to ask him to meet me here, but I'll bring him back to the office. You can go outside and take a break, so you don't have to see him."

He gave her a disgusted look and stood, his big frame filling the small space. "I'll be there," he said, an edge to his voice.

"Deacon—"

"I have to get back out front," he interrupted. "Mary Alice will be here soon. We'll be okay for a while without you, if you have stuff to do."

Recognizing male pride when she heard it, she decided to let it go.

"Wait!" she called when he reached the door. He looked at her again, eyebrows raised in query. "Don't say anything to June or Mary Alice about what happened. I want to tell them myself."

"Should I send them back to the office once Mary Alice gets in?"

"No," she said. "I'll tell them after their shift is over." That way she could come up with some kind of a plan before she talked to them. Maybe.

Deacon frowned at her.

"They're going to hear rumors," he pointed out. "Everyone out there knows the cops were here earlier. The gossip's already spreading."

"I just need a little time." She rubbed her aching forehead.

"What am I supposed to say when they ask me what's going on?"

When, not *if*.

"Just tell them the police were here investigating something."

Deacon shook his head. "They'll want details."

"Okay, fine." She shoved a hand through her hair again, headache pounding. How long did it take ibuprofen to work anyway? "Fine. If they ask you anything, send them to me, and I'll tell them. Otherwise, I'll talk to them at the end of the shift. Okay?"

"I guess." Deacon studied her for a moment and his face softened a little. "You know we're going to work this out somehow, yeah?"

She stared at him across the small office. "We?"

He shrugged. "All of us. We'll figure something out." Then he left, closing the door behind him.

Hannah found herself fighting tears again. *We*, he'd said. *All of us*, he'd said, and he'd meant it. He was right, too. Everyone who worked at the Country Time would do what they could to help. But Hannah was the one who was responsible. She was the one who paid their salaries. And she was the one who'd let George put them all in jeopardy.

She sat down in her chair and planted her elbow on the desk, chin in her hand, her entire body stiff with tension.

Now she had to call Sam.

Lovely.

Reaching out, she fiddled with the black cord on the old-fashioned, slightly greasy, beige phone.

She'd met Samuel Black, Deacon's brother, when she'd signed up as a peer-to-peer English tutor to earn extra credit in high school. She'd been assigned to Deacon, a new kid whose family had just moved into the district. He'd been failing miserably in his junior year English requirement, and the guidance counselor thought he might work harder if his tutor was a girl.

Which was why she'd been sitting with Deacon at the Black family kitchen table, trying to help him slog through *A Tale of Two Cities*, when Sam had come home after football practice.

Hannah could still remember how dazzled she'd been the first time she'd seen Deacon's brother. She'd thought he was simply beautiful—all dark curly hair and big blue eyes. Plus, he was a senior, while she and Deacon were only juniors. His presence had overwhelmed her to the point that she'd stammered like an idiot.

She'd been totally shocked when Sam had flirted with her, but she'd almost fainted dead away when he'd actually asked her out to a movie. He'd kissed her sweetly in the back row of the old movie theater, and she'd drawn a big heart around his name when she'd written about that night in her diary.

The movie theater had been torn down a year later. She and Sam hadn't lasted that long.

Her fault, she admitted now. He'd gotten bored because she'd never been available when he'd wanted to go out.

Well, she had a lot on her plate, even then. She'd been taking care of most of the household chores, something she'd started doing after her mother died in a car crash when she'd been eleven. It had been her and her father for years, and she liked to think she was taking care of him.

By the time high school rolled around, she was working nights and weekends at the Country Time, too. Not serving drinks or anything, but learning the business from the ground up. Between her various responsibilities at home and her father's business, the tutoring, and her school work, there just hadn't been a lot of time to go to football games or hang out at the movies with her boyfriend.

Sam, probably frustrated as hell, had tried to push the physical thing one night in his shiny red Camaro. She hadn't been ready, and he'd backed off. Way off.

After he dumped her for a cheerleader with big boobs, Hannah told the guidance counselor she didn't want to tutor Deacon anymore. She didn't want to take the chance she'd have to see Sam—and Sam's new girlfriend. That had worked so well, she hadn't run into Deacon's brother again until he'd come back to town a few years ago as a big-time lawyer. They'd met, and the old spark had sizzled. This time she hadn't been scared, so the sweet kisses transformed very quickly into wild sex.

Boy, had there been sex.

Hannah sighed nostalgically.

Then lung cancer killed her father and she'd gotten crazy busy trying to run everything. And Sam had nailed Louise, her waitress, in the parking lot.

Good times.

Sighing again, she picked up the phone and called Sam's cell. A part of her hoped he'd changed the number, but he picked up after two rings.

"Hello," he said.

His voice was deep and always sounded intimate.

"It's Hannah," she said abruptly.

There was silence on the other end of the line.

"Hannah Frederickson," she added.

"I know that," he said. Now he sounded intimate and annoyed.

"I need some help," she said.

"You do?" Intimate, annoyed, and shocked.

"I'd rather not get into it over the phone."

More silence. She could practically hear Sam assuming she wanted an excuse to see him again. The truth was, she could have happily lived the rest of her life without seeing him again, but she wanted to look him in the eye when she talked to him. Maybe then she'd be able to judge his real reactions. Maybe she'd be able to tell if he was lying to her.

Right.

"Hannah—" he started.

"I can't come to you. I need you to come to the Country Time. Tonight."

It would be the first time he'd been inside the Country Time since he'd been inside Louise, but what the heck. Seeing Sam again couldn't make the day any worse.

He laughed shortly. "Like I'm going to just drop everything and come running because you decided to call me after two years."

"You will."

More sarcastic laughter. "Please. Why would I?"

"Because you owe me."

"What are you talking about?"

"You had sex with Louise in the parking lot. You owe me."

He huffed out a breath. "I don't owe you anything. You got your payback when Deacon slugged me. I could have sued, but I didn't."

Hannah welcomed the anger surging inside her. It made her feel like she wasn't helpless, wasn't a victim, wasn't dependent on the good graces of a man who had trampled all over her feelings. Twice. She realized she was gripping the phone's receiver so tightly her fingers ached and forced herself to relax before she cracked the old plastic.

"It's not enough," she said through her teeth. "You humiliated me. Everyone in town was laughing at me, talking about me."

"They talked about me, too."

She snorted. "No they didn't. You weren't around for them to laugh at. You were in Allentown or Philadelphia or New York doing your lawyer thing. I was here every day, smiling and acting nice when people came into the bar to ask personal questions or make stupid comments. It took months for the gossip to die down. Months, Sam."

Her stomach roiled because she knew it would all happen again once people found out about George. She wanted to scream. Honest to God, men and their dicks!

"Okay, I understand you're pissed off because you were on the front lines—"

"Pissed *off*?" She was shouting now. Dimly, she hoped the music in the taproom was loud enough so the customers wouldn't hear her screaming at her ex. "I mean, Jesus. You couldn't even drive the car to a different parking lot before you jumped Lou?"

"She only had a half hour break."

Hannah would not dignify that with a response. She took several deep breaths, struggling to rein herself in.

"You owe me," she said, proud of the chill she heard in her voice. "You will come over here because you actually might be able to help me."

"Hannah—"

"You know you really screwed up, and you know I paid the price for it. You know that you owe me some kind of consideration for the time we were together. You *know* that, Sam."

This time he was silent for several minutes, but she waited him out.

"Maybe," he said finally.

"Tonight," Hannah insisted.

"I said, maybe. If I show up, it will be late. And Deacon had better not punch me again."

Hannah could hear the stubbornness and knew pushing him any further would be counterproductive.

"Whatever. Just get here," she said. "Before two." She slammed down the phone and tugged at her own hair. "Aaarrrgh!"

She didn't want to see him again. She didn't want to look at him and know he had lied to her, cheated on her. Twice. She didn't want to talk to him and wonder if he was lying to her again.

Letting go of her hair, she let out a deep sigh and attempted to smooth it back into place.

Well, you couldn't always get what you wanted, could you?

Taking Deacon at his word that she wouldn't be needed out front for a while, and praying he wouldn't send June or Mary Alice back to her office until she knew what she wanted to tell them, she turned back to the spreadsheets on her computer.

Deacon left June to tend the bar, ignoring her pointed questions because he didn't want to get into it with her, and headed out back to the spot they'd set up as a break area for the staff. It wasn't much—just a few plastic lawn chairs on an old cement pad—but the breeze was cool when it brushed against his skin, and the dumpster was pretty far away.

He grabbed one of the plastic chairs, dropped into it, and stretched his legs out in front of him.

Sam. Fucking Sam.

He still couldn't believe Hannah was actually going to call his brother, not after the way the man had hurt her.

Although she was right when she'd said Sam could give her legal advice. Hell, he could freaking smother her with legal advice. Wasn't he admitted to not one, but *two* bar associations? Couldn't he practice law in Pennsylvania *and* New York? Hadn't he graduated from fancy lawyer school *summa cum laude*? Didn't their parents remind Deacon of those facts whenever he tried to talk to them?

Why, yes. Yes, they did.

Deacon huffed out a laugh that had little to do with humor. The bars he was admitted to weren't places his parents bragged about nearly as often.

He crossed his legs at the ankles and his arms over his chest, staring into the scrub trees beyond the cracked asphalt of the parking lot.

He thought Hannah was being overly optimistic to think Sam would fall in with her plans. As far as he could tell, his brother's normal way of dealing with guilt was to shrug it off. Even getting arrested for public indecency hadn't seemed to put a dent in the man's calm self-assurance.

He fisted his hands under his armpits.

God, it was infuriating. He'd been aching to get a taste of Hannah Frederickson for years, ever since high school. It had about killed him to watch her fall for Sam the first time, back when she'd been his tutor—to see the light in his brother's eyes while he'd charmed her, and to know that as soon as Sam had shown up and smiled at her, she'd forgotten all about Deacon.

Hannah had buzzed around in his brain like a wasp the whole time he'd been away; the one woman he'd never been able to forget. When he'd finally come back to Hardy Falls, the Country Time had been his first stop. Lord only knew why he'd decided to hire on as her bartender.

Well, he *had* needed a job.

· · ·

"Holy shit."

Deacon turned around from stacking glasses on the back counter and found himself face to face with Sam for the first time in over ten years.

"Holy shit," Sam repeated. He stood at the bar, obviously surprised. "I didn't believe her when she told me you were back in town."

"Hannah?"

Sam nodded and smiled. "Last night."

It was pretty clear what he and Hannah had been doing last night. Deacon felt his stomach tighten. Stupid.

"You've hooked up again," he said. It wasn't a question.

Sam's grin broadened. "Oh, yeah."

Deacon nodded and tried not to betray his reaction.

"Seen the old man yet?" Sam asked.

"No." He'd only been back in town a week.

"Better do it soon. It wouldn't be good for him to hear about it from someone else."

"Planning on telling him?"

"Maybe." Sam smiled again. "Welcome home." Turning, he headed for Hannah's office.

"Christ." Getting one of the clean glasses, Deacon poured himself a drink.

He'd fully expected Hannah to fire him after Sam's little parking lot rendezvous. Hey, she'd dropped him right quick back in high school when Sam had dumped her the first time. He'd figured she wouldn't want to look at Sam's brother this time around either.

But she hadn't fired him. Hadn't even considered it, as far as he could tell. He'd taken that as a good sign.

And now, after two blissful Sam-free years, now when Hannah seemed to have moved on and finally—*finally!*—

started to see Deacon as more than just the stupid, pimple-faced jerk he'd been back in high school, now when she might even be starting to look at him with a little bit of interest, here came Sam again.

"Shit."

Deacon's cell phone buzzed and he dug it out of his back pocket, automatically checking caller ID.

Sam Black.

What the hell?

He hesitated for another instant, then answered.

"How did you get this number?"

"Never mind that. What the hell's going on over there?" Sam demanded.

"I guess Hannah called you." Deacon settled back in the chair again.

"Yeah, but she just told me to get over to the bar and didn't give me a reason why I should. She hasn't had the time of day for me in two years and now she calls and demands I come over? I don't think so. I've got...stuff tonight."

Deacon stared across the parking lot, smiling a little at his brother's obvious irritation. He had to take his amusement where he could find it.

"I really can't say what she wants," he said with deliberate mildness. "Guess you'll have to come find out."

"Bullshit. I'll be damned if I'm going to jump because she thinks I should. I don't care what happened to her after I got caught with Louise." Sam's voice was tight.

Interesting. It almost sounded as though Sam was acknowledging some sort of responsibility. Deacon frowned. He wasn't sure how he felt about the fact that it had only taken one phone call from Hannah to penetrate his brother's thick protective coating.

On the other hand, Sam's coating could self-seal with amazing swiftness. He might be flailing around a bit at the moment—hence this phone call—but if he kept rationalizing, Deacon had infinite faith he'd work out a reason to justify not showing up.

Too bad that wasn't what Hannah wanted.

"So don't come," he said, keeping his tone careless. "She's got plenty of people here. I'll help her. I told her not to call you in the first place." It might have been years since they'd had a real conversation, but he still knew how to push his older brother's buttons.

"Wait." Sam sounded truly offended. "You mean you think *you* can handle this thing for Hannah?"

"Sure." Deacon said, still casual.

"Yeah, right," Sam sneered. "You'll help her? The place will fold in two weeks."

"I know the business. You don't," Deacon said, feeling resentment grow. No matter what his family thought, he *wasn't* goddamned stupid.

"I'm an attorney," Sam ground out.

"I can look things up on the Internet."

He hadn't meant this conversation to turn into "anything you can do I can do better," but apparently Sam could still push his buttons, too.

"Really? The Internet?" Sam's laugh was derisive. "Oh, I've got a big picture of how that will go."

"We don't need you. Hannah doesn't need you."

"She's the one who asked for me."

Deacon's grip on the cell phone tightened. He wanted this conversation done. "Then why are you even talking to me about this? Are you coming or not?"

There was a beat of silence on the other end of the phone.

"I'll be there," Sam snapped, and abruptly cut the connection.

"Great."

Deacon shoved the phone back into his pocket. Sam probably would show up. That should make Hannah happy, anyway.

Sighing, he stood and stretched out his back, reaching his hands to the sky before dropping them back to his sides. He'd better get inside before June came hunting him. Once the leagues were finished, they'd get busy.

The hell of it was, Deacon thought as he trudged towards the building, he'd told Sam the truth. He really did know the business. He knew the customers and the vendors. He probably could be of help, if given the chance. Maybe even more than Sam.

3

———

Hannah had decided the first thing she should do was figure out exactly how much money she was going to need and when she was going to need it. She felt that would be both mature and logical. Her other option—running around her office bellowing and waving her arms like a gorilla—didn't seem like it would be nearly as useful.

Even if that was exactly what she felt like doing.

It was too late in the day to start calling her vendors, so, for lack of a better plan, she began comparing the accounting records to her online bank statements.

George appeared to have kept relatively up to date with normal operating expenses, which was a relief. He'd probably been afraid the vendors would complain to her if he fell behind. She couldn't find any payments for the last round of deliveries, but she'd expected that.

Still, it wasn't too much of a surprise when she found the first discrepancy. About a month ago the bank statement showed a deposit slightly lower, and then a cash withdrawal slightly larger, than the transactions reflected in her accounting records.

Stomach clenching, she kept looking and spotted another difference. And another. And another.

Once she'd compared deposits and withdrawals for the last six months, she'd found ten discrepancies. Never especially large amounts, which was why she hadn't spotted them before. Of course, since she'd also been under the impression she had a trustworthy accountant, she hadn't exactly been diligent about checking her bank statements. Stupid. So stupid.

Hannah sat back in her chair and ran her hands through her hair so she wouldn't throw the computer against the wall.

It sure looked like good old Uncle George had been stealing from her all along. Yesterday might have been his big score, but he had helped himself to the business's money on a regular basis.

"You bastard."

She shoved her chair away from the desk, tried to breathe, to think past the anger and the hurt. It could be worse, she reminded herself a little desperately. At least the vendors were pretty much up to date. She'd find money to cover what she owed. Somewhere. No worries.

Times like these were when she missed Lou the most. Louise Weber hadn't just been a terrific waitress, she'd been hell on wheels with numbers and coming up with creative ideas to handle problems.

Hannah sighed. She missed Louise for a lot of reasons other than just her business skills. Mostly she just missed her friend. Or rather, the friend she'd thought she had.

She glanced at the phone. She could always call Josie and talk things over with her. Chief Kline was right; if she found out what was going on through the grapevine, she'd really be pissed off. And a pissed off Josie was not a lot of fun.

Still, it would probably be better to wait a day or two before making that phone call. God willing, she'd have more information or a plan or something by then. The last time they'd spoken—jeez, two weeks ago now!—Josie had been involved in some big ad campaign. It was her first after being promoted to a new team at the New York City ad agency where she worked. Hannah didn't want to distract her friend with problems she couldn't do anything about.

Which meant she was on her own.

Rolling back to the computer, Hannah pulled up her calendar to see what deliveries were scheduled in the next couple of weeks. Her eye caught on the current date and held. She froze, staring at the screen in horror.

It was September 9th.

September...9th.

Quarterly estimated taxes were due on September 15th. Quarterly unemployment taxes were due on September 15th. Payroll taxes for last month were due on September 15th. And September 15th was—she checked the calendar—only six days away.

Queasy, she switched back to her bank records. Nope, no tax payments.

Which meant everything was still due.

Plus, the money withheld for payroll taxes from the first pay of the current month was missing too.

And, as Chet had pointed out, the quarterly insurance premiums were due. Even though the policies apparently weren't all that great, she still needed coverage to operate the business.

She was so totally screwed.

Hannah groaned and laid her head on her desk next to the keyboard. The scarred wood bit into her forehead as she rolled it from side to side.

"No. No. No."

George had planned it this way, of course. He'd chosen a time when the bank account was at its highest, and then he'd taken everything.

The office door opened.

"Hey, Hannah, we need you at the grill—" Deacon's voice cut off abruptly. "What's wrong, now?" he demanded.

"There's no money. None at all," she said. She felt hollow inside.

"We already knew that."

She sat up and looked at him. "It's September 9th and there's no money. Quarterly and payroll taxes are all due on the 15th, and there's no money."

"Oh." He paused. "Oohhh," he said again as it sunk in. For a moment he just stood there, absently wiping his hands on a bar rag. "Oh."

"Yeah."

"Can't you get an extension or something?"

"How the hell should I know?" She rubbed her face. "I think there are a lot of penalties if you don't pay on time, and even if I get an extension, I still don't have any money."

"You need a new accountant. Fast."

"Yeah, no shit, Deacon. God." As if she hadn't figured out *that* news bulletin.

"Do you know anybody?"

"No." She tried to tamp down her irritation. "Look, I'm going to the bank tomorrow. Dad took out a line of credit a couple of years ago, but we haven't had to use it since he died. I'm going to reactivate it. That should buy me some time to figure out the rest of this mess." But she was going to have to borrow a lot more than she'd thought she would. And then she'd have to pay it back. Her stomach jittered.

"You still need an accountant."

"Well, I *know* that. But I also need to be able to pay them. Sue me if I don't have an accountant ex-boyfriend who screwed one of my waitresses in the parking lot so I can guilt him into doing work for free."

"Too bad," he said, tucking the rag in the front pocket of his jeans. "I'll come with you to the bank."

Hannah blinked at him, surprised. "What? No. Why?"

"You need another set of eyes and ears while you're dealing with those people. I know almost as much about the Country Time's business as you do."

"I guess," she muttered. It was true. Somehow she'd come to depend on Deacon more and more in the time since he'd started working for her. It was too bad he'd be leaving sooner or later.

Thinking about Deacon leaving made her stomach churn more than it already was, and she spoke without thinking.

"Maybe I should take Sam," she said. "Since he's an attorney and all." Then she winced because she didn't want to piss Deacon off.

He didn't get angry, just crossed his arms over his chest and leaned against the door jamb. "Do you really want Sam to know all the details of your financial affairs? Do you even want to talk to him more than you have to?" He sounded genuinely interested.

"I'll do whatever I have to do. I called him. He's coming over tonight so we can talk," she said with a confidence she didn't really feel.

"Great, but I'm still going with you to the bank tomorrow."

She saw the stubborn set of his jaw and gave up. She didn't know why she was fighting anyway. It wasn't like she *wanted* to go with Sam.

"Fine. You'll come with me," she said grumpily.

"That's what I said."

Hannah rolled her eyes. "Did you come in here for some reason? Maybe you found a million dollars hidden under the bar?"

"Sorry." His face was still grim, but his lips twitched. "June's running the grill, but I need her out front. Leagues are finishing, and the place is busy."

She sighed and hauled herself to her feet. "Okay. Who's got the bar now?"

"Mary Alice. June needed to fill some food orders."

"God." They had to get out there. No way could Mary Alice handle everything by herself.

When she went to push past Deacon to get out of the office, he lifted his hand and cupped the nape of her neck. She stopped at the unexpected contact and looked up at him with some confusion.

"It will be all right," he said, his fingers warm and strong against her skin.

"Thanks." She was only breathless because of the stress.

They stayed like that for another moment, staring at each other. He really did have nice eyes.

"Deacon...?" Mary Alice called from out front, voice quavering.

Shaking off the strange paralysis, Hannah stepped around Deacon and trotted down the short hallway to the main room.

She was gratified to see the taproom had indeed started to fill up with, hopefully, paying customers. Country music blared over on the sound system. Mary Alice looked frantic as she pulled a beer tap.

"The people at the tables are frowning at me," she said, her eyes sky blue and protuberant.

Mary Alice Norton was an artist in the body of a sod farmer. She was as big and broad as an oak tree and as dreamy as a poet. She was always stopping to stare into the distance, then rush off to scribble in her notepad, sometimes forcing the customers to go to extremes to get her attention.

She was also reliable and cheerful, and you pretty much had to hit her over the head with a stick to offend her. But you couldn't exactly expect Mary Alice to multitask.

Deacon moved quickly down the bar and took over filling drink orders.

Leaving Deacon and Mary Alice to deal with the customers, Hannah pushed open the door to the kitchen and stepped inside. She needed to get to work so the bustle and routine of a Wednesday night at the Country Time could help take her mind off her problems.

As the door swung shut behind her, she stood for a moment and watched June Esperanza work.

The older woman moved quickly from grill to fryer, flipping burgers, plating orders, graceful as a ballerina despite the heat and heavy smell of oil. She'd worked at the Country Time since Hannah had been about thirteen, a mass of energy with big, dark eyes, and hair a shining black.

June could do anything. She could run the grill, run the bar, run the world if given half the chance. Yes, her reputation had taken some dings over the years, and yes, she'd been the object of her share of gossip. But she'd always risen above it. Or just ignored it.

There was no denying she was magic when it came to the customers. The regulars loved her. Hannah loved her. June wouldn't have trusted George to handle the business's money. She wouldn't have put everyone at risk. June always knew what to do.

Well, except for when she'd gotten involved with Pat Murphy, the owner of Murphy Lanes. It had been kind of comforting to find out June could make mistakes, too.

"You'd better get out front," Hannah said, stepping into the room. "Mary Alice is panicking."

"Mary Alice always panics." June finished plating the order she was working on and put it aside for pickup before turning to face Hannah.

"It's about time you got in here," she said, wiping her hands on the hem of the chef's apron she wore over her Country Time polo shirt. "I haven't had a chance to come find you. Why the hell were the cops here?"

So much for hoping June hadn't heard about the police visit. Well, that really had been too much to expect.

Trying to give herself a moment to think, Hannah walked to a nearby closet and grabbed another chef's apron, pulling the loop over her head. As she fastened the tie around her waist, she looked up and found June watching her, head cocked like a bird of prey. She felt her shoulders hunch and made a conscious effort to straighten them.

"Umm," she said. The headache, which had gotten a little better, came pounding back.

"Did it have something to do with George skipping town with his slut assistant?" June raised her dark eyebrows. "Or was it the fact that he took all of your money?"

Hannah's hands fell limp to her sides. She collapsed on a stool set up near the prep station.

June leaned back on a counter. "Holy shit. So it's true."

"How—?"

"A couple of women from the bowling leagues came in flapping their jaws right before Deacon asked me to work the grill. I think they were trying to pump me for information, but I didn't know anything." June glared at Hannah accusingly.

"Sorry," Hannah said weakly. "How—?"

"One of them apparently has a sister who's friends with someone who works with Hildy at the Wal-Mart. Sounds like Hildy's been calling everyone she knows and spouting off about George."

Of course she was. Hannah closed her eyes.

"You didn't tell me." June's statement was flat, but Hannah could hear the hurt. *Crap.*

"I'm sorry," she said again. "I was going to tell you later tonight. I wasn't trying to hide anything, I promise. I just..." she shrugged helplessly. "I guess I just wanted to get a better handle on what was going on first."

"All right," June said slowly. She continued to watch Hannah closely, dark eyes alert in her sharp face. "So how bad is it?"

"Pretty bad," Hannah admitted. "He got everything."

June nodded. Hannah waited for her to shout and tell her what an idiot she'd been. June had to know she'd been the one to give her uncle access to the bank account. To her surprise, she just sighed.

"Does Deacon know?"

Hannah swallowed. "He was here when I found out. I kind of lost it."

And then he'd held her.

She wouldn't think about that. She had enough problems.

June nodded again, pushing away from the counter. "We'll figure something out."

We.

"June—"

"Can't let that horny old bastard get away with this, can we?"

They were interrupted when Mary Alice came flying into the kitchen clutching about six food order slips. Her wide, sunny face looked even more crazed than normal.

"Oh, jeepers, June," she said. "That nice Calvin Hardy is looking for you, and Deacon said he could use your help on the bar like right now, and the tables are busy because a big group of kids from the college just came in, and people are getting mad because they're waiting for their food, and I sure hope you're finished in here, and Old Albert yelled at me because I spilled some of his drink." She took a breath. "But then he apologized."

June raised her eyes to the heavens. "Fine, fine. I'm coming." She pulled off her apron and tossed it towards the laundry bin.

"We'll talk more later," she promised Hannah, and stalked out of the kitchen.

Hannah sighed. "Great."

"What are you going to talk to her about?" Mary Alice asked as she gathered the completed orders from the counter. She balanced plates expertly, the prospect of having help at the tables apparently calming her nerves. "Oh, I guess she wants to know about George taking all of the money." She smiled, cheerful once more. "I want to know about that, too." Pushing open the door with her hip, she went back to the main room.

Hannah sighed again. Freaking small towns.

Then she tied her hair back in a knot, put on the white baseball cap she always wore in the kitchen, and got to work.

The next few hours were insane, as people from the bowling leagues and bored kids from the nearby college collided in a perfect storm of demand. To make matters worse, Billy, the dishwasher, had called out sick—again—which left Hannah running the grill and trying to keep ahead of the dishes at the same time. June and Mary Alice helped when they could, the frenzied pace and noise of the kitchen combined with the more muffled sounds of pounding music and voices from the taproom helping to prevent awkward questions.

Oddly, Hannah found herself soothed by the hot, hurried work. This was normal. This was routine. Routine was good.

Once table service ended around midnight, the grill orders finally slowed. Hannah knew she should start on the pile of dirty dishes stacked next to the rinse sink. Instead she headed out to the taproom to escape the kitchen and get off her aching feet for a few minutes.

She slumped down on one of the stools at the end of the bar, vaguely wishing there was a way to erase the smell of grease and cooked meat clinging to her clothes and hair. Oh, well. She was used to it. Hell, the scent of broiled hamburger was probably imprinted in her skin by now.

Country music wailed, and the voices of the customers rose over it. A group of people stood at the bar watching the Phillies wrap up an overtime game on the television. Mary Alice sat at a table, scribbling in her notebook. Chet Hinkle was at another table with his friend Bernie Housemann and some of the other members of their bowling league, all resplendent in lime-green striped bowling shirts that made Chet look like a watermelon.

June was perched on a stool at the far end of the bar flirting with Calvin Hardy, co-owner of Hardy Hardware and descendant of the founder of Hardy Falls. The man was probably around June's age, his dark hair just starting to turn gray and his broad shoulders stretching his denim shirt. June laughed at something he said and swung her legs while he blushed.

"Here," Deacon stepped up opposite her and handed her a bottle of water.

"Thanks." She uncapped it and downed most of it in one long gulp.

He leaned his forearms on the bar next to her and turned his head to look at June and Calvin. June's cackle of a laugh rang out again.

"How are they doing?" he asked.

Much to everyone's surprise, June and Calvin had started seeing each other on a regular basis a few months ago. They had a rocky past, and June had just broken up with Pat Murphy when Calvin had moved back to town. But they seemed to have worked it out somehow.

Hannah shrugged. "Good, I guess. She doesn't talk too much about him, but she gets all soft and mushy when he's around, and he lights up as soon as he sees her. It's cute."

Deacon scowled. "Maybe I should have a little chat with him. Make sure he's treating her right."

Hannah laughed. "Don't worry about it. They're fine." June was a completely different person around Calvin, and the man was obviously gone over her.

"Hmmm," Deacon made a noncommittal sound. He continued to watch the pair, as if daring poor Calvin to make the wrong move. Hannah knew he didn't really have anything against the man; Calvin Hardy was a likable sort of a guy. But Deacon could be a bit overprotective.

"I heard his divorce was bad," he said. "There's got to be a reason."

"There can be a lot of reasons for an ugly divorce," she pointed out. "He and June are good together, and he loves her so much his pupils turn into little hearts when he looks at her. That's what matters. Let it alone, Deacon."

"Hmmm," he made the sound again.

His position leaning on the bar across from her made her realize just how big he was. And solid. And warm. The short hairs on his forearms tickled her when he shifted. She put her hands in her lap, but he probably hadn't even noticed that he'd invaded her personal space.

She remembered that he'd been a little chubby when they'd known each other in high school; like he was still carrying around some baby fat. But the mass of muscle on him now, the calluses and scars on his hands, the deep reserve in his blue eyes, they all spoke of some rough years between then and now.

Of course Deacon had always been somewhat reserved. They hadn't had classes together in high school, but as far as she could tell, he'd never talked much and hadn't been into sports like Sam. She'd really never even noticed him until she'd been assigned as his tutor.

"Did you crack and tell June about George?" he asked, still watching the couple at the other end of the bar.

Hannah sighed. "Not exactly. She found out from a customer."

Deacon shifted and met her eyes, close enough that she could see the dark rim around the lighter blue of his irises.

"I'm shocked. Shocked, I tell you," he said, his voice dry.

"Yes, you were right about the gossip. It's all over town," Hannah pouted morosely. "Not just about the police, but about the whole mess. Apparently Aunt Hildy's been talking."

"Again. Shock, amazement." Deacon had met Hildy on more than one occasion when she'd come into the bar with George. "No wonder people have been trying to talk to me all night."

"Yeah." Hannah took another long swallow of water. "I think I'll have a meeting with the staff tomorrow after I go to the bank and before we open. I'll call everyone in and lay it out." She'd come to that conclusion as she'd worked in the kitchen. It was only fair for the staff to know what was going on. Hopefully she'd have more information and a plan of action by the time she talked to them.

"Good idea," Deacon said. Somebody signaled for a drink, and he left to get it for them.

When he returned, he handed her another bottle of water. She smiled as she took it.

"Hannah," a male voice said from behind her.

Hannah stiffened. Slowly, she turned to face the man who had come up to her, unnoticed among the bar's remaining patrons.

"Hello, Sam."

4

———

***P**retty*. Samuel Black's impact hadn't diminished with time, Hannah thought. He smiled at her with all of his old charm, dark hair artfully curly, eyes deeply blue.

She toyed with the brim of her kitchen ball cap, belatedly realizing it might not have been such a great idea to insist he come over that night. It would have been nice to look like something other than road-kill when she talked to Sam for the first time in two years.

Deacon straightened and braced his hands on the bar, seeming ready to jump over it and defend her honor.

Again.

"Do you want a beer?" she asked Sam quickly, hoping to avoid sibling violence this time.

Sam smiled, although his attention remained focused on his brother. "That would be great. Whatever you have on tap."

Without comment, Deacon got a clean glass, filled it from a random beer tap, and placed it on the bar in front of Sam.

"Enjoy," he said.

The sarcasm, it burned.

"Thanks." Sam lifted the glass and took a long pull before

looking at Hannah. His smile deepened, bringing his dimples into play. She couldn't control an involuntary twitch of reaction at the sight.

"I need your help," she said abruptly, because it irritated the hell out of her to know she still found him attractive.

"That's what you said on the phone." Sam settled on a barstool, but he stared down into his beer instead of meeting her eyes, absently turning the glass this way and that. "You also said I owed you. I think you might be right."

Deacon made a noise deep in his throat, but his expression was unreadable when Hannah glanced at him. She turned back to find Sam watching her, the overhead lights glowing in his eyes.

"Here's the problem," she said abruptly. "Uncle George ran off with all of my money."

Sam blinked. "Huh?"

"George. Money." She made a running motion with her fingers. "Gone. Get it?"

Sam spread his hands. "Okay, that sucks. Why are you telling me about it?"

"Because I need legal advice," she said, trying to hold on to her patience.

"Don't you have insurance?" he asked.

"No." She bit off the word.

Sam quirked his eyebrows, but to his credit, didn't call her an idiot.

"Did you report it to the police?"

"Sure," Hannah said. "Chief Kline is looking into it."

"There you go then. Once she finds him I can sue him for you if you want." Sam shifted as if preparing to leave, and she grabbed his arm to keep him in place. He was wearing a long-sleeved shirt, but the material was thin, and she could feel the hardness of his biceps under her fingers. Well, Sam had always been fit.

"What can Hannah do in the meantime?" Deacon asked quietly.

He was ignoring the customers, but Hannah saw that June had slid behind the bar to take care of drink orders. And probably to eavesdrop. She looked around, noticing all of the bright interested eyes focused on them, and it occurred to her that a public venue was not the best place in the world to be having this particular conversation. She stood.

"Come with me," she ordered, and without waiting for a response, marched into the kitchen. Sam followed her. So did Deacon.

"All right," she said to Sam once the door had swung shut behind the two men. "What are my options? Advise me. And no bullshit."

Sam ran a hand through his hair, rumpling the curls. "Christ, let me think. Off the top of my head, the quickest solution would be to declare bankruptcy. That will get the creditors off your back, and you'll have some protection as soon as you file."

Hannah shook her head. "No. If I declare bankruptcy, I might as well close."

Sam shrugged, "So, close."

She glared at him. "No."

"Anything else?" Deacon asked. He leaned back on the counter they used for completed food orders. The pose was casual, but his shoulders were straight with tension.

Sam frowned, thinking. "Since George ran off with your money, you can probably sue his wife for half of everything she still has."

Hannah pictured the old mobile home and the aging sedan she was certain George had left behind with Hildy.

"No," she said shortly.

"Sure?" Sam raised his eyebrows.

"I'm sure," she said firmly. "Besides, who's to say he didn't take all of their money, too?"

"He probably did," Sam said equably. "But you'd get something out of her. You could likely get part of any future income, too."

Because Hildy made so much as a cashier at the Wal-Mart.

"No," Hannah said. She was not going to ruin her aunt just because her uncle was a bastard.

"Well, I don't know what else to tell you, Hannah," Sam said, impatience peeking through the charm.

"We need to find George," Deacon said.

"Yes, that would be nice, wouldn't it?" Sam frowned at his brother.

"Does your firm work with a private investigator?" Hannah asked. "I thought most of the big ones did."

Sam jingled his keys in the pocket of his trousers, studying her. "We do," he said slowly. "But the guy's not cheap, and you said George stole all of your money."

"Could you arrange some kind of a deal for me?" she persisted.

"Deal?" Sam laughed. "You think I'm a magician?"

"But you could try," Deacon said. "For Hannah." He hadn't taken his eyes off Sam the entire time they'd been talking. His unblinking stare was making Hannah nervous, and she wasn't even on the receiving end of it. Sam didn't appear affected, but he was an attorney and used to bluffing.

The two men stared at each other across the span of the kitchen, braced like gunslingers at the O.K. Corral.

"Tell me again why you're involved in this?" Sam asked Deacon, voice pleasant, but eyes sharp.

Deacon shrugged, equally pleasant, equally deadly, "I work here."

Hannah stepped in front of Deacon. "I'll pay the freight," she told Sam, trying to keep him on track. "I'll need some time to arrange for working capital, but I'll pay it." *Somehow*. "I can't wait for the investigator to start work, though. We need to find George as soon as possible, if not sooner. I need you to get the investigator to start work without a retainer. And maybe give me a discount."

Sam broke his stare-off with Deacon to consider her.

"You're going to apply for a loan, right?" he asked.

"Yes."

"You'll need a new CPA. And you should probably tell the vendors what's going on to see if they'll cut you any slack."

"Hello, Captain Obvious," Hannah waved her hand, "I'm on it."

"You're the one who asked for advice," Sam pointed out. Then, to her surprise, he stepped closer, got right in her personal space. Close enough that she could smell his warm skin and spicy cologne. Close enough to remind her of the days when standing near him like this had been exactly what she'd wanted. He looked down into her face, seeming sober, maybe even serious. Except Sam was never serious.

"I know I hurt you," he said unexpectedly. "I hurt you when we were in high school, and I hurt you even worse two years ago. You were right about me leaving you to deal with most of the fallout and gossip. I royally fucked up and you paid for it." He ran the backs of his fingers over her cheek.

Deacon shifted, and the small movement broke the odd mood. Hannah pulled away, forcing Sam to drop his hand.

"Don't think this is about giving you another chance," she warned him, wanting to be clear. "This is just payback. Nothing more."

Sam considered her for a moment longer, eyes hooded. "How about this," he said at last. "You can call me for legal advice and I'll help out with paperwork or whatever. I'll also talk to Adam Kouris, the private investigator who works with my firm, but I can't make any promises there until I see what he has to say."

"When will you know about the investigator?" Hannah pushed. "George is spending my money as we speak."

Sam sighed and rubbed the back of his neck. "Tomorrow. I'll talk to Adam and get back to you tomorrow."

She nodded. "Fair enough. We'll be here early tomorrow. Team meeting to discuss the problem."

Sam smiled a little at that. "Team meeting?"

She shrugged, "The people who work here are my team."

"Right." Sam looked at Deacon, then back to Hannah. "I'll be in touch." With that, he turned, pushed open the door to the taproom, and left.

"Wonderful," Hannah muttered.

"Hannah—"

Whatever Deacon had been about to say was interrupted when the kitchen door slammed open.

"What the hell was that?" June demanded, storming into the room. "What in the holy hell was that?"

"June—" Hannah warned.

"I mean, *Sam Black*? Really? *Really*? Are you out of your ever-loving mind?"

"June!" Hannah yelled. Uncowed, the other woman crossed her arms over her chest and glared, practically snarling.

"Oh boy, is everything okay?" Mary Alice asked, pushing into the kitchen behind June.

"I'll go handle the bar." Moving fast, Deacon made his escape. Coward.

"Why was Samuel Black here?" June demanded, ignoring everything else. "Why were you talking to him and not scraping his bloody body parts off the floor?"

"That was Deacon's brother?" Mary Alice asked. "Golly, he sure is good looking." Since Mary Alice had replaced Louise, she'd only heard about the drama with Sam second-hand.

June glowered at Hannah. "Don't you even tell me you're going to use him as your attorney."

"June—"

"Oh, my God." June smacked her hands on either side of her head and grabbed her hair. "You're going to work with him?"

"I have to!" Hannah shouted at her. "I don't have a choice."

"Like hell! He isn't the only attorney in Pennsylvania!"

"No!" Hannah leaned towards the other woman, hands clenched, body tense as she struggled not to reach out and shake June by her scrawny neck. "But he's the only attorney who will help me for free."

"Oh, come on. Why would he do anything for free? Guilt?" June snorted. "Right."

Since that was, in fact, the plan, Hannah didn't appreciate her scorn.

"I'm working it out," she said. "Give me some credit."

"Well, I would but your track record hasn't been too great lately."

Ouch.

"Hey now! Hey now!" Mary Alice flapped her big hands and got between them. "Calm down. Both of you just calm down. Take deep breaths. Like this." She drew in a breath to demonstrate, and her robust chest expanded to the bursting point under her polo shirt before she exhaled.

Hannah and June both stared at her.

"I mean, come on June," Mary Alice said earnestly. "If Uncle George took all of Hannah's money, then she needs a free lawyer, right?"

June scowled. "Maybe," she admitted after a moment of edgy silence.

"And Hannah, June is just worried about you." Mary Alice turned those large round eyes on her. "She doesn't want you to get hurt."

Hannah looked down because she knew Mary Alice was right. She scraped the toe of her sneaker across the floor.

"Yeah."

"Say you're sorry," Mary Alice persisted.

Hannah and June glared at each other.

"Come on." Mary Alice put a hand on each of their shoulders and squeezed. "It's just one little word. You can do it."

"Sorry," June muttered after a moment, sounding like she was swallowing nails.

Hannah sighed. "No, I'm sorry."

They exchanged sheepish grins.

"There, that's good." Mary Alice beamed, peaceful and happy. "Did I hear you say that we were going to have a team meeting tomorrow, Hannah?" she asked.

"Yes." Hannah rubbed her forehead, trying to get herself back under control. "I'll call everyone else in the morning. Maybe we can get together around two?" She looked at June. "If that's okay with you. I know you're off tomorrow."

June fisted her hands on her hips. "Tell us now."

"It's better to wait," Hannah argued. "I'll know a lot more after I go to the bank tomorrow."

"Now, come on, June," Mary Alice cooed to the other woman. "That makes sense. Hannah will find stuff out and then we'll all know, and we'll all be able to help. I'll bet Grace will have some great ideas. She's in college. And Jason's going to be a doctor."

"I'll go to the bank with you," June said, ignoring Mary Alice. "I know how to deal with those jerks."

Yeah, Hannah had a big picture of how well *that* would go.

"Deacon's going to go with me."

"He is?" June thought about that for a few minutes. "Okay," she finally agreed. "But you'd better damn well tell us everything tomorrow."

"I will, I promise."

June's expression softened. Reaching out, she touched Hannah's cheek, pushing back a tendril of hair that had escaped from her hair tie.

"I saw you fall for Sam Black twice," she said, quieter now. "I watched him hurt you both times because he couldn't keep his dick in his pants."

"June..."

"I don't care if he is Deacon's brother. I'm going to hate watching you deal with that asshole again."

Smiling at the older woman who'd been one of the constants in her life, Hannah put her hand over the one on her cheek and pressed hard. June could annoy the crap out of her, but she loved her.

"I know," she said. "I won't keep any secrets, I promise. I just want to get some more information first. I'll tell everybody everything tomorrow."

"Damn right you will." June cleared her throat and stepped back. She turned to the smiling and suspiciously moist-eyed Mary Alice and cast her own eyes towards heaven. "Come on, Mary Alice. Since our shift is over, we can get out of here and let Hannah deal with the dishes."

Hannah glanced at the dishes piled next to the rinse sink. "Thanks."

"Bye, Hannah." Mary Alice waved as June took her arm and propelled her towards the back door. "See you tomorrow!"

The two women grabbed their purses, and then they were gone.

Ignoring the dishes for the moment, Hannah went out to the taproom. The place was almost empty now, with just a few of the regulars still hanging around, talking. She sank onto a barstool, and Deacon came to stand opposite her.

"I heard some, uh, aggressive talking," he said.

Hannah put her head down on the bar.

"Uh huh," he said.

After a moment she knew he'd leaned next to her because she could feel the warmth of his arm. It was nice. Maybe she'd just go to sleep here.

"You should have guessed June would be upset," he pointed out. "She said she was going to emasculate Sam after the thing with Louise."

"She was going to use a garlic press."

"I blocked out that part. Thanks for the reminder." Deacon chuckled, the sound deep and unexpectedly sexy.

Sighing, Hannah sat up and found herself face to face with him. Instinctively, she drew back.

"We'll be closing soon. I guess should finish the dishes," she said, a little breathless for some reason.

"Yeah." The humor gone, he watched her soberly. "We'll figure it out, Hannah. We'll know more after we go to the bank."

Hannah picked at the wooden bar top with her fingernail. "You really don't have to come with me, you know. This is my mess."

"I'm going."

She nodded, relieved in spite of herself. "We should meet up at my apartment around ten thirty, then. The appointment's at eleven."

"I'll be there." He smiled a little. "And I promise to look respectable."

"You always look respectable."

His eyebrows lifted, and she slid off the barstool to escape back to the kitchen. But as she started to move away, she found herself pausing to glance back at him.

"Deacon?"

"Yeah?"

He was tall behind the bar, broad and solid.

"Thanks."

He smiled, just a little bit. "No problem."

5

Deacon parked his aging SUV in front of Hannah's squat, square, apartment building, and sat staring through the windshield, tapping his fingers on the steering wheel, thinking.

He sincerely hoped Hannah's agreeing he should go with her to the bank today meant she was starting to think of him as something other than an employee. More than a freaking responsibility. Maybe he'd finally managed to muscle his way past that damned invisible wall she drew so sharply between them. He had to take advantage of the opportunity before she shoved him back into the place she'd assigned him.

If only he knew how she felt about Sam.

Deacon scowled and tightened his hands on the wheel. His brother had hurt Hannah, yet she'd been eager to call him for help. And, yes, she'd had her reasons, but her face had gotten all flushed and glowy when she'd looked at Sam the night before. Hadn't it? Or had that just been from the heat of the kitchen? Had she really looked at Sam as intently as Deacon imagined? Had she stopped seeing Deacon again now that Sam was back in the picture?

Cursing under his breath, he climbed out of the SUV and

slammed the door shut with more force than was strictly necessary.

No, damn it. No. He hadn't imagined the hints of feminine interest he'd seen directed his way over the past couple of months. Last night hadn't been the first time he'd noticed a spark in Hannah's big hazel eyes when she'd looked at him. He liked it. He liked her, liked her strong face and her curvy body; liked her lush lips and wide mouth. He'd dreamed about that mouth since high school, dreamed about her using it on him.

He rubbed both hands over his skull, trying to get some blood flowing north again. It was a little soon to think Hannah might be willing to get her mouth anywhere near him. Women seemed to like him okay, even with his damned receding hairline, but no one was going to see him standing next to Sam and think he was the good looking one.

What did Hannah think when she saw him standing next to Sam?

"Christ," he muttered, thoroughly disgusted with himself. He was almost thirty years old, for God's sake. He should have outgrown this shit by now.

The fact was, he was here and Sam wasn't, and whether Hannah wanted to admit it or not, she needed him. Whatever today was or could be, he'd been given a chance to take a step forward with the obstinate woman. So he'd take it.

He checked his watch: 10:22 a.m. His button-down shirt and khakis wouldn't win any fashion prizes, but for once Hannah would see him in something other than his Country Time uniform. Deacon hoped it would be another reminder that he was a man—not just a bartender.

"Let's get this show on the road," he told himself firmly.

Hands shoved in his pockets, he walked across the parking lot to the main entrance, found the bell for Hannah's apartment in a bank of buttons, and jabbed it with his finger.

"What?" her voice came over the intercom, so sudden and sharp that he started.

"Um, it's me, Deacon."

A chime sounded at the door. "Come up. Apartment 3B." Then she was gone.

"Aye, aye, captain." Deacon snapped a salute towards the panel of buttons, opened the security door, and took the stairs to the third floor.

Hannah opened the door at his knock a few minutes later.

"Hey," he said, then stopped to blink as every thought in his head simply vanished. He'd worked with Hannah Frederickson for two years, and he'd never seen her wearing anything other than jeans or khakis. Sometimes in the heat of the summer she wore shorts or those short pant things that stopped mid-calf, but that was about as fancy as she got. The woman facing him across the threshold was almost a stranger.

She had on what he thought of as a "lady suit" —straight dark skirt short enough to show off her excellent legs, a white blouse with a deep "V" neckline, shoes with pointy toes, and sky-high heels. She had bundled, pinned, and twisted her wonderful golden brown hair until it fell in a contained waterfall down her back. Her eyes seemed deeper, her lashes darker, her lips glistened. He could smell a subtle perfume.

Damn. Just ... damn.

"What are you staring at?" she demanded.

"Nothing," he croaked, mouth dry. "You look good."

She eyed him critically, then nodded.

"You do, too." She stepped aside and opened the door wider. "Come on in. I'll be ready in two minutes."

Not waiting for a response, she turned and marched back across the room. Deacon stepped inside and closed the door, making himself look around the apartment so she wouldn't catch him staring at her ass.

He'd never actually been in her place before. It was nice.

Nothing special really, just a combination living room/kitchen with two doors beyond leading to a bedroom and bathroom. But it was neat and bright, and the furniture, although well used, looked comfortable. It was ... homey.

He thought of the small furnished room he'd been renting over the bookstore since he'd come back to town—the single window, the bathroom down the hall that he shared with three other guys. At least Ms. Gregory, his landlady and the town librarian, was conscientious. He hadn't had to deal with mice, cockroaches, or crackheads since he'd been living in her building, unlike some of the other places he'd been.

Hannah came striding out of the bedroom, the sexy shoes making her legs seem a mile long. When she reached him, she held out a thin, gold chain.

"Can you fasten this for me?"

Deacon took the chain from her. It held a gold cross and looked far too fragile in his rough hands.

"What?" he asked stupidly.

"It belonged to my mother, so I want to wear it for luck, but the clasp sticks and I can't get it on by myself." She turned and presented her back to him, then pulled her hair out of the way. He found himself staring at the nape of her neck.

Something very primal shuddered through him. Her slender neck looked vulnerable. He wasn't sure if he wanted to kiss it or bite it.

Hannah turned her head to the side and looked up at him through her fall of hair.

"Deacon?" she prompted.

Moving slowly, absorbing the warmth of her body, breathing in her unique scent under the light, floral perfume, he reached around her with the necklace. For a moment the fine chain bound them together, her back to his front. It got tangled in her hair, and their hands met as they both tried to work it loose.

Hannah had fallen silent, as if she too was affected by the position, by the nearness. He wanted to twist her around, to pull her up against him, to kiss her, devour her until she forgot everything and everyone else.

She'd probably knee him in the balls if he tried it.

Shaking his head slightly, he struggled to concentrate on his task and finally found the necklace's impossibly tiny clasp. Frowning, he examined it while Hannah held the cross pressed to her chest, then managed to slip the edge of his thumbnail under the little mechanism. After some fumbling, he got the clasp to catch the loop on the other end of the chain.

Carefully, he placed the hooked chain against Hannah's neck. Without thinking about what he was doing, he ran his fingertips over her soft, silky skin, feeling the surprisingly delicate bones underneath. She shivered, then abruptly stepped away.

"Thanks," she said, not meeting his eyes. She was flushed, but he probably was, too.

"No problem," he said. It was a damned good thing he hadn't tucked in his shirt, or Hannah might have gotten an eyeful of just how happy he was to be of service. Breathing deeply, he willed himself to calm down.

Not now. Not yet.

Hannah cleared her throat, adjusted the cross, and picked up her suit jacket from where it was slung over the back of a chair, shrugging into it like she was pulling on armor. He stood there like an ass, clasping and unclasping his hands at his sides.

He wanted to run his teeth all over her.

"Let's go," she said, picking up a slim portfolio case and her purse before walking to the door.

"I'll drive," he said.

Now she did look at him and raised her eyebrows. "Oh, you will?"

"Yes." He had to have control over something.

"You expect me to get up into your SUV wearing this outfit?" She gestured down at herself.

Deacon ran his eyes over her body. Jesus. He felt himself starting to hyperventilate.

"Yes," he said.

She stared at him for a moment longer.

"God." But she turned and walked out of the apartment.

This time he couldn't help watching her go, admiring the sway of her butt in her lady suit.

"Deacon!"

"Coming." He followed, and she locked the door behind them.

They took the stairs in silence and, once they were outside the building, Hannah strode across the parking lot to his SUV without any more arguments. She waited impatiently while he beeped the locks open, then threw her portfolio case and purse onto the front seat and kind of shimmied up after them. Deacon appreciated the move.

"Are you watching me?" she demanded.

"No," he lied and, slamming the door shut behind her, walked around to driver's side. By the time he'd gotten in, she was sitting upright, skirt adjusted. She looked so prim and proper that he couldn't help being a bit of a prick.

"Nice underwear," he said.

"Go to hell."

Deacon laughed, glad they were back on a more normal footing. He started the SUV, and backed out of the parking spot.

"Do you know where you're going?" she asked.

He rattled off the address.

She took a deep breath and nodded. "That's it."

Turning out of the parking lot, he took the road that ran through the heart of Hardy Falls. It was a sunny late-summer day in northeastern Pennsylvania, and a lot of people were out walking around town. Some were window-shopping along the main street, while others were standing in groups talking or striding briskly to get to their next destination.

"It's a good town," Hannah said contemplatively.

"I guess," he said, just to be saying something.

He felt her watching him, her attention like a touch.

"Why did you come back?" she asked suddenly.

He turned his head and briefly caught her eye before turning back to the road.

"Why do you care?" he countered.

He sensed her shrug.

"I never asked before, that's all. You just showed up one day."

"Lucky for you," he said. "You were desperate for a decent bartender."

"I was that."

He knew they were both remembering the rainy day when he'd come in for a drink and asked about a job. She hadn't recognized him, not at first, but he couldn't blame her for that. He'd changed a lot since those months when she'd been his tutor in high school. He'd gotten taller, gained some muscle, lost some fat. Lost a hell of a lot of hair.

If he'd followed his original intentions and stopped at his parents' house first, he might have discovered that Hannah was hooked up with Sam again before he'd hired on as her bartender. Maybe then it wouldn't have been as much of a surprise. Which, he thought, went to show that you shouldn't put things off just because they'll be unpleasant.

"So," she prodded after a moment. "Why?"

"I'd been traveling and wanted to stop for a while." He'd been drifting around for years and thought he'd try coming home.

"That's no answer," she complained.

He was silent for a while, then decided to admit part of the truth. "I thought I might make it up with my family."

"Oh." It was her turn to be quiet. "How's it going?" she asked.

He couldn't help grinning at her. "Could be better."

She watched the town slide past the window.

"My fault."

"Nah," he said. "I would have punched Sam in the face sooner or later."

"But your parents—"

"Here we are," he interrupted as they arrived at the bank. He parked at the curb and turned off the engine before shifting to face Hannah.

"How do you want to play this?" he asked.

She took a deep breath and squared her shoulders. "Just follow my lead."

"You have a plan?"

Hannah considered him through narrowed eyes, like a general sizing up troops before battle.

"The lending officer's name is Allison Arthur," she said in a seeming non-sequitur.

When the name registered, he realized he'd heard the bowling league guys gossiping about the lady now and then. She apparently had quite a reputation.

"Okay," he said.

Hannah's smile was all teeth.

"Do you know her?"

"Not personally." He couldn't tell if that pleased Hannah or not.

"You'll distract her." She sounded brisk and business-like as she gathered up her bags. "It might help. Be charming."

He stared. "Huh?" Was Hannah asking him to … seduce the lending officer?

She sat back in the seat and glared at him. "You heard what

I said. Charm her. You've got the skills, boy. Use them for good." Before he could move, she opened her door and slithered out of the SUV.

Deacon sat for a moment. She thought he had skills?

Struggling to control a pleased and probably foolish grin, he jumped out of the truck and followed Hannah to the old bank building.

They entered through a graceful, arched doorway that spoke of prosperity past, but Deacon noticed the sign on the outside had been covered by a piece of canvas bearing the slogan, "Coming Soon!" Times being what they were, he guessed First National was in the process of being swallowed by a larger predator.

He trailed Hannah across the marble-floored lobby, past the short line of people standing in a roped queue waiting their turn to approach the teller windows. A flat screen television mounted behind the tellers played a rotating series of ads for the bank's services. The people in line watched it without emotion.

They made their way to a largish customer service area where several young women worked diligently at desks lined up behind a fanciful wrought iron fence. Deacon wondered if the fence was there to keep customers out or to keep the employees in. The thought made him smile.

At that moment one of the women looked up. She met his smile and returned it brightly.

"May I help you?" She sounded as if helping them would be the high point of her day.

"Allison Arthur," Hannah said. "We have an appointment."

The young representative's smile noticeably dimmed. "Have a seat." She gestured to some small wooden chairs in front of her desk and picked up her phone.

"She was pretty enthusiastic," Deacon whispered to Hannah as they sat down, "until I mentioned Allison."

"It must have been disappointment. I think she really wanted to be the one to help us."

"Right."

Hannah straightened her skirt. He wished she wouldn't keep doing that. It drew his attention to her legs, which was making it really hard to concentrate. Forcing himself to look away, he stared at the white crown molding on the other side of the room and rested the heel of his shoe on the opposite knee, trying not to jiggle it with restless energy.

"Ms. Frederickson?" Deacon and Hannah both looked up to see the young customer service rep stand and open a gate in the fence.

"Yes?" Hannah got to her feet, and Deacon rose beside her.

The rep smiled. "Come on back. Ms. Arthur will see you now."

"Nice fence," Deacon said as he followed meekly behind the two women. "It's like an English country garden or something."

The customer service rep turned, smiled at him blankly, and shrugged.

"It's been here since the bank opened in 1890," she said. "They're tearing it out next week."

There didn't seem to be a whole lot to say about that.

They went down a short hallway, then took some stairs to the building's second floor. Deacon wondered if there was an elevator. If there wasn't, he wondered what happened if somebody came in for a loan and couldn't climb the stairs. He imagined that if the person had enough money, the lending officer would come down to them. The other schmucks were out of luck.

He thought it was probably a good thing he and Hannah could climb the stairs.

The second floor was full of low cubicles affording no privacy whatsoever; offices lined the walls for those of higher rank. The customer rep led them to one such office, knocked on the jamb of the open door and poked her head inside.

"Here's Ms. Frederickson," she said.

"Yes, come in," a low, sultry female voice called.

Hannah's expression was grim, but her lips twitched in what might have been a smile for the woman who'd led them to Valhalla. Then she straightened her shoulders and marched into the office. Deacon obediently followed.

"Hi," Hannah said, as she walked up to the desk and held out her hand. "I'm Hannah Frederickson. I appreciate you fitting me into your schedule so quickly." The woman behind the desk stood, and they shook hands.

Allison Arthur wasn't as tall as Hannah, but she was very curvy, very blond, and smelled of a lot of perfume. Her blouse gaped open at the neck, exposing quite a bit of cleavage. Deacon snapped his attention back up to her eyes and found her studying him with what could only be called predatory interest.

"Well, well," Allison said, drawling the words, "who is this?"

Hannah's expression tightened.

"This is Deacon Black," she said through stiff lips. "He works with me."

Deacon appreciated the fact that she'd said "works with" instead of "works for."

"Deacon Black," the other woman purred. "Related to Sam?"

He should have guessed she'd know Sam.

"Brother," he said shortly, glancing at Hannah. Her face had taken on the appearance of a stone mask.

"So you're the returning prodigal son. I haven't seen your father since we worked with him on his purchase of the hobby store property, but at that time Dr. Black mentioned you were back in town."

Now there was a shocker. His father had actually told her

about him instead of pretending he didn't exist. Deacon sincerely hoped Hannah's chances for a loan hadn't just taken a nosedive.

"Ah," he said.

She held out a hand. "I'm Allison Arthur."

"I kind of figured," he moved forward to take the hand she offered. He wondered if she might expect him to kiss it or something, so he shook it once and let it go as soon as he could. Her long fingernails trailed along the back of his hand.

Charm, he reminded himself, and gave Allison a smile. She smiled back, then swiped her tongue over her plump bottom lip.

Well, okay.

Hannah settled herself in one of the visitor's chairs. After Allison had reseated herself behind her desk, Deacon closed the office door and sat, as well.

"So." Allison leaned back in her chair, which pushed the plumpness of her breasts against the silk blouse. She swiveled slowly back and forth. "What can I do for you today?" She was still focused on Deacon, but the question seemed directed at both of them, so he decided it was safe to keep quiet.

Hannah cleared her throat, finally drawing Allison's attention. "My business—"

"The Country Time Bar and Grill," the lending officer interrupted. "I looked up the file after you called yesterday."

Deacon had a feeling that, although Allison Arthur might like men, she was too smart to let anyone charm her out of anything.

"Yes, the Country Time," Hannah said. "We have a line of credit that we haven't been using, and I need to reactivate it as soon as possible."

Deacon heard the sharp tension in her voice, but hoped to hell Allison didn't. He suspected the other woman wouldn't be above using any perceived weakness to her own advantage.

He thought Allison was a bit of a shark. Or maybe a piranha.

"Yes. The line of credit," Allison said. She leaned forward and tapped on her keyboard with the tip of a long fingernail. "Unfortunately, that was a personal loan in your father's name, not a business loan. It was closed when he died."

Hannah stared at her.

"What?"

Allison laughed, deep and sensual. "We sent all of the proper notifications."

Hannah folded her lips tightly together, and Deacon could see her clenching her fists in her lap. She drew in a deep breath through her nose.

"How do we go about reinstating it?" he asked quickly before she could explode.

The lending officer turned her attention back to him, and her smile became almost blatantly sexual. But now that he'd had time to absorb her impact, he thought her actions were more automatic than personal. She'd probably smile seductively at Old Albert Cromwell if he came in for a loan.

"I'm afraid it's not that simple," she said. "It was a personal loan, so we can't simply reinstate it."

"Which means?" Hannah demanded.

Allison looked at her with pity. "I'm sure you realize that we're in a much different lending environment now than when your father originally took out the line. In addition, this bank has recently merged with a larger institution."

"Which means...?" Hannah repeated through clenched teeth.

"Which *means*, you will need to apply for a new loan, and the approval process will be handled in accordance with the standards of PFNB." Allison's voice was smooth, like honey.

"PFNB?" Hannah asked, obviously confused.

"It's an acronym for the new banking entity. People First National Bank," Allison told her.

"What paperwork will you need if we apply for a loan?" Deacon asked quickly, before Hannah could make a comment she'd regret.

Allison looked at him, her expression calculating. "Will this be a personal loan or a business loan?" she asked.

"Business," Hannah snarled.

"Hmm." Allison frowned prettily. "Bad time to try to take out a business loan. Especially for a—" she tapped on the keyboard again, "bar and grill."

"We still want to apply," Deacon said. He didn't like the way Hannah was breathing. It sounded like she was pulling in air between her teeth, as if she was a pressure cooker ready to blow. This could get really ugly, really fast.

Allison smiled at him. "If you apply for a business loan, we'll need a complete business plan with a loan application."

"Hannah owns the building. She'll probably have to put it up as collateral, right?" He wanted to be clear on exactly what they were discussing.

Allison inclined her head. "Yes. I don't believe we'll be willing to discuss an unsecured line of credit at this time." She smiled at Hannah with condescension. "I understand your business has suffered some setbacks recently." She tut-tutted. "Frankly, the fact that your uncle embezzled all of your business funds and ran off with his assistant does not inspire confidence."

Hannah opened her mouth. Then closed it. Then opened it again.

"You know?" she squeaked.

"Well, of course I know," Allison said. "Everyone in town knows." She appeared amused. "Were you going to hide it from me?"

"No," Hannah choked.

"Will you give us the loan paperwork?" Deacon asked.

Allison smiled at him. "Certainly."

"Okay." He looked at Hannah, but she was watching the curvaceous lending officer.

"After I apply, how soon before I know whether or not the loan is approved?" she asked, spine straight.

Allison appeared disinterested.

"That depends," she said. "Probably several weeks."

"Several *weeks*?" Hannah shrieked the last word. "I need the money sooner than that."

Allison shrugged her slender shoulders.

"These things take time."

"What am I supposed to do in the meantime?" Hannah asked. The words sounded like they'd burst out of her without her permission.

Allison shrugged again.

"Frankly, that's not my concern," she said.

6

—————

"Not her concern," Hannah said, still fuming over Allison Arthur's comment as she hoisted herself into Deacon's SUV after they'd left the bank. Deacon didn't reply, just stood holding the car door open, waiting patiently for her to settle so he could close it again. "Not her concern. Maybe it's not her concern, but it will freaking be the bank's concern if they lose a good customer. I'll go to another bank," she threatened, feeling reckless. "Hell if I won't. There are plenty of other banks in the sea. We don't live in freaking Siberia." She pulled down the damn skirt of her damn suit, and jammed her seat belt into the buckle.

Deacon closed the passenger door, then walked around to the driver's side and got in. After buckling up, he started the vehicle and pulled away from the curb.

"I'm no expert, but I wouldn't just walk away from First National—"

"PFNB," she corrected, sneering.

"Whatever. I wouldn't leave without applying for the loan," he said mildly, slipping on sunglasses with one hand while guiding the SUV with the other.

"Why?" she demanded.

He shrugged, glancing her way. The glasses made him look tough. But good.

"You told me you guys have been using that bank for years. Seems to me they'd be your best shot at getting a quick loan approval. Even though they're merging, all of your history is there."

"So what." She crossed her arms and scowled out the side window while Deacon drove through what passed for lunch hour traffic in Hardy Falls.

He was right, of course. She couldn't afford to walk away from First National until she found out what they might be willing to offer.

Damn it.

Nothing had gone the way she'd hoped. Nothing. And, on top of everything else, she was having thoughts about Deacon. Interesting thoughts. Tingly thoughts. She kept remembering the gentle roughness of his fingers on her neck, the heat of his body against her back, his breath flowing over her when he bent his head to fasten her necklace.

She flattened a hand on her chest, pressing the gold cross to her skin.

It was enough to give a girl the vapors.

"Will the vendors cut you a break?" Deacon's question broke into her thoughts. Obviously he was still concentrating on the problem at hand, not mooning over an intense moment back at her apartment. Of course, maybe she was the only one who had considered it intense.

"They might," she admitted, forcing her thoughts back on track. "But even if they do, I still need to pay them something. My good looks won't be enough to convince them to keep making deliveries."

"You should meet with them dressed in that suit," Deacon muttered.

She stared at him. "What?"

"Do you have any cash?" he asked. "Any money anywhere you can use as working capital?"

"Not enough," she slumped in the seat, weighed down by the mountain of her responsibilities. "I have a little bit saved, and I'll max out my credit cards. But I won't be able to do everything." She thought about it. "Maybe I can try to get a personal loan or a mortgage, if they won't give me a business loan." Then she shook her head and sighed. "I don't think I'll be able to qualify. The business *is* my income."

They drove in silence for a little while.

"I have some money," Deacon finally said.

"What?" She straightened and twisted in the seat to face him. "No, Deacon—"

"Not enough to save the day, but enough to help." His expression was unreadable behind the dark glasses. "I'd be happy to consider a loan. In fact, there are probably a bunch of people who'd be willing to invest."

Her stomach jumped. First of all, she knew how much Deacon made, and it wasn't a lot. He wasn't even renting an apartment, for God's sake. Second, the thought of him, an employee, lending her money was just freaking awkward. And she didn't even want to consider what would happen if people she knew, friends and neighbors, invested in her business and she still lost everything, including their money.

"I don't think—"

"I said lend, Hannah, not give," he interrupted. "You can pay us all interest."

"No." The word came out sharper than she'd intended, and she tried to gentle her tone. "I'm not going to play Russian roulette with people's savings, especially yours." She realized that might have offended him and hurried on. "Look, I want to try to get a bank loan first. If that doesn't work, well, I'll think about it." Investors, maybe. Taking Deacon's money? No.

He didn't say anything, but his hands flexed on the steering wheel.

"Thank you," she added after a moment. "It's a good idea. That will be my Plan B."

He snorted.

"It's your call," he said.

"Deacon—"

"If you're going to apply for a loan," he interrupted her, "you'll need a business plan. Ever write one before?"

"No," she admitted, glad he'd changed the subject. "But I'm sure I can come up with one. How hard can it be?"

Deacon snorted again. "I'm sure it's not that hard to *write* one," he said. "I'm guessing it's hard to write a *good* one."

She glared at him. "Well, I can't afford an accountant so I'm just going to have to wing it."

This time he sighed.

"Listen," he said passing a mail truck double parked in the middle of Main Street. "I really can help here. We'll write the business plan together."

"We will?" she said, wondering when she'd lost control of the situation.

"Sure," he said. "I've never written one either, but we're both intelligent adults. We both know the Country Time business top to bottom. I'll bet you that together we can come up with a loan proposal good enough to blow Allison Arthur's mind."

Hannah drew in a deep breath and tried to think rationally. The way he was pushing her was extremely irritating, but he was right when he said he knew the business inside out. And it would be kind of nice to have help.

"It will take up a lot of your free time," she warned. Deacon worked almost as many hours as she did.

"Hannah," Deacon said, turning the wheel with his big, competent hands. "You go out of business, I'm out of a job. You can't make the payroll, I don't get paid. My helping you is a no-brainer."

She chewed on her bottom lip. "We're going to have to make it look professional."

"I know a guy who's a CPA in Philadelphia. You can't afford him," he continued when Hannah opened her mouth to say just that, "but we were in the service together and we've been friends for a while. I'll talk to him. I'm sure he'd be willing to look at our plan and smooth out the rough parts." He glanced at her. She felt the look, even though she couldn't see his eyes. "Okay?"

For some reason she was a little surprised to find out he had a friend who was an accountant in Philadelphia, which was just silly. He'd been on the road for a long time. He probably had friends everywhere.

It was just that she didn't know them. And it was a little disorienting to realize there were parts of Deacon she didn't know.

"Hannah?"

She shook off the odd feeling.

"Okay."

"Great," he said. "I'll start digging up information on what we need."

"I will, too," she said, because she didn't want him to think he was in charge of this train. This was *her* business. She was in charge.

"Fine." He didn't sound offended at all and she relaxed a bit.

A few minutes later, Deacon dropped Hannah off at her building and she went up to her apartment to change out of her damned uncomfortable suit. Then, since she wasn't expected at the Country Time for another two hours, she sat down at her laptop to obsess over spreadsheets. Maybe she could massage the numbers and make them look better.

Maybe.

She could hope.

~

After dropping Hannah off at her apartment, Deacon drove around aimlessly for a while, trying to shake off his irritation.

He didn't know why he'd offered to lend her money in the first place. Talk about stupid. It wasn't like he was rich or anything. Yes, he'd made it a habit to live cheaply, so he'd been able to save more than anyone might expect, but he definitely couldn't afford to lose what he had.

Plus, he worked for the woman. If Hannah had taken his money, it might have made things really weird between them. He certainly didn't want that.

So, he'd take her refusal as considerate because he didn't think she'd meant to be condescending. And he'd help her in other ways. That would be better, and they wouldn't have money erecting yet another barrier between them.

He didn't want anything to come between them. Especially not another fucking barrier.

Deacon drove past the Country Time, but didn't stop. Instead he turned off the highway to head into downtown Hardy Falls.

Since he wouldn't be starting his shift at the bar for another couple of hours, he figured he had plenty of time to go to the library and search the Internet for info on business plans. Maybe he'd catch up on e-mails from his buddies while he was there. He could give Quinn Barad, his accountant friend, a heads-up on the situation and tell him he'd be shooting a business plan his way. And he could see if he'd finally gotten an email from Mateo Guerrero. He hadn't heard from the man in months; it was starting to worry him a little.

Mat was a former army sergeant, and, although they hadn't served together, not like him and Quinn, they'd bonded almost instantly when they'd worked on an oil rig in the Gulf of Mexico a couple of years ago. They'd kept in touch after Deacon came home, but the emails and phone calls were becoming less frequent as they both moved on with their lives. Mat had gotten engaged a little over a year ago to a beautiful elementary school teacher in Galveston, Texas. Deacon had never met the woman—Gail—but he'd seen her picture, and Mateo had seemed damned happy.

Maybe Mat was married now. Maybe Deacon wouldn't hear from him again.

It happened.

Maneuvering through the town's haphazard maze of streets, he came to the ugly brick library building and turned into the adjoining parking lot, pulling into a space next to Old Albert Cromwell's rust bucket of a pickup. The old guy spent most afternoons reading the paper and flirting with Ms. Gregory before heading over to Country Time to watch sports and drink beer with his buddies.

If he was lucky, Albert's presence would distract Ms. Gregory and keep her from hovering around Deacon, watching to make sure he didn't surf porn sites. He just hoped he wouldn't have to ask her for help. Since Mathilda Gregory was about a thousand years old, admitting she knew more about computers than he did was humiliating.

He took off his sunglasses and got out of the SUV, stretching a little to loosen up his back. The day was bright, the breeze warm, and the trees were already starting to turn their glorious autumn colors. Birds flew, outlined black against a clear blue sky, and he could hear their loud, chittering calls.

It would be the height of the fall season soon. The tourists would drive through town on their way to Lake Wallenpaupack or the Delaware Water Gap. They'd take pictures of the leaves, shop at the little boutique stores, drink at the Country Time.

Hannah was right. It was a good town.

There was a loud roar, and he turned to see a beige, four-door sedan flying down the street. Even from where he stood he could hear the deep, pounding bass of rap music. It made him smile.

Only in Hardy Falls would a teenager play gangsta rap while driving his grandmother's sedan.

Deacon's grandmother had let him drive her car now and then after he'd gotten his license, but he'd had heavy metal pumping through the speakers, not rap. She and his grandfather had moved to Arizona when he'd been eighteen, right before he'd enlisted and hit the road out of town.

Turning abruptly, he walked into the library, nodding at Ms. Gregory when he passed her station. She smiled absently, but her focus was on Old Albert, who leaned against her counter like he leaned on the bar at the Country Time. Albert spared Deacon a grin, showing off healthy pink gums, which meant he'd forgotten his teeth again. Ms. Gregory didn't seem to mind.

Shaking his head, Deacon made his way to the computers clustered against a wall away from the book stacks. Since it was a weekday afternoon and the kids were in school, he found a vacant station right away, sat, and pulled out his library card to access the system. His father would have been shocked to learn that he not only had a library card, he actually used it on a regular basis.

Maybe, Deacon thought, frowning as he logged in, if Hannah decided to go the private investor route, he should talk to his father about lending her money. After all, they were actually kind of on speaking terms now. Unlike Deacon, Dr. Trevor Black, big-time pharmaceutical research scientist, was rolling in dough, and as the sultry Allison had indicated, enjoyed investing in local property.

His parents had been angry at him when he'd left home to join the army. They hadn't understood why he'd been desperate to make his own way, to go someplace where he wasn't Sam Black's brother or Trevor and Samantha Black's son. When he'd finally come home, they'd been cool to him—especially after the blow-up with Sam.

It was only once the furor died down that he'd spoken to his mother and tried to explain his side of things. She must have intervened with his father, because a few days later Dr. Black summoned him to the family manse. The conversation had been extremely awkward, but it had been a first step. Since then, his parents had even invited him to dinner once or twice.

Maybe if he made it very clear the loan wasn't for him …

No.

Deacon knew it was his pride talking, but he just couldn't do it. His father would never believe he was telling the truth, would think he was begging for a handout. Trevor Black still had definite opinions of his younger son's capabilities.

"I guess you need money," his father said, clear blue eyes staring, unblinking.

Despite the warmth of the sun shining into the great room, Deacon felt chilled. He straightened in the armchair until his spine felt like an iron bar.

"No, sir. I have plenty of money."

His father's expression reflected his disbelief.

"Of course you need money. You barely finished high school. I imagine you've been working shit jobs for years. Well, I'll consider it, but I'll expect to be paid back with interest."

Deacon wondered what he'd thought would happen. Maybe there was only so far he and his father could reconcile. Maybe it wasn't even worth the effort. He took a sip of cognac from the glass he held and told himself to let it go.

"That won't be necessary," he said politely. "Thank you for your offer, sir."

Deacon shook off the memory, forced himself to concentrate and, slowly and carefully, typed his search into the web browser.

7
___

After spending almost two hours massaging the numbers in her spreadsheets, Hannah realized she'd only made them look worse.

Pushing away from her laptop on the kitchen table, she stood and walked to the apartment's big living room window, leaned her hip against the casement, and looked out at the familiar scenery. The mountains rising in the distance surrounded the town and tugged at her, calming her as they always did. A car drove by on the street below, and then it was empty again. There was a machining shop across from her apartment building, and a couple of guys were out taking a break.

Hannah watched them gesture wildly and laugh at each other. She couldn't see their faces, but she thought she recognized one or two of them as regulars at the Country Time.

She could scrape together enough from her personal savings to cover the taxes and insurance premiums, but the fact was, even if she maxed out her credit cards, used every cent of money she had, she wouldn't be able to keep the business going for long without a loan.

Okay, so she'd just have to get the business plan done ASAP and get applying. Then she'd pray for quick acceptance and a decent interest rate.

Or she could do what Deacon had suggested and raise the money she needed through private investors. She'd still need a business plan, but they might cut her some slack, and she'd have more play with the interest.

Hannah sighed and closed her eyes, turning to lean with her back against the wall.

The problem was, taking money from people she knew would add so much more pressure. She was almost buried under responsibility now; she wasn't sure she could handle any more. Far better to borrow from an impersonal financial institution.

If they'd let her.

She rolled her head in a circle, trying to ease some of the tension in her neck.

No matter what, she just knew she couldn't lose the Country Time.

The phone rang. Hannah reached over and grabbed the receiver from a side table without opening her eyes to check caller ID.

"Hello?"

"What the hell, Hannah?"

Hannah's eyes snapped open and she cursed under her breath.

"Hi, Josie."

"What—the—hell?"

Even over the phone's crappy cable connection, Hannah could hear her friend's heavy breathing. Josie sounded like she was either going to explode or let loose a stream of fire like a dragon. She knew that on the other end of the line, her friend's dark eyes were blazing with indignation.

"I was going to tell you," she soothed.

"Oh, yeah? Well, I happen to notice that you *didn't* tell me. I had to find out from Jenny, and you know how much I hate that. I want to know stuff first, goddamnit!"

Hannah sighed. She hadn't even thought about word getting to Josie's older sister, but she should have. Jenny Kline worked part time for a maid service and went into a lot of the bigger houses scattered around town. Whenever Hannah talked to her, Jenny knew everything happening in Hardy Falls.

"I didn't want to bother you." The excuse sounded lame even to her own ears.

"Bother me? Hannah, we're friends! Friends tell friends when life dumps a crap-load ton of shit on them."

"I know, I know." Hannah pinched the bridge of her nose. "But you're in Manhattan, for God's sake."

"So?"

"And," Hannah continued, "you just got promoted to a new advertising team, and you're already stressed. What good would it have done to tell you?"

"I can help," Josie said stubbornly.

"Really?" Hannah challenged. "How can you help from hundreds of miles away?"

"Well, I don't know, but I can at least listen. I can empathize. I can offer goddamn ideas and suggestions. I'm a freaking creative person here, but I can't do anything if I don't even know there's a problem."

"And I'm going to need all of those goddamn ideas and suggestions," Hannah assured her. "I've been to the bank to see about a loan and—"

"You went to the bank without me?" Josie wailed.

"I couldn't wait for you to go with me, now could I?" Hannah all but shouted.

"Oh." Josie was silent for a moment. "Right. But you had to go alone or—" she gasped in horror, "don't tell me you took

June. Do not tell me you subjected some poor lending officer to June Esperanza."

"First of all, the lending officer is Allison Arthur. She's not a 'poor' anything."

"Oh. True."

"Second, I didn't take June. Deacon went with me."

"Deacon?"

"Yeah."

"Good," Josie said with satisfaction. She'd been friendly with Deacon in high school, and since he'd come home they'd run into each other whenever Josie was in town. "I bet that screwed with Allison's concentration."

"It did," Hannah admitted, although she frowned at the memory of the banker's shameless flirting. "He didn't seem impressed by her, though."

"Huh." Josie sounded thoughtful.

"And Deacon's going to help me write a business plan, because we need one to apply for the loan."

"Huuuhhhh" Josie drew out the sound.

Hannah cleared her throat, a little nervous about this next part.

"Just in case Jenny didn't have all of the information, I should tell you that Sam is going to be giving me legal advice."

"Sam?" Josie shrieked. "Are you fucking kidding me?"

Hannah sighed. "It's complicated."

"Complicated? Complicated? So help me God, Hannah Frederickson, if you let that jerk lay one finger on you again, I'm going to ... to ... come down there and cut off his hand. Or his dick."

"Well, thanks for that. But don't worry. Samuel Black isn't going to lay anything on me. This is payback. He owes me."

"Yes, he does. I still can't believe Louise let him talk her into the backseat of her car."

"He's charming and persuasive," Hannah said, although she had a hard time believing it herself.

Actually, that had been the worst part of the whole thing. Sam had already dicked her around once, so she wasn't entirely surprised when he did it again. But Lou had been her friend for years. Heck, Hannah, Josie, and Lou had all gone through school together. To have someone you'd been friends with for that long turn around and make out with your boyfriend in your own damn parking lot? Well, it hurt.

"No excuses," Josie said brusquely. "Crap, I have to go to a meeting in a few minutes. Are you sure you'll be okay? Want me to come there? I can dump this hotdog stand and be there in a couple of hours."

"Josie, no. I've got things under control." All Hannah needed was her friend getting involved, too.

"I'd do it," Josie said stubbornly. Then she sighed. "Except ... well, I really kind of can't. The team I just transferred to handles the firm's biggest client. We're talking multimillions of ad dollars here, and they haven't been satisfied with our results. They're threatening to pull the account, so the team's not only designing a whole new strategy, we're looking at past results and trying to tell them what they'll get in the future. It's huge and a lot of work, and if I leave now they'll think I can't handle the pressure. The dick-wad ad manager I work with will have me pushed off the team before I can spit. I told you about him, right? Donald Corso?"

"Is he still giving you problems?" Hannah asked.

"Nothing I can't handle. Shit, I really have to go. I'll talk to you later, okay?"

"Okay." Hannah smiled into the phone.

"Just ...no more secrets."

"Right."

"Pinkie swear?"

Hannah smiled again.

"I swear. No more secrets."

They hung up. Hannah sighed. It bothered her to hear the stress and exhaustion in Josie's voice when she talked about her job.

But she'd have to deal with that problem another day. Right now she had a business plan to write.

Hannah rubbed her eyes with the heels of her hands, then glanced at the clock. Time to go. Hopefully Deacon had come up with something brilliant after he dropped her off.

His fingers had been warm, his hands calloused and rough. He'd smelled clean, like soap, but with a hint of male spice underneath. Not a lot of cologne, not like Sam.

Unless something had changed in the last two years, Sam's hands were strong, but smooth. You could tell that Deacon had worked at more manual jobs than his brother. Sam had lawyer hands.

Why the hell was she thinking about their hands?

Shaking her head, Hannah pushed away from the wall, then gathered up her things and left the apartment.

When she got to the Country Time, Deacon's SUV was already parked next to the building. She found him leaning against the bar, studying some papers, a cup of coffee at his elbow. He was still in the neat khakis he'd worn to the bank, but now he'd changed into his Country Time polo shirt.

"Hey," she said, sliding onto the stool opposite him.

"Hey." He looked up and smiled.

Hannah drew in a breath at the unexpected impact of Deacon's smile. The color of the shirt made his eyes look bluer, the quirk of his lips full of sensual promise.

Had he always looked at her like that? Had she just never noticed?

Trying to find a way to distract herself, she nodded at the papers he was holding.

"What are they?"

"What?" He glanced at the papers. "Oh, I printed some stuff off the Internet about writing a business plan and putting together a good loan proposal package."

Hannah blinked. "The Internet?"

"Sure." He scowled at her. "I know how to use a computer, Hannah. I can search the Internet. I'm not goddamn stupid."

Terrific. Now she'd insulted him.

"I know you're not stupid," she assured him quickly. "I was just surprised it didn't occur to me to do a search." She'd been too busy obsessing over numbers.

He nodded, but she wasn't sure he believed her.

"Anyway, there's a whole lot of good information out there we can use," he said. "It's going to be a pain in the ass, but we'll manage. There are online templates, but you have to pay for some of them."

"Okay."

"Oh, and I emailed my buddy in Philadelphia. Quinn said he'd be happy to look things over once we pull it all together."

"Okay." Wow, he'd sure put his time to good use. "I've started figuring out how much I owe," she said, so he wouldn't think she was a slacker.

"Good. Apparently you're going to need a new balance sheet, income statement, statement of cash flows, and all that," he said.

"Yeah." She hated accounting.

"But the gurus of business plans," he tapped the papers, "say that you can use the financial statements from the prior year."

"Uncle George was embezzling from me," she pointed out. "How much to do you think I can trust the financial statements he drew up last year?"

"Good point." Deacon stacked the papers together and put them under the bar. "You want something to drink?"

She nodded at his mug. "I wouldn't mind some coffee." Maybe it would clear her head.

"Coming up."

The kitchen door opened, and June and Mary Alice walked in followed by Grace Cooper, their third server.

"You guys are early," Hannah observed. She'd called everyone that morning before going to the bank, but she hadn't expected them to turn up for another half hour.

Grace settled on the barstool next to Hannah. She had beautiful clear skin the color of the coffee Deacon set in front of her, big dark eyes, and a short cap of hair in neat cornrows. She was pretty, friendly, reliable, and a real favorite of the middle-aged men from the bowling leagues.

Since she was a senior at college this year, Hannah would have been worried about losing her, but Grace was an English major. She'd probably be in college for the rest of her life unless she got her PhD and tenure.

Of course, if the Country Time closed it wouldn't be much of an issue.

"I'm so sorry about all of this, Hannah," Grace said, patting her back in a comforting gesture.

Hannah smiled weakly at the younger woman. "I'm pretty sure that's my line."

Grace shrugged. "You're not the one who ran off with all the money."

"No," Hannah sighed.

"Is everyone coming?" June asked. She'd walked behind the bar to get herself a mug of coffee. Mary Alice sat down on Hannah's other side, beaming her bright, slightly insane, smile.

"Almost everyone can make it," Hannah told June. "Jason and Billy will be here. Kevin's at another job today, but we'll fill him in tomorrow." Kevin Barbet, the part-time cook, was working three jobs so he could send money to his family in Haiti.

"Oh, good," Mary Alice sighed. "That means Billy feels better today. He sure gets sick a lot."

Hannah, June, and Deacon all exchanged a look.

"Yeah," Deacon said, not unkindly, "he sure does."

As if conjured by their words, Billy Phillips strolled in the front door, looking more rumpled than usual in a T-shirt that had seen better days and smelled even worse. He slumped on a barstool with a huge yawn, not bothering to cover his mouth. His brown eyes were red-rimmed, his hair standing on end, and it looked like he'd just rolled out of bed—which meant he'd probably been partying hard the night before.

Hannah sighed. She'd been hoping Billy would mature now that he was finally out of high school, but she should have known better. The kid had all the earmarks of someone destined for a long-term career in dish washing.

Grace frowned at him. He grinned sleepily as Mary Alice leaned around Hannah to see him.

"I'm glad you're feeling better, Billy."

He blinked at her. "Um, yeah. Thanks, Mary Alice."

"Here's Jason," Grace said. She smiled flirtatiously at Jason Nguyen, the other bartender, when he came in through the kitchen. He was younger than Deacon, shorter and smoother, with golden brown skin and eyes reflecting his Vietnamese heritage. A lot of the women who came to the bar when he was working seemed to find him interesting. Too bad he was going to be moving on to grad school next year.

Hannah found her eyes drawn to Deacon. He was listening to June, lines fanning from his eyes when he smiled at something she'd said.

A man rough around the edges could be interesting, too.

She shook herself slightly. She really had to stop thinking like that.

Deacon poured coffee for everyone, handling the pot with grace and expertise. Billy took his mug in both hands and held it reverently, as if it contained the cure for cancer. He drank long and deep, then let out a sigh.

"Okay," June said, leaning on the bar beside Deacon, "tell us what's going on."

"Yeah, man," Billy said. "Word around town is Georgie Porgie took off with all of your money and his smoking hot assistant."

Hannah raised her eyebrows. "Georgie Porgie?"

Billy smirked and shrugged.

"And you and Deacon were seen leaving the bank this morning," Grace reported.

Hannah stared at her. "By who?" she demanded.

"Whom. My Dad was in making a deposit and he saw you. One of his cashiers told him about George yesterday. He called me at school to tell me." Grace's father owned the local grocery store.

"Great." Hannah took another sip of her coffee. Freaking small towns.

"And everyone knows Sam was here last night," Jason added. "My mom said all the bowlers were talking about it."

"Great," Hannah repeated. She glanced at Deacon, but he didn't seem inclined to jump in and break the news for her. He caught her eye and smiled a little as he sipped his coffee. She scowled at him, then took a deep breath.

"Okay," she said, "George took all of the money."

"We *know* that," June said.

"Which means there's no money for the taxes that are due in five days. There's no money to pay the vendors. And there's no money for the, well, payroll."

That got their attention.

"Dude," Billy said.

Hannah assumed he was talking to her.

"What are you going to do?" June challenged. "Lay us off? Close the place? Declare bankruptcy?"

"No, no." Hannah waved her hands. "Nothing like that." She hoped. "I've got a plan for now, and Deacon and I went to the bank this morning to see about getting a loan."

Grace was watching her intently. "Don't those things take time?"

"Yes," Hannah admitted. Before she could say anything else, the kitchen door opened, and Sam Black walked in. He strolled up to the bar just like he had a right to be there, powerful and confident in a dark gray pinstriped suit with a bold, red tie, accustomed to being the center of attention.

"You really should keep the back door locked," he told Hannah and dropped his briefcase next to a barstool.

"Well I would have if I'd known you were going to show up," she replied, forgetting for a moment that as of yesterday he was her free attorney.

Sam ignored her and zeroed in on Grace. The younger woman blushed and nibbled on her lips while watching him from under her thick lashes.

Sam's smile turned predatory.

Hannah raised her eyes to the heavens. "Why are you here? Shouldn't you be in court fleecing someone?"

"The judge called the day early because he had to make a tee time."

"Justice," Deacon muttered.

Sam shrugged. "I came to tell you that I talked to Adam Kouris, the private investigator. He's willing to help you out."

Hannah stared at him. It wasn't that she didn't trust him, but … no, that was exactly it. She didn't trust him.

"Just like that?" she asked.

"What private investigator?" Jason asked.

"A guy who works with my firm." Sam sat next to the still-blushing Grace. "Well, *hello* there," he crooned to her.

"Oh, for God's sake." June walked around the bar, grabbed Sam's arm, and pulled him over to another stool. Then she sat on the one he'd occupied, putting her body between him and Grace. Sam and Grace both frowned at her.

Deacon grinned and put bowls of chips and nuts on the bar. He did not offer Sam a cup of coffee.

"What did the investigator say?" Hannah demanded, trying to keep the conversation on track. She craned her neck to see Sam around Grace and June. "How much will he charge me?"

Sam stopped glaring at June to look at her.

"He's going to give you an additional 30 percent discount off the corporate rate."

"What does that mean in dollars?"

Sam gave her a more reasonable number than she'd expected. "He'll start working without a retainer. He'll bill you afterward. We'll figure out a payment plan, then."

Hannah was surprised. The terms were generous and a lot more than she'd expected Sam to be able to deliver. Yes, she'd still have to pay the investigator, which was a little scary, but at least now she didn't have to worry about finding money up front.

"Thanks." She gave Sam a real smile. He smiled back, and his dimples winked.

Deacon shifted behind the bar.

"Give me his information, and I'll get in contact with him," Hannah said, but he waved it away.

"I've already told him what he needs to know to get started."

"Oh." She wasn't sure how she felt about that.

"But he's going to get in touch with you later."

She relaxed. "Good."

8

"Sorry to break into this mutual love-fest," June interrupted, her tone thick with sarcasm, "but maybe you could tell us what happened at the bank? It's only our livelihood. No big deal."

Hannah realized everyone gathered around the bar, with the exception of Deacon, was watching her.

"Like I said, I'm applying for a business loan," she told them.

Casually, Sam grabbed a fistful of peanuts, leaned back his head, and poured them into his mouth.

"Collateralized?" he asked through the nuts.

"I guess. I thought I had a line of credit, but it turns out it was closed when my father died. It sounds like Allison Arthur—she's the lending officer—is going to want collateral for a new loan."

"Ah, Allison." Sam's smile did not belong in public.

"Yeah. She said she knew you," Deacon said.

"Let me get this straight," June said, focusing on Hannah, her eyes sharp and hard. "You'll use the bar as collateral to get a loan to keep the bar running. And if you can't pay the loan, you'll lose the bar anyway?"

Hannah's stomach jittered, but she shrugged.

"So I'll make the payments," she said. *Somehow.*

"How long will it take to get a loan?" Jason asked. He had perched on a stool a fair distance away from the group, but Hannah didn't think he was trying to be a snob. The longer they sat, the more the rankness of Billy's T-shirt became apparent.

"I don't know," she told him honestly. "A couple of weeks, I guess."

Sam snorted. "Try a couple of months."

"Maybe you could borrow some money from regular people," Mary Alice suggested. "Like investors."

Hannah met Deacon's eyes. "I'm not going to do that now," she said. "We'll see about a bank loan first."

Deacon turned away and poured himself another cup of coffee.

"Oh, but if they're rich, they're probably looking for investments," Mary Alice protested.

Hannah realized almost everyone had turned to look at Sam.

He was chewing more peanuts and choked when he saw them all staring at him. Surprise had him coughing and spitting peanut pieces across the bar. June slapped him on the back a couple of times, just a little harder than was absolutely necessary.

"Hey," Sam said when he'd gotten himself under control. "I can't lend her money."

"Why not?" June asked. "You're the fancy lawyer here."

"Well, yeah, but I just bought a condo and a new car. I've got expenses."

Hannah waved her hands to get everyone's attention.

"Sam's not lending me money and neither is anybody else

at the moment," she said, not looking at Deacon. "But I do need to raise some working capital to help keep things running until everything shakes out." Her savings and credit cards would only take them so far. "Anyone have any bright ideas?"

The silence was deafening. Deacon leaned against the back counter and crossed his legs while he sipped his coffee.

"Is there anything you could sell?" Grace asked finally. "I sell a lot of stuff on eBay."

Hannah gestured around her. "Do you see anything worth selling here?"

"Oh."

More silence.

"What about those, like, cage fights?" Billy asked. "You know, mixed martial arts shit? Man, people would pay to see that." He chopped at the air with his hands.

"No," Hannah said, thinking of her insurance premiums. Especially if Billy pissed off one of the fighters, which he was bound to do.

"How about strippers?" Sam said. "I know a lot of people who would come to see strippers."

"I'll bet," Hannah muttered.

"How do you think we would reconcile the whole 'country tavern' image with strippers?" Deacon asked. He sounded sincerely curious.

"Well, you don't have too many families coming in after nine o'clock, do you? And little kids barely come in at all. So the strippers start after nine."

"What about the women?" Deacon shifted and put down his coffee mug. "We get a lot of women in here. They bring their boyfriends and husbands."

Hannah gaped at him. For God's sake, he didn't think hiring strippers was a good idea, did he?

"Oh! Oh!" Mary Alice raised her hand like she was in school. "We could have male strippers."

Grace brightened considerably. "That's a good idea."

"Like I'd come to see that," Jason scoffed.

"Okay, we'll alternate," Mary Alice agreed equably.

"No strippers!" Hannah yelled, and everyone stared at her. "Jesus, why do I even have to say that? Read my lips. No strippers."

"Killjoy," Sam muttered.

"It would bring in money," Mary Alice pointed out. "People like to see strippers."

"No. Strippers. Besides, if there are strippers here, what do you think you'd have to wear to wait on the tables?"

"Oh." Mary Alice and Grace exchanged a look and both grimaced.

"We could have an ... event," June said slowly. "Like a special deal to raise cash."

"Oh yeah, man," Jason said. "They're always doing that kind of stuff at school. Sometimes we even stand at the Wal-Mart and sell baked goods our parents make. My mom makes a bitching brownie."

"Wait." Deacon straightened. "You want to hold a bake sale to save the bar?"

"No, no, more than that." Grace was excited now. She leaned forward. "We do them all the time for my sorority. You have food and drinks and entertainment and people come. Then you charge them for what they eat, and you get them to donate to the cause while they're there."

"Does it work?" Hannah frowned. Yes, it sounded lame, but it beat the hell out of hiring a bunch of strippers.

"Sure. We raised a lot of money the last time we had an event."

"Food?" Hannah asked.

"I'll see if my Dad will donate food from the store."

"Drink we've got covered," Hannah mused. "Entertainment?"

"Well, you've got to have something to make the people want to come buy the food and drink." Grace agreed. She frowned prettily.

"Strippers?" Billy suggested.

"Would you leave off the damn strippers?" Hannah scowled at him. "Do you possibly have any other suggestions?"

He didn't.

"We could rent a moon bounce," Mary Alice said.

Hannah snorted. "Right. I've got a big picture of Old Albert in a moon bounce."

"Actually, it might not be a bad idea to have some things for kids," Deacon said. "We could sell tickets. Like a carnival."

"A carnival." Hannah pondered that for a moment. A vision started to form in her mind. Crazy, but ... "Can a person rent a carnival?" she asked slowly.

Deacon looked worried.

"Hannah—"

"I think you can," Jason said. "Like those volunteer fire company carnivals during the summer?"

Deacon glared at him. Jason shrugged.

"Well, I'm pretty sure the firemen don't have Ferris wheels around all year long," he pointed out. "I guess they hire someone."

"Thanks for mentioning it," Deacon said. "No, really. Thanks."

Hannah ignored them both and turned to June. "You know a lot of people," she said. "Do you have anyone you could call?"

June smirked. "Oh, sure. Let me just check my address book."

"June."

The older woman shook her head and put her coffee mug back on the bar. "Even if you can rent a damned carnival, it's going to be freaking expensive, and you know it."

Hannah continued to stare at her until June heaved a deep sigh.

"Fine, fine. I'll make some calls," she said resignedly. "See if I can find someone who will cut us a break."

Hannah beamed. "Thanks."

"Yeah, right."

"You know, you could have a band, too." Mary Alice sounded tentative, and when Hannah looked at her, her eyes were wide and guileless.

"A band?" Damned if that wasn't a good idea. Even if they tracked down a carnival, not everyone would want to ride rides or play games. "I don't know any bands," she admitted. At least she didn't know any bands who were halfway decent and would work for little or no money.

"My life partner's brother is in a cover band," Mary Alice sounded eager. "Johnny said they're pretty good. I haven't actually heard them all play together, but Johnny's brother comes over to our house and plays his guitar for us. It sounds like he knows all the chords."

Hannah stared at her. So did everyone else.

"What?" Mary Alice blinked at them.

"You're not a ... your life partner is a ... man?" Hannah finally asked.

The other woman's expression was serene. "He is now."

Okay. Hannah decided to let that one go.

"The band is playing in Scranton tomorrow, so you can probably go see them if you want," Mary Alice offered.

"Huh." Hannah was trying not to think about why Mary Alice's life partner was a man ... now. She looked at Deacon, who was watching Mary Alice with a bemused expression. When he caught her eye, he shrugged slightly, as if to say "who knew?"

"Want to go see a band tomorrow night?" she asked without thinking.

Surprise flashed in his eyes, then he grinned. "Tomorrow is Friday night," he pointed out. "Who will tend the bar?"

"I'm sorry," Jason said. "I can't. I work at the country club on Fridays and Saturdays."

"Oh...I didn't...I wasn't..." Crap. What was she doing?

"I'll work the bar," June said suddenly.

"Are you sure?" Deacon asked her. "You'll be alone, and it's going to be busy."

"Please." She waved that away. "I can pull a beer tap. If somebody comes in here and wants a fancier drink, they're in the wrong place anyway."

"I can come in and work," Mary Alice volunteered. "I can wait tables or work in the kitchen or even help with the bar."

"Sounds good," Deacon said quickly.

"Kevin's going to be angry about working alone on a Friday night," Hannah pointed out, still not sure how she'd gotten herself into this situation. "Plus he'll have to do cleanup." Billy had this Friday off, not that anyone would notice.

"Kevin won't mind," June assured her. "We'll help him."

It felt wrong. It felt like she was deserting her post in the hour of need, but the lure of an actual Friday night off was irresistible. And, for some reason, the thought of a Friday night alone with Deacon made it even more appealing.

"Okay," she said, then glanced at Deacon. "We can meet here. That way we'll be around for the early crowd."

He grinned at her. "Sure."

Hannah looked at the people clustered at the old wooden bar.

"So, we're going to do this? We're going to try to pull off an event?" She wasn't sure if she was asking for approval or rejection.

"Save the Country Time," Jason said. "Save a beloved local business."

"When you decide what you want to do, I can ask my sorority to help," Grace said. "We get credit for volunteer work."

"Sah-weet!" Mary Alice gave a fist pump. "I'll tell Johnny to tell Roy that you'll be stopping by to check out the band tomorrow. They'll be so happy. And I'm sure they'll work for free because they're trying to line up some new venues."

"I need a drink," Sam said and suited action to words by walking behind the bar to pour himself a double shot of scotch.

"Man." June knocked back another hit of coffee. "Times like these I'm glad I don't own this joint."

"Yeah," Hannah muttered. "You should be glad."

After that everyone started talking at once, throwing out plans and ideas. Deacon didn't join in. Instead, he turned away from the excited group at the bar and tried to decide how he felt about this whole "event" idea. It was just like Hannah to decide to rent a carnival. A carnival, for crissakes! He shook his head and started to restack glasses that didn't really need restacking.

Hannah Frederickson would always do things her own way, no matter what anyone else said.

Hands busy, he realized he was watching her through the big mirror on the back wall. She and June had their heads together, both of them wearing serious expressions, probably talking about money. Her hair fell brown and wavy down her back, and he knew it would feel like heavy silk against his bare skin.

He drew in a deep breath at the vision of Hannah leaning over him in bed, her hair pooling on his chest as she kissed him.

He didn't want her to consider him a responsibility. He wasn't her damned responsibility.

It was probably a good thing Jason came up to him just then and interrupted his thoughts.

"I have to take off," the younger man said. "Big test tomorrow."

"Hey, good luck." They bumped fists. Jason was a good kid, even if he was studying to be a research biologist. "We're okay with the schedule, yeah?"

"We're good. I'll give you a call if something comes up and I have to shift."

"Anytime."

"Hey, Jason, dude." Billy sauntered over to them, still reeking of cigarettes, stale beer, and old sweat. "Give me a ride home?"

"You're working tonight," Deacon reminded him. He honestly didn't know why Hannah hadn't fired Billy a long time ago. "Don't call out two nights in a row."

"Yeah, because this place has so much room for advancement." Billy laughed at his own joke. "Dude, lighten up," he said when he saw Deacon's expression. "I'll be here. But I'm not scheduled for another couple of hours, so I'll catch me some Zs first."

"Didn't you drive? How did you get here?" Jason took a step back, as if ready to make a break for it.

Billy waved that away. "Ma dropped me off on her way to the grocery store."

Deacon could tell Jason wanted to refuse, and he couldn't blame him; his car would need to be fumigated after Billy got out of it. But the kid caved after a few minutes of expectant silence, which didn't bode well for his future as a scientist.

"Come on," he said, sighing.

"Awesome!"

Jason sighed again, and started towards the back door. Billy flipped Deacon a salute and followed, running to catch up with the other man.

Hannah and June, still talking, headed for Hannah's office. Mary Alice and Grace left a few minutes later, since their shift didn't really start until five. Grace seemed reluctant to go, her brown eyes fastened on the glory that was Sam. But Mary Alice grabbed her arm and pulled her away, unusual determination firming her round face. It was always a surprise when Mary Alice showed good sense.

And that left Deacon alone with Sam.

Shit.

Moving automatically, he began to wipe down the bar and remove the empty glasses and dishes. They'd be opening in a half hour, and the summit meeting had put him a little behind schedule.

When he looked up from what he was doing, he caught Sam watching him. His brother was lounging on his barstool, casually sipping scotch. The expression in his eyes was cool and distant, but his shoulders were straight and tight. It occurred to Deacon that this encounter might be as uncomfortable for Sam as it was for him.

Oddly, that thought settled him. Tucking the rag he'd been using in his back pocket, he got another glass and poured himself a drink from the bottle Sam had used, then turned to study his brother.

He hadn't seen much of Sam since he'd been back. It was a small town, but the only place they would have been likely to run into each other was at their parents' house, and everyone had striven to avoid that possibility.

His brother looked ... older. The lines around his mouth and eyes were deeper than Deacon remembered, and he was pleased to note his hair didn't seem to be as thick as it had once been. It had always burned his ass that he'd been the one to inherit damned receding hair genes. Sam still had a full head, but his curly locks did not appear to be quite as luxurious as before.

Yes!

"Did you really come to tell Hannah about the private investigator?" he asked.

"Sure." Sam smiled, but it didn't reach his eyes. He took another sip of the scotch.

"You could have just called her. Or sent her an e-mail."

"Yup," his brother agreed.

He'd wanted to see her, though. Deacon knew that as if Sam had spoken the words out loud.

They drank.

"I have a date with Sam tonight," Hannah said, eyes sparkling. "Are you sure you're good to handle things by yourself?"

"Of course," Deacon said. He'd only been at the Country Time for two weeks, but it wasn't rocket science. He'd worked in plenty of bars since getting out of the army.

"Great. I think he's taking me to the casino at Mount Pocono. Maybe I'll win a million dollars." She laughed.

Likely all she was going to win was a night in a hotel room with Sam. Deacon fisted his hands at his side.

"Oh, there he is talking to Louise. Do I look okay?"

She looked effervescent.

"You look great. Have fun," Deacon said.

"I will." Hannah laughed again and went up to Sam, taking his arm and pulling his attention away from the plump and pretty little server. Sam smiled down at her, and they left, Hannah cuddled against his side.

Deacon and Louise both watched them go.

"How are Mom and Dad?" Deacon asked when the silence had gotten oppressive.

"Fine, I guess." Sam shrugged. "I don't see too much of them."

A tractor-trailer abruptly geared down out on the highway with a sharp blast of horn. Some idiot must have cut it off.

"You know showing up here today is just going to get you deeper into this mess," Deacon pointed out. "Didn't sound like that was what you wanted yesterday."

"Maybe seeing Hannah again made me remember how good we were together."

"Maybe it would be better if you forgot."

"Look," Sam put his glass on the bar and leaned forward, suddenly intense. "I screwed up. I know that."

"You did." The weeks after the incident in the parking lot had been pretty brutal for Hannah. It seemed like everyone who'd come into the Country Time had wanted to gossip or laugh and make rude jokes.

"I'm trying to make amends," Sam insisted.

Deacon didn't believe it for a minute.

"I know she thinks she needs your help, but don't push it," he said. He put down his drink and planted his hands on the bar, getting right in his brother's face, intent on making his point. "You've already hurt her twice. I'm not going to stand here and let you do it again." He heard the cold warning in his own voice.

Sam snorted and sat back, lips twisted in a sneer. "I'm pretty sure you don't have much to say about it."

"Try something and see," Deacon invited softly.

To Sam's credit, he did not appear terrified. He just stood and pulled on his suit jacket, carefully adjusting the lapels. Then he looked at Deacon, studying him as if he were shit he'd smeared on his expensive loafers.

"Whatever happens between me and Hannah is up to us. Not you," he said, voice cool. "I don't know why you came back, and I sure as hell don't know why you've stayed, but keep out of my way."

He bent, retrieved his briefcase, and walked out.

Deacon watched the kitchen door swing shut behind his brother, listening until he heard the slam of the back door a few seconds later. Then he picked up his scotch and sipped, feeling it burn all the way down to his gut.

"Fuck."

That little confrontation had probably been a mistake. For sure Sam would take his warning as a challenge. He should have just kept his mouth shut.

He stood, drinking his scotch, looking out at the big, empty taproom.

The old oak paneling glowed a warm golden brown, and when he lit the stained glass lamps suspended from the ceiling, reds and blues would merge with the gold. The big mirror behind the bar would reflect them, and the flat-screen television would add a bit of punch.

Later he'd turn on the sound system, and country music would thunder under the voices and laughter of the customers, filling the gaps. But for now it was quiet. Hannah and June must have shut the office door, because he couldn't hear them talking. The endless traffic noises from the highway were muffled.

A good place. A good town.

After a few minutes, he heard the office door open and Hannah's and June's voices echoing in the short hallway. Finishing the last of his drink, he put the dirty glass in the bus tub and took out his rag. He began to polish the bar, trying to look as if he'd been doing nothing else the whole time they'd been gone.

9

Hannah saw Deacon standing alone at the bar when she and June walked back into the main room. Apparently the rest of her staff had scattered until their shifts started, which was only to be expected.

Sam was gone, too.

Settling herself on a barstool, she studied Deacon's closed expression. It occurred to her that she should have run Sam off before she and June went back to the office. She could only hope he'd left soon after she did and the brothers hadn't spent the whole time sniping at each other.

June walked behind the bar and grabbed a mug. "It's a damned mess," she snapped as she poured herself more coffee.

Deacon raised his eyebrows.

"I take it you've seen the books," he said.

"I showed them to her." Hannah sighed, folding her arms on the bar. June had not been pleased when she'd understood the full extent of what they were facing, but she'd had a right to know. "You'll get the show tomorrow when you help me work on the business plan."

He watched her, idly flipping the bar rag he was holding.

"You still want me to help you?" he asked, as if seeking clarification.

"You said you would." She sat up and narrowed her eyes at him. "You're not backing out, are you?"

"Not unless you want me to."

"Of course I don't want you to," she said, throwing up her hands. "How the hell am I going to figure out what I'm doing if you and June don't help me?"

That seemed to please him, because his mouth kicked up and a smile sparked in his blue eyes.

"Okay," he said.

"Good." She didn't want to think about why she felt so relieved. "Um, would you mind coming in early tomorrow? We're not going to have time to work on anything today. I have to start calling vendors, and I expect we'll be pretty busy tonight."

Deacon was still looking at her. "No problem," he said.

June had been drinking her coffee, watching them. Now she bent and put the empty mug in the tub under the bar, then straightened.

"Well, since this is my day off, I'm outta here. I've got to rest up for tomorrow."

"You're sure you're going to be all right?" Hannah asked, trying not to feel guilty—and failing miserably. Fridays were busy even when rumors weren't flying. Tomorrow promised to be manic.

"Oh, sure." June huffed a breath. "With Mary Alice coming in to help, we'll be fine. You guys go and have fun."

"It's just that I need to make a decision about the band as soon as I can. I can't wait." Hannah realized she was over-explaining. "It's work. We're not going to have fun."

"I'm going to have fun," Deacon disagreed mildly. He was leaning against the back counter, arms and ankles crossed. Hannah glared at him and he shrugged. "Well, I am. If you're not, I'll just dump you and pick up some other chick."

"We don't even know what kind of place this is," she pointed out. Mary Alice had told them the name of the bar where the band would be playing, but Hannah had never heard of it before. Frankly, a place called "The Wounded Sparrow" did not bode well. "For all we know, it's a gay bar."

Deacon shrugged again. "Whatever. At least most of those guys can dance."

She studied him. "Can you?"

He gave her a full grin that absolutely lit up his face. "Wouldn't you like to know?"

Hannah realized that, yes, she would very much like to know. Another fizz of anticipation bubbled up her spine.

"See you tomorrow." June looked smug, but Hannah chose to ignore it. She watched her leave, then turned back to Deacon. He looked smug, too.

"Any bright ideas before I go grovel before many vendors?" she asked.

He sobered. "You're going to tell them what's going on?"

"I have to. I'm sure most of them know anyway."

He nodded and thought for a moment.

"Maybe you could offer to send them some strippers."

She rolled her eyes and shoved off her barstool. "Thank you, Deacon. Come get me if you need me."

Strippers. God almighty.

But she was smiling when she headed back to her office.

As she expected, the vendors she managed to contact were less than pleased to hear the news of her financial situation. Fortunately, she didn't have a lot of time to obsess about what might happen next.

In the normal course of life, Thursdays at the Country Time weren't as busy as Wednesdays, but that night the joint was jumping. At this point, word of Uncle George's excellent adventure had spread throughout the land, and the fine townspeople of Hardy Falls had descended *en masse* to try and find out what was going on. At least they made the cash register ring while they were at it. Once table service started, Hannah was too busy at the grill to dwell on the fact that her uncle and his assistant were someplace warm spending all of her money.

Since they had so many customers, she kept things going later than usual and didn't stop food service until a half-hour to closing. Once Mary Alice and Grace finally took themselves off for the night, delighted at the amount of their tips and promising to rest up for Friday, she told Billy to go out front and start clean-up. They had their usual argument, but eventually he shuffled off to the taproom, dragging a mop behind him.

Hannah shook her head and pulled on rubber gloves before turning to the dirty dishes piled at the rinse sink next to the industrial dishwasher. Billy tended to move at the pace of a three-toed sloth, but even if he'd sprinted around the kitchen like a gazelle, they wouldn't have been able to keep up with the dishes that night. She hoped Mary Alice would be able to help Kevin tomorrow, or he'd give her hell on Saturday.

She paused in the act of reaching for the first food-encrusted ceramic plate. She was going to have a night off. Despite everything, she felt almost giddy. A night off. And not just any night, but a *Friday* night.

Her smile faded as she grabbed the plate, rinsed it, and put it in a dishwashing rack before getting another.

Going to the Wounded Sparrow with Deacon should have felt like work. After all, she spent a lot of time with Deacon. And listening to the band *was* work. But it didn't feel like work. It felt almost like a ... date.

Which was crazy.

"Stop it," she grumbled to herself. The rack was full, so she pulled a lever on the side of the big dishwasher to open it. After she'd pushed the rack of plates inside and closed the door again, she jabbed a button to start the machine.

The deep, rumbling noise of the dishwasher filled the kitchen, and Hannah turned back to scraping and rinsing dishware, falling into the familiar rhythm of the work.

Mary Alice and Grace had told her they'd been talking about the upcoming event with the customers, so gossip was sure to spread. In the meantime, they could expect more curiosity seekers to come in. That would certainly help the bottom line. A few more nights like tonight would be awesome.

What should she wear tomorrow?

"Stop!"

"Stop what?" Deacon asked from behind her.

Hannah jumped and turned, still holding a plate. He had pushed his way through the kitchen door, hauling a loaded bus tub. It looked heavy.

He looked really, really good hauling it.

"Nothing. What are those?" She winced as soon as she spoke because it was obvious to a blind gnat the tub was filled with glassware from the bar. Her only excuse was that she was distracted by the sight of the corded muscles in his forearms. Deacon grinned at her a little quizzically.

"Last load of the day. I threw out the customers a few minutes early and locked up. Billy's cleaning."

"Right."

"No, I mean he's really cleaning. Not just pretending to."

She smirked at him. "Sucker."

Deacon laughed.

Hannah swallowed. This was ridiculous. They were together almost every day. It was silly to feel awkward with him just because they'd be going out the next night.

She wondered if Deacon really could dance, or if he'd just been teasing her.

The dishwasher ended its cycle and she turned to pull out

the rack of clean dishes, shove it down to the end of the stainless steel work table, and push in the next load. Once she'd started the machine again, she realized Deacon was still holding the heavy tub, waiting.

"Just put it over there." She indicated a nearby counter with her chin. He grunted and hefted the overflowing plastic bin up onto it, brushing against her side in the tight space as he did so.

"Sorry," he muttered.

"No problem."

Normally Deacon would have gone back out front to keep an eye on Billy and help with the hundreds of little chores necessary to make sure the place stayed relatively clean. But tonight he leaned back against the counter where he'd put the tub and folded his arms, the heat and scent of his body mixing with the steam and chemicals from the dishwasher.

Hannah was pretty sure she was flushed and sincerely hoped he'd think it was due to exertion.

He watched her in silence while she went back to scraping and rinsing dishes, loading them into another rack. When the dishwasher cycle finished, he walked behind her to the other side of the machine and pulled out the clean plates. She shoved the next rack in from her side and started the dishwasher again.

"Where do you want this?" he asked, speaking loudly to be heard over the noise.

"Oh." Frazzled, she pushed her hair back with one of her wrists, keeping the wet gloves away from her face. "Just push that rack down with the other one. Let the plates air dry for a minute."

He nodded and shoved it down the table. "I guess you'd save money if you didn't let the machine dry them at all. It's got to use a ton of electricity."

"Maybe." She hadn't really thought about it. The dishwasher used a hell of a lot of power, and leasing the big machine wasn't exactly cheap. Chewing her lip, she pulled out one of the special racks made for glassware and absently began to load it from the tub Deacon had brought in

"What?" He was way too observant sometimes.

Hannah shrugged.

"I was just wondering whether I should get rid of the dishwasher and do the dishes by hand," she admitted.

Deacon leaned a hip against the table on his side of the machine while it rumbled. "So you're going to cook, do the dishes by hand, and run the place, too?"

"No, Billy's going to do the dishes by hand."

"Oh, right." He laughed at her.

Hannah glared at him. When the dishwasher stopped working, the relative silence seemed thunderous.

"Don't be stupid." Deacon pulled out the rack of clean white plates and pushed them down the work table.

"I'm not stupid." She shoved the glasses into the dishwasher and only realized she'd forgotten to pre-rinse them after the machine started running. Oh, well.

"You're still going to have to spend some money if you expect to keep this place open," he said, his voice so reasonable that she wanted to kick him. "Besides, there's no point in killing yourself."

"I'm not killing myself." Another cycle finished. He pulled out the rack of glasses. She pushed another one in. The dishwasher started again.

"Bullshit. Look how you've been pushing yourself all day today."

Okay, maybe he had a point there. Her lower back ached like a sore tooth. With a groan, she stretched, twisting this way and that. She stopped abruptly in mid-twist when she realized he was staring at her.

"What?" she demanded.

"Nothing." He began to unload dry dishes from the racks, stacking them carefully on the shelves. Hannah remembered the glasses she'd forgotten to pre-rinse and, after stripping off her rubber gloves, walked to stand next to Deacon. She picked up one of the glasses and examined it carefully in the light. No stains. *Victory.*

The dishwasher stopped running, but she ignored it and put the glass she held back with the others. Then she turned to face Deacon.

"You don't have to come with me tomorrow." She didn't know why she'd asked him in the first place.

"I'm coming." He didn't look up from what he was doing, continuing to sort and stack dishes. She put a hand on his arm to stop him and he turned to her.

"I didn't mean to put you on the spot like that," she said.

He considered her for a moment. "Are you saying you don't want me to go?"

She gulped. "No." She wasn't exactly sure what she was saying, but she was suddenly certain she wanted to spend Friday night with Deacon.

He studied her for another moment in silence, then smiled slowly. Hannah found herself intensely aware of the warmth of his skin under her hand, the hair-roughened texture, the strength of muscle, the jump of his pulse.

"Did you change the oil in the fryer?" he asked, voice soft and low.

"Um, no."

"I guess Kevin will have to deal with it tomorrow."

"I guess."

What were they even talking about? Hannah felt hypnotized by the heat she saw flaring in his blue eyes. He was looking at her as if she was a dessert he wanted to slurp up.

"Anything else?" he murmured, and, reaching up, trailed his finger down her cheek.

There was a noise out in the taproom and a loud curse from Billy. Hannah jumped, reminded of where they were. She dropped her hand and hastily retreated to her side of the dishwasher, out of touching range.

What was she doing? This was *Deacon* for Pete's sake.

"You'd better go see what's wrong. I'm almost finished here," she said, trying to sound steady and in control, and failing.

Deacon watched her silently, then nodded. His smile had faded, but it still flirted with the edges of his hard mouth, hiding in the corners. She had the distinct impression he wanted to laugh at her.

"Sure."

When he strode off to the taproom, there was just the hint of a swagger in his step.

Hannah pulled up a stool and sat down hard.

"Crap."

10

The next morning, Hannah pulled her little red compact into a parking spot behind the Country Time and turned off the engine. Her jaw cracked wide in a huge, involuntary yawn.

Man, she needed coffee.

Rubbing her face hard to get the blood moving, she dragged herself out of the car and, groaning, stretched her tired muscles, taking a moment to enjoy the cool, fresh air. It was *way* too early for her to be back at work, but there'd been no point in staying home.

Straightening, she slammed the car door shut and absently jingled her ring of keys on her finger.

She hadn't slept well at all, but she'd expected that. More troubling was the reason she'd been tossing and turning. It hadn't been money troubles keeping her awake; it had been the memory of her encounter with Deacon in the kitchen. Every time she'd closed her eyes, her mind had insisted on replaying the incident in loving detail.

If Billy hadn't knocked over a chair and reminded her

where she was, if she hadn't backed away, would Deacon have kissed her?

Hannah drew in a deep breath and let it out slowly.

She was pretty sure he would have. She remembered how his face had looked—skin pulled taut over cheekbones, that sensual mouth hard yet wonderfully full, blue eyes narrow with arousal.

Yeah. He would have kissed her.

More, she would have kissed him back. Hell, she might even have dragged him down to the kitchen floor and had her way with him. Why hadn't she ever noticed how...delicious he was?

Well, because it would cause problems, that's why. She was his boss. She was in charge. She'd dated his brother. She shouldn't think about him *that* way.

She shouldn't.

She was thinking about him *that* way.

"Arghh!" Hannah smacked herself on the forehead, then rubbed the spot because it hurt. What the hell was she doing? "Come on, Frederickson," she muttered. "Get your mind off the hot bartender and focus on your real problems." Like writing a business plan and saving her business.

She wondered when Deacon would show up.

"Gah!"

Irritated at her own lack of sense, she marched toward the building. The sun, bright and clear, highlighted all of the flaws and cracks in the old brick facade. She'd always meant to have it repointed and repaired, but there'd never been enough money.

There sure wasn't enough money now.

After unlocking the back door and stepping inside, she flipped on lights in the kitchen before moving through to the taproom. Hitting those lights as well, she went behind the bar to the big coffee maker.

Ah. Salvation.

She'd make a full pot. Even if she didn't drink it all herself, Deacon would want some. She'd forgotten to arrange an exact time for them to get together, but he'd likely show up soon.

Hannah frowned as she rinsed out the pot, filled the machine with water, and scooped coffee into the filter basket.

Seriously, hotness aside, when had she gotten so dependent on Deacon?

She started the coffee and headed to her office. It was chilly in the building and she was glad she'd worn jeans with a thick fleece hoodie. There'd be plenty of time to pop back to her apartment and change before going to check out the band.

With Deacon.

While her computer booted up, Hannah leaned back in her chair and pulled her hands through her hair, then laced her fingers behind her head and stared at the ceiling.

Friday night. Dancing. With Deacon.

She was certain he'd be a good dancer. He was graceful for such a big guy.

Fortunately for her peace of mind, the coffee maker burbled in the taproom, which meant the brew cycle had finished, praise Jesus. She went out to the bar, poured herself a huge mug of the lifesaving liquid, and drank it standing where she was, burning her tongue in the process. Then she poured another mug and took it back to the office. A miracle had occurred and the computer had finished booting up, desktop screen proudly displayed.

Tah dah!

After draining about half of her second mug of coffee, Hannah brought the balance sheet up on the computer, then cracked her knuckles and concentrated on the joys of accounting. She didn't surface from that fourth level of hell until she heard a rustle of movement in the taproom some time later.

"Hannah?"

Deacon's voice. Her stomach shouldn't flutter at the sound of his voice. Stupid stomach. See? This was why noticing him was such a bad idea.

"Back here."

A moment later he walked into the office, carrying a mug of coffee in one hand and a lot of paper in the other. He was wearing jeans and a black T-shirt that looked like it had shrunk over the years, because it clung to his chest and those well-developed shoulders.

Yeah, Deacon sure wasn't soft anymore.

"Hey," he said.

"Hey yourself." She shouldn't get breathless just because he'd come into the room. Stupid breath.

He dropped the stack of papers on her desk, and settled into the chair opposite her, sipping his coffee.

"Tired?" he asked.

"No," she snapped. "Why?"

"With everything going on, I thought you might have had trouble sleeping, that's all."

His hand against her skin. His body, large and warm, standing close to hers.

"No," she said, voice strangled. "No problem."

Deacon nodded and sipped more coffee. "Good."

She thought she saw the gleam of some emotion in his eyes, but it was gone so quickly she'd probably imagined it.

"Is that the stuff you printed off the Internet yesterday?" she asked, hoping to change the subject.

"Yup. There's a lot of good information."

"Like what?"

He put down his coffee and picked up the papers. "Right, we should probably get busy. So you're working on the financial statements?"

"Unfortunately. What else do we need?"

He flipped some pages.

"It says here that for a kick-ass business plan, you need an executive summary."

"Executive summary? What the hell is an executive summary?" Hannah leaned forward and folded her arms on the desk.

"Wait a minute." He read a little. "It looks like an executive summary is an overview of the business."

She nodded. "Uh huh. So kind of like a summary. From an executive."

"Smart ass." He frowned at the paper. "The first bullet point they list under executive summary is 'objectives.'"

"Objectives?"

"For the business," he added helpfully, and she rolled her eyes.

"Well, of course objectives for the business. Duh. Okay. How about 'to dig myself out of the hole wherein Uncle George left me'?"

"I like the 'wherein' part, but I think you're going to have to be a little more specific."

"Okay, okay." Hannah pulled out a sticky note and wrote 'Objectives.' Then she stuck the note to her monitor. "Let's skip that one. What's next?"

He quirked his eyebrows at her. "Don't you even want to give it a try?"

"I want to think about it before I commit. Come on, we don't have all day."

He sighed and looked at the paper he was holding. "The next bullet point says 'mission statement.'"

"Mission statement." Hannah ran her hands through her hair. "What the hell kind of list is this?"

"I got it from a reputable website. I think." Deacon shook the papers at her. "What's your mission statement?"

"Well, I don't know!" Hannah threw her hands wide and waved them in the air. "Serving beer to bowlers since 1876?"

"I don't think you're taking this seriously."

"How can I take this seriously? Mission statement." She snorted. "How about 'to dig myself out of the hole wherein Uncle George left me'?"

"That's the same as your objective," he said loftily.

"If you don't like it, you come up with one."

"You don't think I can."

She crossed her arms over her chest and sat back in the chair. "That's right, sonny boy. Put up or shut up."

"Okay." Deacon stared at the ceiling, thinking. "How about 'To provide a comfortable atmosphere, good food and drink, and a place for the community to gather'?"

"Not bad," Hannah admitted. "But we can jazz it up some. Let's try, 'a local establishment to facilitate the gathering of the community in joyous camaraderie whilst ingesting exceptional grilled or fried food and adult beverages.'"

Deacon just looked at her.

"Hey," she shrugged, "my father always said that you should baffle them with bullshit."

"Uh huh." He looked back at the paper. "Why don't we skip the mission statement for now?" He read for a few minutes. "It says that we should provide a background of the principle owners and how they're qualified to run the business."

Hannah sighed. This stupid list wasn't making her feel very optimistic.

"I guess, 'grew up in the back room of a bar, started waiting tables at fifteen, and basically ran the place since age twenty-one' doesn't cut it."

Deacon put down the papers. "What's wrong with that? It shows you have experience."

"I've never been to college," she pointed out. "Never even took any business classes."

"A business degree doesn't mean you know how to manage a business."

"People who have a degree have the right qualifications."

"You have a degree in life, baby. Just like me."

Hannah laughed. "Neither one of us knows how to write a business plan," she pointed out.

"Which only goes to show how stupid they are. If business plans were smart, people with a degree in life like us could write one in five minutes."

"Right." She reached over and tapped the papers. "What else?"

"Well." He picked them up again and frowned. "You're going to need demographics."

"Jesus. Demographics?"

"Who you think will come to your bar."

"Bowlers. College kids. Old Albert Cromwell and his friends."

"I can look up the town demographics on the Internet. They've got to be there somewhere." He took her pen and made a note on the printout. "There's all kinds of shit like this, but if I read our girl Allison correctly, she's going to focus on the financial statements. Especially since the business is already up and running."

"I know." The thought did not improve Hannah's mood.

"Are you finished with the balance sheet?"

"Almost. It's not pretty. George really did a number on me before he took off for parts unknown."

"The Internet god of business plans says here," Deacon held up the papers, "that the statement of cash flows is the most important part of the plan. How long is it going to take you to finish that one?"

"Just a few minutes. Let me pull it right out of my ass."

"An attractive image. Come on, it's not that hard."

She stared at him. "You think it's not hard? When's the last time you did one?"

"About six years ago, I guess." He smiled when she gaped at him. She'd expected him to say he'd never prepared any kind of accounting statement. "Money comes in, money goes out."

"What if all the money went out?" she muttered.

"More will come in. Why don't you show me the balance sheet and what you've got on the cash flows so far?"

"It's rough." She gestured and he got up, moving around the desk to stand next to her. "It's been kind of hard to figure out which numbers are real."

He planted his hand on the desk by the keyboard and leaned forward until she was blanketed in the heat of his body and the clean scent of the soap he'd used that morning.

Unable to resist, she studied his profile, noting the way the light brought out his high cheekbones and the dark shadow of his eyelashes. Had his eyelashes always been long? He glanced at her, and from this angle his eyes seemed to be a darker blue, the curve of his mouth more defined.

For a moment they just looked at each other, neither one moving. Hannah knew that if she turned just a little bit, her body would be pressed against his, against the soft cotton of his shirt and all of the strength beneath it. She wondered if he'd mind. She wondered what he'd taste like...

"It looks great," he said.

She blinked at him.

"Huh?"

"The balance sheet." He straightened away from her and his mouth twisted into a secret little smile. "You've done a great job. Quinn, my CPA friend, should be able to work with it."

"Oh." Hannah struggled to pull herself together. What in the hell was she doing? "Good. That's good." She winced when her voice came out all bright and cheery.

Deacon's strange little smile deepened and he went back around the desk to settle in the visitor's chair again.

"I'll tell you what. Since there's only one computer in here, why don't I work longhand? I'll rough out the mission statement and objectives and that kind of thing, while you're working on the statement of cash flows." He hesitated deliberately. "Unless it will bother you if I stay?"

Hannah caught the challenge in that normally quiet face.

"Of course it won't bother me," she lied.

"Great." He beamed at her. "I'm going to get more coffee."

"Great," Hannah muttered as he left the room. "Freaking great."

He came back a few minutes later with another mug of coffee for himself and one for Hannah as well. After putting them carefully on her desk, he grabbed a yellow legal pad of paper she had lying around. Dropping into the visitor's chair, he balanced the heel of one battered running shoe on the opposite knee, propped the pad on his leg, and was soon muttering to himself, scratching away with a pen he'd scrounged up from somewhere, apparently oblivious to any strange vibrations that may or may not be resonating between them.

Of course, maybe he didn't feel them.

Good. That was good.

"Are you okay?" Deacon asked suddenly, making her jump. She realized she'd just been sitting there staring at him.

"I'm fine," she snapped. "Damned numbers," she added.

"Sure."

He smiled and seemed inordinately pleased with himself, which just pissed her off more, so, with an effort of will, she turned her full attention to the statement of cash flows.

If the balance sheet was the fourth level of hell, Hannah decided the statement of cash flows must be the heart of the fiery inferno. After she'd interrupted Deacon with questions for the billionth time, he gave up on the mission statement and pulled his chair around to her side of the desk so he could look over her shoulder.

It felt good to be working together like this, even though the flutters in her stupid stomach erupted every time he leaned forward to point out something or other. Amazingly, that stone bitch of a cash flow statement was pretty well roughed out by the time Deacon had to leave to get the bar ready.

At least something had gone right today.

Once Deacon had gone, Hannah tried to keep working but just couldn't concentrate. She finally gave up and decided she might as well go home to get changed. That way she'd be ready whenever they decided to head out to the other bar.

And, she thought as she drove to her apartment, if they got an early start, they could come back to work once they were finished. After all, this wasn't a date. It was business.

Still, it seemed to take her an awfully long time to decide what to wear, and she spent way more effort than usual on her hair. She even put on makeup. Then, because she never used makeup, she ended up looking like a sad clown and had to clean it all off her face. That was when she forced herself away from the mirror and back to the bar.

After she'd parked her car behind the Country Time again and gotten out, Hannah hesitated, smoothing down the silk blouse she now wore. It was dark green and looked good with her coloring, but maybe it was too much. Maybe she shouldn't have bothered changing at all. It was highly unlikely a place named "The Wounded Sparrow" had any kind of a dress code. Deacon might think she'd dressed up for him.

Which of course she hadn't.

She'd tell Deacon to just go home after they checked out the band, Hannah decided, walking to the back door. Then he would know she hadn't meant anything by getting dressed up, that she wasn't offering him anything.

He wouldn't go, though. If she came back to work, he would, too. He had just as much devotion to the place as she did.

Biting her lip, she pulled open the back door and slipped

into the heat of the kitchen. Kevin was already there, getting things set up for the Friday night crowd. He didn't notice her right away because he was changing the fryer oil and cursing loudly in Creole. Tiptoeing in her short boots, she tried to sneak past him, but he looked up and caught her.

"You." He pointed a thick finger at her. "You left this for me."

"Yes, I did," she admitted and stopped. "Sorry."

"And you do not work with me tonight. You leave me alone with that crazy woman."

He meant June. Kevin was a little scared of June. Most people were.

"It's business," she protested.

"Yes, yes. I know." He waved his big hand, then wiped the sweat off his forehead and grinned, his smile splitting his broad, brown face. "You go with Deacon, yes?"

"Yes."

"Good. Is good." He nodded. "Why you all dressed up?"

"What?" she looked down at herself. "No reason. No...too much?"

"*Non*." He kissed his fingers. "Just right. You look pretty."

"Thanks, Kevin."

"I practice my English with Gracie and Mary Alice when we are not busy. Next time you need to go out for business, I take you." He shoved his thumb against his chest and laughed, a booming sound in the small room. Hannah laughed with him.

"Honey, you don't need to speak English for that," she teased.

"No, because I can move." He swiveled his hips and his solid, stocky frame shifted behind the grease-spattered apron. "You should wish that skinny ass Deacon can move like me."

"I should," she agreed. "And how is your wife going to take it if she finds out you went dancing with me?"

"Ah. She will understand, no?" He flicked that away.

"Someday she will meet you and she will see that my boss lady is beautiful. She knows I cannot resist a beautiful woman."

Hannah laughed even as her heart sagged under renewed guilt. Kevin had told her that, once he became a citizen, he was going to send for his wife and kids. He wanted his children to grow up in the United States. If he lost his job...

"Hey." Kevin had moved closer without her noticing. He tapped his finger on her cheek. "What is bothering you, boss lady? Is it the bar? You worried because that asshole ran off with your money?"

"So you heard all about it, huh?"

"Sure. People talk. Especially in the kitchens." He shrugged, then smiled. "It will be okay. You'll see."

She blinked rapidly against unexpected tears. "What if I can't do it?" she whispered to the big man. "What if I can't save the Country Time?"

"I know you, eh? You will pull it off. And if you cannot, it won't be because you did not try." His smile was gentle.

"Oh, Kevin." She moved to hug him, but he took a step back.

"*Non*. I have grease all over me from this goddamned fryer. You look too beautiful to mess up. Now," he waved both hands, "get the hell out of my kitchen. My lazy boss lady left me to do dirty work while she goes out dancing with another man."

Hannah laughed.

"You're crazy."

"Sure am." He chuckled again and turned back to the fryer.

Hannah went into the front room and was surprised to find Grace and June already seated at the bar, drinking coffee. Deacon was leaning across from them, laughing.

He'd changed at some point, too. Instead of the old T-shirt he'd been wearing while they worked on the business plan, now he had on a light blue oxford shirt that highlighted the color of his eyes. The sleeves were rolled up to his elbows, exposing those strong forearms. His jeans, as she'd already had occasion to note, fit him very well indeed. He looked big and broad, and she wanted to climb all over him.

Down girl.

"There you are," June said. She looked like a cat who was stuffed full of canary, although Hannah couldn't imagine why.

"Hi, Hannah!" Grace called and waved at her.

Deacon straightened slowly and studied her from head to toe. His smile was quiet, but something burned in those bright blue eyes. Hannah knew she was blushing. Deacon's smile deepened.

"Why are you frowning?" he asked innocently. God, he was such an ass.

"I am not frowning," she growled.

"You know, it kind of looks like you're frowning," Grace offered.

"Yup, that's a frown all right," June agreed, voice bland. She took another sip of her coffee.

"Why are you here already?" Hannah demanded of the other women.

"I work here." June said sweetly.

Grace nodded. "I thought maybe I could help Kevin until table service starts, but he told me to get lost until he was finished cleaning the 'goddamned fryer.'"

"Oh." Great, now she felt like a real bitch. "Um, thanks," she muttered.

"When do you want to leave?" Deacon asked, drawing her attention back to him. "Mary Alice said the band plays their first set around eight, but it's going to take a little while to get to the place. And you'll want to take your car back to your apartment, right? I was assuming I'd drive."

"Okay." It was easier not to argue. Besides, if she came back to work, she'd just drive in again later.

"If you want something to eat, you should probably leave at

five thirty or so," June volunteered. "Might as well have dinner out while you can." She fluttered her eyelashes at Hannah.

"Sounds good to me," Deacon said, and Hannah saw him watching her intently.

"I'm ready whenever you are," she said.

This time Deacon's slow smile made her gulp. June cackled. Grace giggled.

Deciding it was well past the time to beat a graceful retreat, Hannah took a step away from the bar.

"Okay, well, I'm going to work on the business plan," she told Deacon, trying to hold on to some semblance of professionalism. "Let me know when you want me."

His eyes darkened into an expression not entirely appropriate for the workplace.

"Sure."

She practically tripped over a barstool in her haste to get away from him.

Back in her tiny office, sitting safely behind the barricade of her desk, Hannah stared blindly into the glare of her computer screen and tried to breathe. Just thinking about Deacon's smile was enough to make her toes curl. The heat in his eyes when he'd looked at her had nothing to do with work and everything to do with the bedroom.

He wanted her.

She might not be the smartest person in the whole world, but she knew that much with absolute certainty. Deacon Black wanted her. Worse, she wanted him back. And she didn't know when it had happened. Had he always looked at her that way and she'd just never noticed? Or did it have something to do with Sam being back in the picture?

She frowned at the thought and picked at the peeling varnish of her desktop with her fingernail.

The timing was a little suspicious, wasn't it? She had absolutely no desire to be fought over by the two brothers like some kind of bone.

Well, it didn't matter anyway, she told herself. No way would she take things further with Deacon. It was bad enough that they were coworkers. It was worse that she was his boss. If they got involved and people in the town found out, the gossip would be unbearable.

It wasn't fair, but people would laugh at Deacon and think he was sleeping with her because she paid him. Like he was a gigolo or something. Hardy Falls could be a town without pity, as she'd discovered on more than one occasion.

Hannah's frown deepened into a scowl. What if they got involved and he sued her for sexual harassment?

Okay, no. Deacon wouldn't sue her.

But what if they hooked up for however long and things went wrong? Even if things didn't implode with a lot of drama, like her and Sam, what if they just drifted apart? How would they be able to keep working together if they broke up?

What would happen when he left?

"Stop." She realized she was gripping the edge of the desk so hard her knuckles had turned white. She made herself relax; she did not need this stress right now. Wasn't it enough that all of her money had been stolen?

But oh, that *look*.

Deacon Black was a lot more dangerous than she'd ever suspected.

"It's always the quiet ones."

Sighing, she shoved a hand through her hair, messing up whatever style she'd managed earlier, and pulled up the income statement spreadsheet on the computer. She used to know what she was doing. Now figuring out a business plan was going to be a hell of a lot easier than figuring out her own life.

11

On the road to Scranton, Deacon guided his SUV around a slow-moving truck and tried to focus on his driving rather than the woman sitting next to him. It was hard. All he wanted to do was pull over onto the shoulder of the interstate, grab Hannah, and kiss her until neither one of them could think straight.

He glanced at her and saw she was staring out the side window, profile highlighted by the ambient light. What in the world was spinning around in that agile brain of hers?

Frowning, he turned his attention back to the road.

He'd been happy with the progress he seemed to be making. Last night at the dishwasher, today in her office, the way she'd gotten all flushed and flustered after coming back from her apartment. Hannah Frederickson had definitely started to notice him.

But then there'd been an early rush of customers, and he'd ended up working the bar while June helped Grace and Kevin. He and Hannah hadn't been able to leave nearly as soon as he'd hoped, and he was pretty sure the extra time had given her a chance to have second thoughts.

Hell, who was he kidding? She was rebuilding her walls faster than a damned stonemason.

He tightened his grip on the steering wheel and shifted a little in the seat.

Easy, boy. Patience.

He shot a look at her again. God, that face. Strong nose. Stronger chin. Wide mouth. She just did it for him. Hannah wasn't fragile, she was a real woman and he wanted her. He flexed his hands.

"Are we almost there?"

Deacon started when her soft question broke the silence.

"I think so," he said. Mary Alice had given him directions the night before, which was a good thing. The Wounded Sparrow wasn't exactly high profile.

"I forgot to tell you that I was able to get in touch with most of the vendors." Hannah stirred and turned to him. It put her face in shadow, but he could see the gleam of her eyes when he glanced at her.

"And?"

She sighed, just a light exhalation of breath. "They're wary."

"Shocking."

"I know."

With that, she fell back into a brooding silence. Deacon let it go until he saw their turn up ahead.

"We're here," he said. "Hey, it doesn't look as bad as I thought it would."

"That's not saying much," Hannah muttered.

Laughing, he turned into the parking lot and slid the SUV into an empty spot at the far end. The Wounded Sparrow was a long, low building, bigger than he'd expected, with the requisite neon beer signs scattered across the front. A larger sign with the name of the bar flashed above the main entrance. The place didn't look like anything special, and wasn't nearly as nice as the Country Time, but it didn't seem all that bad either.

"Huh," he said, turning off the engine and pocketing his keys. "Maybe Roy's further up the food chain than I thought he was."

"Johnny and Roy," Hannah mused. "I wonder if their parents were fans of that old TV show? *Emergency*?"

"You know *Emergency*?" Deacon grinned at her, foolishly pleased.

"Sure." She shrugged. "Dad and I used to watch the reruns all the time on cable when I was a kid."

He pointed at her. "See? That's why I like you. You know the classics."

Hannah grimaced. "It's always good to have a skill. If the bar closes, maybe I can get on a trivia game show." She tried to laugh, but it fell flat.

Deacon leaned closer, wanting to kiss the worry and stress off her face.

"It will be okay, Hannah," he said. His voice came out raspy, but there wasn't much he could do about that.

Hannah smiled, her eyes dark pools in the dim light, and touched his arm. "I'm glad you came with me tonight."

"Me, too."

He was intensely aware of the movement of her breasts as she breathed, the clean scent of her skin. He wanted to bury his face against her neck and run his teeth all over her.

He shifted back instead.

"We'd better go in," he said. Without waiting for a response, he jumped out of the SUV while he still could.

By the time he'd gotten around to the passenger side of the car, Hannah had slid out and was standing, pulling the strap of her tiny purse over her head and across her body. Damn it, he'd wanted to open her door for her. How was he supposed to show her that he had some freaking class, if she never gave him a chance to prove it?

Shaking it off, he quirked his eyebrows at her. "So, are you ready to take on the Wounded Sparrow?"

Hannah sighed. "I guess."

Side by side, they started towards the building. The dull thud of country music pounded across the parking lot, and there was a cold bite of fall in the air, mixed with the tang of cigarettes from a group of smokers huddled near the door. In spite of the lingering buzz of sexual tension, on his part at least, Deacon realized that this felt right. Talking with Hannah, being with her, was normal and it was good.

He shoved his hands in the pockets of his jeans and frowned down at the asphalt. Would everything change if they took things to the next level?

Of course it would; it would have to. Then what would happen if they broke up?

It wasn't the job he cared about so much. He could get another job. It was Hannah. Over the past two years he'd become friends with everyone who worked at the Country Time, but Hannah was special. He really didn't want this thing brewing between them to screw that up.

People always said it was possible to stay friends after a breakup, but he'd never seen it happen. God knew it had never happened in *his* life.

"What's wrong?" Hannah asked. He glanced at her and found her watching him.

"Nothing."

"Bullshit."

Jesus, she was persistent. Deacon flailed around for an answer that did not involve discussing his hopes and fears in the parking lot of the Wounded Sparrow.

"I, um, I was thinking about the business plan and the financial statements."

"Oh." She made a face. "Me too."

Well, hell. He didn't want her thinking about business

plans. He wanted her to be thinking about him the way he was thinking about her.

A few more steps and they were at the Wounded Sparrow's main entrance. This close to the building the music was loud enough to deafen. The smokers clustered a few feet away eyed them speculatively in the strange neon half-light. Deacon drew Hannah closer to his side, meeting their stares with his own until they turned away.

Hannah muttered something he thought sounded a lot like "caveman."

A big, muscled guy was perched on a tall stool at the door. Deacon paid the cover charge and they stepped inside, the noise level immediately ratcheting up to epic proportions.

The Wounded Sparrow was one big, dark room with more neon signs on the walls, a few tables, and an enormous bar manned by two bartenders. In the gloom, the mirror behind the bar seemed to glow, as reflected light from the signs bounced off shelf after shelf of glass bottles.

A small stage that didn't look big enough to hold a gerbil was set up off to the side, and Deacon could see instruments and microphones already set up waiting for the band. He sure hoped Roy and his friends were thin or they'd probably fall off.

Two women wiggled in front of the stage on a postage-stamp-sized area he guessed was supposed to be the dance floor. He thought they were trying to do a line dance, but mostly they shook their butts and giggled. A number of men stood nearby, holding beer bottles and watching the women.

"Looks like it's a neighborhood hangout," he shouted to Hannah.

"Who else would come here?"

Deacon grinned.

"I don't think they have table service," Hannah yelled up at him. "Do you want to go to the bar and get something to eat?"

Deacon felt his stomach clench at the mention of food. He was starving.

"Hope to God they have something decent," he muttered.

"What?"

"Come on," he shouted at her just as the music coming through the sound system cut off. The people standing nearby turned to look at him, and Hannah, the witch, started laughing.

"Come on," he repeated and pulled her towards the bar.

They found an empty barstool and Hannah settled on it, Deacon standing beside her. He saw four guys get up from one of the tables and climb onto the small stage, but the level of noise in the room didn't change, so he wasn't sure anyone else noticed. The drunk women on the dance floor still shook their butts, even though the music had stopped. The men still watched them.

The band—he guessed it was the band—strapped on their instruments and stood at the mics. There was a loud spurt of feedback, inspiring yelled curses from the patrons. Then, without any introduction, the guys began to play. It wasn't country, it was "Land of a Thousand Dances."

And it was pretty good.

Deacon raised his eyebrows.

They weren't terrific. But the guitar player, who also sang lead, had a decent voice and was handling the riffs pretty well. What the other guys lacked in finesse they made up for in enthusiasm. A big drummer twirled his drumsticks and shook his shaved head to the beat, grinning. Soon the two women on the dance floor were lost in a crowd as other people joined them.

Deacon looked down at Hannah.

"They'll work for free?" he asked.

She shook her head, obviously as surprised as he was. "That's what Mary Alice said."

"Think she's right?"

She shook her head again. "Maybe we'd better make sure."

One of the bartenders finally noticed them, and Deacon ordered two beers. The song segued into "Old Time Rock & Roll," and he watched as the tiny dance area turned into some sort of twisted, cowboy-flavored mosh pit, the floor shaking under the thunder of pounding boots.

Deacon thought the band members might have been a little surprised by all of the excitement, too. The lead singer exchanged a somewhat nervous look with the keyboardist, who gave a subtle shrug and launched into an intricate solo that was only a little bit beyond his abilities.

"Do you want something to eat?" Deacon asked Hannah when the beer came.

"Not yet."

He nodded and ordered cheese fries with extra cheese for himself.

"Extra cheesy cheese fries?" She poked him in the stomach. "Why don't you have a gut?"

"Clean living." He tried to ignore the fact that she'd touched him, just like he was trying to ignore the fact that he could feel the heat of her body pressed against his side.

"Right." She drank her beer, studying the band. "They're not bad."

"I think you might have yourself a winner. They'll be a good fit for us."

"Maybe."

"They're probably free."

She grinned up at him. "You're right. If they're free, they're an excellent fit for us."

For a few minutes they listened to the band without trying to talk over the music. The beers and fries came, but Deacon didn't really pay that much attention to them. He found himself leaning closer to Hannah, breathing her in. Just her. Hannah.

The music changed, became slow and rhythmic. "My Girl."

"Dance with me," he said suddenly, hoping she wouldn't notice the roughness of his voice. He had to get his hands on her, had to touch that strong, supple body, had to feel her moving against him.

"What?" She blinked at him owlishly. "Why?"

"Because I want to dance with you." *Want* was too tame a word. He made himself smile and spoke close to her ear. "Come on. I have to prove that I can move." *Over her. In her.* He drew in a deep breath and tried to wrestle himself back under control.

Hannah shivered a little, but laughed and pushed away from the bar. "Okay, I guess we might as well."

Before she could change her mind, he led her out onto the tiny dance floor, crowded with the bodies of swaying couples, and pulled her into his arms.

God, he was finally, finally, *finally* holding her. Not trying to offer comfort. Not being a friend. Just holding her. Man and woman.

He knew the exact moment when she realized what was happening. She stilled and he could practically see her rethinking the entire situation. *No, no. Don't think.*

"Relax," he said, and tugged her resisting body a little closer. He started to move with her, swaying with her as the other couples were swaying, circling her in the middle of the warm, humid dance floor.

It took a few minutes, but, as "My Girl" ended and "Unchained Melody" began, Hannah's body lost some of its rigidity. A moment later her arms crept around his neck, her breasts lifting against his chest, their bodies perfectly aligned.

"Now I'm hungry," she said, obviously striving for normalcy. Almost like being this close to him made her uncomfortable. He turned his head to hide his smile in her hair.

"I'll feed you later," he murmured close to her ear.

"What?" She sounded a little distracted, and he couldn't have been more pleased.

He let his face drop into her hair, burrowed through it until he could kiss her neck, smell her skin. She shivered.

"Deacon."

She might have meant his name to be a protest, but it came out as a sigh. He smiled against her and nibbled her earlobe.

"Hannah," he breathed into her ear, and she shuddered again.

"What are you doing?" she asked. And he felt her swallow hard when he nuzzled her temple.

He was quiet for a minute, debating his answer. Losing Hannah, losing what they'd come to mean to each other over the years, would kill him. But if he let her go—if they both walked away from the potential he could feel bubbling right under the surface—well, that would kill him, too.

So he guessed in the end there really wasn't much of a choice. Whether she knew it or not, everything had changed already.

He drew in a deep breath of his own.

"I'm seducing you," he said.

Her breath hitched, but thank God she didn't pull away.

"Seducing me?" Her voice was so quiet that he barely heard it.

Again, he hesitated, unsure of how to proceed. But the music was winding around them, separating them from the other people, isolating them. Suddenly Deacon knew that this moment, this woman, demanded honesty.

"I want to make love to you," he said, voicing the desire he'd harbored since he'd been an awkward teenager and opened his front door to see her for the first time.

She didn't say anything for so long he was afraid he'd ruined everything.

"We can't." Her voice was still quiet. And she still hadn't moved away.

"We can."

"It's wrong."

"It's not."

Now she did pull back far enough to look up at him. Her eyes—*those eyes*—were clouded, her brow creased with a frown.

"I'm your employer."

"You're not my keeper."

Her frown darkened into a scowl, even as the freckle-faced lead singer hit an unfortunate high note that signaled the end of the song. The next one was also slow. "When a Man Loves a Woman." Deacon decided he'd do whatever he could to ensure Hannah gave Roy and his friends the chance to play at her event.

"Are you doing this because of Sam?" she asked, and the question made absolutely no sense. He tensed.

"Sam?" What the fuck did his brother have to do with any of this?

Hannah's chin was set in a stubborn way he knew very well. "You sure didn't show any interest before he came back on the scene."

"Oh, I was interested."

She snorted in a way that told him she didn't believe him. "Right. Your brother shows up after two years and suddenly you're making moves on me? Please. I'll bet this is all about competition. I just got in the way."

She was getting herself all worked up and he felt her pulling away from him, physically and mentally. He had to shut her up before she could talk herself into pushing him back in the friend zone.

He did the only thing he could think of.

He kissed her.

~

Deacon kissed her. Right there in the middle of the dance floor with other people crowded around, all of them moving to the slow, wailing music.

And at the first touch of his mouth, Hannah's mind exploded off its axis and went twirling into space.

His kiss wasn't tentative, it was hot and hard, demanding in its intensity, his lips soft and full. Moaning a little, she opened to him, wanting more. He tasted like beer and fries and cheese, and she forgot where she was, what she was doing. She forgot everything but him and her sudden, overpowering need to get closer to him.

After a moment, he pulled her off the dance floor and pressed her into a shadowed corner, his broad, masculine body shielding hers from view. He kissed her again, his hands strong and sure as they moved over her, tugged her in tighter to the hardness of his arousal swelling under the soft cotton of his jeans. Well past the point of rational thought, Hannah wrapped her arms around his neck and returned the kiss, digging her fingers into his short hair to anchor him where she wanted him.

With a groan, he pulled her impossibly closer as their tongues tangled, battling for control. It was as if he was trying to climb into her through her mouth, and for a moment she let him sweep her away.

Deacon.

God, it was *Deacon*.

She was probably saved from completely embarrassing herself in a dusty corner of the Wounded Sparrow by a sudden burst of feedback blasting through the speakers overhead. She and Deacon both jumped, the sound cutting through the erotic haze of the kiss like a machete through butter. Hannah thought she might have bitten his tongue. Deacon raised his head and she realized the band had stopped playing when country music pounded through the room.

Deacon looked down at her, his eyes glittering in the semi-darkness, his chest rising and falling rapidly. Hannah stared back at him, her own breathing quick and uneven.

Oh God, oh God, oh God.

She was in soooo much trouble.

She drew in another shaky breath, drew in the scent of him—the slight tang of sweat, the soap he used, the barest hint of aftershave.

So much trouble.

"We can't," she squeaked.

Despite the gloom, she saw Deacon's nostrils flare as he breathed, saw his absolute focus on her. He leaned down, ran his lips over her cheek, let her feel the roughness of his jaw before he pulled back a little to look at her again.

"This isn't about Sam," he said, his voice harsh. It took her a moment to process what he was saying. "Sam has nothing to do with it. This is about you and me."

You and me.

"I'm not your responsibility," he continued, tightening his grip until she was sure she'd have bruises. "I'm not a child. I know what I'm doing, and I know what I want."

She licked her lips and his eyes followed the gesture. Her insides turned hot and molten, echoing the desire she saw plainly written on his face.

"What do you want?" she asked, just loud enough for him to hear.

"You." He didn't hesitate, didn't look away. She thought her legs might collapse under the power of that gaze. "The question is, what do you want, Hannah?"

What did she want? How was she supposed to know?

She couldn't think when he was holding her like this, pressed against the strength of his hard body. She couldn't think when he was looking at her with eyes full of heat, as if he wanted to strip her naked and have her right there on the dance floor.

How was she supposed to think?

What was she supposed to do?

Almost against her will, she flexed her hands on his shoulders, shaped the curves of muscle under her palms.

She could stop everything right now and walk away. She probably *should* walk away. Then they could try to go back to being friends.

Except she'd have to forget what he tasted like, what he felt like. And she wasn't entirely sure she could.

He was going to leave. Not now, but someday. Did she want to get involved with him, knowing it wouldn't last forever?

Hannah stared into Deacon's eyes, into his hard, determined face.

She could walk away. Or she could believe him when he said he knew his own mind, when he said his attraction to her had nothing to do with Sam.

The possibilities blew through her until she was dizzy with them. She slid her fingers up into his hair again. God, she wanted to bite his sexy mouth, sniff his skin like a puppy, run her hands all over his body.

"If we take this step," she heard herself saying, "and something happens—"

His eyes flashed. "We'll deal with it."

We.

In Deacon's mind, they were always "we."

Maybe in her mind, too.

She drew in one deep breath. Then another. And took a step over that line.

"Let's go," she said. "I have beer at my place."

He smiled, slow and full of masculine promise, before bending his head close to her ear.

"Good," he whispered.

12

Hannah didn't bother talking to the band. She'd get their number from Mary Alice and call them later. Right at the moment she didn't give a damn about the band. All she wanted was to leave the Wounded Sparrow. With Deacon.

I'm seducing you.

She half-expected him to jump her as soon as they got in the SUV, but instead they drove back to her apartment in relative silence. Just music playing low on the radio, the drone of the tires on the road, and a humming anticipation bubbling under the surface. She found herself breathing deeply, felt her breasts swell, fully aware of her skin and her body within it.

I want you.

As he drove, he touched her. Little touches, almost casual. Her hand. Her arm. Her leg through her jeans. She touched him as well. Traced the tendons in his forearm. Brushed his shoulder. Learning his shape, his feel. Learning him in this new context.

Finally he pulled into the parking lot of her apartment building and turned off the engine. He didn't say anything, just looked at her.

The tension between them grew so taut she could almost see it, tight as a harp string. She curled her fingers into her palms to keep from reaching for him. If she touched him now, she was going to rip his clothes off.

"Do you want me to come in?" he finally asked.

His low voice made her shiver when it touched places deep inside her, but Hannah wondered what the hell he was talking about. Either he came in or they were going to follow Sam's and Louise's example here in the car.

She started to reply, then stopped, studying Deacon's face in the harsh light of the floodlights, seeing the hunger in his expression. And the determination.

Then she got it. He didn't want there to be any room for misunderstanding or recriminations. He was telling her that whatever happened next would be her choice.

God, he knew her so well.

"Yes," she said. "I want you to come in."

And he kissed her.

No hesitation, no easing in. He just launched himself across the seat and took her mouth in a way that had her toes curling inside her boots and her whole body clenching with desire.

"Thank fucking Christ," he said when he let her come up for air. Before she could respond, he kissed her again. She grabbed his head and pulled him closer to feast on him, felt his fingers flex and dig into her hips, bringing her tighter up against his body.

The gear shift jabbed painfully into her thigh, but she didn't care. All of the buried attraction, all of the unwanted lust she'd felt for him for the past two years had reached flash point, and the fire turned everything else to ash.

Another thought struck and, breathless, she broke away.

"You'd better have a condom with you." She hadn't needed to stock those for a while.

"Or?"

"Or we're heading to a drug store. Right now."

He grinned. He looked happy and turned on and sexy with his lips swollen and a flush riding his sharp cheekbones.

"I might have a few with me," he admitted.

She raised her brows. "A few?"

He smiled.

"Come on." Impatient, she twisted away from him, opened the passenger door, and jumped out. Her knees buckled and she almost did a face-plant into the blacktop.

Deacon laughed and got out as well, then strode around to help her steady herself. She had to kiss him again. Had to taste that mouth. But when he pushed her up against the side of the SUV, she pulled away.

"Inside. God, inside."

"Okay."

Giggling like two children, they raced for the apartment building. As she put in her passcode to open the main entrance, he groped her and chewed on her collarbone.

It took forever to climb the stairs to her floor because they kept stopping and mauling each other. She had to force herself to concentrate so she could hold the key and get them inside the apartment.

As soon as the door closed behind them, Hannah found herself crushed back against it, Deacon's mouth on hers. Dimly, she heard the keys clatter to the floor as she reached for him, wound herself around him.

She wrestled with his shirt, desperate to get her hands on him. He struggled with hers. They both got trapped and broke apart, laughing.

"This isn't going to work," she panted.

Deacon didn't bother to answer. He just stepped back, stripped off his shirt with quick efficient movements, and threw it towards the kitchen.

Hannah paused, absorbed the view, appreciated. God, he

was all solid muscle. Forgetting her own clothes, she stroked his hot skin until he grabbed her hands and kissed her again.

It was slower this time. Deeper. Maybe a little dangerous, with more than a hint of teeth.

"Deacon!" she protested when he released her mouth to kiss her jaw, her neck. "Let me—"

Her words broke off with a sharp breath because he let go of her hands and lifted her off her feet, pulling her legs around his waist and shifting her until she rode the long, hard, ridge of his erection. Moaning, she wrapped her arms around his neck, sucked on the skin under his chin.

With a growl, Deacon turned and stumbled into her bedroom. He paused to flick on the lights at the doorway, then walked over to her bed and unceremoniously dumped her onto it. She giggled as she bounced, feeling rumpled and incredibly excited.

"Lose the clothes," he ordered as he unbuckled his belt and pulled it through the loops. His voice was deeper than normal and so rough she barely recognized the words.

"I will if you will." Hannah had to lick her lips to keep herself from drooling. Without the belt, his jeans hung low at his lean waist. She wanted to run her tongue all over that intriguing shelf of muscle where his groin met his hips, wanted to trace the veins disappearing beneath his waistband.

He toed off his shoes and then, keeping his eyes on hers, slowly drew down the zipper of his jeans. He stepped out of them, and got rid of his briefs and socks in a few quick movements. Bending, he grabbed the pants again and dug through the pockets until he pulled out a strip of condoms. He dropped it on the nightstand and threw the jeans across the room.

Hannah inhaled when he turned to her, gloriously naked, totally aroused. Deacon did not have the body of a boy, just as he didn't have the face of a boy. He was hard and muscled—and all man.

He shifted under her stare, then walked over to the bed.

"I guess I'm not like Sam," he said.

She blinked at him, so caught up in watching the play of lamplight over his skin that she didn't catch what he'd said at first.

"Huh?"

He rubbed a hand over his head, then let it drop.

"Nothing. Stupid." He started to reach for her, but she pulled back a little bit and he sat on the bed beside her instead. "Just forget it."

"No." She sat up and kissed him, caressing his tongue with hers, tasting him. When she ran her hands up his arms, over his chest, she felt the play of the muscles under his skin. He wasn't extremely hairy, and she liked that. But he wasn't smooth either. She liked that better. She scraped her palms over the hard points of his nipples, and he let out a broken curse.

Still dressed, she practically crawled into his lap and laved the tendon where his shoulder connected to his neck, her fingers kneading the hard planes of his back.

"Hannah." He gasped her name and moved his large hands up her body, under her hair, to hold her head as she drew his skin against her teeth and marked him. "Hannah."

She was too intent on what she was doing to answer. For a while, she tormented his earlobe, enjoying the sound of his heavy breathing, the feel of his pounding heart matching the throb of her own. He clutched at her shirt and she guessed he was thinking about just tearing the damned thing off her body. The idea sent a jolt of excitement shooting through her.

She moved back a little until she could touch his impressive erection, pull at his length with her hands. She loved the feel of him, all silky smooth skin with hardness beneath. When she tightened her grip, he groaned deep and long, and pushed into her hold as if he couldn't help himself. Laughing, she burrowed her face against him to breathe in his scent.

When she looked at him again, his face was flushed with desire, his eyes narrowed and somewhat glassy with passion, closing when she moved her hand.

"Get me naked," she murmured, "I don't want to have to kill you."

He opened his eyes and smiled. Humor, and a hint of devilry, sparked in his face.

"As you wish," he said.

It was as if a coiled spring had been released. Suddenly he had a hundred hands and they were all over her, fighting to get her clothes off. Since she refused to stop touching him, he had a bit of a problem, but she knew he could handle it.

When she was finally naked, he forced her to lie back on the bed and cuffed both of her wrists over her head with one large hand. She writhed against the spread they'd forgotten to turn down.

"Deacon!"

"My turn."

He used his mouth on her. All over her. Face. Neck. Breasts. Torso. He kept her in place with his hand on her wrists and the weight of his body even as she tried to buck and touch him.

While he lavished attention on her, he moved his free hand down, down, between her legs, into the wetness and heat pooling at her core, arousing her with his fingers, with his lips, with his strength.

"God!" Hannah cried out when he pulled her nipple between his teeth and rolled it with his tongue. "Please!"

Slowly, he pressed two fingers inside her body and rubbed the ultra-sensitive bud of her clitoris with the heel of his hand.

Hannah screamed, arched against him, and shot into a mind-blowing orgasm.

Before she fully came down from the high of her release, Deacon let go of her wrists and grabbed one of the condoms, sheathing himself quickly. Then he gripped her hips, raised her legs, and pushed into her.

It had been awhile and she was tight, but she was oh, so ready. His face was in shadows, the heat from his body flowing over her in waves as he thrust forward. It seemed to take forever until he was seated in her as deeply as he could go.

Slowly, he pulled back. Rocked forward again.

His big body trembled with the need to let go, to take, but she could feel the brutal control he held over himself. As he moved, grinding against her with each down stroke, the sensations built inside her again, growing in intensity until she felt like she had to come or she'd die. Squeezing her legs around his waist, she tried to urge him forward.

"Deacon!" It was a wail and a demand.

He managed one more slow thrust and retreat. She lifted herself to him, raked her nails down his back.

He broke.

All of Deacon's restraint vanished in an instant, as if it had never existed. He drove into her, pounding her into the mattress with sudden ferocity. The tension coiled tighter inside her, spiraled up and up until it finally crested with an almost audible snap. She came, teeth bared, hands clenched on his hard shoulders.

A moment later, Deacon shouted out his own release.

They held each other, both of them flying on the sharp edge of feeling for long, exquisite seconds. Then, with a grunt, Deacon collapsed on top of her.

"Jesus Christ," he muttered into her ear. It sounded like a prayer.

Eyes closed, Hannah just smiled, panting and satisfied beneath him.

With obvious reluctance, Deacon shifted his weight off her and pulled out of her body. They both groaned at the loss of him. Hannah heard him removing the condom, tying it off.

"I have to get cleaned up." The bed dipped as he moved and got up.

Turning onto her side, she pillowed her head on her arms, content to stay exactly where she was for, oh, about a year or so.

And Deacon had been worried about Sam? Please.

She heard water run in the bathroom, the flush of the toilet, and opened her eyes so she could watch him walk back across the room to her.

Yeah, baby.

"God, you're beautiful," he said, looking at her.

"You think so?" She stirred and stretched, every muscle feeling loose and relaxed. It made her tingle to know he was watching her.

"Why don't you give me a minute and I'll show you what I think," he suggested.

She looked at him and saw rekindled heat in his bright blue eyes.

"You're staying, right?" she asked.

"You want me to?"

She rolled her eyes.

He grinned at her.

She laughed, then shivered when a cold draft blew across her naked body.

Deacon tilted his head. "I see goose bumps all over that soft skin of yours, and I'm going to assume you're not shivering with delight at my manly physique."

He was wrong. She was shivering at the sight of him. But—

"I am a little cold."

He moved forward and gestured towards her.

"Under the covers, Frederickson. We'll spoon and snuggle for a little while. You girls like that shit."

"Wow. You sure know how to romance a woman."

On the other hand, she *was* cold, so she got up and turned

down the now-rumpled bed. As she was bending over to straighten the pillows, he came up behind her and wrapped his arms around her. He toyed with her breasts while he kissed her neck, and she felt that he was not quite soft when he pressed against her body.

"You seem to be willing to postpone the snuggling," she said, moving against him.

"I'm getting there." He used his teeth on her shoulder. "I'm not eighteen anymore, but I've been wanting you for a long time, Hannah."

"Really?" She reached up behind her and clutched the back of his head. The change in position gave his hands more room to play. He tweaked her nipples, pulled them until they were hard and throbbing.

"Really," he said.

One of those clever, clever hands moved down her body, between her legs, touching her, and just that quickly she was desperate for him again. She squirmed, gratified to feel his arousal growing against her butt.

"Christ." Ignoring her protests, he backed away and turned her into his arms. His mouth got very busy on hers before he pushed her onto the bed and landed on top of her.

After he'd brought her to yet another orgasm by licking her until she screamed, she pushed him onto his back, straddled him, and kissed every inch of his delicious body. Once his erection was rock-hard and straining, she sheathed it in a condom. Smiling into his glittering blue eyes, she took him into her mouth.

"Hannah!" His fingers dug into her hair, urging her on as her head bobbed up and down. Then, moaning a little, he pulled her off him, flipped her onto her back, and filled her.

There was no finesse. He battered her into the sheets. She grabbed at him, scratched him, and marked him. That seemed to drive him crazy, and his hips pistoned faster and faster. She felt herself rising towards her peak, and when she exploded around him, he finally ground out his own climax.

Their muscles gave way, and they were once again a jumble of arms and legs on the soft bed.

Hannah nuzzled into his neck, loving the weight of his body covering hers, smelling sweat and the heavy musk of good sex. Their hearts pounded together, like they'd break free and fly away.

"God," she gasped.

He didn't speak, but he did pull out of her. When he moved, she rolled to her side again, listening to him stagger to the bathroom. He must have walked into a table because she heard a crash and some violent cursing. Hannah smiled, but didn't raise her head. She wasn't sure she could.

She knew he was back when she felt him looking at her.

"Come to bed," she murmured.

"Won't be able to perform. Not for a while. Maybe years," he warned.

"God, I hope not. I'm not an 'inflate-a-mate.'" She opened her eyes and looked at him. He seemed a little unsure of himself, and that fact had the haze fogging her mind backing off a little bit.

"Come to bed, Deacon," she said. "Stay with me. Sleep with me. Just sleep."

He hesitated a moment longer, then walked around the bed and climbed in beside her. He shifted, spooning her, and pulled the covers up over both of them.

Wrapped up in his warmth, his scent, feeling his breath on her cheek, she slept.

13

Hannah woke slowly, comfortably wrapped in warmth, the sound of rhythmic thudding under her ear. Hair-roughened skin gently scraped her cheek when she moved.

Her eyes snapped open.

Deacon.

She was practically lying on top of him, legs tangled with his. His arm was around her waist, hers was draped over his side, her face against his chest.

"Morning."

Deacon's voice was rough with sleep. He moved his hand up and down her back in a slow, petting motion.

Everything inside Hannah stilled, then sped up again.

"You're awake," she said to his chest.

"So are you." She heard the amusement in his voice and raised her head to look at him.

Boy, he sure was scruffy and gorgeous in the morning. His eyes were narrowed against the sunlight streaming into the room because she'd forgotten to draw the black-out curtain the night before. His chin was dark with stubble and what little hair he let grow on his head was mussed, although you could hardly tell.

"Why hello, Hannah," he said and bent forward, obviously intending to kiss her.

"I have morning breath," she warned.

"Me, too. We cancel each other out." He tightened his arm around her waist and cupped her naked ass, pulling her closer to him. He was hard, and his morning erection felt hot and glorious against her stomach as he kissed her. She pulled back after a minute.

"Let me go," she said. "I have to pee."

Obediently, he loosened his hold and she sat up, shooting him a look over her shoulder when he traced a finger down her spine to the crack of her butt.

"Hands off, buddy. This is an emergency."

Still naked, she sprinted for the bathroom.

After she'd tended to necessary tasks, she brushed her teeth. She was just finishing when she looked up to find Deacon lounging in the doorway watching her, still naked, still hard. Turning, she spat toothpaste into the sink.

There really wasn't a sexy way to spit out toothpaste.

"I'm done," she said, then rinsed the toothbrush and her mouth.

There wasn't a sexy way to spit out water either.

Really, there just wasn't a sexy way to spit, period.

"I need to use the facilities," he said.

"Okay. Sure." She wished she'd thought to grab a robe. Except she didn't own a robe. She wished she wasn't naked. She wished he wasn't naked. She wished she'd told him to go after they'd finished balling each other's brains out last night.

She wished she was touching him again.

"Hannah," he said patiently. "Do you want to watch me piss?"

"What? Oh. No. Sorry."

She fled back to the bedroom and pulled on a sleep shirt. Why was she nervous now? It was a little late for that. Talk about locking the barn door after the cow had gone to the Wounded Sparrow and then had amazing sex with a bull.

The toilet flushed and water ran in the sink. She wondered what he was doing.

She was losing her mind.

Goddammit, this was ridiculous! This was *Deacon*. There wasn't any reason to be uncomfortable with him now. Or second-guess what they'd done. She'd give him breakfast and he'd leave and then she'd work on the—

"Hannah." Deacon was standing in the doorway to the bathroom. Still naked. Still aroused.

She gulped.

"I have to work on spreadsheets," she blurted out and immediately wanted to smack her head into the wall.

He cocked his eyebrows, a slight grin flirting with the edges of his mouth.

"Okay." He paused. "Want to take a shower first?"

She studied him. "Alone?"

"No."

"With you?"

"Yes."

Hannah watched him watching her and felt heat flare down deep inside. She couldn't breathe.

"All right," she heard herself saying. Then she stripped off the sleep shirt and walked to him.

It took them some time to get to the actual showering part of the program, so Hannah felt as shriveled as a prune when she was finally dressed and standing in the kitchen area of her tiny apartment. At least she was an incredibly satisfied prune with whisker burn in some interesting places.

Since Deacon was busy making use of a new disposable razor and the shaving cream she used when shaving her legs, she poked her head in the refrigerator and wondered what in the world she could give him for breakfast. Er, brunch, she amended, after a glance at the clock. She usually just had an apple or something in the morning, but she had a feeling that wouldn't be enough to satisfy the big guy.

"I'll make something," Deacon said from behind her. She straightened and looked at him. He was clean-shaven now and smelled a little floral. Hands on her hips, he nudged her away from the refrigerator.

"Really?" she asked, a little surprised. He'd dressed in the clothes he'd been wearing the night before, but he'd left his shirt hanging out of the jeans and he was still barefoot. He had very nice feet.

"Sure. You're not the only one who can cook."

She fluttered her eyelashes at him. "Tell me about it, babycakes."

He grinned at her and looked in the fridge. "Jesus, Hannah, there's nothing in here. What do you eat?"

She tried to see around him.

"What are you talking about?" she said. "There's stuff in there."

He looked at her over his shoulder. "Excuse me. I should have said there was nothing resembling real food in here. Fake butter. Fake eggs." He pulled out a loaf of bread. "This is probably fake, too."

Hannah crossed her arms and frowned at him.

"Hey, I have real food. I just don't run to bacon around here."

"You should run to bacon. Everybody should." He pulled out a carton of milk. "1% milk? Why bother? You should use water and pretend."

Hannah's frown morphed to a scowl. Just because the man had given her a good time last night—and this morning— didn't mean he got to mock her groceries.

"You know, if all you're going to do is complain, then maybe you should—"

He waved a hand, interrupting her. "I'm not complaining. I'll figure something out."

She looked down her nose at him, which wasn't easy to do since, even barefoot, he was about five inches taller than she was.

"Please do not do me any favors."

He grinned at her and winked. "I thought I just did."

"Pig."

"Absolutely." He laughed. "If you want, we could talk about the business plan while I work."

That put a little hitch in her stride.

"Now?" She'd kind of expected him to cut and run, although she wasn't sure why.

"Sure." He'd already turned to the counter, but glanced back at her. "We have to pull this thing together, right?"

We.

"Right," she said.

Deacon began muttering about essential fatty acids while Hannah went to sit at the kitchen table.

"It was a relief that the band was good," she said while she waited for the laptop to boot up. "They were good, weren't they?"

"They were," he agreed, his back to her. She indulged herself by watching the play of muscles under his shirt. He looked really good cooking.

"I was surprised," she admitted. "It's not that I don't trust Mary Alice, but...well, I was surprised."

Deacon laughed and bent to rifle through her kitchen cabinets. He looked really good bending.

"What do you need?" she asked, trying to keep from offering herself as a substitute for whatever it was.

"A frying...found it." He pulled out a pan and set it on the stove.

"So, tell me the truth. Do you really think we should have a carnival?" she asked.

"Well, I don't know about a carnival, but you might as well try something." He found a bowl and began putting stuff into it. "It might take a little time for the loan to go through."

"Yeah." Hannah stared at the laptop screen as it blinked to life. Well, they'd found the band. Now she just needed to figure out...everything else.

Deacon made a facsimile of French toast, and soon the kitchen filled with the warm smell of fake butter and fried bread. He seemed a little resigned when he bit into the first piece, but she thought it was great. Plus, she actually had some real maple syrup to go with it. Deacon looked like he might cry when she produced the dusty bottle.

"Why do you eat this shit, Hannah?" he asked as he speared a forkful of the fake French toast. "You could at least have real eggs."

"I'm not going to apologize to you." She pointed her fork at him before taking another bite. God, he was right about the maple syrup. After a moment of reverential chewing, she swallowed. "My hips are on a mission to spread across the country. Only constant vigilance keeps them within state boundaries. It not like I'm trying to be a twig, for God's sake."

"I like your hips." He leered at her. "And your butt's pretty good, too."

She shook her head, chewing. He did seem to enjoy squishing her squishable parts. But men were not exactly choosy in certain situations.

"Enough about my hips," she said.

Deacon looked disappointed and she pointed at him with her knife this time.

"We are going to talk business."

His look turned soulful.

"I mean it, Deacon." But she had a hard time choking back the laughter.

"So, you've got the financials pretty well under control?" he asked after he'd swallowed. He'd switched to work mode; she tried not to be disappointed.

"I think so," she said. "The balance sheet is finished, and that bitch of a statement of cash flows is roughed out. I have to get the income statement done, and then that part will be in pretty good shape."

"Did you have a chance to work on the marketing plan, goals statement, that kind of thing? We didn't do much with them yesterday."

"Do I look like Wonder Woman?"

He considered. "Not really. Although if you wore metal bracelets and had a rope—"

"Good, because for a minute there I thought you'd gotten the two of us confused. I'm a bar owner, not a miracle worker, damn it."

He ticked the air with a finger while he chewed and swallowed. "Props for the oblique 'Star Trek' reference. How about you finish up the financial statements and I'll work on the other stuff."

Hannah chewed her lip. "I know you already started on them yesterday, but it feels kind of like cheating. If I'm the owner, shouldn't I come up with all of that crap?"

Deacon cocked his head and studied her before wiping his mouth with a paper towel.

"Do you want to come up with it?"

"I'd rather scrub Old Albert's dentures."

"There you go then." He got to his feet and picked up his plate before rounding the table and getting hers, stooping to give her a quick kiss in the process. "Get working on your spreadsheets and let me help you."

Hannah gave in so quickly, she knew she'd been counting on him saying something like that.

When he came back to the table, they got to work and eventually settled into a companionable rhythm, bouncing ideas and questions off each other, occasionally getting up to see what the other was doing. Deacon always stole a kiss when they were on the same side of the table, and Hannah found she tangled her feet with his beneath it when he was across from her. It felt good, she thought. It felt...right.

"We got a lot done," she said a few hours later as she powered off the laptop. "I think it's ready for your friend to take a look at it." She was sure the guy would have questions, and the numbers weren't exactly encouraging, but at least the spreadsheets looked pretty.

"I'll give Quinn a call," Deacon said. He was neatly stacking papers and pencils next to the computer.

"Thanks." She stood and stretched, her body all loose and limber. Remembering why she was feeling so good got her motor revving again. She sashayed around the table to where Deacon sat, grabbed him by the front of his shirt, and leaned over, kissing him with a sudden, fierce hunger.

As soon as her lips touched his, he opened his mouth to deepen the kiss, his tongue stroking hers. He wrapped his hands on her waist and pulled her down until she was straddling him.

Moaning, Hannah rocked against him, but when he would have pulled her tighter into his body, she found the strength to plant her hands on his chest and ease him back a little bit. If they kept it up, she was going to forget all about work and just drag him off to the bedroom.

"That will have to hold us until the shift is over," she panted.

"Tease," he said, his face flushed.

"That too." Feeling a little giddy, she smacked another kiss on his lips, then twisted off his lap and headed towards her bedroom to get changed for work. Deacon stayed where he was at the kitchen table.

"So, does this mean you're inviting me to come back here tonight?" he asked quietly.

She stopped in the doorway to the bedroom and turned to face at him. He appeared calm, but she could see a fine tension in the straightness of his shoulders.

Another choice.

"Do you want to come back here tonight?" she asked, because where they went from here was his decision as well.

"Yes." No hesitation.

Hannah swallowed.

She could back away. She could call a halt.

But why? She didn't want to and neither did he. Why was she fighting?

"Okay," she whispered.

"Okay what?"

Pushy bastard.

"Okay, I want you to come back here tonight."

Deacon smiled and his face lit up. He nodded.

"All right," he said.

Hannah felt herself blush, and hurried into her bedroom.

"We'll drive in together, right?" Deacon called from the other room. "It seems silly to take two cars when I'm just going to come back here."

Hannah froze in the act of stripping off her T-shirt, her heart slamming erratically in her chest.

If people found out they'd driven to work together, they'd probably assume Deacon had spent the night. There'd be speculation. There'd be no way to hide.

If she wanted to hide.

But why should they hide? It would be a waste of time. The speculation had probably started the moment she'd asked

Deacon to go with her to the Wounded Sparrow. If they were going to do this, they might as well just get it out in the open.

"Or not. No big deal," he said when she took too long to answer. "I'll have to stop by my place to get a few things, anyway."

Despite the words, a note in his voice told her it was a big deal to Deacon.

"No," she said. "I mean, yes, I think we should go in together."

Now it was Deacon's turn to pause.

"Good," he said.

14

Hannah let Deacon drive them to the Country Time in his SUV because, as he pointed out, it would take a can opener to get him out of her compact. When they pulled into the parking lot, she was surprised to see June's and Kevin's cars already there, sitting behind the building.

Meaning, of course, that June and Kevin were inside. Which pretty much killed any hope she might have entertained of getting settled before she had to deal with knowing glances and teasing innuendos.

"Why are they here?" Hannah said, frowning. "Neither of them should be in yet."

Deacon parked and turned off the engine.

"Having second thoughts?" he asked, expression neutral.

She turned her frown on him. "No." She wasn't a coward.

He smiled at her and seemed to relax. "Good."

"Besides, for all they know, you just gave me a ride to work."

His smile broadened and he patted her hand where it rested on her knee. "There's my little dreamer."

Huffing, Hannah got out of the car.

They walked into the building together and Kevin, naturally, spotted them as soon as they entered the kitchen. He propped hands the size of small hams on his hips and gave Hannah a thorough once-over before turning his gaze on Deacon.

"Uh huh," he said.

"Hi, Kevin." For once Hannah didn't stop to chat with the big chef and moved quickly past him to the front room. Deacon followed at a more leisurely pace.

June was in the taproom, working on setups. She was wearing tight jeans, cowboy boots, and her Country Time polo shirt, her hair glistening black in the low light. When the door opened, she turned and grinned at them. It was a sharp smile, full of teeth.

"Well hell," she drawled. "Isn't it convenient that the two of you should show up for work at exactly the same time?"

"Shut up," Hannah muttered. Deacon, looking amused, slid behind the bar to begin his preparations for opening.

"Just an observation." Tossing aside the rag she'd been holding, June went to settle on a nearby barstool.

"How did things go here last night?" Hannah asked, determined to change the subject.

June cackled. "I'm more interested in finding out how things went with the two of you last night. Did you have fun?" She waggled her eyebrows suggestively.

"I had fun," Deacon volunteered. Hannah scowled at him.

"It was fine," she said, turning back to June. "The band was pretty good. I'm going to call them today and see if they'll do it."

"Right." June crossed her legs and leaned an elbow on the gleaming bar top, swinging one boot-shod foot. "Good band."

"Yeah." Hannah retreated behind the bar to get a bottle of water. She twisted off the cap and took a long swallow, intensely aware of June's stare.

"And afterward?" the other woman prompted.

"June," Deacon said, walking to stack some paper napkins

near the beer taps. "Are you asking Hannah if we spent the night together?"

"Deacon!" Hannah smacked his shoulder with the back of her hand.

"What if I am?" June asked, ignoring her.

Deacon smiled.

"I would tell you it was none of your business," he said pleasantly.

June studied him for a moment, then, to Hannah's shock, nodded.

"Fair enough."

Hannah only wished she could shut the woman down as efficiently.

A pot of coffee was already brewed and simmering on its burner. Deacon got a mug from the rack, filled it from the pot, and took it to June, patting her arm when he placed it in front of her. June snorted, picked up the mug, and drank.

And it's just that simple, Hannah thought. *Sheesh.*

"Come on. How did things go last night?" she demanded of June, coming around the bar to perch on another stool. "Was everything okay?"

"What am I, an amateur? It went fine."

Hannah scowled. She knew bullshit when she heard it.

"Then how come you and Kevin are here already? Neither of you are supposed to start for a couple of hours," she pointed out.

June took another sip of her coffee. "I called for a team meeting," she said, casually. "Jason couldn't make it, but Mary Alice and Grace are coming in, and Billy's probably going to show up, fat lot of good that will do."

"Team meeting?" Alarmed, Hannah set the bottle of water down on the bar. "Why?"

"I don't want to get into it until...here they are," June said as Mary Alice and Grace walked into the taproom from the kitchen. They were followed by Kevin, who had a firm grip on Billy's skinny shoulder, probably to keep the kid from running away.

"Coffee's made," Deacon told them.

"Coffee." Grace said the word like a prayer and leaped for the pot.

"Um, hi, Hannah." Mary Alice sidled up next to her. "So, um, did you have fun last night?"

"Oh, for God's sake! Do we really need to get into that now?" Hannah exploded. Had everyone in this place spent the evening gossiping about her and Deacon?

Mary Alice's protuberant eyes widened alarmingly.

"Was the band that awful? Johnny told me they were going to try really, really hard."

Hannah frowned at her. *The band?*

Deacon made a sound that might have been a muffled laugh.

"Easy there slugger," he said, reaching over to pat her arm. "Mary Alice was just asking if we liked the band."

"Oh." Hannah wanted to sink through the floor. "Uh, yeah," she muttered. "They were great. I need a phone number so I can call and ask them if they want the gig."

Mary Alice's wide, plain face brightened with relief as she smiled.

"Yay! I'm sure they'll do it."

"What you want us all here for, June?" Kevin asked, a twinkle in his dark eyes telling Hannah he knew damn right well he was changing the subject. He propelled Billy to a seat and shoved him down onto it. The kid wisely didn't protest, but he rolled his eyes and sighed dramatically. Kevin smacked him on the back of the head, then stepped away and crossed his arms over his massive chest, patient and implacable.

June shifted. "Okay, here's the deal—"

She broke off, frowning, when the door to the kitchen opened again and Sam strolled into the room.

"Hi, everyone," he said, smiling his attractive, lazy smile.

"What the hell are you doing here?" June demanded before Hannah could speak.

Sam shrugged and, just like he had the right, walked behind the bar to help himself to some coffee.

"I heard you telling everyone to come in early for a meeting," he said over his shoulder. "I was curious."

"You heard her? What are you talking about?" Hannah clenched her hands into fists and glared at her ex-lover's back. "What the hell is going on?"

"That's one thing I wanted to tell you," June said, her expression sour when she glanced at Hannah. "Sam showed up last night."

"I have a right to drink where I want to drink," Sam protested, pious in his righteousness.

"You were freaking serving customers!" June snapped. "I had to stop you from juggling bottles, for Christ's sake."

"I wanted to help," Sam turned and opened the small refrigerator under the bar.

"If somebody doesn't explain what's going on, I might just kill all of you," Hannah said with as much calmness as she could manage under the circumstances. Which, she admitted, wasn't much. "Sam, why the hell were you here last night?"

Sam pulled out a carton of half-and-half and doctored his coffee before meeting her gaze.

"I was here because I couldn't find the place where you'd gone to hear the band," he said, as if it made perfect sense.

Hannah blinked. "Huh?"

"Well, I had *planned* on helping you check out the band," Sam said reasonably. "Unfortunately Mary Alice gave me the wrong directions. Unless the band you want to hire plays polkas at a senior center." He glared at Mary Alice, who gave him a beatific smile.

"Oh, gosh, I told you I was sorry, Sam," she said and shrugged. "I get messed up sometimes."

"Uh huh." Sam drank some coffee before walking around the bar and dropping onto a stool. Grace, who'd been standing to one side sipping her own coffee moved as if to sit next to him, but June grabbed her arm and pulled her to another seat.

Hannah noted the byplay but remained focused on Sam. He watched her in turn, blue eyes brimming with innocence.

"Let me get this straight," she said at last. "You thought you'd help with the band, even though I didn't ask you to, and when you couldn't find us, you just came here and started...working?"

He thought about it, then smiled and nodded.

"Pretty much."

Hannah threw up her hands with so much force she almost toppled off the barstool. "What the hell, Sam? I mean, seriously. What the hell. What are you trying to prove?"

"I'm trying to help." Sam's face was the picture of wounded dignity.

June snorted with derision.

Sam turned to her, obviously ready to defend himself.

"Why don't you tell us what's going on, June," Deacon interrupted. "Why did you ask everyone to come in today?" He was leaning against the back counter in a casual pose, but he was watching everything, body tense.

Hannah took a moment to appreciate how his shirt stretched across his shoulders, remembered the feel of all of that muscle under her hands. Taking a deep breath, she forced herself to look away. It was goddamn lowering to realize that, despite all of the other crap going on around her, she was close to grabbing him and wrestling him onto the floor so she could touch him again. Pathetic.

Now June sighed.

"I guess it's good Sam's here," she admitted reluctantly. "Hell, maybe he might even have something useful to say."

"I did go to law school." Sam pointed out.

"You and a whole lot of other horse's asses."

"June," Deacon said, voice quiet. "What's up?"

June huffed out a breath and faced Hannah fully. "Okay. So, Pat Murphy came into the bar last night."

Hannah straightened, Sam's odd behavior forgotten.

"What? Are you okay? Did he try to hassle you?"

Although at one point he'd come in regularly, Pat Murphy hadn't set foot in the Country Time since June had broken up with him a couple of months ago. It was a bit of an understatement to say Pat hadn't taken the ending of their relationship very well.

"No, no." June flapped her hand to dismiss the thought. "He didn't bug me. I stayed out of his way, if you want to know the truth. And Calvin was here to keep an eye on things. But Pat was definitely looking around, and it sounded like he'd made sure to come at a time you wouldn't be here."

"How the heck did he know I wouldn't be here?" Hannah demanded.

"He said one of the league players mentioned overhearing you talking about going out Friday night. Probably Bernie," Sam volunteered. Everyone turned to look at him. He smiled at Grace, who fluttered her eyelashes and smiled back.

"Jesus," Hannah muttered.

"Did he tell you anything else?" Deacon asked his brother.

Sam shrugged. "He claimed it was just a friendly visit, but he was definitely trying to get more information about your plans."

"Mr. Murphy was acting like a spy or something," Mary Alice put in eagerly. "When we were busy and I was helping

Grace wait on tables, he frowned at me and asked about the specials."

"What specials?" Grace asked, craning her neck so she could see around June.

"I told him we could give him another pickle if he wanted," Mary Alice said. "He smiled, so I guess he must like pickles."

"Listen to me. There's more," June said, apparently thinking they were getting off track, which they were. "Calvin isn't in a bowling league anymore, but he's still friendly with some of the people who are. He said Pat's been telling everyone the Country Time is bound to fail, that you can't possibly recover from all of the problems you're having. Besides, Pat says he's fixing up the bar and grill at the bowling alley, so it's just a matter of time, anyway."

The past couple of months, Pat had been working hard to convince the league players to do their eating and drinking at the bowling alley bar, not the Country Time.

"He only serves one kind of beer, and he doesn't even have a grill," Hannah pointed out a little desperately.

"Yeah, *now*," June agreed. "But Calvin said his friend Milo told him that Pat ordered a bunch of new equipment for the restaurant to handle an expanded menu. And Pat's cousin will be there next week to paint and put down flooring and that kind of thing. Hell, he's talking about table service, and he knows someone he wants to hire as manager."

Hannah knew Pat wasn't above jerking Calvin around in the hopes rumors would get back to June. But if he was actually spending money...if he was talking about hiring a manager...

She tried not to panic.

She failed.

True, the Country Time was right next door to the bowling alley and, since the parking lots were joined by a thin strip of grass, literally steps away. But if Pat finally got his head out of his ass and upgraded the bowling alley bar and grill, human laziness was bound to win out. Especially if she had to back off on what she could offer at the Country Time. They'd probably lose some of the league business. Maybe most of it.

The Country Time depended on the leagues; they pulled in a decent crowd otherwise, but the league players regularly coming over before and after their games kept them going.

Unable to sit still any longer, she got up and started pacing.

"Well, it's going to take time, right?" she said. "Renovations don't happen overnight. How soon can he expect it to be finished?"

"Pretty soon," June said dryly. "Sounds like he wants to be up and running for a grand reopening at Halloween."

15

June's announcement sent a chill through Hannah.

Halloween was only about seven weeks away. With the money she had on hand, there was no way in hell she'd be able to compete with a newly renovated bar right next door.

She realized everyone was watching her, obviously expecting her to spout pearls of wisdom. Trying to give herself a moment to think, she walked over to the front doors and stared out through the old, leaded glass.

Pearls of wisdom continued to elude her.

Damn Pat Murphy. He wanted to steal her business, and now he'd been handed a freaking golden opportunity on a golden platter. For all she knew, he'd given George the idea to embezzle her freaking money in the freaking first place.

The more she thought about it, the more it made a twisted kind of sense. George might have been raiding the till for years, but he really didn't have the brains to come up with this scheme all on his own. Plus, he and Pat had been drinking buddies, despite the fact that Pat was about twenty years younger than her uncle. They'd probably talked, maybe shared a few laughs about Hannah's gullibility, and Pat had, oh so casually, pointed out that George was missing a much bigger score. No way would George have been able to resist the temptation.

She clenched her fists, felt anger bubbling, determination solidifying. Those bastards were *not* going to win. She would *not* go down without a fight.

Turning, she marched back to the people clustered around the bar.

"You." She jabbed a finger at Sam. "Have you heard from the investigator yet?" She glared at him suspiciously. "You did hire an investigator, right?"

Sam held up his hands, palms out, as if to ward off evil. "Of course I hired the investigator. He's already talked to Hildy and said he'd give you a call on Monday, but he'll report through me."

"Why?" Hannah snapped out the word.

"Because I hired him as though it's a case for my firm. Because," he continued when she would have interrupted, "my senior partner agreed that was the way to give you the lowest rate and biggest discount. As far as Adam's concerned, he's working for me and you're one of my clients."

"But I'm paying the freight," she pointed out.

"Honey, what do you think other clients do? You'll get an invoice from the firm, like everyone else."

"Oh." Well, she guessed that would be all right. "What has he found out?"

"He's tracked George and his former assistant, one Crystal Fields, to Las Vegas, but lost them once they got there. He's looking, but it might take some time."

Sam didn't bother to add the obvious fact that, since George certainly hadn't gone to Vegas for the weather, Hannah's chances of recovering any of the money he'd stolen were somewhere between slim and none.

She began to pace again, hands clasped behind her back, feeling vaguely like General MacArthur addressing the troops.

"Deacon and I have been working on the business plan," she told them.

"Among other things," June muttered. Hannah ignored her.

"We'll have the information out to his accountant friend tomorrow." She looked at Deacon. "Right?"

Deacon snapped to attention and saluted.

She scowled at him before turning her attention back to the others. "Once the business plan is submitted to the bank, there'll be a time lag before we know if the loan was approved."

"I'll say," Sam agreed and drank some coffee.

"Taxes will be paid. Payroll will be met." And her credit cards would scream the screams of the damned to accommodate the charges. "But if Pat Murphy is trying to steal our business, the event we've been planning has become even more important. We need working capital and we need it now."

"Right." June agreed amiably. She was leaning back against the bar, elbows propped on the wooden surface behind her. Mary Alice was watching Hannah with eyes so wide they looked like they might fall out of her head. Grace had shifted away on her barstool. Kevin stood quietly by the kitchen door, a mountain waiting for instructions. Billy just looked bored and drew a design on the knee of his jeans with a pen.

Hannah pointed at Grace. The young woman's golden brown eyes widened and she inched further back. "Did you ask your father about food?"

"Um, yeah." Grace darted looks to June and Mary Alice, as if seeking support. "He said he could give us a bunch of stuff. And he'll let us run a tab for the stuff he can't give. I think he'll give us a discount for the stuff he can't donate."

Hannah nodded. She'd follow up with Grace's father about what "a bunch of stuff" meant.

"What about the carnival?" she shot at June.

"What about it?" June asked, not bothering to straighten.

Hannah clenched her teeth.

"Have you found one yet?"

"Oh, sure." The other woman flicked that away. "Just pick a date and come up with enough cash to pay them."

Hannah's jaw tightened to the point of pain.

"I don't *have* cash," she snarled. "That's kind of the point of this whole thing."

June swung her legs and gave a small shrug. "Doesn't matter. They're going to want to be paid."

Hannah tried to resist the almost overpowering urge to wrap her hands around June's neck and squeeze.

"Find one," she said slowly and distinctly, "that takes credit."

June threw back her head and laughed.

Hannah realized she was growling. Deacon had sidled to the end of the bar and looked like he was ready to leap around it and pull her back if she jumped the older woman. Fortunately Sam spoke before she could do anything stupid.

"There's also the small matter of permits," he said.

"Permits?" Hannah whirled on him, glad to have a safer outlet for her anger. June would have kicked her ass. "What the hell are you talking about?"

He smiled at her. "Hannah darling, you're talking about putting on a public entertainment along a major roadway. Chances are good you're going to need some kind of permit, even if you are having it on your own land. That's the way our lovely 'burb works."

God! She'd never even thought of permits. Hannah clenched her hands in her hair and tugged. "How long will *that* take?"

Sam shrugged. "Don't know. I'll find out."

"Can you rush things through?" Deacon asked. He was once

more leaning against the back counter, arms crossed over his impressive chest. "You know people."

Sam kept his focus entirely on Hannah. "Don't worry. I'll work it out." His smile broadened. "You'll owe me."

Once upon a time, Samuel Black's smile coupled with his full attention would have curled her hair and her toes and everything in between. Those days were long gone. Hannah dropped her hands and stared back at him.

"It doesn't even begin to scratch the surface of what you already owe me," she told him quietly.

Sam's smile dropped away, as did his eyes. Hannah shook her head, rolled her shoulders and went back to planning the op.

"Once we find out if we need permits and how long it will take to get them, we can come up with a date for the thing." She glared at June. "We need that carnival, damn it."

"Uh, if you like, I can help with the carnival, too," Sam interrupted and spread his hands when they all looked at him again. "No offense to June's capabilities."

June snorted.

"What are you talking about?" Hannah demanded.

"I know a guy who runs one."

"What?" Hannah stopped pacing and stared at him, jaw slack. "You actually know someone who runs a carnival?"

"I do."

Hannah forced herself to draw in a deep breath and not give in to the urge to punch him right in his pretty face.

"Why didn't you mention this before?"

"Maybe he's lying." Deacon said quietly from his position behind the bar.

"I'm not lying." Sam gave his brother an irritated glance before turning back to Hannah. "I didn't tell you because I wasn't sure he still had the thing. I talked to him yesterday and he's still running it."

Hannah was surprised. "You already talked to him?"

" I wanted to get the facts before I told you. He runs it like a turnkey operation, so there wouldn't be any setup required on your part. His guys would put up and run the rides and the games. He can do food and drink, too, if you want, but that's up to you. Plus, he carries his own insurance for the rides. He's in the area this weekend if you want to check him out."

Hannah watched Sam's face, trying to see any signs of deception. "Sounds perfect. And just a little too good to be true."

Sam ran a hand through his dark tumbled curls. "I keep telling you I want to help. What do I have to do to prove it to you?"

"I'll let you know." Hannah shook her head. Could the man really want to make amends? Or was he just playing another game? Instinctively, she glanced at Deacon, but his expression was closed and unreadable, his eyes moving between her and Sam, his body stiff with tension.

June leaned forward, dark eyes intent.

"Who is this guy?" she asked. "Maybe I've already talked to him."

"You probably have." Sam pushed aside his now empty coffee mug. "His name's Chuckie Scanlon."

"Chuckie?" Deacon muttered.

Hannah frowned at him, then turned back to Sam. "His name's familiar," she said. "Didn't he have something to do with the volunteer fire company's carnival this summer?" She had a vague memory of a large man shouting at one of the carnies when the funnel cake booth collapsed.

Well, in all fairness the lack of funnel cake *had* been pretty tragic.

"Could be," Sam shrugged. He lounged against the bar, tie undone and the first two buttons of his shirt unfastened. His eyes were very blue as he watched her. "Fire company gigs are kind of his specialty."

"Yeah. I talked to him." June grinned, and it wasn't pretty. "He was a real douche bag."

Sam actually laughed. "Yup. That's Charming Chuckie."

June looked at Hannah. "Calvin gave me his name so I checked him out. When I *finally* managed to get him on the phone, he told me to take a hike, called me some creative names for bothering him, and hung up on me. Apparently he knows Pat and has heard all of the gossip about George."

Hannah crossed her arms and glared at her ex. "What the hell, Sam?"

"Look, I know he's a jerk." Sam held up his hands in a placating gesture. "But trust me, I can get him to do your carnival, and I can get him to do it on credit. Hell, he might even give you a discount."

"Why?" Hannah demanded.

Sam shrugged. "He owes me. Big time."

Deacon let out a harsh breath that might have been a laugh. "In other words, you'll blackmail him."

"I'll be calling in a favor."

"And you'd be willing to do that? For us?" Deacon asked, straightening to stand with feet braced.

Sam flicked him a look.

"For Hannah," he said.

Turning away from both men, Hannah looked at June. The older woman's mouth twisted sardonically and she shrugged her thin shoulders.

"If you're dead set on doing this without paying anything up front, I'm going to have a hard time finding someone. I'm not a miracle worker."

Hannah nodded and started to pace again.

Of course, she didn't *need* to have a carnival, but she did have to find a way to raise money. And if Sam could be believed

—*big* if—this might give her a chance to make a carnival happen without shelling out a lot of cash up front.

If she could trust Sam.

Did she have a choice?

Coming to a decision, Hannah turned to Sam. He quirked his eyebrows inquiringly, but she knew he knew he had her.

"I want to see his setup," she said. Out of the corner of her eye, she saw Deacon shift position and drop his hands to his sides.

"Hannah—" he said.

"I want to talk to this guy before I commit," she said to Sam. "But it is a good idea," she said to Deacon.

He scowled, but didn't argue.

"Chuckie has a gig at a fireman's carnival tonight," Sam said. He looked satisfied. "It's somewhere close. I'll get the directions and we can go check it out."

"Today's Saturday," Hannah pointed out. "We'll be busy, hope to God."

"It won't take long."

"I'm going with you." Deacon stared at Sam like a wolf stares at prey, his teeth bared in a pseudo-smile. "Another set of eyes."

Sam shrugged. "You have to tend the bar," he pointed out. "It's Saturday night. It will be busy here."

"I can handle the damned bar for a couple of hours," June said. She swung her foot back and forth and took a sip of coffee. Hannah could tell she was amused.

Sam's expression turned petulant and Deacon relaxed a little bit.

Hannah sighed.

"Okay, find out where this guy is," she told Sam. "You, Deacon, and I will go check him out and get back here as soon as we can."

Sam made a disgruntled noise deep in his throat. He got to

his feet and drew a sleek cell phone out of his pocket, then stalked off, muttering under his breath.

Hannah studied Deacon's hard expression as he watched his brother walk away and sighed again before turning her attention back to the rest of her staff. They were all staring at her with varying degrees of fascination.

"I think we've nailed things down as much as we can for now," she told them. "We can't pick a date for the event until Sam finds out about permits anyway. Grace, I'll talk to your father and see what he's willing to donate."

"Okay." Grace sounded relieved.

Hannah looked at Kevin where he stood at the kitchen door, massive arms folded across his chest.

"Can you handle the kitchen alone tonight while I check out this carnival?" she asked.

His wide face split into a grin. "I see you do not ask me before you make plans. *Non, non,*" he held up his hands when she would have protested. "I will be fine. You go and have fun, no?"

"It shouldn't take long." She returned his smile, then glanced at Billy. The dishwasher was still busily drawing on his jeans. "Billy."

He jumped when she said his name and drew a blue slash across his knee through a lopsided skull and crossbones.

"Um, yeah?"

"Do you have any bright ideas to contribute?"

"Um, no."

"Shocker. Okay, let's break this up. We need to get ready to open."

"Hey, Hannah?" Mary Alice flapped a hand to get her attention. "Since June's going to be tending the bar, do you want me to stay and help out again tonight? I can if you want me to."

"That would be great, Mary Alice. You're the best." Hannah smiled at the woman with real gratitude. Yes, it was true she couldn't afford to pay more overtime, but it was equally true that she couldn't risk annoying the customers by not having enough staff working on a Saturday night.

Mary Alice blushed at the praise, then she, Grace, and June began chattering. Kevin lumbered back into the kitchen. As soon as the big chef was gone, Billy made a break for the front door. He wasn't really supposed to be on shift for another couple of hours, so Hannah didn't try to stop him. She was amazed he'd shown up in the first place.

Shaking her head, she pushed away from the bar and headed to her office, figuring she might as well try to review the business plan again while she had a moment. She hadn't gotten far when she heard footsteps behind her, then Deacon grasped her upper arm in one big, calloused hand and ushered her down the short hallway. He tugged her into the office and shut the door behind them.

"Are you out of your damned mind?" he demanded as soon as they had some privacy. "Sam's friend's carnival? Really? *Really*?"

"It's a good idea," she insisted, pulling away from his hold to turn and face him. "It will be a godsend if Sam can work a deal so I don't have to shell out the money up front."

"Do you think Sam actually wants to help you? You're just putting yourself in his debt. You can't be stupid enough to trust him again." Deacon crowded further into her personal space. Unlike the night before, the flush riding his high cheekbones had nothing to do with passion and everything to do with anger. His eyes, normally such a calm blue, were flashing. Hannah struggled to hold on to her own temper with difficulty.

"I'm not stupid," she said through clenched teeth. "I am trying to save this damned bar."

He looked down at her with an extremely unattractive smile marring his features. "Yeah? Sure you're not just looking for an excuse to hook up with Sam again? Third time's the charm."

Hannah gaped at him. "What?"

He shrugged, a quick jerk of his shoulders. "All I'm saying is you were awfully quick to jump at his offer."

"Oh, for God's..." Hannah tugged at her own hair and paced away from him, then strode back and jabbed a finger into his chest. "Listen, you ass. I don't want to have anything to do with your brother. I wouldn't even see him again if I had an option, but I don't. And if he can give me some help to pull this thing off, I'll take it. So if you want to be a jealous prick about it—"

"I'm pissed off," Deacon shot back, stating the obvious. "Just pissed *off*, that you're listening to Sam. That you're even talking to him."

"What the hell am I supposed to do, huh?" Hannah jabbed at his chest again. "Ignore him if he offers up something we really need?"

"Yes," Deacon snapped. "Ignore him. Exactly."

Hannah stepped back and stared at the ceiling, breathing deeply, trying not to say something she'd regret. When she had herself under more control, she met his angry gaze again.

"I need you to be able to deal," she told him. "And if you can't because now we've slept together, well—"

"Yeah, we slept together." Deacon's tone was sharp, his eyes electric. "Then the next thing I know you're running off with Sam to some fucking carnival. You're *excited* about it."

"Jesus!" She threw up her hands and waved them in the air. "It's business, Deacon. Business! I'm not going to let him buy me some damned cotton candy or grope me on the rides. What the hell do you take me for?" If he thought she would jump out of bed with him and run off with Sam, if he thought she *could* do that...

Deacon let out a deep sound of intense frustration.

"God!" He spun away from her and rubbed his hands roughly over his scalp, then turned back. "I know, okay? I fucking know you wouldn't do that. I know you're not like that. I know it's business." He looked at her again and she saw the anger finally beginning to fade, replaced by sheepishness. "But I guess…yeah, I'm…jealous."

She wanted to stay pissed off at him, she really did. But seeing the worry, understanding how difficult it must be for him to admit it, had her rolling her eyes instead. Honestly. *Men.* She went to him and, standing on tip-toe, wrapped her arms around his neck to bring her body flush against his.

"Deacon, you have to believe me when I tell you that you are the only one I want groping me."

He pulled her into a tight embrace, practically crushing her. Then he bent his head and kissed her, long and slow until her brain dissolved.

"Good," he murmured when he pulled away.

It took her a moment to remember what they'd been talking about. She blinked, bringing him back into focus.

"Do you trust me?" she asked.

He searched her face for a long moment.

"I do," he said. It sounded almost like a vow.

"I'm glad. You should."

He kissed her again.

After a few minutes she stepped back towards her desk, grabbing the edge to steady herself when her legs would have given way.

"You need to…and I'm…" She paused to clear her throat. "I'm going to work on bookkeeping things until it's time to go." She looked at him. "Are we good, now?"

He was watching her, his lips reddened and slightly swollen from their kiss. She imagined hers looked the same. "We're good." He smiled and it was a miracle she didn't just swoon. "I'm going to get things set up for June. Then I guess we can take off."

"Come get me when it's time?" she asked. It was strange, but she didn't want to let him go. She wanted him to stay with her, to keep touching her.

She thought he might have read that thought on her face, because his eyes darkened.

"Count on it." He opened the door and was gone.

Hannah stayed where she was for a moment, running a finger over her lips, remembering his kiss. Remembering how his strength felt crushed against her. Remembering the previous night.

Then she realized she was wasting all of her time daydreaming and walked around the desk to power up her computer.

16

Deacon had to fold himself up like a freaking pretzel to get into Sam's little convertible. He'd assumed he would drive them all to the carnival in his SUV, but when he'd mentioned it, his brother had smiled and said Deacon could meet them there if he'd be that uncomfortable in the smaller car. Deacon didn't argue because there was no way in hell he'd take the chance Hannah would ride alone with her former lover in a car the size of a peanut.

In the end, Sam hadn't gotten what he'd wanted, either. He'd been clearly annoyed when Hannah insisted Deacon take the front seat while she scrambled nimbly into the back. So, that was something, anyway.

After Deacon had crammed himself into the car, he stared resolutely out the side window while Sam assumed the driver's seat. It wasn't easy to ignore his brother, especially since he was practically sitting on his lap, but he tried. Sam strapped in, then gave Deacon a rough shove to push him further out of the way.

"Saaaam," Hannah warned from the back. She sounded alarmingly like their mother.

Sam muttered a curse under his breath and put the car in

gear, pulling away from the Country Time with a screech of gears and the spit of gravel. Deacon held his breath until they'd merged safely onto the highway.

Jesus.

For a day that had started so spectacularly, it sure was ending up in the crapper. And, yes, part of that was on him. He'd completely lost it listening to Hannah make plans to spend the evening with Sam, even though he knew full well she wouldn't hop out of his bed to jump into that of another man.

Although, technically it had been her bed they'd hopped out of, not his.

And that was the real problem, wasn't it? He couldn't even invite Hannah back to his place, assuming she'd agree to come. He sure didn't want her to see the dark room over the bookstore he rented for a song. The best he'd be able to do would be to get a motel room for the night. Maybe he was concerned—not afraid, *concerned*—that the more time she spent with Sam, the more she'd remember what his brother brought to the table.

Deacon shifted in the tiny seat. When had he gotten so insecure? He was annoying himself.

After what seemed like an eternity, they finally arrived at a fireman's carnival somewhere out in the butt-crack of nowhere. Hannah, of course, took one look at the bright, colorful setup and decided it was perfect and exactly what she wanted for her event at the Country Time. When Deacon pointed out, sensibly he thought, that there was no way this much stuff would fit in her parking lot, he got the cold stare of death.

Sam jumped in, claiming to know Mr. Clark, the man who owned the field adjoining Hannah's property. That field had to be at least seven or eight acres, and Mr. Clark hadn't planted a fall crop this year. Sam was sure he could get the man to let her use his land for the day, especially if she mowed it for him.

Hannah glowed.

Deacon contemplated fratricide.

They paid the entrance fee and walked into the carnival, the look in Hannah's eyes as she took in their surroundings making Deacon distinctly nervous.

"There's the office." Sam gestured toward an old, battered trailer sitting off to the side behind some booths. "Chuckie said he'd meet us there."

"Let's go." Hannah rubbed her hands together and took off, weaving her way through the crowd. Sam smirked and followed, jogging to catch up with her.

Deacon started after them, but found himself blocked by a harried looking woman surrounded by a flock of kids screaming for fried corndogs. Once he'd finally maneuvered around the group and caught up with Hannah and Sam, he saw his brother had a proprietary hand on the small of Hannah's back. She didn't seem to mind.

Deacon wanted to rip that hand off at the wrist and toss it to the kids for a snack.

He settled for pulling Sam's hand away and replacing it with his own. And, yes, okay, maybe the tactic was a bit of a caveman move, but he didn't think he deserved another cold stare of death from Hannah. Shouldn't he be the one who was upset? Wasn't she letting her ex-lover touch her? Wasn't Deacon her current lover?

But, no. Instead of cuddling into him or something, Hannah twisted out of his hold and marched off, hips swishing.

Man, those were some pretty great hips.

Deacon realized he wasn't the only one appreciating the view; Sam was obviously riveted by the sight, as well. Deacon growled out a warning, but his brother just laughed and went after Hannah.

Shit.

Deacon shoved his hands in the pockets of his jeans and followed.

This really wasn't how he'd thought things would go after he'd finally managed to get Hannah Frederickson into bed.

When they'd reached the old trailer, Deacon saw a torn paper sign taped in one of the windows claiming it was indeed the office. Still ignoring him, Hannah trotted up rusted stairs to the door, knocked, and went inside, Sam at her heels. Deacon stepped into the place behind them and found himself in a sizable room sporting dark wood paneling on the walls and thin, brown carpeting on the floor. There was a small kitchenette at one end, a bank of dented file cabinets at the other, and a variety of chairs scattered around an ancient metal desk in the middle.

A big man with a buzz-cut sat behind the desk, smoking a cigarette and staring at a laptop. The overflowing ashtray at his elbow, and the thick blanket of smoke smothering the room, were clear indications he'd been at this activity for quite some time. Deacon didn't know what the hell brand the guy was smoking, but it smelled a lot like manure. Or toxic waste.

He took a shallow breath and pushed the door open a little wider behind him. A breeze blew in, stirring the smoke into eddies, but it didn't improve things too much otherwise.

The man stubbed out his cigarette and pushed heavily to his feet, hiking his jeans up around a hard, round beer gut. He was wearing an Ozzy Osbourne tour T-shirt that looked like it might be the same age as the trailer.

"Hey, you must be Hannah Frederickson," he said to Hannah and leaned over the desk to offer his hand. "I'm Chuckie Scanlon."

Hannah mumbled something and they shook hands. Chuckie greeted Sam deferentially, barely acknowledged Deacon, and offered them all seats. Deacon held his breath and lowered himself into a fragile looking side chair. It creaked in protest, but at least it didn't dump him on his ass. Maybe things were looking up.

Once they'd all settled with Chuckie behind the desk again, the man lit up another cigarette, then planted his elbow on some papers and considered Hannah, blowing a stream of smoke out of the side of his mouth.

"So, Sam said you needed something," he said, shooting Deacon's brother a look. "What's up?"

Hannah told him. Chuckie was not impressed, especially when she told him she wanted to handle the event on credit. She hadn't even finished her spiel before he sat back in his chair and shook his head.

"I remember this deal. Some broad called me a couple of days ago," he said, disgust evident. He looked at Sam. "What the fuck, Black? I'm not a fucking charity here."

"That's right," Sam said, his voice as cool as his expression, "but you owe me, Chuckie."

"Yeah, I do." The other man considered him in silence for several long moments. "So, if I do this gig, we'd be even? All debts discharged?"

"Sure." Sam smiled pleasantly.

Chuckie looked from him to Hannah and back again. Finally he shrugged. "Okay, then. Credit."

"And a discount," Sam said, holding up a finger.

"Jesus. Okay, fine. It'll be worth it to finally get you off my back."

"When would you be able to do it?" Hannah asked with undisguised eagerness. Deacon saw she was sitting on the very edge of her own rickety chair.

The carnival owner pulled his laptop closer and clicked around on the keyboard for a minute.

"I've got the last weekend in September open," he said looking at Sam, not Hannah. "I can't do more than two days, but I can fit it in then."

"That's only about two weeks away." Deacon shook his head. "It's too soon."

"I'm fully booked otherwise," Chuckie said, still looking at Sam. "Besides, we go too late and it might snow. Best I can do."

"I'll take it," Hannah said quickly.

"Hannah—" Deacon started and Hannah turned to him.

"We need to pull this thing off before Pat Murphy finishes his renovations," she said. "This is perfect." The stubborn set of her jaw told Deacon any argument would be a waste of breath.

"Right," he said. "Perfect."

Chuckie grinned, showing off large yellow teeth. "Great."

Deacon watched without further comment as Hannah and Sam made arrangements with the carnival owner, who promised to get a contract for the job to Hannah the next day. She was beaming freaking rainbows and kittens when they finally got out of there, jumping down the rusty stairs to give two enthusiastic fist pumps while wiggling her butt.

"I can't believe it!" she crowed. "This is awesome!"

Sam chuckled, indulgent. "Glad I could be of help."

Hannah punched him companionably in the shoulder, then rubbed her hands together. "Hot damn. Now we can finally get moving."

Deacon wanted to point out that even with a discount, Hannah was taking a huge risk.

"That's great." Sam looked down at Hannah, smiling as if they were alone. He tilted his head towards a nearby booth. "They have cotton candy. You used to love that stuff, right? Why don't we celebrate? I'll buy you the biggest cone they've got."

Deacon froze, waiting to see what she would do.

Hannah's smile faded and she studied Sam in silence for a moment. Then she shrugged.

"Sorry. Saturday night, remember? We need to get back to the Country Time."

Deacon wondered if she really regretted the fact.

Sam just grinned. "Maybe next time."

They all trooped to the convertible and, after Hannah

vaulted into the back, Deacon twisted himself into the front seat again. His balls were going to fall off from lack of circulation, but at least they were heading home.

Sam started up his little deathtrap and set it bumping back down the country road towards the highway. He and Hannah kept up a running conversation about her plans for the event. Deacon stared out the front windshield, listening to the notes of their voices rather than the words themselves. Hers were light and excited. Sam's, deep and intimate.

It sounded like before.

"So, you think Hannah Frederickson is cute, don't you?" Sam said, lounging against the door to Deacon's bedroom.

"She's okay." No, Deacon didn't think she was "cute." He thought she was stunning. But he knew better than to admit it to his older brother.

"Yeah, you're just lucky you're such a dumbass. If she didn't have to tutor you, she'd never have given you the time of day."

"Shut up," Deacon snapped, although he knew it was true.

"She let me kiss her at the movies. With tongue." A smirk. "I'll get to second base next time. Maybe further."

"Get lost, asshole."

Still smirking, his brother wandered off. Deacon lay back on his bed, hands clasped behind his head, and frowned at the Metallica concert posters he had taped to the ceiling.

Someday, he vowed, Hannah Frederickson would look at him, not Sam.

And she had looked at him, he reminded himself. It might have taken twelve years, but not only had she looked, she'd liked the view. So why should he care if Sam was hanging around again? Why did it matter to him if Sam had come up with some ideas she seemed to like? Deacon was the one who would be going home with Hannah Frederickson tonight.

Unless she dumped him for acting like a jealous dipshit.

He was being stupid. He might not like the idea of a carnival, and he might hate the fact that Sam was involved, but Hannah was firmly on that train now and they were heading into the station. It would be better to just man up and participate in the festivities before she decided to shove him onto the tracks and wave goodbye.

He'd told her he trusted her, and he did. So if Hannah said she didn't want Sam groping her, if she said she was only using his brother because he had resources she needed, then he should believe her.

With that realization, he actually started listening to the conversation the other two were having, and even offered a few suggestions of his own. When he did, Hannah, who was leaning through the space between the seats now, turned to smile at him, bright as the sun. He smiled back. Deep inside him something tightened, almost painfully, then relaxed.

Sam might have been Hannah Frederickson's past, but Deacon was going to be her future.

End of discussion.

17

A half hour later, thanks to a well-placed elbow jab in Sam's ribs when they'd gotten out of the car, Deacon was right behind Hannah admiring her ass as they walked back into the Country Time. In fact, he was so focused on the view that he almost mowed her down when she stopped abruptly right inside the taproom door.

Tripping a little, he caught himself before he walked on her heels, looked up, and blinked.

What the hell?

The place was packed, which was great, but it wasn't exactly the normal Saturday night crowd. True, he could see some college students and bowlers, but most of the people jammed into the big room seemed to be senior citizens. It was like gazing out over a sea of gray and silver, with the occasional improbable black or red head mixed in like a buoy.

Voices thundered, drowning out all but the bass of thumping country music. June was behind the bar slinging drinks, not so much smiling at the customers as hissing at them. He saw Mary Alice and Grace squeezing through the crowded tables, platters balanced high over their heads, faces red with exertion.

"What in the world is going on?" Hannah asked, almost reverently.

"It's really busy," Deacon said stupidly.

She looked back at him.

"Well, I can *see* it's busy, Deacon," she retorted acerbically. "The question is, why?"

"Maybe it's just a good turnout," Sam said, having come up behind them. He managed to push Deacon aside and slid in next to Hannah. "I'm sure people are still gossiping about you."

Hannah shook her head. "These aren't people from town, and I can't believe I'm a top news story outside of Hardy Falls."

"Tourists?" Deacon suggested.

She snorted. "Right."

"Well, it looks like we won't be able to talk any more about the carnival tonight," Sam said.

Hannah cocked an eyebrow at him. "Really? You think?"

"Yeah." Sam ignored the sarcasm. "So, uh, I guess I'll see you tomorrow. If you survive." He turned, and before Deacon could stop him, vanished through the front door.

Ass.

"It didn't take long for him to bail. What a wimp. Good thing we're stronger and more courageous," Hannah said. She smiled up at him and his breath caught in his throat. He stared down into her face. *That face.*

"Maybe he thought we'd put him to work," he said absently.

"Maybe he was right." She looked around with some wonder. "Come on. We'd better find out what's up."

They had managed to make their way to the bar before Mary Alice spotted them. Her plain face burst into a sunbeam smile of relief.

"Oh, golly. I'm so glad you guys are back."

"Where did all of these people come from?" Hannah asked, gesturing around the room.

"There are two busloads of senior citizens here because one of their buses broke down on the way home from the casinos at Mt. Pocono, and the driver of the second bus was kind of new so he didn't know the route well enough, and so he wanted to wait until the first bus driver had a different bus, and they could drive back together, and they were right near here when the bus broke down, so they figured they could wait here, and then on top of that there was a football game at the university, and I don't know what else." She drew in a deep breath. "I'd better get these orders in." Smiling again, she skittered past them and pushed through the kitchen door.

Hannah looked at Deacon. "Wow."

June came to stand behind the bar opposite them.

"Deacon, if you don't get back here and help me, I'm going to pluck out your liver and fry it up for these old goats. They'll eat it, too." Her dark eyes glinted when she smiled.

"Coming." Deacon swallowed hard and slid behind the bar. June could be scary.

"I'll go help Kevin," Hannah said, shook her head again, and disappeared into the kitchen.

For a little while, Deacon didn't think. He couldn't think. All he could do was react to shouted demands.

"The college kids aren't bad, but the bus people are insane," he said to June when he reached behind her to grab another bottle of tequila.

"Bus company's comping them," she told him. "They're eating and drinking like it's the apocalypse. Keep your diaper on, I'm coming," she snapped at a customer and moved back down the bar.

Even June's considerable aplomb had a breaking point. When she looked like she was going to get into a smack-down with an elderly woman over beer nuts, Deacon sent her outside for a few minutes.

She came back calmer and was soon cracking jokes with a couple of old guys who were busy admiring her various assets. Deacon took the coffee pot over to the two bus drivers who sat huddled together as far away from their passengers as they could get.

"When's the mechanic supposed to get here?" he asked, topping off their mugs.

"Soon." One of the drivers looked at his watch with more hope than expectation. "He's bringing another bus so we can transfer the passengers who were on the breakdown."

"Assuming he can find the place," the other driver put in. "Isn't much of a town."

"At least everyone seems happy," Deacon said, waggling his thumb towards the raucous crowd in the taproom.

"I thought they'd all be asleep by now," the first driver said, shaking his head. "Free food just does it for them."

Deacon laughed and went to fill some more drink orders. When he was finished, he turned to see Old Albert Cromwell at the bar with two women who looked ancient enough to be dead. They were staring at Albert with identical gleams in their rheumy eyes. It was kind of creepy.

"More beer, Albert?" Deacon shouted into the man's good ear.

"Set me up, Deacon," Old Albert shouted back. "These here are twins. I might be getting me some twin action tonight!"

The two women tittered.

Deacon forced a smile. "Great." *Jesus*. And he'd thought Albert's fling with Ms. Gregory was disturbing. He focused on the twins and found them considering him thoughtfully. He was kind of glad he had the bar to protect him. "Can I get you ladies anything?"

After setting Albert up with a beer and his dates with boilermakers, he gladly left them to their wooing and went to lean against the back wall, trying to take some of the weight off his aching feet.

Things seemed to finally be calming down, thank God. He thought the bus people might have actually reached saturation point and were descending into a holding pattern. The tab for the bus company was going to be astronomical. At least that would make Hannah happy.

June walked over to him and dropped onto a stool they had set up behind the bar for nights such as these.

"How did the carnival thing go?" she asked. It was the first time they'd had a chance to talk.

"Fine. Hannah's going to book him. He has a date open in two weeks."

"Holy Mother of God."

Deacon went to fill some drinks.

"Two weeks? Is she crazy?" June asked when he was standing next to her again. She'd crossed her legs and Deacon saw some of the men admiring them. One or two of the women were, too.

"Pretty much. But she's determined."

"Damn." June sighed. "I'll talk to her." She hesitated. "How was Sam?"

"He was a dick," he said.

June didn't reply. Deacon went to fill some more orders.

"Hannah is determined to save this bar," she said when he came back.

"Yeah, I kind of got that."

"I think her father loved her, but he piled a whole shit-load of responsibility on her." June shook her head. "Now she's afraid this place will just fall apart around her."

"I know," Deacon said. "We won't let it."

June nodded and shot him a look. "Sam's making himself pretty useful to her."

Deacon felt his shoulders tense. "He's playing her."

"'Course he is. He doesn't give a shit what happens to the bar."

"He's trying to piss me off."

"'Course he is."

Deacon drew in a breath and looked at June, ignoring a white-haired woman who was waving at him. "And he wants Hannah."

"'Course he does," June snorted. "Sam wants nothing more than whatever he can't have."

"I'm not sure he can't have her," Deacon admitted.

"Bullshit."

June left to wait on the woman, who'd been growing increasingly agitated. When she came back, she stood, scowling at Deacon.

"Get this straight, Deacon Black," June said. "Hannah wants *you*. No way would she have gone to bed with you if she didn't feel something for you. Don't fuck this up."

"I'm trying not to."

"Well, try harder. She doesn't want Sam, but he's slippery and he's got charm to spare. Don't push her towards him because you decide to put on your ass hat."

"I don't have an ass hat," Deacon muttered.

"Hell you don't. Every man on this planet has at least one. Some have a boxed set. Your brother's being useful, so you've gotta be useful, too. She likes useful. Plus, you're the one who really cares about the bar. For Christ's sake, don't let Sam get the upper hand now."

Deacon considered her. "Are you saying you're on my side?"

"I'm saying if you two can work things out, you might be good for her. But if you hurt her, I'll chop off your dick with a rusty hatchet and scoop out your balls with a melon baller."

Deacon winced.

"Ouch."

"Go. Take a break." June nudged him towards the door. "I'll look after these people. Hey!" Her potent smile flared. "There's Calvin."

"Humph." Deacon frowned at her. "Do I need to worry about you two?"

"Nah. I can take care of myself."

"Okay," he said and touched her cheek. "But you're not the only one who can handle a hatchet. Just saying."

June laughed and shoved his chest. "Get outta here before I change my mind." She walked up to the bar and got a beer for Calvin.

Happy to obey her dictates, Deacon stretched his back then walked around the bar and into the kitchen, waving at Kevin when the chef looked up from the grill. Hannah stood at the sink rinsing dishes, her back to him. He went to her and bent down to run his mouth over the sensitive place where her shoulder met her neck.

She jumped about five feet and slammed her shoulder into his jaw.

"Ow." Holding his chin, he backed away.

"Sorry, sorry." Laughing, she turned and stood up on tiptoe to give him a solid kiss on the mouth. "You snuck up on me."

He was happy that none of his teeth seemed to be loose. Happier still that she'd kissed him without any hesitation. "Aren't you supposed to sense me coming up behind you because you're so finely attuned to my presence that all of the hairs on the back of your neck stand up when I walk into the room?"

She stared at him. "Have you been reading romance novels?"

"Mary Alice is reading the *50 Shades of Grey* series."

"Great. That's all we need." She smiled up at him, so obviously pleased to see him that any remaining jealousy he might have felt towards Sam simply evaporated.

"What are you doing here?" she asked.

"June sprang me for a few minutes. Want help with the dishes?"

She laughed. "No, go take your break. Kevin and I have this on lockdown, don't we Kevin?" she called to the chef.

"Sure thing, boss lady," he called back. His hips were shifting as he worked, moving in time to an internal beat that didn't have much to do with the country music playing in the front room.

"See?" Hannah pushed back her hair with a gloved hand. "Take your break before June changes her mind."

Deacon didn't want to go, but there was a limit to how much he could do when they were so busy and Kevin was watching. So he just bent and gave her another lingering kiss before leaving her to her dishes.

Outside, he made his way to the little makeshift rest area behind the building and settled on one of the plastic lawn chairs, sighing at the pure pleasure of getting off his feet for a minute. It was relatively cool and quiet there, away from the turmoil of the kitchen and the taproom, the two tour buses hulking shadows at the tree line.

Deacon stretched out his legs and gazed into the darkness beyond the lights, towards the field Mr. Clark owned. The thing was, he could actually see how the whole carnival idea might work. Rides and food. Adults and kids.

It was just like Hannah to jump into the deep end. He wouldn't be surprised if she set up circus tents and brought in elephants. Anything to keep the Country Time afloat.

Be useful.

June was right. Sam was making himself useful, but Sam was a fancy lawyer with money and connections. Deacon was a bartender. What could he do? Mix Hannah a strong drink? He'd already offered her a damned loan. Not too many employees would do that for their employers.

But he'd never felt like an employee, not with Hannah, not even before their relationship had changed.

The late summer breeze brushed past his skin, pleasant after the heat of the overcrowded bar. He heard the thumping music from inside and crickets singing in the underbrush, slow and lazy at this time of year.

This place might have been Hannah's home for most of her life, but over the past two years it had become his as well.

Except, he thought now, maybe it wasn't the place at all. Maybe it was the woman.

And wasn't that enough to scare a man shitless?

"Hey."

Still lounging, Deacon turned his head and watched Hannah walk over to stand beside him. She looked good in her jeans and button-down shirt. She'd looked better naked in her bed with her hair tousled and her arms reaching for him.

"Hey," he replied.

She smiled at him and he actually felt a "click" somewhere deep inside himself.

Yup. Scared shitless.

"The new bus will be here in a few minutes," she said.

"Good. We need to spring the wait staff and get cleaned up."

"Yeah." She studied him. "I just wanted...we're not mad at each other anymore, right?"

"I'm too tired to be mad." It had been one hell of a long day.

"Tell me about it." She hesitated. "Um, so the carnival was good, right?"

Danger, Danger! Landmines ahead! Evasive maneuvers!

"I guess," he said carefully, "but two weeks isn't a lot of time, Hannah. Have you ever run a really big event before?"

"I was chairman for the band bake sale in middle school." She put her hands on her hips. "I'll figure it out."

He grinned at her, distracted. "You were in band? I didn't

know that." And he'd thought he'd known everything about her.

She made a face. "Clarinet until I was in tenth grade. I did not shine."

"I'll bet you looked awfully cute in your uniform, though."

"Our uniforms were black and pea green. Nobody looked cute in them. And you're changing the subject."

"I got sidetracked by the thought of you in your band uniform."

She shook her head.

"*Anyway*, I will run this event and I will pull it off in two weeks because I have to. You'll still help me, right? Even though you maybe don't agree with everything I'm doing?" He heard a thread of vulnerability in her voice, as if she was expecting him to say he wouldn't. Please. When she looked at him like that he'd give her anything she wanted.

He shrugged, deliberately casual. "Sure. I'm still going to help you. I figured I could handle the regular business while you pull the thing together, but let me know what else you need me to do"

Hannah grinned. "You're pretty great, know that?"

"True. Very true."

Laughing, she straddled his lap, draped her arms around his neck, and kissed him. Taken by surprise, he gripped her hips and pulled her even closer, tasting her mouth warm and wet on his. She took her time, deepening the kiss with languid pleasure and leaning against him to tease him with her breasts before chewing on his bottom lip and releasing him.

"I need to get back," she said, sounding breathless.

"Uh." His fingers flexed. "Um..."

Smiling down at him, she rocked a little on his growing erection. Deacon's eyes crossed. He dug his fingers into her, urging her on as he thrust up to her.

"You're still coming home with me tonight, right?" she asked.

"Uh...well," he gasped. "I kind of...um...have to. We drove in together so...you don't have a car."

"True." She watched him, biting her lip as she rocked, her eyes dark pools in the poor lighting. She was so fucking sexy. "And when we get back to my apartment? Will you come inside?"

"Oh, hell yeah." His hands tightened, kneading her ass.

Hannah leaned down and gave him another, longer, deeper kiss. Then, to Deacon's disappointment, she swung off his lap like she was dismounting from a horse and stood, twisting free from his grip when he tried to pull her down again. He sank back in the chair, breathing hard. She grinned at him.

"I have to go in." Her smile turned wicked. "You might want to take a minute."

"Right," Deacon panted. He was hard enough to pound nails and the little witch knew it.

Hannah's laugh was breathy and seductive. Then she turned and sauntered back into the bar.

Deacon blew out a breath.

"Well, hell."

He sat, staring at the buses, trying to think calm thoughts. It didn't work. All he could see was Hannah, naked, riding him.

"Christ."

She wanted him.

There was an awful lot to be said for the fact that she wanted him.

An awful lot.

Boy, was there a lot.

He wasn't calming down much.

"Okay," Deacon muttered to himself, "if you don't think of something else you'll never be able to get back to work."

Sam wanted Hannah. He just wished he knew how Hannah actually felt about Sam.

Didn't matter. Just fucking didn't matter.

Because Deacon was the one going home with Hannah Frederickson tonight.

A loud rumble shook the earth and a third bus pulled up behind the other two, interior lights shining in the darkness, a cloud of diesel fuel belching into the cool night air. Deacon pushed to his feet, adjusted his pants and polo shirt to hide the lingering effects of Hannah's little lap dance, and went to tell the two bus drivers their relief had arrived.

18

T he Tuesday after The Night of The Bus People, Hannah strode into the Country Time, took a brisk lap around the perimeter of the taproom, decided she was still freaking angry, and walked around it again.

"Problem?"

She looked to the bar where Deacon stood finishing his preparations for opening. Tuesday was his night off, but Jason had a test, so he'd come in to cover. She could always count on Deacon Black.

Hannah was a little surprised at how happy she was to see him. It wasn't like he hadn't spent every night with her since the Wounded Sparrow. And today she'd been with him until she'd had to leave to keep an appointment with Allison Arthur at First National Bank...no, PFNB, now.

"What makes you think there's anything wrong?" She walked over to the bar and kicked the base of one of the barstools several times.

"Wild guess." He smiled one of his slow smiles and her simmering fury transformed into a completely different emotion.

God, he had a great smile. She loved the way it started in his eyes and then moved to his full, sensual mouth. Over the past couple of days she'd found she lived for ways to make that smile break across his normally quiet features.

Deciding to put her energy to good use, she went behind the bar, pressed herself up against him, and yanked his head down for a long, hot kiss. He responded with gratifying enthusiasm, his lips devouring hers as he clasped her hips and pulled her more tightly into the frame of his big, muscled body.

"Well," he said when they finally broke apart, "hello to you, too."

Hannah laughed and relaxed for the first time since she'd left him that morning. She laid her head on his chest, breathing in the clean, crisp scent of him, listening to the steady "thump" of his heart.

"Would I be correct in assuming something happened at the bank?" Deacon asked after a moment. "Did our girl Allison have a problem with the business plan or loan application?"

Hannah jerked a shoulder. "I don't think so. She really didn't say too much. I think I was only in her office for about five minutes."

"Uh oh. How long did you have to wait to see her?"

"Like, forty-five minutes."

"Yikes. And you had an appointment and everything."

"Yeah." Hannah looked up and made a face at him. "I'll bet I wouldn't have been left cooling my heels for that long if you'd been with me."

Deacon appeared skeptical but she'd only been telling the truth.

"Did she give you any idea about when they'd make a decision?" he asked.

"She'll get back to me." Hannah's stomach churned. She certainly hadn't expected the loan officer to give her an immediate answer, but she'd been hoping for at least a clue as to how long it would take to hear back from the bank. Instead, Allison had glanced quickly through the documents, smiled without warmth, and said she'd be in touch.

Be in touch. What the hell did that mean?

The only good news was that now the business plan was finished, tweaked, and vetted by Quinn Barad, Deacon's accountant friend, which should make things a little easier when she applied for a loan at other banks. And since, after today's non-meeting with Allison, she had a sneaking suspicion her past history with First National was going to mean dick, applying at other banks had just moved way up on her to-do list.

Well, after she'd finalized arrangements for carnival supplies with Grace's father, since she'd decided it would be more profitable to sell the food themselves instead of going through Chuckie Scanlon's operation. And ordered in more beer, alcohol, and other drinks because they were going to sell those, as well. And figured out where everyone was going to park and how things would be laid out. And after she'd made sure Roy and his band were ready and planning to show up; bugged Sam about contracts, insurance, and other legal crap so she wouldn't lose everything she still had in a lawsuit if somebody sued; checked in with Adam Kouris, the private detective looking for George, to see if he had any news; and ran the kitchen by herself that evening since Kevin wasn't working. And—

Hannah burrowed deeper into Deacon's chest. He stroked his hand down her back, soothing her.

"I'm here for you, Hannah," he said. "Anything you need."

"I know," she said. But this was her responsibility. Deacon was being wonderful, but she was the one who had to make things right.

"I want to help," he persisted.

"You are helping." And he was. She didn't know how she'd

tackle everything that needed doing if he wasn't taking care of the bar. June was great, but it seemed like Deacon was the one she counted on to hold things together. She leaned back a little and met his eyes, such a beautiful blue.

"You are helping," she repeated and kissed him, slow and soft.

"Are you two at it again?"

The masculine voice had them starting apart. Hannah turned to find Sam standing in the kitchen doorway with a tall, dark-haired man she didn't recognize. The stranger was watching them, an amused expression on his pretty, narrow face.

"What are you doing here?" Hannah asked Sam. "And who are you?" she asked the other man.

"I brought you some papers to sign." Sam sauntered further into the room and dropped onto one of the barstools, letting his briefcase thud to the floor. "Adam hitched a ride."

"Adam? Adam Kouris?" Hannah's heart pounded. She focused on the other man as he followed Sam into the room, letting the kitchen door swing shut behind them. She'd spoken to the detective, and they'd exchanged some emails since he'd taken her case, but they'd never actually met. That he had come here now...her breath hitched with excitement, and she took a step forward. "George?"

"No." Adam smiled, apology evident in his brilliant dark eyes. "Nothing yet."

"Oh." Hannah tried to hide her disappointment and took the hand he extended to her across the bar.

"I'm sorry," Adam said when he released her hand. "George must be using cash and staying out of trouble. It makes things a little difficult. But I'm still looking."

For what that was worth.

"Okay. So, um, what can I do for you?" she asked

Adam settled on a stool and folded his long, khaki-clad legs under the lip of the bar.

"I wanted to have a chance to meet you in person, see the place for myself. When Sam said he was coming out this way, I figured I'd tag along and get the lay of the land, so to speak." He shrugged, wide shoulders rolling under his button-down shirt.

Hannah was honestly a little surprised he'd gone to the trouble. She certainly couldn't be one of his bigger clients.

"Do you have any leads?" Deacon asked.

Adam tapped his forefinger on the old wood of the bar. "I've been in contact with the police in Vegas, and I'm working with a couple of people I know out that way to see if they can find anything." He looked at Hannah. "I'm trying to keep your costs down, so there's a limit to the manpower I can put on the case."

"I know," Hannah sighed.

The expression on Adam's lean face was kind. "You don't want me on this much longer, Hannah. The more days George is missing, the less reason there will be to pay for a private detective."

Because the longer her uncle eluded them, the greater the likelihood he'd have gone through all of her money by the time they found him.

She swallowed hard.

"Am I being stupid?" she asked him. "I mean, yeah, I want to nail George's balls to the wall, but maybe it's a lost cause at this point. If we'd found him right after he left, I might have recouped some of the cash eventually. But now..." She shook her head. "Maybe I should just let the police do their work and hope for the best."

Adam pursed his lips thoughtfully. "If you can give me a couple more days to pull the leads I have in Vegas, I'll have a better idea where we stand. And I can do some of the work *pro bono*."

"Oh—" Hannah started to protest, but Sam reached across the bar and touched her arm.

"Let him," he said, more gently than she would have expected. "Adam wouldn't offer if he wasn't sure."

"Okay." She blinked back unexpected tears and smiled at the detective. "Thank you."

He smiled back. "You can repay me in beer."

"Done." Deacon drew him a draft from the tap and set it in front of him.

Adam lifted the glass, sipped, and sighed his pleasure. "Thanks."

With some difficulty, Hannah shoved her worries about George away so she could focus on other issues. Looking at Sam, she raised her brows inquiringly. "You brought me papers to sign?"

He lounged against the bar and grinned at her. "Special delivery. I wanted to get them to you as soon as they were ready."

"How helpful," Deacon murmured.

Hannah took a moment to glare at him before turning back to Sam. "Thank you," she said, meaning it. "Why don't we go back to my office?" Then, thinking Deacon might be upset if she just went running off with his brother, she went to him and kissed him softly on the mouth. It was funny how easy it was to kiss him in front of other people now. "Call me when you need me."

He patted her on the butt. "Sure."

Hannah studied his face for another moment, but couldn't judge his mood. She looked at Sam.

"Come on, counselor."

Smiling, Sam pushed off the barstool, grabbed his briefcase, and followed her down the short hallway to her office.

Once there, Hannah sat behind her desk in the position of power, such as it was, and gestured for Sam to take the visitor's chair. He dropped into it, crossed one ankle over the opposite knee and adjusted his dark trousers so the crease fell into sharp lines. Then he balanced his briefcase on his lap, opened it, and handed her a sheaf of legal-looking documents.

"What are these?" she asked, taking the papers from him and flipping through them.

"First, the contract for the carnival, including payment arrangements," Sam said, closing his briefcase and putting it on the floor. "Chuckie's giving you a thirty percent discount and accepting credit terms. Everything's all spelled out."

The discount was a lot more than she'd expected. Hannah felt almost...hopeful.

"He has us booked for the last weekend in September, right?"

"Yup. In a week and a half." Sam nodded at the documents. "There's also the contract for your use of Mr. Clark's field, as well as a rider for your insurance policy covering the whole mess, like we discussed. And Chuckie carries insurance for the rides themselves."

"This is great. Thank you," she said.

Sam frowned. "Because of the short timeframe, I had to draw all this up before we got the actual permits required to hold the event. There are escape clauses in the contracts if we need them." He cleared his throat. "But you should know Pat Murphy is fighting the carnival. He doesn't want the town council to let you have it."

Hannah stared at him. "What? Why?"

"He says it will interfere with his business," Sam said.

"But...but..." she sputtered. She understood Pat wanting to take advantage of her misfortune to steal her customers, but this seemed a little extreme. "It will probably bring him business, too," she protested. "You can't tell me people won't check out the bowling alley while they're here."

"Maybe, maybe not." Sam shrugged. "Regardless, Pat says

it's going to jam the road with traffic. He's also concerned people will park in his lot."

"Oh, for..." Hannah sat back. "What an ass. We're not even going to set up on his side of my property. With Mr. Clark's land, we'll have plenty of room for the carnival and parking." The Country Time's lot was pretty big as it was, and Mr. Clark's land spread out on the side opposite Pat, then wrapped around back behind both businesses. "We'll make sure we don't go anywhere near the bowling alley, and he can put up a damned sign if he's that worried about the parking."

Sam's smile wasn't pretty. "Don't worry. I'll get the permits. Pat wants to hold his own event soon, so he won't push too hard in case it backfires. I just wanted to let you know."

She relaxed a little bit. "Okay, good. Thank you," she added, sincerely.

His smile changed to something warmer. "No problem."

Hannah studied Sam sitting opposite her, absently flicking the edges of the papers he'd given her with her fingers. Deacon was right. He really was being awfully helpful. Generous with both his time and expertise. Just how many people owed him favors, anyway? And did he consider her to be one of them now?

Somewhat belatedly it occurred to her that she might have agreed to more than she'd bargained for. Yes, she'd asked him for help, and she knew she couldn't have pulled this off without him, but what was in it for him? For her it was payback. Did he consider his help a debt he'd collect on later, as he had with Chuckie Scanlon? Or did he expect her to give him something else?

In the turmoil of the last few days, she'd kind of forgotten she didn't trust him.

"What are you getting out of this?" she asked abruptly. She needed his help, but she sure didn't want to put herself in a worse situation by accepting it.

He arched his brows, his handsome face guileless. "This?"

"Helping me like this. What do you think is in it for you?"

"Nothing." He spread his hands.

"You don't do anything unless there's something in it for you." Deacon had tried to remind her of that fact, but she hadn't listened.

Sam dropped both feet to the floor and leaned forward, gaze intent.

"I've already told you why I'm helping. When you called, you said I owed you for what happened between us. I thought about it and realized you were right. I screwed up. I want to make things up to you."

Hannah snorted.

"You screwed up *two years ago*," she pointed out, "and I haven't noticed you breaking down my door to apologize before now."

His eyes slid away from hers and he squirmed a little in his chair. "Maybe I never would have admitted I'd been wrong if you hadn't pushed the issue. But seeing you again..." He looked at her directly. "It hit me harder than I thought it would. You and I...we were good together, Hannah."

Uh oh. She drew in a deep breath and tried to gather her thoughts.

"Let's just get a few things straight," she said. "Your help in this? It's to settle a debt, not to create a new one. And don't make the mistake of thinking you can use this situation as an excuse to get close to me again. It's not going to happen."

"Because of Deacon." His blue eyes sparked and his mouth firmed. "You know he's not going to stick around. I don't know why he's stayed this long."

"It doesn't matter," Hannah insisted. "This is about me, not him." Still, her heart clutched at the thought of Deacon leaving.

Sam was silent for a moment.

"I never meant to hurt you, Hannah," he said at last. "Either time. Back in high school, well, I was a kid and thinking with my dick."

"You were thinking with your dick two years ago, too," she said.

"I guess." He looked down at the floor. "The thing with Louise, it just…happened. I never expected it to."

"But you didn't turn away from the opportunity either."

"No," he admitted. "I mean, I knew you'd be upset if you found out, but I guess I didn't think we were all that exclusive." He shrugged helplessly and rubbed the back of his neck. "Or, yeah, maybe I just wasn't thinking with my brain. I got…caught up. Then Louise was gone, too."

The tone in his voice when he said that last bit was interesting. Maybe Sam hadn't emerged from the train wreck of their relationship unscathed after all. And, Hannah thought, maybe they'd been on different pages the whole time anyway, maybe from that first moment in the Black's kitchen when she'd looked up from *A Tale of Two Cities* and fallen under the spell of curly black hair and big, blue eyes. If she'd believed they were in a serious relationship, and he hadn't considered them "that exclusive," well…

Pushing out of her chair, she paced over to the little office window and stared out at the parking lot. Clouds had rolled in since she'd gotten back from the bank, and the weather forecasts were calling for rain later. That was fine, as long as it didn't rain in a week and a half.

"We weren't good together, Sam," she said without looking at him. "Neither of us had any idea what the other one wanted. We never knew what the other one was thinking."

"Hannah—"

She turned to face him. "It's not just you. I mean, yeah, you were an asshole—both times we were together—but if I'd paid more attention, I would have seen what was happening. I would have noticed that big-boobed cheerleader hanging around in high school. I would have seen something growing between you and Lou. I guess if we'd really had what I thought we had, you wouldn't have done what you did, and I wouldn't have been shocked that you did it. I never let myself admit something was missing. I didn't even notice it wasn't there."

Sam shrugged with an unusual awkwardness.

"I really am sorry," he said.

Hannah considered him. He seemed sincere. Maybe he even meant his apology. But she wanted to be absolutely clear on one important point.

"I appreciate that and everything you're doing to help me. But please don't think you've got a chance with me, Sam," she said quietly. "That ship has sailed. You and me, we're not going there for a third time."

He held her gaze for a long moment and she thought he was going to argue. Then he nodded slowly.

"Fair enough," he said. "Let's look at the contracts."

She wasn't sure she'd gotten through to him, but Hannah walked back to the desk and settled in her chair, picking up the stack of papers he'd brought with him.

By the time she'd read everything she was supposed to read, questioned everything she was supposed to question, and signed everywhere she was supposed to sign, she felt drained of all life, spirit, and humanity.

"I don't know how you do this every day," she told Sam, dropping back in her chair.

"You get used to it." He gathered the signed papers and stuck them back in his briefcase, snapping it closed. He looked at her, his eyes very blue. "I guess I just miss you, Hannah."

She didn't know how to answer that, so she didn't say anything.

He waited, then drew in a deep breath and let it out as he pushed himself out of the chair. "I'd better get going." He looked down, fiddled with the briefcase lock before throwing the strap over his shoulder. "I'll make sure Chuckie and Mr. Clark get signed copies of the contracts."

"Thank you."

Sam smiled faintly. "It's the least I can do." He turned and left the office.

She watched him leave, because he really did have an excellent ass, then sighed and straightened in the chair.

The zombie apocalypse must be coming soon, she thought, as she pushed the mouse to wake up her computer. Samuel Black actually seemed to be turning into a decent guy.

19

Deacon brooded. He brooded as the afternoon wore on and people started coming in for after-work or pre-bowling brews. He brooded when Sam finally came out of Hannah's office and left with the private detective guy. He brooded as he pulled beer taps and mixed drinks. He brooded as Hannah went back to the kitchen to handle the food orders. He brooded as thirsty bowlers came in after leagues, as he listened to the country music playing through the sound system, as voices rose and fell, as the Phillies lost the last game of the post-season series.

People tried to talk to him. Normally, he would have leaned on the bar and engaged in some idle gossip to pass the time. Tonight he just smiled, filled drink orders...and brooded.

He was man enough to admit—to himself—that he was jealous. Sam was slick and slippery and attracted women like flies. He didn't like his brother in Hannah's orbit, not one bit.

On the other hand, he understood Sam had chopped up Hannah's trust like kindling and fed it to the fire. Deacon might not know exactly how Hannah felt about Sam, but he was pretty sure she wouldn't jump into bed with the asshole, especially since she was currently jumping into bed with Deacon.

On the *other* hand, he wasn't entirely sure she didn't want to, eventually, at some point, jump into bed with Sam.

Hence, the jealousy.

But he didn't think jealousy was the only uncomfortable feeling he had churning around in his gut.

Hence, the brooding.

Calvin Hardy returned from the men's room and slid onto a bar stool across from him. Deacon handed him a beer without being asked, and the other man smiled.

"Thanks." Calvin turned his head, sipping the beer, the back of his neck a leathery tan under thick dark hair threaded with silver. Deacon saw he was watching June move through the tables, joking and laughing with the customers.

Thank God, he thought. Here was something he understood.

"You realize I'll kick your ass if you hurt June, right?" Deacon said conversationally. It wasn't a threat. He just wanted to make his position clear.

Calvin turned to look at him with some surprise, then put his glass carefully down on the bar.

"I'm not sure June would thank you for getting involved," he said.

Deacon shrugged. "Doesn't matter."

Calvin frowned, but before he could respond Deacon had to leave to wait on a few customers, take some money.

"I don't want to piss you off," he said to the other man when he got back. And he really didn't. Calvin might be older than him, but the guy looked tough. Still, Deacon had been in his share of fights. He knew how to handle himself.

Calvin eyed him, expression harsh and unreadable. "Mind telling me why you feel the need to get in the middle of something that's none of your business?"

Deacon shrugged. "You and June have a history. I know you hurt her when you guys were involved the first time around."

The other man's dark eyes were calm, but they seemed to hold a hint of grief. "Maybe I did."

"I won't let you do it again," Deacon said simply. "June is my friend." And he had her back. No matter what.

Calvin was silent for a moment, then nodded. "I can respect that."

"Good." Deacon went off to help more customers.

When he came back, Calvin was staring into his beer, face somber. He looked up when he sensed Deacon opposite him.

"I respect what you're saying," he repeated. "But you don't have to worry. I'll do everything in my power to make sure I never hurt June again."

It was a vow.

Deacon inclined his head. "Fair enough."

He felt kind of bad for reminding the man of something that was obviously as painful for him as it was for June, but he'd wanted to get it out there. It occurred to him that he'd never really talked to Calvin before. Well, they'd *talked*, but they'd never had a true conversation.

Deacon just knew what he'd heard; that Calvin had moved back to town to help his father with the hardware store when his mother's Alzheimer's had gotten so bad she couldn't be left alone. They had home health care workers coming in now, but most of the burden was still on them.

The older man toyed with his beer glass, turning it this way and that on the top of the bar. His knuckles were chapped, as if he washed his hands a lot.

"I never expected her to talk to me again," he said, almost to himself. "Not after I left and got married, and she stayed here working for Fred. She was so beautiful and the whole town thought they were having a thing." His lips quirked. "They weren't."

"What was he like? Fred Frederickson?" Deacon wiped up some liquid so it wouldn't stain the wood. He thought he might have met Hannah's father once or twice when he was a kid, but Fred had been dead of lung cancer before Deacon had come back to town.

"He was a bastard," Calvin said, then flushed a little and met his eyes. "Sorry."

"No, that's fine." His interest piqued, Deacon put his rag aside and leaned on the bar. "Why do you say that?"

Calvin studied him. "Got a thing for Fred's girl, don't you?" he said.

Deacon nodded slowly. "I guess I do."

The other man lifted his beer, took a drink, and put it back down. June's laugh cackled out over the music. Deacon had to go fill a few orders. When he returned, Calvin looked at him, his face set in hard lines.

"Fred was about twenty, twenty-five years older than me, so I didn't know him all that well. I knew Hannah's mother better because she was closer to my age. Fred was a lot older than her. All I can say is, what I knew of Fred Frederickson, I didn't like very much."

Deacon waited, but he didn't offer any further explanations.

"Hannah sure feels obligated to keep this place open," he said, bending over to sort and stack glasses in the bins under the bar.

Calvin snorted. "I don't doubt it. Fred was training her to run the Country Time from the moment she was born, as far as I can tell. I think if he hadn't gotten cancer, he would have dumped the place on her and taken off just like George did."

Deacon looked up at the other man, an ache in his chest at the thought of Hannah deserted by yet another person she should have been able to depend on.

"Didn't he want it?" he asked.

"If he did, he sure didn't act like it. Practically drove the place into the ground and worked Hannah to death as soon she was old enough to be of any help. My father said his old man made him take it. Now there was a true, cold-hearted bastard." He laughed without humor. "Whatever Anton Frederickson wanted, Anton Frederickson got. And he wanted the bar to continue in the family."

"And Fred?" Deacon asked.

Calvin shrugged broad shoulders. "He was the same way. Whatever Fred wanted, Fred made sure he got. And if he didn't get it, he got nasty."

Deacon was startled by the depth of anger in the other man's eyes.

It stayed with him as he went to ring up a customer wanting to pay her tab. When he came back, he tried to refill Calvin's beer, but the other man shook his head.

"No thanks. Too much alcohol's not a good idea for someone my age. I don't want to take any chances." He blushed bright red.

Deacon hid a grin. Sounded like somebody was hoping to get lucky tonight.

Well, that made two of them.

"How are things were going here?" Calvin asked after Deacon brought him a cola. "June said Hannah's going to try to pull this carnival thing off in, like, a week."

"A week and a half," Deacon corrected.

Calvin shook his head and sipped his soda. "Kinda rushed."

Deacon felt his hackles rise, even though he'd said pretty much the same thing to Hannah.

"She needs more money if she's going to keep this place open," he snapped.

Calvin smiled and held up a placating hand. "Easy, I'm just making an observation. June said Hannah applied for a bank loan, but the climate's not great for them right now. I can understand why she's looking at other options."

"Yeah." Deacon settled a little. "Plus that bastard Pat Murphy is fixing up the bowling alley and badmouthing her all over town. She's worried."

Calvin's mouth compressed into a thin line. "Pat's had a hard-on for the Country Time since he and June broke up."

Deacon was called away to take care of customers, then came back, leaning on the bar opposite Calvin again.

"So Murphy's going to sabotage this place just because June dumped him?" he asked. "What is he, thirteen?"

Calvin shrugged. "Pat doesn't forgive easily, and the breakup was pretty public. He's still royally pissed. I'm not sure I'd call it sabotage, though. Seems a little strong."

"Well, what else would you call it?" Deacon demanded.

"Business." Calvin shrugged again. "Pat thinks Hannah's weak. Sprucing up your operation to take advantage of the fact a rival's in trouble is normal. Hell, we did it when the Moynahan boy took over his father's hardware store a couple of years ago." His smile was sharp. "Kid always was an arrogant prick. Hardy Hardware just...helped the customers to see the light. We reworked our store, ran some nice sales, and grabbed people who used to shop with Pops Moynahan and were dissatisfied with his spawn."

"But is it normal to go all over town trying to undermine the rival's business?" Deacon persisted.

"Well..." Calvin rubbed his jaw. "I have to say it isn't exactly kosher, but it happens."

"What about having conversations with your rival's uncle, who is also your rival's accountant, right before he runs off with all of your rival's money?"

"Wait." Calvin held up a hand. "Are you saying Pat encouraged that idiot George to do what he did?"

"I don't know," Deacon admitted. He'd only been voicing a suspicion he'd had rambling around in the back of his mind.

"But George hung out at the bowling alley an awful lot. And he was friends with Pat."

"He was." Calvin looked thoughtful. "Now that you mention it, he and Pat seemed tighter than usual right before George ran off."

Deacon had to go ring out more customers. This group was pretty chatty, and then there were more drinks to see to, so it was several minutes before he got back to Calvin.

"Listen," the other man said as soon as he returned, "if you really think Pat encouraged George, you might want to give Hannah a head's up. June told me Hannah applied for a loan at First National Bank, or whatever the hell it's called now. Pat's extremely chummy with some of the guys who survived the merger. They're in the rotary, and I see them hanging out together at the meetings. I think they play golf or something."

Shit.

"Do you think he'd try to fuck with her loan?" Deacon asked.

Calvin tugged his ear. "I wouldn't have thought so. But if you're right and he actually encouraged George to embezzle, why wouldn't he?"

"Hey, you."

Their conversation was interrupted when June sidled up to Calvin and smoothed a hand over one of his thick biceps.

"Hi, honey." Calvin's smile could have lit up the room.

Despite the seriousness of the situation, Deacon couldn't help but grin. Calvin looked positively giddy, and maybe a little stunned. Deacon was glad. June deserved someone who'd act stupid over her.

June shifted to lean her hip against Calvin, a platter of dirty dishes balanced perfectly in her opposite hand.

"What are you two talking about? Looks intense." She stared at Deacon with her sharp, dark eyes.

He smiled innocently.

"I was telling Calvin he'd better watch how he treats my best girl," he said.

June barked out her rowdy laugh. "Bullshit. We both know who your best girl is, and it isn't me." Leaning down, she ran a kiss over Calvin's cheekbone. "Don't you be listening to him, love machine. You treat me just fine in *all* the right ways."

"Okay." Deacon held up his hands, palms out in surrender. "That is way too much information."

June laughed again and straightened, her free hand caressing Calvin's back.

"I'm off shift now," she told him. "Just give me a minute to get rid of these plates."

"No problem," Calvin said. "We're still on for tonight, right? Dad said he's fine watching Mama."

"Oh, yeah," June breathed, and the look she gave the other man really did make Deacon feel uncomfortable. She ran her hand over Calvin's thick, dark hair, then turned to hurry into the kitchen.

Calvin watched the door slap shut behind her, longing written clearly on his face.

"I never thought she'd look at me twice again, you know?" he said, his voice so low that Deacon had to strain to hear him over the ambient bar noise. "Not me. Not after I—" he broke off and shook his head, smiling a little when he glanced at Deacon. "Sorry."

"But she did look at you," Deacon said, thinking about himself and Hannah.

"Yes, she did." Calvin smiled. "Don't know how long it's gonna last, but I'll take what I can get." He pushed back the barstool and stood, discretely adjusting his pants with another shy smile. Then he looked at Deacon and his expression sharpened. "Let me give you a little advice. Make sure your woman knows how you feel."

"How?" Deacon asked, ignoring a customer who was trying to get his attention.

Calvin pulled his wallet out of his back pocket and tossed some bills on the bar. "It's hard and talking's not always enough. Most of the time you have to show them. Don't leave any room for doubt." He winked. "Why, I think I'll go do that right now."

Tipping his head to Deacon, he headed for the kitchen.

Deacon mulled over what Calvin had said while he soothed the irritated customer he'd been ignoring and served others.

He couldn't deny that hearing Pat Murphy was tight with higher ups at First National Bank was a concern. There were plenty of other banks around, but how much influence did Pat have? And what was he trying to prove? Yes, he was a dick, no question. But was he merely capitalizing on a rival's misfortune, or was he actively trying to put Hannah out of business?

Maybe it was time for him to have a little chat with Patrick Murphy. Find out what game he was playing.

"And then stomp his ass," he muttered, wiping down the bar top.

"Talking to yourself?"

He looked up to see Hannah sliding onto a barstool across from him, mussed and flushed from the heat of the kitchen. She wasn't wearing the ball cap she normally wore while cooking, and her thick brown hair was starting to come out of its tail, the curls wild around her face.

He smiled, watching as she reached back to tighten her hair tie. The position thrust out her breasts and highlighted her strong, toned arms.

Deacon drew in a deep breath and snapped his gaze up to meet her eyes. She grinned at him.

Yeah, she knew what she was doing to him, all right.

"Smart ass," he said and handed her a bottle of water from the mini-fridge under the bar. She twisted off the top and took a long, long drink, then finally lowered her head to smile at him again.

Something shifted inside him.

He didn't want to think about what that meant.

"How are things back in the kitchen?" he asked.

"Fine," she shrugged. "Billy burned his hand on the dishwasher, so I sent him home."

Deacon sighed. "Hannah…"

"I know, I know." She turned the water bottle on the bar. "I'll deal with him."

Deacon shook his head. "Sure you will, you big softy."

He turned away to take care of some college kids who were getting pretty rowdy. By the time he got them paid up and out, she had vanished back into the kitchen.

The last few hours passed with the comfort of routine. When Hannah finally re-emerged from the kitchen, the place was nearly empty and it was fifteen minutes to closing.

He handed her another bottle of water. Ordinarily he would have started cleaning up the main room, helping Billy if the loser was actually working. But tonight he walked around the bar and perched on the stool next to Hannah, positioning himself so he could keep an eye on the last patrons—Old Albert and his three equally ancient friends.

"So, what did Sam have to say, anyway?" he asked. He was just curious

That's right. *Curious.*

"He brought me the contract for the carnival and some other papers to sign," Hannah said.

"Oh. Good."

The four men at the other end of the bar laughed at something on the television, but Deacon wasn't paying much attention to them. Hannah had turned to face him, her knees pressing against his when she moved closer. He wrapped a hand around her thigh, felt the heat and soft, round strength of her through her jeans.

He wanted to kiss her, but restrained himself. She was still uncomfortable with public displays of affection in front of the customers, and he guessed he understood. She didn't want to be the subject of gossip; she was the boss and he was the employee.

It seemed kind of silly to him since everyone in town already knew, but what the heck. He wouldn't push her. She might not be broadcasting the fact that they were sleeping together, but she wasn't hiding it, either. That was saying a lot.

Baby steps, he reminded himself. Slow and easy. He wasn't going to be impatient and lose this fish when he'd just gotten her on the hook.

Hannah swiveled to look down the bar.

"Time to close, guys," she called to the old men. "Go home and watch your own televisions."

"I would, but my wife's there," Harry Newman, one of the four, yelled back. The others laughed, elbowing him and each other.

"She's always there," Martin Scanner another of the men guffawed. "His wife ain't even set foot outside their house in ten years."

"That's because she's so satisfied," Harry snorted. "She's got all she needs."

"Nah," said Joe Horton, the fourth man in the quartet. "It's because she's waiting for Albert to come over and bang her."

"How can I bang her?" Albert protested. "I'm always with you assholes."

"Unless you're with twins," Joe winked broadly.

"Or Mathilda Gregory," Martin put in.

"I wish Albert would come over and bang my wife," Harry muttered. "Then maybe she'd get off my back."

That set them all laughing again.

Chuckling with them, Deacon reluctantly pushed to his feet and walked around the bar to pick up the remote and click off the television.

"Get out of here, you old perverts."

There was a chorus of protests, but the men obediently pulled their creaky asses off the barstools and shuffled over to the cash register to pay their tabs. Deacon rang them out, smiling his thanks over the completely unnecessary tip each man solemnly pressed into his hand. He'd add the money to the communal jar later.

Still razzing each other, Martin, Joe, and Harry pulled on their coats and headed for the door. Albert hesitated, waiting for his friends to move away. He looked down the bar, and, when Deacon followed his glance, he saw Hannah had retreated to the kitchen.

Albert leaned forward, his faded eyes sharp and piercing.

"You hurt that little girl," he said, "and you'll answer to me."

Deacon did not disrespect the man by laughing at his threat or pretending not to know what he was talking about. Albert's eyes might be as old as the rest of him, but they still worked.

"I'm going to do my best not to hurt her," he promised. Was this the way Calvin had felt? "Hannah's lucky she has people like you watching out for her."

Albert's chest puffed with pride, and he nodded. "Just so you know." He grinned, showing he hadn't bothered to put in his teeth for the evening, and hurried to join his friends.

Deacon shook his head and locked the door after the old man before walking around to shut off the decorative lamps and neon beer signs. Then he went behind the bar to grab the last tub of dirty glasses. He'd deliver these to Hannah and get the rest of the closing routine done so they could get the hell out of there.

He paused when he realized he was assuming he'd be

invited back to Hannah's apartment. He might have even been taking it for granted.

That made him a little nervous.

Since the first time they'd slept together, Deacon had driven Hannah to and from work. Every night had followed the same routine. He'd take her back to her apartment building. Hannah would look at him with her fathomless eyes, and she'd ask him to come upstairs.

He went.

But today she'd brought her own car so she'd be able to keep her appointment with Allison Arthur. Somehow the fact that they were here at the Country Time instead of in the parking lot in front of her apartment building made the chance she'd invite him home with her seem a lot less certain.

Would she ask?

And what would he do if she didn't?

Deacon muscled the heavy tub of glassware out from under the bar and headed back to the kitchen.

Lots of people seemed to be worried that he'd hurt Hannah, he thought. There might be more danger the other way around.

He took the overflowing bus tub to Hannah at the dishwasher and left her scowling at it to go finish the familiar closing chores. When everything was finally in order, he went back to the kitchen in time to see her stacking the last of the clean dishes on the appropriate shelves.

"Thank God that's done," she said as she stripped off her big yellow rubber gloves and tossed them on the counter. Untying her chef's apron, she threw it towards the laundry basket, raked her hands through her hair, then glanced at him from under her lashes.

"So, you'll follow me home?"

And just like that he could breathe again.

"I will," he said.

He guessed she heard something in his voice because she tilted her head to the side and looked at him quizzically.

"You do want to, right?" she asked, and he could sense her hesitation.

For the first time he realized he wasn't the only one feeling a little uncertain about this relationship, and Christ, it was a relief. He went to her, grabbed her, pulled her up against his body, and kissed the hell out of her, sucking on her bottom lip before releasing her a fraction of an inch.

"I want to go home with you," he said, his voice a low and scratchy growl.

"Okay." She was clinging to his shoulders as if her legs wouldn't support her. He couldn't have been more pleased.

"I will always want to be in your bed, Hannah," he said, deciding to put his cards on the table. "That's one thing you can count on."

Her breath caught.

"Let's get out of here," she said.

Later, back at her apartment, after he'd stroked her soft skin until she moaned, after he'd feasted on her beautiful body until she'd screamed, after his own orgasm had blown through him with the force of a tsunami, Deacon lay with Hannah on her bed and let himself relax for the first time in hours.

It was only then that he remembered his conversation with Calvin and what the man had said about Hannah's father.

"Do you ever regret running the bar?" he asked, smoothing his hand down her back.

Her face was against his shoulder, and for a moment he thought she might be asleep. Then she shook her head.

"Not really," She began petting his chest absently, distracting the hell out of him. "Well, not now, anyway," she added after a moment. "I wanted to travel when I was younger. Get a van and hit the road. Maybe see the country, go to college." She nuzzled him and breathed deeply. "But my dad told me I was going to take over the business and that was that. By the time I realized I might actually have had a choice, he was sick and I was in charge."

He thought about how trapped she must have felt. How burdened by her responsibilities.

"Why didn't you go after your father died?" he asked. "Just sell the place and leave. No one would have blamed you."

She jerked her shoulder in a shrug, her fingers gentle, caressing him. "I don't know. I thought about it, but it didn't seem right."

He turned until they lay face to face, legs intertwined. "Hannah, this thing with George is bad, but maybe it's your chance to do something else."

"I'm not running away, Deacon." She gripped his biceps and looked up at him, her eyes large and dark in the ambient light coming from the lamp in the living room they'd forgotten to turn off. "Not now. People depend on me for a paycheck, and I'm not going to let them down, especially since this entire situation is my fault."

Suddenly, inexplicably, he was angry at her. No, not angry. Furious.

"This situation is *George's* fault. You're not responsible for every damn thing and every damn person. You're not our fucking mother."

She frowned at him. "I realize that."

"Do you? Do you really? Who am I to you?" he demanded, pushing even though he'd sworn he wouldn't push.

"I don't know." She sounded more than a little breathless, but he could tell it wasn't from fear. Not when her hands were clutching at him and her legs were wrapped around his thigh. "Who are you to me?"

"I'll tell you who I am," he said, the anger changing as quickly as it had come, morphing into an even darker passion. A moment ago he'd thought he was sated, but now it felt like he'd never had her. He was instantly hard, instantly ravenous. "I'll tell you. I'm your fucking lover, that's who." He kissed her, deeply and passionately, before he pulled away. "And I'm the one who's going to make you come your brains out in a minute," he muttered into her ear.

"Good." She pulled his head up so she could kiss him.

He rolled her onto her back and devoured her mouth. God, he was hungry for her. Hungry for her to be as desperate as he was, hungry for her to admit that he was more than an employee, more than her goddamned responsibility.

Finally he tore his mouth away from hers and looked down into her shadowed face.

"Deacon—" She gripped his shoulders and tried to pull him back, but he braced himself and settled his thick arousal against her.

"Say I'm your lover, Hannah," he demanded. "Say it." He needed this acknowledgment from her, this recognition that they were more than friends.

Her knees crept up his sides, but he still refused to move.

"Yes!" she gasped. "Yes, damn you. You're my fucking lover."

Deacon took her lips in another urgent kiss. He fingered her, testing her readiness until she cursed him and yelled so loudly he was afraid they would hear her outside on the street.

Reaching over her head, he scrabbled around on the nightstand and grabbed a condom. He ripped it open with his teeth, sheathed himself, and thrust into her with one stroke.

They both groaned.

Deacon pulled out, pushed back, his pace quickening, control shot.

Hannah was panting, her heels crossed behind his back to hold him close. Her magnificent eyes were closed, her head thrown back. He bent and licked the strong column of her throat, twisting his hips with each down stroke to rub sensitive places, desperately trying to prolong the sensations. He didn't want this to be quick, damn it. He wanted her to cry for him. To moan. To understand he would take care of her.

God, she felt good.

"*Deacon!*" She wailed his name. It was a demand and a plea all wrapped up in one word.

He started moving faster until he was slinging his hips into the cradle of her body, straining towards his own completion as well as hers.

For several moments he hung on to that edge, pumping furiously, mindlessly. Then she screamed, arched, and shattered.

And, with a shout, he joined her.

20
—————

The next morning, Hannah woke up around nine feeling surprisingly energized, considering her activities the night before. She stretched a little and yawned, debating what needed to be done first. The choices were practically endless.

Then Deacon shifted in his sleep beside her and pulled her closer to his hard, warm body.

She decided she should probably wake him up.

He appreciated her efforts.

After they'd recovered, shared a shower, and gotten dressed, Deacon made the coffee. They drank in companionable silence until he put his mug in the sink and told her he needed to leave to run some errands before work.

"Oh." Hannah sucked in a breath, more than a little disappointed. "Okay."

"I have to change my clothes, anyway." He smiled at her and waited. He'd been doing that a lot lately; saying something and then waiting for her response. Almost as if he expected something from her.

This time she knew what it was. Deacon had a razor and a toothbrush at her apartment, but everything else was still in his room over the bookstore. Usually they stopped on their way in to work for him to get clean clothes and other essentials. That had to be a pain in the ass for him.

But if he started keeping more things at her place, it would almost be like he was moving in, and she wasn't ready to take that step. She might never be ready.

The sad fact was, Deacon was probably going to leave someday, maybe someday soon. Sam had been right when he'd said it was surprising he'd stayed this long. Hannah had a good idea what Deacon's life had been like; he couldn't possibly be content to remain here in this small town with his estranged family.

No, he was bound to go. And the more she let him into her life, the more it would hurt when he was gone.

It was already going to hurt plenty.

When she remained quiet, he let out a deep breath. His obvious disappointment made her heart hurt, but what else was she supposed to do?

"Okay," he said after a moment. "Should I come back and pick you up later? We could carpool to work?"

"All right," she said, even though it was silly for him to drive back there when she could certainly get to work herself. But she didn't want to disappoint him again.

This time she was rewarded with a smile and he took her hand, tugging her through the apartment to the door. Once there, he gave her a sultry kiss, running his big hands through her hair.

"I'll see you at two," he murmured when he lifted his head.

"Good." She pulled him back down for another, longer kiss.

He went with it for a while but eventually broke away with a soft sound of regret.

"I really do have to go."

She pouted, pushing out her bottom lip and making her eyes go all sad.

Deacon grinned.

"We could always pick this up at work later," he suggested casually. "It would be like dinner theater."

"Um, that would be a no." She tried to sound stern.

"Are you sure?" He quirked an eyebrow at her. "We do there what we've been doing here and we'd get way bigger tips."

"No, go." She shoved him back a step.

"Party pooper." He kissed her again before opening the door and stepping out into the hall. "I'll see you later. Don't forget to lock up."

"I won't." She smiled at him and watched him walk down the hallway towards the stairwell.

Sam wasn't the only Black brother with a truly excellent ass.

Deacon turned at the stairwell door and grinned when he caught her watching him. She rolled her eyes and blew him a kiss. God, she was such a sap.

Stepping back into her apartment, she closed the door, locked it, then braced her back against the wall and slid down until she was sitting on the carpet.

"Holy shit," she muttered, "the man sure has some moves on him."

Would it hurt to let him keep some shirts and underwear here? Maybe empty a drawer for him or something?

Hannah shook her head. Not yet.

The phone rang, startling her from her thoughts.

Rather than getting up, she crawled to the end table and pulled the handset out of its charger.

"Hello?"

"Hannah!" Josie's buoyant voice came through the receiver.

"Hi, Josie." Resigned, Hannah settled on the floor with her back against an armchair. She hadn't talked to her friend in a couple of days, although they'd exchanged a few e-mails.

"How are you?" Josie asked. "I had a minute, so I wanted to get an update. What's going on?"

"Don't you know?" Hannah hedged. "I thought you kept up with everything happening in Hardy Falls."

Josie sighed, the sound long and deep. "I haven't had time for *anything* but work. I'm seriously thinking of just setting up a cot in the office and sleeping here. I only had time to call you now because the computer system went down."

"Really?" Hannah frowned, distracted from her own worries by the exhaustion in her friend's voice.

"Welcome to the glamorous world of advertising." Josie sighed again.

"I don't know what you do, but that doesn't sound right," Hannah said. "Is that Donald Corso guy dumping on you?"

"Sure." She could almost hear Josie shrug. "That's the way it goes. I'm the newest member on the team and extremely low on the totem pole, so I get all of the crap nobody else wants to do. On the other hand, if we can pull this campaign off, it will make a huge difference to my career. And don't think I didn't notice you changing the subject. What's up?"

What *wasn't* up? Hannah thought.

"We're having a carnival," she said.

There was a long pause.

"Okay," Josie said at last. "I've got to admit I wasn't expecting that one. Want to tell me why you're having a carnival?"

"To make money because my bastard uncle emptied all of my accounts. Why do you think?"

"I assumed you'd be more focused on a bank loan," Josie said slowly, "but way to think outside the box. Where the hell did that idea come from?"

Hannah shrugged her shoulders uneasily, even though Josie couldn't see her.

"It just came up."

"Oh, please. A trip to the mall just comes up. 'I'm going to have a carnival' takes some thought."

Hannah let her head roll against the arm of the chair.

"I need to get some short-term working capital together fast." She hesitated. "Pat Murphy is fixing up the restaurant at the bowling alley."

"Shit."

Josie was always quick to grasp the implications of a situation.

"Yeah." Hannah rubbed her eyes. The weight of responsibility that had lifted during her incredible night with Deacon settled back on her shoulders. "Pat's telling everyone in town that I'm failing."

"What a dick. But that doesn't mean people believe him."

"No," Hannah admitted, "but if he fixes up his restaurant, if the bowling league people don't come in after their games...I'm in trouble."

"True," Josie agreed. "Honestly, I don't know why he's focused on the bar. He should hype the good, clean family fun of bowling, instead. You two don't have to be rivals."

"Huh." Hannah had never considered that before.

"So when is this carnival, anyway?" Josie asked.

"A week and a half."

"A week and a...are you crazy?"

Hannah felt her back go up.

"No," she snapped, "just desperate."

"A week and a half." Josie sounded dazed. "Man, when you make a decision, you don't mess around, do you?"

"Have you listened to anything I've said? I need working capital, fast."

"I wish I had money to give you." Josie's voice softened. "But it's pretty expensive to live here."

"I know." Her friend had found an extremely tiny apartment in Manhattan. It was very convenient to where she worked, but the rent was more than a lot of the mortgages in Hardy Falls. Regardless, Hannah knew she would have turned down Josie's offer of money, just as she had Deacon's.

Deacon.

If Josie hadn't talked to anyone in town lately, she didn't know about Hannah and Deacon.

"You're still going for a bank loan, right?" Josie asked.

"Yes." Hannah closed her eyes. She had to tell her about Deacon, didn't she?

"Good. There are a ton of banks out there. One's bound to lend you money."

"I know." Hannah chewed her bottom lip. Yeah, she had to tell her. Josie was her best friend. If she thought she was keeping another secret, especially one this big, she'd never forgive her. Better to get it out in the open.

"Plus you could always look for individual investors."

"Right." Hannah cleared her throat. "Um, so I started sleeping with Deacon."

"Just because—" Josie broke off mid-sentence. "Excuse me?"

"Deacon and I started...a thing. An affair," she qualified, although she winced a little at the word.

"Deacon Black?" Josie asked, as if seeking to confirm her understanding. "Your bartender? Sam's brother?"

"Yes." Hannah swallowed. "Deacon Black. My bartender. Sam's brother."

"Huh." Josie sounded a little stunned, but not as surprised as Hannah had expected.

"That's all you have to say?" she demanded.

"Well, yeah. I mean, no. Wow. That's huge."

"Yes." Hannah's sigh was a trifle carnal. "It is."

"Oh, shut up! You are such a bitch." Josie laughed, then sobered. "I guess I just didn't think you'd actually go there. Not with an employee, anyway."

Hannah shifted uneasily.

"I don't know how it happened," she admitted. "One minute we were watching a band, the next we were in bed."

"I'm not judging you," Josie said hastily. "I always thought you'd hooked up with the wrong Black brother, even when Deacon was a cute little dweeb back in high school. But now that he's back, all grown up and buff, with those shoulders...*Yawwwrrr*," she growled.

"Hey!" Hannah straightened.

Her friend laughed uproariously before stopping to catch her breath. "Deacon's a really great guy, Hannah," she said, sounding more serious. "He always was."

Hannah slumped. "I know." He was just a really great guy who probably wouldn't be around much longer.

"I know you do." Josie's voice held a smile. "So," she added after a moment, "I'll come to help you with this carnival deal."

"No! Absolutely not. If you leave now, the assholes you work with will take the credit for all of your work. You know they will."

"Yeah, yeah, yeah." Hannah could actually hear her friend roll her eyes. "You need me—"

"I'm fine. I'm handling it. I swear if you come here, I will kill you."

"Well...okay." The other woman sounded reluctant, but a little relieved. "If you're sure."

"I'm sure."

"You're right, you know," Josie said in a quiet voice. "We're working seven days a week to prepare for our presentation to the client's board of directors. If I take any time off, Donald will steal credit for the work I've done and try to push me off the team. But things should get better after the meeting. I'll be able to go home for a couple of days and see you."

"Good," Hannah said, glad she wasn't going to have to argue.

Josie was quiet for another moment before she spoke. "I'd better go. I want to call my mother while the computer system is still down."

"Have fun with that," Hannah said with real sympathy. Chief Kline had always been protective of her children, but she'd taken things to a whole new level after Josie moved to Manhattan.

They said their good-byes and hung up, but Hannah didn't move right away. Instead she sat with her head resting on the overstuffed arm of the chair, thinking about friends and men and the way life could twist and turn on you.

21

Friday afternoon, Hannah sat in her office staring at her computer screen, trying to decide whether or not she'd ordered enough beer for the carnival. She was pretty sure her original order would be okay, but if they ran out and people got angry...

What the hell. Better safe than sorry. It wasn't like the expense would make much of a difference.

The phone on her desk rang just as she hit the button to submit a supplemental order, and she glanced at it absently. Then she froze, staring at the caller ID screen.

PFNB.

Oh, God. It was the bank. Her heart stuttered, then started pounding wildly. Already? They'd only had her loan application since Tuesday. They couldn't have made a decision yet. Could they?

The phone rang again and she grabbed the receiver.

"Hello?"

"Hannah Frederickson?" a familiar female voice asked.

Hannah swallowed. "Yes, it's me."

"This is Allison Arthur from PFNB."

"Okay. Um, I mean, hi." Hannah wrapped the cord of the old fashioned phone around her fist so tightly it cut off circulation. "How are you?"

"Fine, fine." The other woman sounded distracted. "I'm calling about your application."

"Oh." Hannah breathed in and out. "Is there a problem? Do you need more information?"

"No. That is to say, yes, there is a problem, but I don't need more information."

Hannah's chest tightened.

"What can I do for you?" she asked carefully.

Allison cleared her throat on the other end of the line.

"Unfortunately, the bank lending committee has decided to decline your loan."

A roaring storm whirled through Hannah's brain, and even though Allison kept talking, only random phrases penetrated: "*...too much risk...bad economy...business value...blah, blah, blah...*"

When the swirling noise finally faded, she realized Allison had stopped and was waiting for a response.

"Thank you," Hannah said, because she couldn't think of anything else appropriate.

"Naturally, I felt you deserved a personal phone call instead of a form rejection letter," Allison said smoothly. "After all, you have been a good customer with us for years."

Right, Hannah thought.

"I appreciate your consideration," she said.

"Of course, just because our bank considers you a poor risk does not mean you won't find another lending institution willing to take a chance on your business."

"Of course," Hannah murmured.

"You'll be receiving a formal acknowledgment letter in the mail detailing our decision," Allison said.

"Okay."

"I think that's all." Allison sounded content, Hannah

thought. Relaxed, now that an annoying task had been completed. "Thank you for being a valued customer of PFNB."

"Sure," Hannah said.

The line went dead as Allison broke the connection. Hannah sat holding the handset for a moment, then placed it carefully in the cradle. She stared at it, unseeing.

She'd been in contact with some other banks, and yesterday she'd submitted applications at three of them. This wasn't the end of the world. In fact, based on the way Allison had acted at their last meeting, she'd known the decision was a distinct possibility, if not a probability.

But the empty pit in her stomach told her she'd still apparently hoped for a different outcome.

There was a brief knock on the door jamb, and Deacon walked into the office.

"Hannah, did you order more—" he broke off when he saw her face. "What's wrong?"

"The bank called," she said. "Allison Arthur."

"Yeah?"

"Yes." She swallowed. "So, they kind of, um, made a decision."

Deacon was silent for a moment. "I didn't think you'd hear back from them until next week, at the earliest."

"Me, either."

"Based on your expression, I'm guessing it's not good, huh?"

She shook her head. "No, they..." To her horror, she felt her eyes filling with tears. "They declined me."

"Hannah. Hey, hey, Hannah."

He moved around the desk and pulled her into a tight embrace. She wrapped her arms around his waist and buried her face in the hollow between his chin and shoulder, struggling to get herself under control while she breathed in the now-familiar scent of his skin. For several minutes she just held on to him as he ran his hand ran soothingly up and down her back.

God, this was ridiculous. Why was she crying? There was no reason to get so upset.

After another moment, he cupped her face in his hand and gently nudged her to look at him.

"Are you okay?" he asked, when she finally met his eyes.

She shrugged as she tried to sort through her emotions. "I'm okay. Hearing her say it...it was such a huge let-down. I guess I hoped they would come through after all, or at least try to work with me since I've been a customer so long. When she rejected the loan without giving me a chance..." She shook her head.

"Good thing you've already contacted other banks."

"Yes," she sighed. "I'm just not sure they'll seriously consider me. Or if they do, I'm afraid they'll give me a really high interest rate."

"You'll work it out." He ran his hands up her arms and cupped her shoulders.

She drew in a deep, shuddering breath and tried to smile.

"At least I have a business plan now," she said.

He returned her smile and rubbed her upper arms.

"And a carnival next weekend to bring in some ready cash. Everything will be fine."

An emotion Hannah was afraid to identify welled up inside her. *Look at him*, she thought, *propping me up. Caring what happens to me.*

Impulsively she leaned forward and took his mouth in a long, sizzling kiss that had him clenching his hands on her arms and pulling her closer.

"Thanks," she whispered when she pulled back.

"For what?" He breathing was harsh.

The fact that he really didn't know how special he was astounded her, and she went in for another kiss, this time sucking and chewing on his bottom lip before releasing it when they both needed air.

"For being here," she told him.

Deacon's eyes were a little glassy.

"You're welcome." He sounded hoarse.

Hannah giggled, which fifteen minutes ago would have been unthinkable.

Deacon had just pulled her closer and dipped his head for another kiss when there was a knock on the door.

"Hannah—Christ. Are you two at it again?"

As one, Hannah and Deacon turned to look at June standing in the doorway. The older woman cocked out a hip and crossed her arms.

"Might as well just—" Her smirk quickly changed to a frown when she got a good look at Hannah's face. "What's wrong?"

A little embarrassed, Hannah stepped away from Deacon and grabbed a tissue from the box on her desk.

"The bank turned down my loan," she said after blowing her nose and disposing of the tissue. "Allison called."

June straightened. "Son of a bitch. Did she say why?"

Hannah shrugged. "Risk. Poor economy. Those were the highlights."

June fisted her hands on her hips. "So what now?"

Hannah shook her head and sank wearily into her chair. "I'm applying at other banks, so we'll see what they say."

"Maybe you should cut and run," June suggested.

"Not going to happen. Besides, the carnival is next weekend. That'll bring in enough money to keep things going until I get a loan." Hannah tried to sound positive and in control even as her stomach rolled.

Deacon touched her shoulder, before moving around the desk towards June. "Did you need me?" he asked her.

June frowned at Hannah for a moment longer, then seemed to decide to let it go. Her stance became a little less militant.

"We're starting to fill up already. Want me to man the grill?"

Hannah gave a guilty start.

"I'll be right—"

"I can run the damned grill," June interrupted her. "Been doing it for years, haven't I?"

"Mary Alice—"

"Mary Alice will be fine handling the tables for a while. You take some time to get your head together."

Hannah drew in a deep breath, felt her eyes filling again.

"June—"

"Sheesh, don't cry." June looked disgusted. "It's my job too, isn't it? You need time to figure out what you're doing, you've got time." She looked at Deacon. "You, on the other hand," she said, "get your butt out front."

"Yes, ma'am." Deacon bent and kissed June's cheek. She punched him in the stomach and made him grunt.

"No funny stuff," she said. "Calvin wouldn't like it."

"Oh, *really*." Deacon drew out the word.

"Shut up." June turned and marched off.

Deacon looked back at Hannah and winked.

"We've got this. You take your time."

Then he followed June out to the bar.

Hannah decided to take Deacon and June at their word and spent the next few hours researching banks and dealing with a variety of things for the carnival.

Finally acknowledging there was nothing more she could do that day, she headed out to relieve June at the grill. Then she proceeded to work herself into the ground for the rest of the night, barking orders at Billy so forcefully he actually kept up with the dishes.

After they'd closed, she and Deacon returned to her apartment. Deacon made love to her slowly and sweetly, as if he knew she needed the comfort as much as the passion.

Later, she snuggled close to his side and laid her head on his chest so she could listen to his heartbeat. Deacon's arm came around her and she sighed, content to be right where she was.

"Try to sleep," he murmured.

"You, too," she said.

They lay in silence for several minutes. Deacon's heartbeat was steady, his chest rising regularly with each breath, but she knew he was awake.

"I don't want to upset you," he said into the quiet, "But have you given any more thought to individual investors? Like a group of them?"

She felt some of her relaxation ebb.

"Yes," she admitted. "It's just...then I'd have more responsibility." More people depending on her. More people counting on her to succeed.

"Ah." He stroked her hair and moved his hand down her back to cup her butt. "I can understand you wouldn't want more of that, especially seeing as how you're kind of obsessive about the whole responsibility thing in the first place."

"Hey!" She pinched him and he jumped.

"Ow." He smacked her playfully on the butt in retaliation, then stroked her again. "What you really need," he continued thoughtfully, "is a bunch of people who can all invest a little. Then it's not as big a deal if something happens."

"I need pretty much money, Deacon, especially if Pat Murphy's trying to steal all my business," she pointed out.

"So you need one or two people who can afford to invest a lot, and a bunch of us who can invest a little."

She sighed, smoothing her hand over his chest, feeling the strength and the muscle under her palm.

"Maybe I should send Sam to ask your father." Actually, she

mused, that might not be such a bad idea. Dr. Trevor Black was kind of a jerk, but he was really wealthy. Hadn't Allison mentioned he was buying property in town or something?

She realized Deacon had gone still under her, his hand no longer moving. She raised her head, trying to see his face in the darkened room.

"Deacon? What's wrong?"

He didn't answer and she hauled herself up until she was staring down at him.

"Deacon?"

Suddenly he pulled her back to him, rolled over on top of her, and kissed her, hard and thoroughly.

"You're thinking too much. You need a distraction," he said.

"Yeah?" She gulped.

"Yeah." And he proceeded to distract the hell right out of her.

That morning, Deacon stood at the window in Hannah's bedroom, holding back the heavy black-out curtain to watch the light of a new day bleed through trees on the mountain, setting the fall colors on fire.

He loved mornings, but the jobs he'd had since leaving the army ensured he didn't see too many of them. He shouldn't have seen this one—it was way too early for him to be up—but he hadn't been able to sleep. Hannah, on the other hand, was down for the count.

He thought she was being a little short-sighted about not going the whole private investor route, especially now that her primary bank had turned her down. Even though he understood she would feel responsible to the individual investors, he was very much afraid she didn't have a choice anymore if she wanted a reasonable interest rate.

Would she ask Sam to talk to their father about investing in the Country Time?

Apparently she wouldn't ask Deacon to talk to him.

Outside, the light strengthened and birds sang enthusiastically. He heard voices and laughter and then saw a couple of guys walking into the machining shop across the street, ready to clock in.

If he had a job like that, or if he'd gone to college and gotten a job in an office, he would see a lot more mornings.

On the other hand, if he saw more mornings, he might not have gotten to know Hannah Frederickson. To his mind, it was a fair trade-off.

Sheets rustled behind him, and he turned, guessing the echo of voices outside had disturbed Hannah. But he saw she was still asleep, her head burrowed in the pillows. Letting the curtain fall back to block out the sun, he walked over and sat on the edge of the bed, watching her sleep in the shadows.

To be honest, money or no money, he didn't want his father getting involved with the Country Time. This was the first place Deacon had really felt at home. Hannah was the first woman who had really mattered. He didn't want his father inserting himself and spoiling things with his coldness and harsh judgment.

He certainly didn't want to be the one to go to the man and ask for help, to be seen as begging or desperate to keep his job. To be viewed as lacking. Again.

He had his pride, after all.

Besides, if Hannah decided to approach his father, it would be smart to get Sam to present her proposition. After all, he was the attorney and the favored eldest son.

Except that would be one more time when Sam swooped in and saved the day while Deacon stood around like a jackass.

He watched the even rise and fall of Hannah's back as she slept.

Be useful.

Well, he could always forget his pride and go talk to his father first.

No room for doubt.

This might be his chance to prove to Hannah he was more than an employee and a bedmate. It might be a way to really help to her.

He drew in a deep breath.

What the hell did his pride matter, anyway? He knew who he was; so what if his father judged him again? It wouldn't be the first time, and it sure wouldn't be the last.

Deacon frowned, thinking it through. He'd go see his father today, before Hannah applied at more banks, and show him the business plan. Then, if he seemed interested, Deacon would go back to Hannah, offer up the possibility, and let her take it from there. Having an investor lined up might even improve her chances with a bank because she wouldn't have to borrow as much money.

Yes, it might be better to have Sam do the asking, but Deacon had been getting along pretty well with his parents recently, and they had always seemed to like Hannah. He thought he had a good chance.

Reaching out, he touched Hannah's tangled hair, smoothed the soft skin of her shoulder. She sighed and shifted until he could see her profile against the plain white pillowcase.

That face.

Not pretty by normal standards, perhaps. But he thought she was beautiful.

Deacon drew in another deep breath and let it out slowly.

He was in love with Hannah Frederickson. He always had been.

So he'd humble himself for her.

She stirred again and her sleepy eyes blinked open.

"Hey." She smiled and moved to see him better. "What time is it?"

"Early."

"Are you leaving?"

"Yeah." He needed to clean up and get some things together before he went to see his father.

Suiting the action to the word, he got off the bed and gathered up his clothes from where they'd been tossed haphazardly around the room, pulling them on swiftly.

Hannah sat and watched him, the covers pooled at her waist, her naked breasts pale and round.

"You could stay for a while," she offered. "If you can't sleep we can try to find ways to...relax." She drew a hand through her hair and down her body.

"Stop." Deacon zipped up his jeans before shrugging into his rumpled Country Time polo shirt. "I have some things I need to do." He bent to tie his running shoes, then straightened. "I won't be able to take you to work today."

"Oh. Okay." She hesitated, obviously waiting for more information, but he didn't say anything. "So, uh, I'll see you later."

He couldn't stand her uncertainty and bent to kiss her softly.

"Don't worry. I'll be on time. Probably even early."

"Good."

Smiling, he went to a chair and picked up the nightshirt she wore in the mornings, holding it out to her. "Come on. You need to lock up after me."

Gloriously nude, she got out of bed and walked over to him, her smile feminine and mysterious in the dim light as she reached for the garment.

"Well, if you're sure."

Deacon drew in air through his nose so he wouldn't start panting.

"I'm sure," he squeaked.

Hannah laughed and pulled the nightshirt over her head, then led the way through the darkened apartment to the door. She held it open for him as he moved past her into the hallway.

"Remember to lock up," he told her, drinking in the sight of her flushed face and sleepy hazel eyes.

"I will. I'll see you later." Hannah leaned forward and kissed him gently. He returned the kiss, deepening it, drawing in her taste. He was going to need to hold onto the memory as a talisman later.

"Lock the door," he repeated when he pulled back and gently disengaged her hands.

"Okay," she gasped, eyes unfocused.

He laughed and pulled the door shut between them.

After a moment the deadbolt clicked on the other side of the door.

Deacon stood there for another moment, then turned and headed for the stairs.

22

A few hours later, Deacon pulled his old SUV to a stop at the curb in front of his parents' large home.

This wasn't the house where they'd lived when he'd been a teenager—that had been a regular, old-fashioned split level on a quiet street in Hardy Falls. But once Dr. Black's career had taken off, thanks to a particularly lucrative patent, Deacon's parents had moved to a more suitable estate, complete with a white colonnade, long, serpentine driveway, and wide sweep of meticulously manicured lawn.

Considering the stately house perched high on a hill, Deacon tapped his fingers nervously on the steering wheel.

He could do this.

He took a deep breath, put the SUV back in gear, and drove up the driveway, parking where a hedge of boxwoods framed the spacious front porch. Before he could change his mind, he jumped out of the car, ran up the stairs, and rang the bell next to a pair of large, glossy black double-doors. A deep "gong" echoed inside the house.

Classy.

While he waited for someone to respond to the summons,

he adjusted the collar of his button-down shirt and smoothed his dark jeans. Nobody answered the bell, so he rang it again, shifting the folder of printouts he held from hand to hand until he remembered the security cameras and forced himself to stop fidgeting.

He wouldn't put it past his father to be sitting inside watching the monitors. He knew the man was home; he'd been sure to call before he'd come over.

Finally one of the doors was opened by a young woman with white-blond hair dressed in a traditional maid's uniform. She must have been new because Deacon didn't recognize her from the last time he'd been invited to dinner. That wasn't much of a surprise. When he'd been younger, his parents had never had household staff, now they seemed to rotate through the place on a regular basis.

"May I help you?" the woman asked coolly in a thick Slavic accent.

"I'm here to see Dr. Black," Deacon said with equal politeness.

"And you are?" she asked emptily.

"His son," Deacon said. "I believe he's expecting me."

The woman didn't even blink.

"Follow me," she said.

Once Deacon had stepped inside, she closed the door behind him, then turned and led him down the main hall to the great room. It was a beautiful space, with dark maroon walls and light natural wood, soaring high to exposed beams in a vaulted ceiling. On the few occasions he'd visited in the past, Deacon had thought of the room—the whole house, really—as magazine perfect, as if at any moment a television crew would walk in and start filming.

He liked Hannah's small, cluttered apartment a lot better.

He followed the maid to the far end of the great room where there was a seating area in front of big windows overlooking the gardens. Deacon's father was ensconced in a tall wingback chair reading the paper, while three men spread mulch outside in preparation for winter.

As Deacon approached, Dr. Black looked up, his eyes a cold blue, bald head gleaming in the late morning light. He uncrossed his legs, then crossed them again, casually sophisticated in black slacks and a white polo.

"Deacon," he said in his smooth, emotionless voice, folding the paper and setting it aside on a small table.

Deacon nodded. "Sir."

Dr. Black considered him for a moment longer, then looked at the blond.

"That will be all, Ilsa," he said.

Without any show of emotion, she glided from the room.

"Sit down," his father directed, gesturing to another wingback chair.

Deacon sat.

"How is Mother?" he asked, just to say something.

"Fine. She's in Scranton supporting a campaign for literacy."

"Ah," Deacon said. Although she'd never worked outside the home when he'd been younger, Samantha Black had recently become involved in local politics. He cleared his throat, anxious to get to his reason for being there.

"Thank you for the taking the time to see me, sir," he said formally.

His father settled back in his armchair and steepled his fingers.

"I am extremely busy, of course, especially now that the lab has received additional funding for my long-term genetics project."

"Congratulations," Deacon said, and meant it. His father was a brilliant scientist. Although most of his work was done for the pharmaceutical industry these days, his research into the genetics of obesity and diabetes was world renowned.

"Thank you." Dr. Black inclined his head. "I generally work on Saturdays, however, you happened to catch me at a good time. I'm not due at the lab until later today."

Which Deacon had known because he'd called the lab before he'd called his father.

"On the phone you mentioned a business proposal," Dr. Black continued.

"Yes, I—"

"I hope this won't be a complete waste of my time," his father said bluntly. "What did you wish to discuss?"

Don't get insulted, Deacon reminded himself. *You got the audience, that's what mattered.*

Leaning forward in his chair, he set the file folder he was still holding on the low coffee table between them. Opening it, he rifled through the papers to give himself a moment to gather his thoughts, then pulled out a paper copy of Hannah's business plan, printed half an hour before at the library and neatly stapled by Ms. Gregory.

He looked up to find his father contemplating him as if he were a sample on a microscope slide.

"As I'm sure you are well aware," he said, "Hannah Frederickson is the owner of the Country Time Bar and Grill, where I am employed."

"As a bartender," his father sneered.

"Yes. As a bartender." Deacon knew he sounded stiff, and sincerely hoped his father wouldn't realize he was already getting to him. "You may also be aware Hannah recently suffered a...reversal of fortunes."

"When her uncle ran off with all of her money." Dr. Black's lip curled.

"Yes." Well, he'd known his father would have heard the

story by now, Deacon reminded himself. "I'd like to propose that you become an investor in her business."

"You want me to give her money?" His father's heavy dark eyebrows shot up.

"No. I'm asking you to consider lending money to a well-established and extremely profitable local business in exchange for a mutually agreeable rate of interest. Here is the business plan." He pushed the papers across the table to his father.

"I see." Dr. Black frowned, making no effort to take them. "I wish you'd given me more details on the phone before you bothered to come out here. Although, admittedly, I should have guessed what your proposal would be."

"Don't you even want to look at the business plan?" Deacon controlled his temper with difficulty. "This is a good opportunity, sir. Hannah is a good manager."

His father snorted. "A good manager who did not realize her accountant was stealing her money until it was too late. A good opportunity to lose whatever I might choose to invest." He studied Deacon over his steepled fingers. "I admit I'm a little surprised you would go this far to keep a job. After all, I offered to lend you money when you first came to town, and you refused. Rather than go to this extreme, I would expect you to simply pick up stakes and move on again."

Deacon drew in a long breath and let it out slowly, trying to ignore the way his stomach twisted. "This isn't about me, Father. I'm offering you a chance to make money."

"Which only serves to demonstrate your lack of understanding."

"I understand plenty," Deacon shot back.

His father didn't seem to have heard him. He was staring out the windows, mouth pursed, idly watching the laborers in his garden.

"Still," he said, "you are correct when you say that the

Country Time is a very popular business and could make quite a bit of money if handled properly. Too bad it's such a risk."

Risk. Trevor Black didn't know anything about risk.

"Right," Deacon said. "Too bad."

"If I decided to move forward, an outright purchase or majority partnership would probably be wiser," his father mused, as if Deacon hadn't spoken. "I prefer to have some measure of control when investing in local businesses. Perhaps I should speak to Hannah about those options."

Deacon rolled his eyes. "Sure. You just go on ahead and do that." Like Hannah would ever sell the Country Time.

Dr. Black frowned thoughtfully. "I really don't have the time."

Honest to God, the man's arrogance knew no bounds. "So you won't even discuss the possibility of becoming an investor?" Deacon persisted, because that was why he had come.

His father's frown turned to him. "Of course not. I thought I made myself clear."

Anger churning, Deacon pushed to his feet, because if he didn't get out of there he was going to give in to the temptation to punch out his own father. Besides, there was obviously nothing to be gained by staying. This had been a huge mistake.

"I have to leave now, Father. Thanks for seeing me."

"Good-bye." Dr. Black nodded and picked up his newspaper again.

Deacon turned and strode out of the room before he said or did anything he'd regret. The silent Ilsa was at the front door, holding it open for him as he stormed out. Without a backward glance, he got into his SUV, revved the engine, and sped down the driveway and into the street.

"Fuck," he said.

He didn't know if he was angrier at his father or himself. What the hell had he been thinking? That he could expect the man to give him a fair hearing just because they'd had dinner together a couple of times?

Deacon slammed the flat of his hand on the steering wheel several times.

Could he be more of a fucking idiot? Thank God he hadn't told Hannah where he was going when he left her apartment.

Except, he thought as he drove, if she asked Sam to talk to their father, he'd have to tell her, wouldn't he? He'd have to tell her and his brother that he'd already given Dr. Black the business plan and been rejected. Then Sam would go be the hero again.

Christ.

Impotent fury—at himself, at his father, at the whole damned situation—tightened into a knot in his gut and threatened to burn him from the inside out. His mood was not improved when Murphy Lanes came into view up ahead, squatting like an ugly concrete gargoyle a few hundred yards from the Country Time, neon bowling pin sign flashing haphazardly alongside the road.

Fuck business as usual, who was Pat Murphy to mess with Hannah's chances of saving the Country Time? If Calvin was right, Pat had probably badmouthed Hannah to the First National lending officers. Who knew what role that had played in their decision to deny her loan?

What if he was causing trouble other places they didn't even know about, yet? If he kept flapping his jaws, Hannah might lose the place that was her home, and with it the people who were her family.

And Deacon would lose his home and family, too, because he was certain his parents' whitewashed mausoleum wasn't home. His father had made it abundantly clear on more than one occasion that Deacon was not considered family.

He clenched the steering wheel so tightly it made his hands hurt.

If the Country Time closed, he'd lose everything.

He'd lose Hannah.

Angrier than he'd been since the day he'd hightailed it out of town at the age of eighteen, Deacon acted on impulse and swung his SUV into the bowling alley's parking lot.

Here was something he could do, he thought. Here was something he could take care of. He could make sure Pat Murphy knew once and for all that if he messed with Hannah, he was messing with Deacon.

Feeling reckless, he had just enough presence of mind to park behind the building, so Hannah wouldn't see his SUV. Then he got out, hitched up his jeans, and swaggered around to the main entrance.

Once inside, he paused to let his eyes adjust to the lower light. The rumble of balls and the crash of pins thundering through the long, low building almost drowned out the pounding bass of classic metal rock coming over the sound system.

Deacon saw a group of college aged kids sprawled over several lanes, whooping and laughing as they pretended to bowl. He doubted very much that the beverage in their large plastic cups was soda. He also doubted most of them were of legal age.

A makeshift bar area was set off to one side, surrounded by hanging drop cloths. The whine of power tools behind the coverings added to the noise and confirmed that Pat really was fixing the place up.

"Help you?" A surly male voice shouted over the din.

Deacon turned and saw Pat Murphy himself sitting in his accustomed place behind the shoe rental counter. The older man's face was a harsh wedge under short blond hair, his body bulked up with muscle, eyes expressionless.

Deacon walked over to him, and they studied each other for a moment across the counter.

"What are you doing here?" Pat asked ungraciously.

"Wanted to talk to you for a minute."

Pat settled back in his chair. It creaked ominously.

"Go ahead."

Deacon leaned forward, arm braced on the scarred Formica.

"I hear you've been spreading some ugly talk around town about Hannah and the Country Time."

Pat didn't move, just watched Deacon with his hard, flat eyes.

"I've been saying nothing but the truth," he said. "Facts are facts."

Deacon's temper heated still more. "I know you were talking to people at First National Bank."

The other man's eyes narrowed. "You do, do you?"

"I think whatever you said to them screwed with Hannah's chances of getting a loan."

Pat shrugged broad shoulders. "Loans are hard to come by. Especially for someone in Hannah's position."

"You're using what happened for your own benefit." Deacon shifted and grabbed the counter, wanting to vault over it and pound Pat's head into the wall. The old, ridged aluminum edging bit into his palms.

"Of course I am," Pat barked out a laugh. "That's business."

Deacon breathed through his teeth. "I know you like spreading rumors, and I think you're taking this thing way beyond business. I'm telling you to stop. Stop badmouthing Hannah. Just stop."

Pat looked at him for a long moment.

"Or?" he asked.

"Or I'll make you." Deacon stared right at him, let him see the truth of the statement.

"Is that a threat, boy?" Pat asked, holding his gaze.

Deacon leaned closer. "No, it's a promise. Lay off Hannah and the Country Time or you'll answer to me."

"Oh, really?"

"Really."

Pat smiled slightly. He didn't appear intimidated. In fact he looked...pleased. "I think you'd better leave now, Deacon."

Deacon pushed away from the counter.

"Fine. I've said all I wanted to say."

Turning, he left the bowling alley and walked around the building to get to his SUV.

He should have felt better. After all, he'd taken a stand and made his position very clear. But now that he'd blown off some of his anger and was thinking more clearly, he remembered Pat's smile and wondered if he'd just made yet another huge mistake.

23

After he'd made it to the Country Time, Deacon threw himself into his work and tried to forget everything that had happened since he'd left Hannah's apartment that morning.

He was not entirely successful, but at least he didn't think Hannah noticed his distraction. She'd been busy solving a crisis with the tents she was renting for the carnival and dealing with reluctant vendors before starting up the grill. For the first time since he'd known her, he was glad they hadn't been able to talk.

The bar was starting to fill up when Police Chief Kline and another younger officer stepped up to the bar.

"Chief." Deacon nodded at Josie's mother, acutely aware that they were the focus of attention of the other patrons at the bar. "Have you tracked down George?" Hannah could use some good news.

"I need to speak to you and Hannah about something, Deacon," Chief Kline said, dark eyes sober.

Uh oh. Deacon straightened, flipping the bar rag he held from hand to hand as he studied the woman.

"This isn't exactly a good time," he said. "Saturday night, you know. We're starting to get busy and Hannah has to handle the grill. Kevin doesn't work tonight."

Chief Kline's expression was kind, but firm.

"I won't keep you long." She glanced around, noting the interested spectators. "We should probably have a little more privacy, too."

Muscles tight, Deacon looked for June, not surprised to see she'd already come behind the bar and was eying the two police officers with unveiled suspicion. He waved her over.

"Hannah and I need to talk to Chief Kline for a few minutes," he told her when she approached. "Can you and Mary Alice hold down the fort?"

"Sure." June's sharp features were hard as she stared at the chief. "You find that worthless piece of shit who stole Hannah's money?" she demanded.

Chief Kline remained calm, although her younger officer shifted uneasily.

"No ma'am," she said.

"Then what's this all about?"

"With all due respect, June, that's between me, Hannah, and Deacon."

Uh oh, Deacon thought again. "Send Hannah back to her office," he told June. Throwing down the rag, he walked around the end of the bar. "Follow me, please."

He'd just gotten them all down the short hallway and into the tiny office when Hannah rushed in behind them, looking flushed and harried and all kinds of beautiful.

"Hi, Chief Kline," she said to Josie's mother.

The chief's expression remained stern, but her eyes softened a little as she stepped back to make room for Hannah to squeeze around her desk in the tight space.

"Why don't I wait outside, Chief?" the younger officer asked.

The chief nodded. "Good idea, Harry. Thanks."

Harry left. Deacon immediately shifted so he was standing closer to Hannah, aligning himself with her against whatever news Chief Kline had come to deliver.

"Did you find Uncle George?" Hannah looked hopeful. Chief Kline sighed.

"No. I need—"

"Then why are you here?" Hannah removed her kitchen ball cap and fiddled with the rim.

"I'm trying to tell you," the other woman said calmly.

"Oh." Hannah threw the cap on the desk and sat in her chair. "Sorry. I get nervous when the cops show up."

"Most people do." Chief Kline dropped into the visitor chair on the opposite side of the desk and sighed. "Hannah. Deacon," she said. "You two have gotten yourselves into one hell of a mess."

Hannah stiffened. "You said you hadn't found George."

"We haven't." The older woman cleared her throat. "Pat Murphy came in to see me. He wants to file a complaint against Deacon and the Country Time for harassment."

Shit, Deacon thought.

Hannah's mouth opened, closed, and opened again.

"Excuse me?" she squeaked.

Chief Kline pulled out a small notebook and flipped through the pages, then paused to read her notes.

"He said, and I quote here, that he's been the victim of threats and feels intimated."

Hannah jumped to her feet, slapped her hands down on her desk, and leaned forward. "What kind of bullshit is this?"

Unperturbed, Chief Kline continued to read her notes. "Apparently Deacon went to see Pat earlier today and had a little conversation with him."

Hannah went very still, then slowly turned to face Deacon.

"Deacon?" she said quietly.

Shit, he thought again.

"Pat's been spreading some ugly rumors about you and the Country Time, Hannah," he said. "I went to tell him it needs to stop."

"And did you threaten him?" she asked, still quietly.

His spine stiffened. "I was just being clear."

Chief Kline had been watching their byplay with sharp-eyed interest. "Pat also wanted to file a restraining order against Deacon and all employees of the Country Time," she said. "I talked him out of that and out of filing a formal complaint, but he only agreed because I told him I'd make sure you knew to cease and desist from any and all similar actions. So that's what I'm saying."

"What about Pat?" Deacon demanded. "Are you going to tell him to cease and desist, too? The rumors he's spreading are really screwing with Hannah's business."

"There's no law against gossiping, as long as it doesn't turn into slander," Chief Kline pointed out calmly.

"He is—"

"No," the chief said. "He's speculating on known facts and offering opinions. You threatened him physically, Deacon."

"You threatened him physically?" Hannah squawked. "Are you out of your damned mind?"

Deacon glared at her impatiently. "What? Am I supposed sit back and watch him put you out of business? So yeah, maybe I told him he'd have to deal with me if he didn't stop."

"Oh, my God!" Hannah clenched her hands in her hair.

"I didn't just hear that," Chief Kline said to no one in partic-ular. She pushed to her feet and adjusted her gun belt. "That's all I had to say. I'll let you two get back to work. And Deacon?"

Deacon looked at her, struggling to remain impassive. "Yes, ma'am?"

"Don't talk to Pat again. Don't go anywhere near him, you hear?"

Deacon nodded. "I hear."

Chief Kline studied him for a moment, then let out a deep breath.

"Off the record, I think he's acting like an asshole, too. But I'm not sure I'll be able to talk him out of filing formal charges a second time."

"Don't worry," Hannah said before Deacon could speak. "We'll stay out of his way."

Chief Kline continued to look at Deacon.

"Deacon?" she prodded.

Deacon nodded and forced a little smile.

"Don't worry," he confirmed.

The chief nodded and turned to go. "See you remember that." She left the office, closing the door softly behind her.

Deacon turned to find Hannah watching him. For a moment they looked at each other in silence.

"What the hell, Deacon," she said at last. "What the hell?" Her voice was calm, but he could see she was furious.

"I was angry," he said, trying to explain. "He's been spreading rumors again, just like he did with June. I'm pretty sure he talked to the PFNB people and screwed up your loan."

"And you thought threatening him would help? Are you stupid?"

He jerked, felt the blow as if she'd punched him in the gut.

"I'm not stupid," he said through clenched teeth. "I had no intention of going to see Pat when I left you this morning. It just happened."

"Just happened. Right. So I guess you left me early this morning to go grocery shopping and decided to see Pat when you were in the frozen food aisle. Jesus."

He wanted to argue, but couldn't bring himself to tell her about his real errand. She was angry enough as it was.

When he remained silent, she laced her fingers behind her head and paced to the other side of the office, staring out the little window.

"God, Deacon, don't you know you've made things worse? Now Pat's going to go out of his way to make my life a living hell."

He shook his head to deny the accusation, although he was afraid she might be right.

"Pat had his fun reporting me to Chief Kline," he said. "He'll get over it."

"Pat never gets over anything and he already didn't like me much." Hannah dropped her hands and turned to face him again. "Okay, if you didn't plan this, why didn't you tell me about it when you came in to work?"

Deacon shrugged helplessly. "You were busy, and I thought I'd taken care of it."

He saw her expression close up tight and knew at once he'd said the wrong thing.

"You had no right to take care of anything without checking with me first," Hannah said icily. "This is my business and you went behind my back. If Chief Kline hadn't talked Pat out of filing formal charges, I would have had a real problem."

"I was trying to help." Couldn't she see that?

"But I'm in charge. If you can't accept that, then..." She stopped abruptly and drew in a deep, shuddering breath. "Well. Then."

Then she would tell him to leave.

He absorbed that blow, too, knowing he deserved it, refusing to look away from her. "I know you're in charge. I was trying to help, that's all, not take over. I can't tell you how sorry I am."

Hannah nodded. She ran her hands down her face and sighed, sounding beyond tired. "This is what I was afraid would happen if we got involved. It makes everything more complicated." Her smile was ghastly.

"Hannah." He took a step towards her, but stopped when she held up a hand. "Look, I screwed up," he said, almost desperately. He could feel her pulling away from him, retreating behind the walls he'd thought he'd knocked down. "I was wrong. I know it. I swear I was only trying to help. I should never have talked to Pat."

But she was shaking her head from side to side. "I just...I can't do this now. I need to think."

"Hannah—"

"No." She shifted, met his eyes. "You should get back to the bar."

Deacon recognized her "boss" voice. She'd never used it on him before. Billy, Grace, even Mary Alice and Kevin. But not him.

"Hannah—"

"Go, Deacon." She'd pulled herself up straight. He could almost see the armor plating wrapped around her body.

He wanted to fight, argue, shout, but that would only make things worse. So he nodded his head in affirmation and left the office, an empty pit inside him growing with each step he took away from her.

He'd wanted to do something to help, but now she thought he didn't understand she was the boss in this situation. She might even think he was trying to use their new intimacy to gain control.

And her response was to shove him away. To take a step back.

He could understand that, even sympathize with it. Too bad he hadn't thought about it earlier and kept his fucking mouth shut.

She thought he was stupid.

She was right.

For the rest of his shift, Deacon busied himself with the regular Saturday night crowd. When he was shutting down after they'd closed, he waited to see if Hannah would invite him back to her apartment.

She didn't.

24

Hannah hadn't asked too many questions when, true to his word, Sam had pulled whatever strings he'd needed to pull and gotten the appropriate permits from the town council for the carnival. She only cared that The First Ever Country Time Bar and Grill Carnival was able to open for business right on schedule and that Saturday had dawned bright and clear, without a cloud in the sky.

She ought to know—she'd been awake to see that dawn and was still going strong as the day drifted into late afternoon.

Well, maybe "strong" wasn't quite the right word. Maybe "upright" was more accurate.

Honestly, between last-minute arrangements, crises of various kinds, supervising Chuckie Scanlon's installation of equipment on Mr. Clark's field, applying for more bank loans, and keeping up with day-to-day business operations, she figured she'd gotten a total of eight hours of sleep in the last week.

See? She'd been busy. Her restlessness had nothing at all to do with Deacon.

Sighing, she slumped against the Country Time's old brick

facade and looked out at the rides, tents, and people. The carnival had been gratifyingly busy ever since they'd opened at noon. Pat Murphy had put a "no parking" sign in his lot, but otherwise left them alone, once his attempt at blocking the permits failed.

Word of mouth, as well as the ads they'd placed in *The Hardy Falls Gazette*, Ms. Gregory's online newspaper, seemed to have worked; the field was full of people.

Roy and his band were already there and would start playing later. The breeze was warm, the customers were happy, the rides were whirring, the food and drink were being consumed. She hadn't checked with June at the refreshment ticket table or Mary Alice and Grace at the gate in the last hour or so, but she imagined sales remained brisk.

So far, the carnival had been a rousing success and showed every sign of repeating the performance on Sunday. Indications were she'd pull in enough money to pay Chuckie and the vendors and still make a profit. She should be feeling relieved. Triumphant even.

Instead, she felt like crap.

Hannah let her gaze track across the milling throngs of people to an open-sided tent canopy on the far side of the parking lot at the edge of Mr. Clark's field. From where she stood, she could see Deacon and Jason under it, working opposite ends of the temporary bar they'd set up for the occasion.

Deacon was smiling and chatting, filling drink orders and schmoozing with the customers, moving competently from task to task. If she'd been closer, she could have seen how the blue of his Country Time polo shirt intensified the color of his eyes, as it always did.

But she hadn't really been close to Deacon for days, had she? They hadn't made love. She hadn't invited him back to her apartment. He still worked, still did his job, helped her, even supported her, but it hadn't been the same. There was a line between them now. Or maybe a moat.

Or maybe an ocean.

Her fault, Hannah admitted and closed her eyes. She'd slapped him back hard. Had she overreacted?

No, she assured herself. She'd been entitled to be pissed off at him. He'd gone behind her back and caused an incident that could have really impacted her business. She'd had a right to feel angry.

And hurt.

And betrayed.

She sighed again and opened her eyes to watch Deacon move behind the bar. He smiled at one of the regular bowling league guys and handed him a beer from the big keg.

God, she missed him.

She was sure that somewhere deep inside that complicated male brain of his, he'd thought confronting Pat was a good idea. She believed him when he said he'd only been trying to help and hadn't meant to push her aside. His apology had been sincere.

But the fact remained that he *had* pushed her aside, intentionally or no.

Still, if it had been anyone else, she would have confronted them by now and hashed things out one way or the other. Why hadn't she done that with Deacon? Why had she continued to keep him at a distance?

She was afraid.

Hannah ran her hands through her hair, then dropped them, the sounds of the carnival blurring to background noise.

This wasn't all her fault, she told herself. There were two people in this relationship, weren't there? Deacon hadn't made much of an effort to talk to her either, had he? Okay, yes, he'd tried to explain himself once or twice, but when she'd shut him down, he'd just backed off. Of course, she would have gotten even angrier if he'd tried to force the issue.

Was she pushing him out of her life?

Was that what she wanted?

Hannah drew in air.

No.

A new surge of energy flowed into her, and she shoved away from the building, hands fisted at her sides.

No. She didn't want to push Deacon away.

She chewed on her bottom lip, thinking.

Okay, so here was what she'd do. She'd start by, casually, checking on the bar and actually talking to the man. After the insanity of the carnival was over and she was basking in newfound, if temporary, solvency, she'd get Deacon alone somewhere and they'd have it out. All of it. Then, no matter what happened, she would at least know she'd tried.

Feeling better than she had in days, Hannah set off down the hill towards the tent and the bar. And Deacon.

Deacon made small talk and served drinks at one end of the long, makeshift bar while Jason worked and flirted with college girls at the opposite end. The tent canopy overhead had protected them from the worst of the sun, the open sides allowing a nice breeze to blow through now and then as the customers drifted in and out.

From where he stood, he could see Kevin busy at a large portable grill, sweating and laughing while two of Grace's sorority sisters took tickets and delivered food to people waiting in line. Billy was missing in action, but the rest of them had been working pretty much nonstop all afternoon. Hannah would be happy.

He smiled at Bernie Housemann and Chet Hinkle, giving

the men cups of beer from the keg in exchange for the appropriate number of tickets, while vaguely responding to their cheerful comments. Once they'd finally moved on, Deacon stretched his neck and rubbed his shoulder, wishing he could sit down for one damn minute.

What with his crazy work schedule and missing the hell out of Hannah the past couple of nights, he hadn't gotten much sleep.

After the carnival, he'd try to talk to her again, apologize again. He'd make her to listen to him this time.

An elderly woman came up to the bar and was delighted to find she could get a gin and tonic instead of beer. He made her the drink and handed it over in a plastic cup, watching her toddle off towards the tables set up under another tent canopy between the bar and the grill.

The problem was, he thought, Hannah seemed to have put him firmly back in employee territory and he wasn't sure what do to about it. There was a wall between them now, one he couldn't seem to break through. Had his stupidity ruined everything? Thank God she didn't know he'd gone to see his father, too.

Someone called for attention and Deacon turned, grinning when he recognized Albert's friends, Martin Scanner and Joe Horton.

Joking with the old men, he got them each a bottle of beer from the ice chest and they headed off to the tables, obviously scoping out the woman with the gin and tonic. Albert had come with Ms. Gregory, so maybe his friends were jealous and wanted a little action.

Deacon wasn't sure if he found it comforting or appalling to know the mating instinct was still going strong in Albert and his cronies.

Turning, he caught a glimpse of Hannah, leaning against

the side of the Country Time, motionless for the first time in days.

He shifted. Well, *his* mating instinct was sure going strong. It was just extremely target-specific.

Sighing, he waited on more customers.

He didn't blame Hannah for being angry with him. Hell, he was angry with himself. It had been a completely boneheaded move for him to confront Pat. What he couldn't understand was why she wouldn't cut him any slack, wouldn't even talk to him. Didn't she want to work it out?

Deacon realized he was mixing rum with club soda instead of whiskey. He threw the drink away and started over, managing to do it correctly this time. After giving the customer their requested whiskey and soda, he just stood and breathed for a few seconds.

What would he do if she decided they were over?

Fight, he realized, bending over to grab some more napkins from under the bar. He wouldn't give up without a fight.

"Hey."

Deacon looked up, jerked out of his thoughts by an unexpected gruff male voice. Incredulous, he gaped at the man standing on the other side of the bar. Holy God, it was Mateo Guerrero, his friend from the oil rigs. True, he hadn't heard from the guy in months, but he'd expected an email, not a visit.

"Mat?"

The other man smiled and shrugged. "Surprise."

Deacon found himself grinning like an idiot and stood, holding out his hand with real pleasure. "Damn, it's good to see you."

"Right back atcha," Mat Guerrero's smile broadened, his teeth white against the dark stubble of beard. He took the offered hand and yanked Deacon close enough to slap him enthusiastically on the shoulder several times before shoving him back. "Fuck, it's been too damned long."

"You can say that again."

Still somewhat shocked, Deacon studied his friend. When they'd worked together on the oil rig, Mat Guerrero had been big and healthy, muscles bulging on his large frame.

Now his skin seemed stretched too tightly over his bones, his dark eyes sunken and red-rimmed, his face etched with deep lines. Even his black hair was liberally sprinkled with strands of silver.

In short, he looked like shit.

"What the hell are you doing here?" he asked, concerned now.

Mateo shrugged again and looked out over the crowd.

"Sounds like a nice town whenever you talk about it. Lots of trees and mountains and crap. Thought I'd finally come see it."

"Right." And that was a load of horseshit. "I don't—damn, hold on." He left to take orders from a group of college kids who'd crowded up to the bar, carefully checking IDs before handing over the beers.

"Always a boy scout." Mateo shook his head sadly when Deacon came back to him. "I thought I broke you of that years ago."

"You tried." Deacon wiped his hands on a bar rag and tucked it back in his belt. "Come on, man, seriously. What's up? I'm glad to see you and all, but I haven't even gotten an email from you in months."

"Sorry." Mateo shoved his hands in his pockets and looked down at his feet in their big, scuffed boots. "Things...happened."

Deacon was interrupted again by a man further down the bar. "Shit. Hold on." He waited on the customer and came back.

"Is Gail with you?" he asked quietly, because he thought he might have an idea what this was all about. Mateo was here, but where was the beautiful schoolteacher?

Mat shook his head, lips twisting. "We're done."

Well, that explained a lot. Deacon pushed a bottle of beer over to him. "Sorry, man."

Mat jerked his shoulder and picked up the beer. Taking a sip, he settled down on one of the stools set up for people who preferred the bar to the tables.

"I knew you'd been working here, but I wasn't sure if you'd still be around," he said. "It's just after things...after Gail..., I guess I had itchy feet. I wanted to see someplace I'd never been, get away from where I was. I figured I'd take a shot you hadn't moved on, yet. When I got into town yesterday, people were all worked up about this carnival deal." He looked around. "Sure is something."

"It's something, all right." Deacon pulled some beer for himself off the keg and tapped his plastic cup against Mateo's bottle. "I'm glad you came," he said, meaning it. "It's really fucking good to see you again."

Mateo shifted on the barstool obviously uncomfortable. "Jesus, don't get all emotional on me." He drank deeply, then gestured with his chin. "Should we worry about that old guy over there? He's gonna give himself a heart attack."

Deacon looked to the open area they'd left for a dance floor and saw Old Albert doing the "Chicken Dance" to the country music blasting out of the speakers. Some kids were hooting and laughing and cheering him on as he waggled his arms and moved his head back and forth, but Deacon noticed Ms. Gregory standing a few feet away, arms crossed, looking severe. He had the feeling Albert would be flying solo before the evening was over.

"What can I say?" he said, turning back to Mateo. "Carnivals get him going."

"I'll say." Mateo raised his eyebrows when Albert executed a particularly enthusiastic dance move. "Whoa."

Deacon laughed and Hannah walked up to the bar.

25

Deacon straightened away from the bar, Hannah's presence like a kick in his gut.

"Hi," he said.

"Deacon." Her smile was slight, but there was a spark in her eyes he hadn't seen for days. She glanced at Mateo. "Sorry, I didn't mean to interrupt."

"No problem. This is Mateo Guerrero." Deacon nodded at the other man. "He's an old friend of mine."

She held out her hand to Mateo. "Hi. I'm Hannah Frederickson. I own the Country Time."

Mat returned her smile, his haggard face transforming with unexpected charm.

"The pleasure's all mine," he purred and took her hand.

Hannah blushed.

Deacon snarled, and Mat, the asshole, grinned.

Fortunately, for the other man's health, he let go of Hannah's hand to gesture around at the carnival. "You've got a wonderful event going on here," he said sincerely.

"Thanks." Her face lit up.

"Did you want something, Hannah?" Deacon asked

abruptly, his tone sharper than he'd intended. She looked at him with some surprise.

"I just wanted to see how things were going."

"Oh." He cursed himself for acting like a jealous dick. Out of the corner of his eye, he saw the humor in Mateo's face fade to sympathy.

"Hey, I can clear out," his friend offered. "I'll catch up with Deacon later."

"No, no." Hannah's hands fluttered. "It's fine. Totally. I can see for myself that everything's...fine."

Hmmm.

Deacon studied her. She wore her bland business-owner expression, but underneath it he thought he sensed a fine tension. Was Hannah...nervous?

"Jason can watch the bar for a few minutes while we review things," he offered casually, resisting the urge to leap over the bar and grab her.

"Well—"

"Hi, Hannah! Hi, Deacon!"

Deacon bit back an oath when he saw Mary Alice coming towards them, rumpled in her Country Time polo shirt and holding hands with a lean, dark-haired man who looked at her as if she'd made the sun rise that morning. The infamous Johnny, no doubt. Deacon didn't know what the guy's deal was, and didn't much care, but liked him immediately just for the way he was watching Mary Alice.

"Hi, Mary Alice," he said when the two got closer. "You look nice."

"Thank you." Mary Alice's radiant face took on deeper color. She pushed a strand of wildly curling hair behind her ear and smiled at the man next to her. "This is Johnny." Her protuberant blue eyes filled with so much devotion, Deacon felt like he was intruding.

"Hey." Deacon waved in greeting.

"It's nice to finally meet you." Johnny waved back. "Mary Alice talks about you all the time."

"Only good things, I hope," Hannah said, shaking the man's hand when he offered it. "What are you guys up to?" she asked Mary Alice.

"Oh!" Mary Alice's face lit with joy. "Johnny and I can't wait to ride the roller coaster. Grace said she'd watch the gate so we could do it while I was on break."

Deacon thought about the portable roller coaster Chuckie's workers had set up in the field the other day.

"You're really going to get on that thing?" he asked, alarmed.

Johnny beamed at Mary Alice. "We're kind of thrill seekers," he told them.

"I'm sure you'll find plenty of thrills riding *that* roller coaster," Hannah said.

"Eh," Johnny shrugged. "Beats the spinning teacups."

Deacon left to wait on more customers. When he got back, Mary Alice was tugging on Johnny's hand.

"We have to get going," she said anxiously. "Grace needs to take a break, too."

"Okay." But Johnny paused and looked at Hannah. "I wanted to thank you for giving Roy and his guys a chance to play here. I know it's not a paid gig, but they'll get exposure and they think they might even pick up some business. This crowd is a lot higher class than the one they're used to."

Deacon figured most crowds would be.

"I'm glad," Hannah said and patted Johnny's arm. "They were good when we went to listen to them."

"They're really jazzed about the whole thing," the other man said. "And the best part is, they're so worried about making a good impression they won't drink as much as they usually do. They'll be fine."

"Wait. What does that mean?" Hannah held up her hand.

"Oh, when they get drunk they play an extended dance version of 'In-A-Gadda-Da-Vida,'" Mary Alice said.

"They love Iron Butterfly," Johnny agreed. "But it does tend to annoy the customers."

"I think it's cute," Mary Alice said, elbowing her boyfriend in the ribs. She looked at Hannah. "Johnny told me that Animal, the drummer, really blisses out. Sometimes he refuses to stop playing, even after the bar closes."

Hannah gaped at her.

"I'll keep an eye on them," Johnny promised, apparently sensing Hannah's distress. "No worries."

"Come on, Johnny." Mary Alice tugged at him again. "There might be a line."

Johnny agreed, they said their goodbyes, and strolled off hand in hand.

Hannah, eyes wide, turned to Deacon.

"Deacon—"

"It will be fine," he assured her, although he honestly wasn't sure. Mateo, still seated at the bar, shook with silent laughter.

"But the band drinks for free," Hannah wailed.

"And they've been taking advantage of it," Deacon admitted, trying to remember what they'd already gotten. "I'll make sure they don't get served any more alcohol. At least not until after they're finished playing. I gave them a round of beer already. No, make that two." He frowned. "Possibly three. But it will be okay. I'll make sure Jason knows."

"How long was the original 'In-A-Gadda-Da-Vida' anyway?" Hannah wondered.

Deacon frowned. Iron Butterfly had been popular well before his time.

"Maybe fifteen or twenty minutes?" he said.

"How long would an extended dance version be?" Mateo wondered.

Hannah turned to the other end of the bar. "Jason!" she shouted.

The young bartender looked up from flirting with a college girl and jogged over to her.

"Yeah, boss?"

"No more alcohol for the band until they're finished playing," Hannah instructed.

"Okay." Jason looked worried. "But that drummer Animal just came in and got a rum and coke. You don't want me to go try to get it back, do you?"

Since Jason was approximately five foot ten and Animal was the size of a house, Deacon had a pretty good idea of how *that* would go.

"No, just don't give them any more. I'll tell them so they won't get mad."

"Okay." Jason sounded relieved and returned to the other end of the bar.

"Hannah," Deacon said, "look—"

"Hi, Hannah. Deacon." Roy walked up to the bar, apparently still sober. "I don't suppose you could spare another round for the band?"

"No," Hannah said.

"I have to cut you guys off for a while, Roy," Deacon said, more diplomatically. "We're running a little low on booze, so I want to save it for the paying customers."

Roy's eyes got almost as big as Mary Alice's.

"Running low? Oh, man, I had no idea you guys were in such bad shape. We're good for a while." He hesitated. "Um, do you think we'll be able to get another round later, though?"

"After you play," Deacon promised. "A round of whatever you want. On me."

Roy beamed. "Thanks, bro. I'll tell the rest of the guys." He waved and left.

"The real thrill will be seeing if we get through the evening without Iron Butterfly," Deacon muttered.

Hannah pointed at him. "Exactly!"

They smiled at each other and Deacon relaxed a little more.

"Deacon—" Hannah began.

"Hey." Billy walked up to the bar and sat on a stool. The bandana they insisted he wear when he worked had come loose and several strands of limp brown hair were hanging around his face.

Hannah frowned at the young man. "It's not time for your break yet."

"Yeah, see, it's like this." Billy scratched his ear. "I kind of quit an hour ago."

She blinked at him. "What?"

"I quit an hour ago. Then I realized I forgot to tell you. So, I figured I should, you know, do that."

Deacon had to leave to wait on a customer. When he got back, Hannah was all up in the kid's face.

"What the hell do you mean you quit an hour ago?" she demanded.

Billy shrugged. "I'm joining the carnival."

"And you can't wait until Monday?" she shouted.

Frankly, Deacon wasn't sure why she was upset. It wasn't like Billy was adding any value to the proceedings.

"No, see, Mr. Scanlon says I can empty the trashcans over there this weekend. And they're gonna teach me how to set up and tear down the rides."

"You're supposed to empty *our* trash cans!" Hannah looked like she was going to punch him in the face. Deacon shifted, ready to intervene if necessary.

Billy, the idiot, just shrugged again instead of running away. "No can do, Hannah. I work for the carnival now. Mr. Scanlon said someone would take care of the trash on this side."

"Yeah, and that would be *you*, you shit!"

Apparently Billy did have some sense of self-preservation after all, because when she made a move like she would grab his T-shirt, he jumped off the stool and backed away, dirty hands raised.

"Sorry, Hannah. Um, you can send the pay you owe me to Ma. She'll know where I am. Maybe I'll, like, see you around." He turned and beat a hasty retreat.

"Yeah, you'd better run, you asshole!" Hannah yelled after him. "What?" she demanded of the people staring at her and, with a snarl, dropped onto a seat. "I cannot believe that little bastard! After everything I did for him."

"Maybe you should have fired him," Deacon said, unable to resist.

"Oh, just shut up." She dropped her chin on her fist.

"Is it really that big a loss?" Mateo propped his arm on the bar. "Not to be rude, but I've been in latrines cleaner than that kid."

"I guess it's not," Hannah admitted, even as she sighed. "Except who's going to do his job for the rest of this weekend? I'll handle what I can, but I have to help Kevin with the food and keep an eye on everything."

She did have a point. Deacon rubbed the back of his neck, thinking. "I'd offer to take over, but the bar's been busy. Maybe we can rotate?"

"What was his job?" Mateo asked.

"Mostly he was just supposed help out where he could," Hannah told him. "Make sure everyone had supplies, take anything that needed washing into the dishwasher, empty trash cans, pick up bottles, that sort of thing."

Mateo lifted his shoulders. "I could do that."

She said grimaced. "It's going to be pretty nasty. I never gave Billy work that required...personality."

"Not a problem," Mateo assured her. "You don't want to know some of the things I've had to do in my life."

Truer words, Deacon thought, had never been spoken.

Hannah studied the other man for a moment, then nodded. "Okay," she said. "We sure could use you. I don't think Grace's sorority sisters are up for emptying trash cans. How about I pay you what I would have paid Billy?"

"Fair enough." Mat smiled.

"You'd better get going," Deacon told Hannah. "Kevin's got a long line for food." He was glad Mat would be helping out, but he wasn't exactly thrilled by all of the smiling going on.

"Oh, crap." Hannah looked over to the food station and got hastily to her feet. "You'll be able to figure out what you need to do?" she asked Mateo.

The other man rolled his shoulders as if preparing for battle. "No problem. Deacon will give me the 411, right?"

Deacon grinned slyly. "I think the garbage first. Billy wasn't exactly keeping up with it."

This time Mateo rolled his eyes. "Great."

"You asked for it." Laughing, Hannah headed towards the cook tent to help Kevin.

Deacon watched her go.

26

Hannah jogged to the food prep area, patted Kevin on a massive shoulder to let him know she was there, then went over to a stack of linens and quickly pulled on an apron. Kevin smiled at her as he plated burgers and passed them off to one of the college kids serving customers at the counter.

"We're pretty busy, boss lady," he said, turning back to the grill. "The people are hungry."

"I meant to help sooner, but I got held up." Hannah stuffed her hair in a ball cap. "Billy quit."

Kevin turned to her, the spatula he held in one large hand dripping grease onto his apron. "He quit? Now?"

She nodded and slipped behind him to grab a pack of hotdogs from the little refrigerator they'd brought outside for the occasion. "Apparently he quit an hour ago. But he "forgot" to tell me until now."

"Huh." Kevin thought about that for a moment, then shook his head. "I saw you yelling at him, but I did not know why. You should not be upset—it is not as though we will miss him too much."

"I guess not." Hannah opened the hotdogs and started

arranging them on the roller grill. "He's joining the carnival. They're going to teach him to set up and tear down the rides."

Kevin stared at her, then burst out laughing. "I wish them good luck with that," he said, and, still chuckling, went back to the burgers.

Hannah started laughing, too. Kevin was right, she thought. Good luck, Chuckie Scanlon.

For a while, time flew by in a parade of wings, meat, dogs, and buns. She and Kevin fell into their accustomed rhythm, working in relative silence until the line of customers waiting for food finally dwindled.

"Why don't you take a break," she told Kevin, twisting to stretch out her back. "Take a walk. Eat something. I've got this covered and you've been here for hours."

He flipped burgers, then cocked his eyebrows at her. "You sure?"

"Yeah. Better go now. It'll get busy again once the band starts playing." She hoped.

He grinned at her. "Okay, I will. I very much want to see this roller coaster I hear so much about."

Hannah sighed. "Not you, too."

"Sure! I might even ride it, since our Billy did not set it up. It will be something to tell my wife and children, no?" He laughed as he handed a plate to one of the sorority sisters, then took off his apron and walked away, whistling. Hannah thought the song was "We're Coming to America," but she couldn't be certain.

Kevin was an interesting man.

Mateo came through to see if she needed anything and she sent him up to the Country Time for more supplies. He was back in a few minutes with everything she'd asked for, replenishing the stock without being reminded. Then, he headed off to work the bar so Jason could take a break.

Hannah watched him go. She noticed the college girls were watching, too.

By the time Kevin returned, the sun was setting in a glorious burst of reds and oranges. Someone—probably Deacon—had switched on the temporary lighting they'd set up, so the parking lot and adjoining field glowed bright against the backdrop of deepening autumn twilight. Little white lights twinkled in the canopies and booths and around the makeshift stage Deacon and Jason had banged together earlier in the week.

All in all, the place looked pretty damned good.

Kevin, still whistling, tied on his apron and stepped back up to the grill, jostling her away with a grin. Hannah was about to ask him if he'd braved the roller coaster when the country music booming through the sound system cut off abruptly and Roy and his band climbed onto the stage. Roy strapped on his guitar and grabbed a microphone.

"Hello, everyone," he called, his voice ringing through the speakers. "We're the Bounty Hunters!"

Hannah didn't think that had been the name of the group when she'd seen them at the Wounded Sparrow. In fact, she wasn't entirely sure they'd had a name then.

"We're happy to be here!" Roy yelled.

Nobody seemed to care.

Roy looked crestfallen.

Great, Hannah thought. Freaking great.

"So, um, I guess we'll play now," he said, not quite as loudly.

Nobody noticed.

Roy and the band went into a huddle.

"I think they are going to run away," Kevin observed.

Hannah thought he might be right. It was a pleasant surprise when Roy turned back to the microphone and squared his narrow shoulders.

"We're gonna play a song now," he yelled defiantly.

Atta boy, Roy, she thought. *Go get 'em, tiger.*

The band launched into a surprisingly rollicking version of "Twist and Shout." To Hannah's relief, some people in the crowd drifted their way, and a few minutes later a few were actually dancing. Roy's face lit with new confidence as he attempted a complicated guitar riff. The crowd was not critical and more dancers began to move.

"See?" Kevin yelled over at her. "Everything works out."

Hannah sure hoped so.

She got back to work chopping up more lettuce and tomatoes for toppings. Soon her hips were shifting to the beat of the music, her mind wandering as she worried about inventory and made plans for the next day.

She didn't want to desert Kevin, but she really needed to check the rest of the stations and make sure things were still running smoothly. June and Deacon would be on top of things, but she wanted to touch base with everyone, especially Mary Alice and Grace at the gate, and she should probably talk to Chuckie Scanlon to see how things were going in the carnival proper. Should she mention his new employee? Or wait and see if he brought it up? And maybe she could get Mateo to come over and help Kevin on the grill so she...

Her rambling thoughts trailed off when she realized the band had shifted to a slow set. They were playing "Unchained Melody," and the sound of Roy's wobbling voice brought back vivid memories of the Wounded Sparrow.

Deacon holding her against him as they danced. His strength. His scent.

His taste.

Hannah shook her head to clear it.

After the carnival, she promised herself. They'd talk and get things—

"Hannah."

Hannah jumped when a deep voice spoke unexpectedly on her left.

Wrong brother.

"What are you doing here?" she asked Sam, then scowled at Kevin when she caught him watching them.

Kevin grinned.

"I need a minute," Sam said, shoving his hands into the pockets of his khaki trousers.

"Busy here." She wiped the sweat from her forehead with the back of her wrist before pulling the next batch of fries out of the fryer.

"Please," Sam said.

Still holding the fry basket, she turned to gape at him. "What did you say?" She hadn't thought the "p" word was in Samuel Black's vocabulary.

He shifted. "I said please. There's someone here who wants to talk to you."

Hannah put the fries back in the oil and considered him. For the first time in all the years she'd known him, Sam seemed almost...uncomfortable. What the hell was going on?

She exchanged another look with Kevin and the big man rolled his shoulders in a shrug.

"Might as well go," he said. "Things be good here and you deserve a break anyway, eh? Tiffany and Janice and I will handle this, yes girls?" He grinned roguishly at the two college student volunteers, and they tittered in response.

"It'll just take a few minutes," Sam assured her.

"God, okay." Hannah stripped off her gloves, soiled apron, and ball cap before turning back to him. "Who is it?" she demanded.

He didn't answer, just led her away from the grill. They headed to one of the tables where Hannah was surprised to see Sam's father sitting and watching the band with obvious disinterest.

"Dr. Black?" she asked, trying to figure out why he was there.

Dr. Black turned to frown at her.

"Hannah. I'd like to talk to you for a moment, if you'd be so good."

"Um, sure?" Hannah said, even more confused.

"Father? What are you doing here?"

Hannah saw Deacon striding up to the table, his frown every bit as thunderous as his father's.

Dr. Black merely raised his eyebrows at his younger son. "Aren't I allowed to patronize this establishment?" he asked.

"Of course." Hannah jumped in before the conversation could disintegrate further. "Did you need something?" she asked Deacon.

He glared at her. "Jason's back so I'm taking a break." He bit off the words. "I was going to ask you to dance."

"Father was hoping he could talk to Hannah," Sam put in quickly. "Is there anywhere we can go that's a little more private?"

Hannah saw the rigid set of Deacon's shoulders as he crossed his arms.

"This really isn't a good time," she said to Sam.

"I know." He ran a hand through his hair, rumpling it. "I mean, obviously you're busy, but—"

"I wanted to reach out to you now," Dr. Black said. He fiddled with the seam on his perfectly pressed eggshell trousers, then folded his hands in his lap again. "I prefer to initiate these sorts of discussions in person as soon as I've made the decision to be proactive in my pursuit of an opportunity. As I was here to observe your handling of the carnival anyway, it seemed the best time. I'm a busy man, after all."

"What?" Hannah asked, totally lost. "What are you talking about? Sam?"

Sam looked distinctly frazzled now.

"If we could just go somewhere more private for a few minutes," he said again. "Then you and Father can talk and we'll get out of your hair."

Hannah saw Bernie and Chet watching them with avid interest. They were attracting quite a lot of attention from people sitting at the other tables, as well. Great. Just great.

"Come with me." Turning, she marched off toward the Country Time. Deacon, Sam, and an elegantly unruffled Dr. Black, followed.

She led them through the building to the break area set up out back, the color and noise of the carnival fading under the harsh light of the ancient floodlights. Coming to a stop, she faced the men and crossed her arms over her chest.

"Okay, now we're more private," she told Sam and his father. "What's going on?"

Deacon shifted closer to her; close enough that she could feel the heat radiating from his body as he wordlessly allied himself with her.

Dr. Black, hands in the pockets of his linen trousers, glanced toward the overflowing dumpster at the other end of the building. His thin-lipped mouth curled into a sneer of disgust.

"Lovely."

Hannah shrugged. "It's private. Please explain what you were talking about, Dr. Black."

The older man met her eyes, his own an icy blue.

"Very well. I shall start at the beginning. I contacted Sam after I spent time contemplating a few interesting points Deacon made when he came to see me last Saturday."

Hannah stared at him. "Wait, what?" Deacon had gone to visit his father? Why hadn't he told her?

Deacon went very still beside her.

"He mentioned that you were looking for investors and asked if I would consider becoming one," Dr. Black continued.

"Naturally, I knew he didn't understand what he was talking about, so I discussed the matter with Sam."

The night hung suspended for one humming second.

"He said what?" Hannah asked quietly, certain she'd misunderstood.

"Apparently Deacon went to Father to see if he'd be interested in investing in your business," Sam said. He shrugged. "It's actually a pretty good idea."

Hannah dropped her hands to her sides and stepped away from Deacon, shifting so she could see him better. He was glaring at his father, his jaw so rigid it resembled a blade.

"Deacon?" she asked, even more softly. "Is this true?"

He glanced at her. "Yeah."

"You went to see your father without telling me." Every cell in her body felt empty, as if her blood had drained through the soles of her feet into the broken macadam.

"Yes." There was impatience in Deacon's eyes when he looked at her this time. "You'd been turned down for the bank loan. I figured if we could get a couple of bigger investors, it would give you some options before you applied at other banks. Father enjoys investing in local businesses. It seemed like a good fit."

"Did it." Hannah's head spun. It was one thing for Deacon to go behind her back and confront Pat Murphy about the rumors he was spreading. But this...this seemed worse somehow.

"It really was a good idea," Sam put in. He shut up when she looked at him.

Dr. Black watched them as if they were specimens in his laboratory, an expression of mild annoyance on his face.

"When I spoke to Deacon, it did not appear to be the kind of business opportunity I would wish to pursue," he said calmly. "However, upon further reflection and discussion with Sam regarding certain legal issues, it seemed there might be some merit in the suggestion after all. I reviewed the business plan Deacon left with me and wished to see what kinds of efforts you were making to raise capital. I decided to visit the carnival, and I must say I'm impressed."

"Thanks." Hannah's shock was fading, rapidly replaced by anger.

"There's more," Sam warned. He tugged at the collar of his shirt, then ran a hand through his hair.

"What more?" Hannah demanded. What more could there be?

"As Sam well knows," Dr. Black said, "I like to have control over my investments. Investing in your business would involve a great deal of risk in that I would be putting substantial funds into something over which I'd have no say. This possibility makes me a trifle nervous."

Sam cleared his throat. "Father seems to think you might consider selling him the business."

"He what?" Hannah stared at him. She couldn't have heard him correctly.

"He, um, wants to talk about buying in as a majority partner or just buying you out altogether," Sam said.

"With appropriate protections," Dr. Black added, raising a finger like a stern schoolteacher.

Hannah opened her mouth, then closed it, then opened it again.

"Hey, this wasn't my idea." Sam held up his hands, palms out. "But you might want to think about it. If Father bought you out, you'd have enough money to do whatever you want to do."

"I am not expecting you to make a decision today," Dr. Black said, eying her coolly. "I know perfectly well these things require thought. I only wished to express my interest in exploring the possibility of purchasing your business, assuming we can come to terms, of course. Deacon indicated you would be open to an offer."

"What?" Hannah thought she shrieked the word.

"Bullshit!" Deacon thundered. "No way in hell did I say that to you."

His father studied him with indifference. "I believe you said I should explore the possibility of purchasing the business, did you not?"

"No!" Deacon shouted.

Dr. Black shrugged his shoulders. "That was not my understanding."

"What did you say to him?" Hannah rounded on Deacon, her frayed temper breaking with an almost audible snap. "Did you go to him to sell him my business? What the hell?"

"No," Deacon snarled at her. "I was trying to *help*. Yeah, I went to him to see if he'd be interested in becoming an investor. He started talking about needing control and maybe he should look into buying the place instead. I made some sarcastic remark. It didn't mean anything!"

Hannah stepped back. "Obviously it did."

"Hannah!" He grabbed her arm. "I swear to you. I wasn't trying to sell your goddamned business."

Hannah was sick of this, sick of them all, sick of everything. She shrugged Deacon's hand off her arm.

"Right," she snapped. "*My* goddamned business. *Mine*. Not yours. You ran off to talk to your father and Pat Murphy without even talking to me, without asking me what *I* wanted to do." She rubbed her hands over her face. "Maybe I'll want to sell to your father," she said more quietly. "Maybe I won't. But the decision will be mine to make. *Mine*."

Deacon held himself very still, his face so closed only his eyes seemed alive.

"You don't believe me," he said.

Hannah sighed, suddenly tired. "I don't know what I believe."

"I thought we were partners."

She looked at him, at the hard face and the strong body.

"So did I," she said. She glanced at Dr. Black. "I can't think about this now," she told him.

He inclined his head, bald scalp glistening in the reflected light.

"Of course. Perhaps we could set up a meeting."

"Come to the Country Time on Monday. Around five," Hannah said. Without waiting to hear the response, she turned and walked back to the lights and noise and people.

Deacon watched Hannah go, then spun to face his father and brother, fists clenched at his sides, ready to rip them both to shreds. Why had they come now? Why today when she'd just started talking to him again? What the hell were they trying to prove?

"The timing of the offer wasn't ideal, but the idea was sound," Sam said before Deacon could tear into them. "You should have told Hannah you had talked to Father. Given her a heads up."

Abruptly the fierce flare of anger died, leaving Deacon weary beyond measure. Because Sam was right. This was his fault.

He rubbed the back of his neck, let his hand drop.

Yes, he'd wanted to help, to be of use. But he should have discussed his plans with Hannah first. At the very least, he should have told her what he'd done once he'd gone and done it. His stupid pride had kept him quiet.

But she hadn't even let him explain.

"Honestly, when Sam told me you were involved with Hannah Frederickson, I did not believe him," Dr. Black said.

Deacon pulled himself out of his thoughts to see his father

contemplating him as if he were a particularly disappointing lab rat.

"Whatever." His father's opinion really didn't matter.

Dr. Black shook his head. "It's always a mistake when management gets involved with the rank and file. These circumstances do not reflect well on Hannah's judgment. She would have been better off seeking attachment with another professional. Her relationship with Sam was much more acceptable."

Sam shifted, but didn't say anything.

Deacon drew in a deep breath and let it out slowly.

"I have to get back to the bar," he said, needing to be away from both of them. He turned to go, but then looked back. "Don't worry about Hannah's judgment," he told his father. "It's fine. In fact, it's a lot better than yours."

Dr. Black drew in a sharp, insulted breath. "Well, really."

"Yeah. Really." Deacon caught Sam's eye and cursed under his breath. "What?" he demanded. His brother was not smiling or smirking. In fact, he was watching Deacon with a sober, almost haunted look.

"Talk to her," he said.

It was the last straw. Deacon just shook his head and left.

Back at the bar, he tried to avoid Mateo's and Jason's questions, finally getting rid of them with a few harsh words. Through the crowd, he saw June watching him, but thank Christ she was too busy to come over. Hannah was nowhere in sight.

Deacon moved mechanically from one task to the next until the familiar routine soothed him enough that he could think again.

He knew once she'd calmed down, he'd be able to convince Hannah there was no way in hell he had actually tried to sell her business behind her back, even if it had been possible. She knew him well enough to believe that much.

Still, her first response had been to shove him away again.

Deacon considered the matter as he mixed drinks, pulled beer from the taps, handed over bottles, collected tickets, and smiled without really hearing what was said.

So. He could stay or he could go.

He'd screwed up because he'd wanted to play the hero. He could talk to her, explain, grovel.

But if he stayed, would Hannah keep putting the business between them whenever there was a problem? Would he go too far again because he was trying to be a partner to her, and she didn't see him that way? Could he keep working for her if she refused to see him as a helpmate in all aspects of her life?

Probably not, he admitted, smiling absently at Chief Kline's brother and handing him a bottle of beer. Hannah meant too much to him. He would try not to keep things from her in the future, but he was bound to overstep if she didn't feel the same way about him that he did about her.

A big group of regulars came up to the bar, laughing. Deacon fell into a blur of activity for a few minutes. After they'd all been served and gone to the tables, he stood, staring at nothing, and wiped his hands with a bar rag.

Should he go? Just run away? Get out of town?

He frowned, then tried to moderate his expression when one of the bowling league guys backed away, hands raised.

No, he thought, getting the guy a beer from the tap. No, he wouldn't leave town.

Hannah Frederickson was his and he wasn't going to run away from her.

So maybe he couldn't work *for* her. Fine. But he was damn well going to work *with* her.

Hannah's voice came suddenly over the loudspeaker, telling everyone that the carnival was going to be shutting down for the night in half an hour. Roy and his band were finishing their last set and Deacon thought he recognized the beginning chords of "In-A-Gadda-Da-Vida" before the music cut off in a loud burst of static.

Craning his neck, he saw Johnny up on the stage talking to his brother, gesturing frantically. After a moment of silence, the band started up again, this time playing "Mony, Mony."

See? Deacon thought, turning back to the last customers as people started moving towards the exit. Sometimes things worked out.

And he was going to make goddamn sure they worked out for him and Hannah.

27

Monday afternoon, Hannah sat staring at her computer screen, but she couldn't focus on spreadsheets or finances or supplies, or any of the million things she should be doing.

Sighing, she glanced at her clock.

Dr. Black would be there in a few hours. He'd called to confirm the appointment and everything, so she was sure he'd be right on time.

Why had she bothered to tell him to come? It was pointless.

But he probably wouldn't have accepted a flat-out "no" on Saturday, anyway. He would have assumed she just needed time to think about his offer. And the fact was, maybe she should think about it.

She looked around at her tiny, shabby office—at the ancient PC, the even older phone, the scarred wooden desk and dinged metal file cabinet. Why was she bothering to hold on and fight? Her uncle had probably thought she'd cave long ago. Why try and prove him wrong? Why not just give up and give in?

She stood and walked over to the small, narrow window, and looked blindly across the cracked parking lot to the scrub trees beyond. She could hear the muffled noise of machinery as Chuckie Scanlon and his workers finished packing up the carnival equipment, getting ready to move on to the next town. Was Billy was helping, or had he already called out sick?

The First Ever Country Time Bar and Grill Carnival had been a rousing success, even if some people had come on Sunday just to see if there'd be more drama. Hannah didn't give a damn why they'd come, she only cared that she'd ended up with enough money to pay Chuckie's fee, satisfy her suppliers, and cover operating expenses for a while.

Too bad everything else hadn't worked out as well.

After the confrontation with Deacon, Sam, and Dr. Black, she'd just focused on doing what needed to be done, putting one foot in front of the other, getting through.

June, Kevin, and the others had noticed of course, but they'd been busy enough that she could avoid long conversations, and she'd been bitchy enough that they'd given her space. She'd expected June to push, but the other woman had surprised her by backing off. Hannah didn't expect that situation to last, but she'd been grateful for the reprieve.

Her mood had been so foul that she hadn't even cared when Roy and his boys broke into "In-A-Gadda-Da-Vida" at the end of their last set both nights. Johnny hadn't been able to stop them on Sunday, and she'd been forced to shut off their microphones after fifteen minutes. Then, exhausted, she'd gone home to lay awake for hours staring at the ceiling.

Hannah reached up and touched the window glass, trailing her fingers through layers of dust.

There was no way Deacon would have suggested his father try to buy her business. Once she'd calmed down and really thought it through, she was sure he'd told her the truth. He'd been trying to help, said something he hadn't meant, and his father had either misunderstood or just willfully took it the wrong way. Dr. Black had always been kind of a dick.

That didn't make it right though. He'd still gone to his father without talking to her, basically shoved her aside as he had with Pat.

Maybe he'd done it because he wanted to help her, but she was very much afraid it was because he didn't respect her.

And if that was true, where did it leave them?

"Okay." June's voice came from the doorway. Hannah jumped and turned to see her standing hip-shot and belligerent just inside the office. "I didn't want to bother you when you were all wrapped up in that carnival deal, but today you and me are going to have a little chat. What the hell is going on between you and Deacon?"

"Nothing," Hannah said automatically. "Why are you here? You don't work tonight."

"Bullshit nothing." June stepped forward and closed the door behind her. She dug into the pocket of her tight jeans, pulled out a pack of gum, and, after peeling off the wrapping, folded a piece into her mouth. "What's up with you and Deacon?" She chewed her gum ferociously for a moment. "It's something to do with his father, isn't it?"

Hannah gaped at her. "What do you know about that?"

"I know Dr. Stick-Up-His-Butt came to the carnival on Saturday with Sam. Everybody knows, and I saw them myself, didn't I?" June settled in Hannah's visitor's chair. "I hear he was spouting off about some kind of a business deal before you yanked them away from the tables. Is that the problem?"

Crap, Hannah thought. She walked back to her desk and sat down across from June. "That has something to do with it."

"Well, what did Deacon do?" June's jaws worked. "Did he pull some boneheaded stunt like when he went after Pat?"

"You know about that, too?" Hannah put a hand to her forehead.

"Sure. Even if I hadn't heard you yelling, you think Pat kept it a secret? Trust me, Deacon wasn't using his brains when he went after the man."

"See? That's what I told him." Hannah leaned forward and jabbed a finger at her. "I told him he'd been stupid."

June stopped chewing for a blessed moment. "You called him stupid?" she asked.

Hannah hesitated. "Maybe," she said.

June reached across the desk and flicked Hannah's ear.

"Ow! What was that for? That hurt."

"Haven't I taught you anything about men?" June demanded. She started chewing again. Soon Hannah was going to take her gum and shove it down her throat.

"What's the matter with saying he's stupid?" she countered. "He *was* stupid."

"Well, yeah, but don't call him that, you moron. Don't call any man stupid, but especially not Deacon."

"Why not?" Hannah kept a wary eye on the other woman in case she decided to flick again.

June rolled her dark eyes. "Oh, for Christ's sake. You've known him longer than I have. Don't you know anything about him? His jackass of a father has been calling him stupid since the day he was born. The last thing he needs is to hear you say it, too."

Hannah frowned. "He got the cops called to my place."

June sighed. "Yes, he did, but I'll bet he just wanted to help, and talking to Pat seemed like a good idea."

"That's what he said," Hannah muttered. "He's just freaking *full* of helpful ideas."

June chewed and considered her for a long moment. Then she took out the gum, wadded it up in a tissue and threw it away in the trash can beside Hannah's desk.

"What happened with his father at the carnival?" she asked seriously.

Hannah toyed with the cord of her phone, twisting it into

coils on her desk. "Apparently Deacon went to his father to ask if he wanted to invest in the Country Time."

"Huh." June sat back and crossed her legs, swinging one booted foot back and forth. "And he didn't tell you."

"No." Hannah looked at her, then back down at the desk. "I think Dr. Black must have said he wasn't interested, but then he changed his mind and called Sam. He came to the carnival to offer to buy me out."

"Whoa, whoa. Wait." June sat bolt upright and waved both hands. "Trevor Black wants to buy the Country Time?"

"Or become a majority partner. He said Deacon suggested it."

"No way in hell," June said without hesitation. "There is no way Deacon would have gone that far without talking to you. His asshole father must have misunderstood."

"Yeah." Hannah smiled at her. "I figured that out myself. Eventually."

"Okay." June settled back again. "So Black got his panties in a wad about something because he's an arrogant prick who doesn't listen to what people say. What does that have to do with you and Deacon?"

Hannah stared at her. "Did you miss the part where Deacon went behind my back again? First he confronted Pat without telling me and then he went to his father." She shifted restlessly in the chair. "He needs to respect me, June. He can't just take over and go do whatever he thinks is best without telling me." And that, as far as she was concerned, was the crux of the matter.

"Hannah Frederickson, I don't know what Deacon thought he was doing, but that man respects the hell out of you, and you know it. Don't you trust him?"

"No...yes." Hannah shifted. "Of course I do. I trust him as much as I trust you. Or Josie."

"Then you need to believe him when he says he was trying

to help, don't you?" June shrugged. "I mean, I get why you're pissed off at him. If Calvin did something like that, I'd ream him a new one. But I don't get why you've shut Deacon out."

"I'm haven't—"

"Hell you haven't. I've been with you two the last couple of days. You wouldn't even look at the man on Sunday. You're treating him like a leper."

"He's my employee and he tried to go behind my back!" Hannah said desperately, shoving to her feet. She paced over to the window again.

"He's your lover," June responded, not moving. "Your *lover*. And he means a lot to you. Why won't you just admit it?"

"Admit—"

"Jesus, I've got eyes, don't I?" June snapped, sitting forward. "I see how it is. Mary Alice and Grace see it. Kevin sees it. Hell, even Old Albert sees it."

"It's not—"

"Don't lie, Hannah. Not to me. I know Deacon was an idiot, but there's more here. Usually you bend over backward to try and work things out. Look at how many chances you gave that twerp Billy. With Deacon, you run for the hills. What the hell?"

"He's going to leave, okay?" Hannah whirled to face June, the words bubbling up and out of her mouth before she even thought about them. "Someday he's going to get tired of this place or of me and he's going to leave. So, yes, maybe I'm backing off a little bit. So what?"

June's face softened. "Honey. Maybe he won't leave. What then? Have you ever considered that?"

"You know what his life has been like." Hannah sighed and walked back to the desk, dropping into her chair. "It's only a matter of time before he hits the road again."

"Maybe," June said, "nobody ever asked him to stay."

Hannah blinked.

"Ask him to stay?" she repeated dumbly.

"Listen to me now," June said, leaning towards her, all vestiges of humor gone from her face, her eyes stark and black. "Deacon made some mistakes. People do. You have a right to be angry at him. You have the right to be angry for the rest of your life. But if you push him away hard enough and long enough, he really will leave. And you'll be left without him. Is that what you want?"

No.

Hannah drew in a breath. "He might hurt me again."

June nodded and got to her feet. "He might," she agreed, walking around the desk. She leaned down to plant a kiss on Hannah's cheek. "You have to decide if you're willing to take a chance."

Hannah watched her stride out of the office, dark hair flowing down her back, hips swaying.

June had taken a chance on Calvin. Was Hannah willing to try with Deacon?

Could she?

28

A little while later, Hannah was at the office window staring out at the parking lot when there was a knock on the door jamb. Surprised, she turned and drew in a sharp breath when she saw Deacon standing there, watching her. His eyes were very blue, his face drawn and hard, his shoulders broad under the neat Country Time polo shirt.

"I was wondering if I could see you for a moment," he said, and it made her heart hurt to hear him use that stiff, stilted tone of voice with her.

"Sure."

Nodding, he walked into the office, and after shutting the door, seated himself in the visitor's chair.

She hesitated for a moment, then moved back to her desk and sat down across from him.

God, they were so awkward with each other. It was awful.

He considered her, then smiled without humor. "I was hoping we could talk for a minute before you meet with my father. June seemed to think this might be a good time."

Goddamn June.

"Okay," she said.

She didn't know what to say to him, how to break through the wall between them, even though she'd pretty much put it there.

Deacon looked down, picking at a loose string on his jeans. "First, I wanted to make sure you knew that I told you the truth on Saturday. I only wanted to help." He met her eyes again, his own blazing with sincerity. "I went to my father to see if he would be interested in investing in your business. He's got money, and he's always looking for ways to make more of it. You're a great manager and this is a great business. It's just the kind of thing he'd be interested in."

"Why didn't you tell me you were going to see him?" she asked.

Deacon ran his hands through his short hair before letting them drop. "Because I didn't know how he'd take it, and I didn't want to get your hopes up." He shifted in his seat. "And maybe I didn't want you to know if he laughed at me."

"And you didn't tell me after you'd gone because..."

"Because he *did* laugh at me." Deacon shrugged. "Look, I asked him if he wanted to consider investing. He laughed and said he'd never risk that much money without having control. I told him good luck with that. He said some other things. I left. I swear that's all. I don't know where he got the idea you'd be willing to sell, because I sure never gave him that impression." He grimaced. "Or at least, I didn't mean to."

"I believe you," she told him, because she did.

His eyes locked with hers. "Good." He smiled again. "Besides, there's a limit to what I could have done even if I'd wanted to. This is your place, your business, and your responsibility."

"Deacon—"

"There's something else." He interrupted her. Standing, he pulled a folded piece of paper out of the back pocket of his jeans before resuming his seat. He unfolded the paper carefully and laid it on her desk. "I'm handing in my resignation."

"Your—" she pulled the sheet towards her with nerveless fingers and saw it was a neatly typed letter with Deacon's bold scrawl at the bottom.

"For my file," he said.

"You're just going to leave?" There were shards of ice in her chest, the sudden pain almost leveling her in its intensity. This was her nightmare. "Just like that? We have one little fight and you're going to run off without even trying to work it out or even *talk* to me?"

"Hannah—"

"I can't believe you're leaving!" *No, no, no. He couldn't go. He couldn't desert her.* She picked up the paper and waved it around. "Running away like a coward. I mean I know you've been here longer than you'd expected, and I know I've been a jerk about Pat and your father and everything, but you're just going to go? You're not even going to try and work it out?"

Hannah realized that, although she'd thought she'd been prepared for him to leave, the reality had blindsided her. How was she supposed to do this without him? The hell with the business, how was she supposed to get through life without him? The concept was incomprehensible.

Understanding crashed through her like a wave.

Deacon was essential.

He tilted his head, studying her. "Where do you think I'm going?" he asked interestedly.

"Away! Somewhere." Practically hyperventilating, she shook the resignation letter in his face. "See? Resignation. You're leaving me!"

Deacon settled back in his chair. Oddly, the more agitated she became, the more relaxed he seemed.

"Well, I'm not leaving town," he said mildly.

"I mean, yes, we have issues. You need to—"She stopped. Blinked. "What?"

"I said, I'm not leaving town," he repeated, patience in every syllable.

Hannah gaped at him for a moment.

"Then what the hell is this all about?" she shook the letter at him again.

"I'm leaving the Country Time. Mateo would work out fine as a bartender, by the way, if you decide to hire him."

Hannah stared at him, crushing the resignation letter in her hand without really being aware of what she was doing. "You're staying? You're still going to stay in town?"

"Well, of *course* I'm still going to stay in town." Deacon heaved a deep sigh and leaned forward until they were almost nose to nose with the desk between them. "You're here, aren't you? I worked damned hard for two years to get you to even look at me. I'm sure as hell not leaving you without a fight." Reaching up, he stroked a gentle finger down her cheek and it was only then she realized she'd been crying. "You're worth fighting for, Hannah Frederickson."

"Oh." Her mind buzzed like a hive of bees. It took a minute for her to process what he'd said.

He was...staying?

She stared at him

"You're staying."

He smiled. "Yes."

Suddenly the distance between them was unendurable. Hannah launched herself at him, caught his mouth in a kiss, and the flavor of Deacon exploded across her tongue. She was desperate to get to him, to touch him. It had been so long. So damned long. She grabbed his head, his short hair tickling her palms, and deepened the kiss.

When they finally broke apart, they were both panting, papers, folders, her empty coffee mug, and the computer mouse and keyboard were all lying scattered on the floor, and Hannah was stretched across the desk with her arms around Deacon's neck. He huffed out a laugh and stood, pulling her the rest of the way over to him, before sitting again and settling her in his lap. She tried to kiss him, but he stopped her to frown into her face.

"I can't believe you thought I would just leave."

She pushed at him. "Then why are you resigning from the Country Time?"

Deacon shook his head. "The business, the fact that I work for you, has gotten in the way from the beginning. I thought if I took the employee part out of the equation, you and I could focus on figuring out this thing between us."

"You being an employee has been a little strange, but..." she drew in a deep breath. "When you did what you did, went behind my back that way, I thought you didn't respect me. And it hurt."

He kissed her, long and deep. Hannah returned his kiss, reveled in his touch, drank him in as if she were parched earth. Finally he pulled away, his lips lingering before leaving hers.

"There's no one on earth I respect more than you," he said softly. "No one."

Hannah moved her hands from his shoulders to run her fingertips over his firm jaw, those sharp cheekbones, mapping him.

Deacon's gaze was intense as he passed a hand over her face, his calloused fingers rough on her skin. "I'm so sorry for the way I screwed up, Hannah. I hope you believe me. I don't know what more I can—"

Hannah reached up and kissed him to stop his words.

"I don't need rescuing Deacon," she said when they'd pulled apart. "I don't need a white knight to ride in and save my poor little self."

He smiled a little. "I know."

"I don't need a rescuer," she whispered, "but I could use a friend and a partner. I can't do this alone." She pulled back. "I can't do this without *you*," she emphasized.

He looked a little wary. "Even though I'm only a bartender? And not all that smart sometimes?" The vulnerability he usually kept hidden shone in his eyes.

"You're plenty smart." She tightened her grip around his neck. "And you're not 'only' anything. You are the most important person in the world to me."

He looked shocked, and that in turn shocked her. Didn't he know? Couldn't he feel it?

Or maybe, she thought, he needed the words.

She drew in a deep breath.

"I love you, Deacon Black," she said, then laughed as wonder exploded inside her. She leaned forward to pepper kisses on his face. "I love you, love you, love you."

He swept her closer, buried his face in her hair.

"I love you, too," he whispered in her ear. "I love you Hannah. I always have. I always will."

Bursting with joy, Hannah grabbed his ears, pulling him so she could kiss him again.

They were interrupted by a knock on the door. Before Hannah could tell whoever it was to go the hell away, it opened and Dr. Black, looking professional in a dark suit with a briefcase under his arm, strolled in, a full hour early.

"I realize I'm early, but this time fit better into my—" He halted abruptly, frown thunderous when he saw the disarray of the office and Hannah sitting in the circle of Deacon's arms. She could only imagine how disheveled and flushed they both looked.

"What is going on here?" Deacon's father demanded.

"I believe that is none of your business, Dr. Black," Hannah said. Deacon made a move to get her out of his lap, but she tightened her grip on his arms and stayed where she was.

"As a potential buyer, I have a right to know."

Hannah shrugged.

Obviously at a loss as to how to deal with her lack of concern, Dr. Black turned his frown on his son. "I had assumed this initial conversation would only be between the two of us."

"You were wrong," Hannah said quietly. "Deacon is well aware of all of my financial concerns and has the right to be involved in any and all business conversations. He's my partner."

Deacon stiffened.

"Your partner?" Dr. Black sounded like he'd just stepped in garbage. "That hardly seems wise."

"On the contrary, it's incredibly wise." Hannah felt the warmth inside her expand and grow. "Deacon is one of the best men I know."

"Hmm." Dr. Black's scowl deepened until his heavy dark brows formed a line across his bald skull. "That is most troubling. I did have concerns before, naturally, but this raises serious doubts about your judgment and management skills."

Hannah shrugged. "Whatever."

Dr. Black's mouth dropped open in shock.

"Young woman, I demand that you treat me with respect."

"Respect," Hannah said, "must be earned."

Deacon's father drew himself up to his full height. "I withdraw my indication of interest."

Hannah nodded. "Understood. I wasn't all that interested in your interest, anyway."

"Humph." Dr. Black hesitated, then turned and stomped out of the office.

Once the echo of his footsteps in the hallway died, Deacon pulled her around to stare down at her.

"Partner? Hannah, you—"

"I can't do this without you, Deacon," she told him, wrapping herself around him like ivy. "Any of it. If you leave, I'm closing down the Country Time."

"But...but...I mean, yeah, I have some money, but I'm sure I don't have enough to buy in as a partner."

"We'll work it out," she said into his chest. "All of it. We'll find a way. We'll figure it out. But this business is as much yours as it is mine, now. I want you to be my partner in everything."

"It just seems—"

She looked up at him. "Tell me you're willing to try."

He was silent for a long moment, just looking at her.

"Tell me," she pleaded.

"If it doesn't seem to be working out, then I quit again," he said finally.

Hannah's breath escaped in a "whoosh."

"Deal."

Pushing away from him, she leaped up from his lap, found the crumpled resignation letter, and ripped it into tiny, tiny pieces. She threw the shreds into the air and they floated down like confetti.

Then, with a broad grin, she jumped him.

EPILOGUE

"Oh, it's just so nice to see you and Deacon together, Hannah." Mary Alice, seated at the bar, clasped her large farmer's hands to her ample bosom, and beamed at them both with big, damp eyes.

"Thanks, Mary Alice." Standing with Deacon on the other side of the bar, Hannah leaned against him and smiled when his arms came around her possessively.

It was the Wednesday after the carnival, and things were changing. For one thing, she and Deacon had decided he would move in with her the following week. Mateo Guerrero was taking over the room Deacon had been renting above the bookstore. Mat was also their new dishwasher and second bartender, Jason having left to focus on his studies.

It was a laughable state of affairs—Mat was so overqualified, it was ridiculous. But he seemed happy about it, so who was she to judge?

No one had heard from Billy since the carnival, but June had told Hannah on Tuesday she'd heard he'd gone to Florida with some of the carnies. His mother seemed very happy and was busy cleaning out his room.

Hannah stirred in Deacon's arms. He reluctantly let her go and she went to the coffee maker to pour herself another mug of coffee. When she turned back, she met June's dark eyes. The other woman, perched on a barstool at the end of the bar, shot her a wink. Hannah grinned at her.

Looking at the rest of the group, her heart warmed. They were all there. Mateo, Mary Alice, and Grace sitting at the old wooden bar with June. Kevin standing next to Deacon, arms crossed over his broad chest.

Her team.

Her family.

Reminding herself that they actually did have business to discuss, Hannah got her head back in the game.

"It looks like we did pretty well at the carnival," she told them. "We more than covered our expenses and it bought us a little breathing room."

"Hooray!" Mary Alice gave an enthusiastic fist pump. "Roy said he and the guys would play anytime you were interested in having them, Hannah. They got three wedding gigs out of the carnival."

"Great." Hannah filed that information away for the future. "In-A-Gadda-Da-Vida" aside, Roy's band was pretty good. "Anyway, I wanted to let you know that Deacon's going to be making more of the decisions and we're looking for a way to formalize that." She met Deacon's eyes and he smiled. They were still fighting about the partnership thing, but he was ready and willing to play a bigger role in the running of the business.

Kevin shrugged. "Eh, big deal. He was in charge, anyway."

"Hannah just didn't think so," June smirked.

"Now if she'd only let me invest," Deacon said ironically.

Hannah grimaced. She wanted to make him a partner without a formal buy-in. God knew the man had earned it over the past two years. Deacon insisted that instead of a partner, he become an investor to the extent of his ability. They'd had an entertaining...discussion about it that morning before coming in to work.

But the makeup sex had been terrific.

"Oh, an investor pool is a really good idea, Hannah," Mary Alice piped up. "I mean, there's risk, but lots of small businesses can't raise capital from banks and go to individuals. You just have to make sure everything is legal and structured properly. Johnny can help with that. I know he and I would love to participate." She blinked when she saw them all staring at her. "What?"

Hannah shook her head to clear it. "Nothing."

"I'll bet my father would invest," Grace put in. She shrugged. "I can't."

"I cannot invest money either, boss lady," Kevin said, then grinned. "I will invest the power of my cooking, no?"

Hannah smiled at him. "Yes," she said.

"I'll bet Calvin will want to invest," June said.

"You think?" Hannah asked. As co-owner of Hardy Hardware, Calvin was definitely a good prospect.

"Sure." June cracked her gum. "I can get him to agree to damn near anything." Her dark eyes sparkled. "All it takes is a little chocolate sauce and—"

"Ahhh!" Hannah put down her coffee mug and clapped her hands over her ears. "Too much information."

June cackled.

"Haven't I told you to lock the kitchen door?"

Hannah turned quickly to see Sam walking in from the kitchen, looking elegant in a dark navy suit.

"Oh, lord," June muttered. "He's back."

Hannah went to stand beside Deacon and he immediately draped an arm around her shoulders, pulling her close to his side. Sam obviously noticed the gesture, but he didn't make a sarcastic remark.

Which pretty much indicated hell was freezing over.

"What are you doing here?" she asked him.

"I have some news from Adam," Sam said.

Hannah's heart stilled, then started pounding, and she huddled closer to Deacon. She might not need him to ride to her rescue, but it was awfully nice to be able to lean on him now and then.

"Did he find George?" she asked.

Sam shook his head. "No, but they found Crystal Fields."

"George's, uh, assistant?" Deacon sounded amused.

Sam snorted. "Yeah. *Assistant*. Right. She started using her own credit card again, and Adam tracked her down to the Four Queens Hotel on the old strip in Vegas.

"George dumped her, huh?" June shook her head with reluctant admiration as she sipped some coffee. "Damn. Who knew the old goat had it in him? I figured she'd be the one taking him for a ride."

Sam flashed his charming grin. "Adam went to Vegas and interviewed Ms. Fields personally. It's his opinion that her intentions at the beginning of the affair were not, shall we say, honorable. George just dumped her first. Apparently he'd had a run of luck at the tables. Nothing major, but enough to build up a pretty nice stake, plus he'd worked deals so they'd been eating and staying at the hotels basically for free."

Hannah shook her head in amazement. *Uncle George, you dog.*

"One morning she woke up and he was gone." Sam spread out his hands. "That's all she knew."

"So she doesn't have a clue where he went?" Deacon asked.

"No." Sam sobered when he looked at Hannah. "I need to know if you want to keep pursuing this. Even with the deal I worked out, it's getting damned expensive."

Hannah sighed, sagging against Deacon. "It's a lost cause, isn't it?"

"Maybe. Probably." Sam frowned. "But Adam seems kind of

invested in it, now. I think it hurt his pride that an accountant managed to give him the slip. He *really* wants to get George, and he said again that he was willing to do some *pro bono* work."

Hannah frowned. "It just doesn't seem right not to pay him."

Deacon bumped against her side and kissed the top of her head. "Let the guy help you, Hannah."

Hannah looked at Deacon, then Sam, and finally her crew.

"Okay," she said. "We'll call off the investigation. If Adam is willing to keep looking on his own time, it would be awesome."

Sam nodded. "I'll talk to him, and we'll get you the bill."

"Wonderful," Hannah sighed. And there went the cushion she'd gotten from the carnival.

"I know a lot of people in Nevada," Mateo said, breaking his long silence. "I'll ask around, too." He'd heard the whole story by now, of course.

"Thanks." She tried to shake off her disappointment. Well, she'd known there hadn't been much hope of getting her money back.

"Can I talk to you?" Sam asked her. His glance flicked to Deacon, then back. "Just for a minute."

Deacon's arm tightened, but he let her go. Hannah wondered if he'd always be jealous of his brother, even when he had absolutely no cause. She reached up and kissed his cheek, getting a sheepish smile in return, before turning back to Sam.

"Come on," she said and led him down the short hallway to her tiny office. "What do you need?" she asked after he'd followed her inside and closed the door.

He studied her in silence for a moment. "I heard through the grapevine that you and Deacon worked things out," he said at last. "You really love him?"

"Yes," she said. "I really do."

He nodded. "Thought so. You never looked at me the way

you looked at him. Even when you didn't know you were looking at him."

"Sam—"

Sam held up his hand to stop her. "I wanted to tell you I was sorry about Saturday. Father got it in his head he wanted to see what you were doing before deciding about the business. I had no idea he was going to make an offer right then and there and try to force the issue."

"Okay," Hannah said warily.

Sam nodded. "You don't trust me. I get it."

"You've been a big help these last couple of weeks." Hannah shrugged. "That's a start."

He nodded again and shoved his hands in the pockets of his slacks.

"I hear Father withdrew his offer," he said after a moment.

"I wouldn't have accepted anyway."

"I'm glad." Sam rocked on his heels, then smiled. "I'd better go. That was all I wanted to say."

Hannah returned his smile. "Thanks." Samuel Black might not have been her dream man anymore, but he had been an important part of her life. She hoped he found whatever it was he was looking for.

He turned to go, and then looked back at her over his shoulder.

"He's always loved you," he said. "Deacon. Even when we were in high school. He never said anything, but I knew. I've always known."

Hannah's smile widened. She'd probably always loved Deacon, too, but she didn't think she needed to say that to Sam.

"You two look good together," Sam said.

"I know."

He left and Hannah stood for a moment, hugging herself.

Yes, she still had problems, but she'd deal with them somehow. The investor pool was probably a good idea, if she could get past her fear of everyone losing their money. And she wanted to get her hands on George.

Then there was Josie, who hadn't sounded like herself the last time they'd talked. And the gossip Pat Murphy was continuing to spread, the way he was trying to undermine her and trying to steal her bowlers.

Problems, problems everywhere.

But she had the most important thing now. She had Deacon.

What else mattered?

"Everything okay?"

The man himself walked into her office, big and broad and hard, except where she was concerned. She melted. She seemed to do that every time she saw him these days.

Impulsively, Hannah leaped at him, grabbed him, and kissed him.

"Wow," he said when she let him go so they could breathe. "I should ask Sam to visit more often."

"I really love you," Hannah said. "I really, really do."

His beautiful blue eyes softened and he ran his hand through her hair and down her back.

"I really, really love you, too."

"Are you sure?" she teased. "I own a business with a butt-load of problems."

"We'll figure them out together."

Together. What a wonderful word.

Hannah kissed him, slowly and with intent.

"Do we have time to—" he gasped a few minutes later.

"Don't you two get busy back there," June yelled down the hall. "It's time to open, and we can't wait for you to get your rocks off. I'm not gonna run this place by myself!"

Hannah and Deacon jumped apart, then laughed.

"Buzzkill," Deacon yelled back and kissed Hannah again.

"You should probably go," she said breathlessly. "And I should get some paperwork done."

He smiled down at her in that slow, sweet way of his.

"It's okay. We'll make up for it later."

"Yes," Hannah said, smiling up at him. "We have all the time in the world."

And they did.

THE END

Turn the page to read the an excerpt from

Trusting Love
Welcome to Hardy Falls, Book 3

TRUSTING LOVE
WELCOME TO HARDY FALLS, BOOK 3

A little trouble might be just what they need...

When Josie Kline seeks shelter from a surprise blizzard at her best friend's tavern, she expects to be on her own for the night. Instead she comes face to face with a grumpy and darkly handsome stranger who claims to be there to run the generator.

Trapped by the storm, power out, Josie finds herself intrigued by her attractive and irritating companion. A really bad move considering the current state of her life. She needs to figure out her future and get out of town again, not waste time thinking about the sexy man she just met.

It still amazes Mateo Guerrero that he somehow ended up working as a dishwasher/bartender in a small town in Pennsylvania. He certainly does not need an annoying, tempting, beautiful woman blowing into his world and messing him up even more.

In *Trusting Love*, overwhelming desire and scorching passion compete with the ghosts of the past as two people try to move forward into the promise of the future. Will they be brave enough to take the chance?

~

Chapter One

"Oh, crap!" Josie Kline tightened her mittened hands convulsively on the steering wheel of her aging sedan as it started to slide off the snow-packed highway—again.

"Salt, people!" she yelled at the absent road crews, who apparently thought a late-October surprise blizzard wasn't worth the effort. "Salt is our friend! And some freaking snowplows might be nice, too."

Shoulders tight with tension, she guided the car back onto the road. Well, where she thought the road should be. It was kind of hard to tell exactly where the hell you were driving when all you could see was snow whipping into your windshield by a gale force wind. Heck, in this ocean of white, the only reason she was pretty sure she was still on the highway in the first place were the occasional mile markers.

"I mean, I get that it's not even freaking Halloween yet, but this is the freaking Pocono Mountains, you jerks! Pennsylvania! We get freaking snow, for Christ's sake."

Yelling at the nonexistent road crews didn't help much. She felt like a rubber band wound too tight and ready to snap.

And yes, yes, yes, she shouldn't have been driving in these conditions in the first place. She'd meant to get an earlier start, but it had taken her longer than she'd expected to pack up her things, get the car out of the garage where it was stored, and leave New York City.

Even so, the stupid weather forecasters she'd listened to before heading out had all insisted the storm would only drop a couple of inches of snow, even in the Poconos. Josie had grown up in this part of Pennsylvania. Driving in snow and avoiding deer were two of her best life skills. She could make her car dance through a couple of inches of snow without even breaking a sweat.

Too bad this was not a couple inches of snow.

Once she'd realized the storm was going to be a lot worse than anticipated, she should have stopped and found somewhere to spend the night. Even the truck drivers seemed to be giving up. But it hadn't gotten really, *really* bad until she was about ten miles away from Hardy Falls. And since Hardy Falls, Pennsylvania, was her ultimate destination, she'd kept going. Ten miles, she'd reasoned, would be nothing at this point.

Wrong!

She tapped the brakes gently as the car rocked in an especially strong gust of wind. All this wind was bad because the trees still had most of their leaves, and the wet, heavy snow was weighing them down. Broken branches and falling trees would take down wires and block roads, just a few of the many reasons why storms like this could be deadly in the mountains. Her mother was the chief of police in Hardy Falls, so Josie had heard lots of stories about what could happen.

She shouldn't have trusted the forecast. She should have stayed in New York. But who knew they'd be *this* wrong?

"Not like I had an apartment to stay in, anyway," she muttered, hands gripping the wheel, giving the car more gas so it could get up an incline, and praying when she felt the tires spin, the tail shimmy. "Or a job. Or anything except this stupid car." She breathed again when the road leveled out.

"Kicked to the curb, remember?" The sound of her own voice was soothing, even if what she was saying sucked. "Laid off and thrown out of the apartment. Way to go, Josie."

In fairness, she knew that if she'd asked, her former roommates would have let her stay another night. The girl they were replacing her with wasn't due to move in for a couple of days, anyway. But Josie had just wanted to get home. After the blows of the past week or so, she needed to reinvent her life—needed to see where she was going and where she wanted to go. She needed to *think*, goddamnit, and home was a good place to do that. A safe place to start over.

Assuming she could get there.

Drawing in another deep breath, she put her car in the lowest gear possible and crept down a hill that felt like a ski slope. She wished she could see landmarks so she'd be able to tell how much further she had to go. On this wooded, lonely stretch of highway, everything looked the same in the unending, swirling whiteness.

This was not a snowstorm. This was a snowpocalypse. Beware, the end of the world is nigh for it is covered with frozen precipitation.

Giggling a little hysterically, Josie struggled to keep the sedan under control.

Maybe she should stop. Pull over and wait it out. As much as she hated to give them any credit, the crews would be through sooner or later. This was a major road, so they'd be out tending it when they could. But she couldn't be that far away from Hardy Falls, and if she stopped, she'd never get started again. Besides, she might get hit by someone else stupid enough to be out driving in this insanity.

It would have been nice if she could have called her mother to get some advice. Jacqueline Kline would at least know what the road conditions were like ahead. But cell service, which was never great, had already been knocked out.

Well, it was probably for the best. She'd wanted to make her explanations in person, so nobody knew she was on her way. If her mother found out how idiotic she'd been, she'd come riding to the rescue and then they'd both probably get stuck.

Josie suddenly noticed a different quality to the snow and stared in amazement as a squat, square building sitting at the side of the road came into view. It was a bar, with lights glowing in the windows and neon beer signs flashing red, blue, and yellow out front.

What the hell? They were *open*?

Most importantly, she recognized the place. This was the Country Time Bar and Grill, a tavern on the outskirts of Hardy Falls, owned by her best friend in the whole wide world, Hannah Frederickson.

Josie was home.

Home.

She blinked hard to keep from breaking down in tears of relief and gratitude and, distracted for one crucial moment, stepped on the brakes way too hard.

"Oh, God. Oh, crap. Oh, shit."

Hands clenched on the wheel, her stomach knotted as she felt the tires slide into a slow motion turn. The brakes did nothing to halt her forward momentum, as the car did a graceful, inevitable 400-degree spin and came to a stop in the middle of the highway pointing directly at the Country Time.

So, *that* was a sign. *Stop, you moron.*

Wheezing a little from the adrenaline, Josie decided that she wasn't going to argue with the universe any longer. She was done. There was determined, there was stubborn, and there was bone-deep stupid. No way in hell was she going to make it, regardless of how few miles it was across town to her mother's house. For whatever unknown, harebrained reason, someone was obviously inside the Country Time, and she had a hunch that someone was Hannah. More than likely, Deacon Black, Hannah's bartender-boyfriend, was there too, and that was fine. Heck, they could be having sex on top of the bar for all Josie cared. She was getting off this hell-road and waiting out the rest of the storm with her friends.

Sadly, the universe did not appear to be impressed with her decision because when she hit the gas, the wheels of the car spun uselessly. For a few moments it slid back and forth, but it never actually went anywhere.

Great. Now she was going to have to slog her way through the snow and get Hannah to help push her off the road.

Not willing to face the cold just yet, she put the car in reverse, then in drive, repeatedly rocking it back and forth. A thrill of triumph washed through her when she felt the wheels finally gain traction and the vehicle lurched forward. Weaving like a snake, she slid into the Country Time's parking lot.

Then she tried to stop again.

"No!"

For one breathless moment, she was sure she would crash into the brick building. The irony of totaling her car in the parking lot of her best friend's business flashed through her mind, along with most of her life. In the end, it was close, but the old sedan finally came to a stop with its bumper kissing the wall.

"God."

Panting, Josie let herself slump over the wheel before raising her head to look around. Murphy Lanes, the bowling alley next door to the Country Time, was dark, as was the gas station across the street. Why in the *hell* was Hannah open? Surely she wasn't expecting any customers.

On the other hand, what did it matter? Someone was in there.

Suddenly and irrationally terrified that her friend would leave before she got inside—where the heck would she go?—Josie braced herself, grabbed her purse and a duffel bag from the backseat that contained more of her clothes, and opened the driver's door.

The cold slap of wind knocked the breath right out of her body, but she managed to stand and muscle the car door shut behind her. Forcing her way through the wall of the storm to the front entrance, she pushed open one of the wooden double doors, stumbled inside in a whirlwind of snow, and wrestled it closed again.

Then she was inside the Country Time's taproom.

And it was warm.

And bright.

And not snowing.

Josie felt weak from the sudden release of tension she'd been carrying for miles—days, weeks—and for a moment she was a little afraid she'd faint. She shook her head to get her brain working again and immediately regretted it when ice rained down from her knit cap.

"Are you nuts, lady? Why are you out in this?"

Trusting Love

ALSO BY BETSY HORVATH

WELCOME TO HARDY FALLS

Believing Love

Handling Love

Trusting Love

Expecting Love (novella)

Choosing Love

LOVE'S MOST WANTED

Hold Me

ABOUT THE AUTHOR

Betsy Horvath was raised on a steady diet of old MGM musicals, Nancy Drew, and Harlequin romances, so nobody should have been shocked to discover that one day she would be writing romance novels of her own. Especially not once became clear that, when given the opportunity, she could sing the entire soundtrack from the *Sound of Music*, regardless of whether or not anyone asked her to (nobody ever did), and that the only books she ever wanted to read were the ones with happy endings (which made things interesting in college).

Let's face it, Betsy is a hopeless romantic. But she's good with it.

www.BetsyHorvath.com
betsyhorvath@betsyhorvath.com

www.ingramcontent.com/pod-product-compliance
Lightning Source LLC
Chambersburg PA
CBHW010347170726
48284CB00011B/2815